The Louisiana heat can [illegible] your heart . . . and your [illegible]

"So where y'all goin' at?" Etienne asked, but his gaze was on Miranda. She told herself that the rush of heat she felt was merely from the sultry air.

Answer him—you're being totally silly. The truth was, she'd thought about him all day long and had watched for him to show up. Now here he finally was, looking as only Etienne could look, staring as only Etienne could stare, and her heart was skipping a beat, and she couldn't come up with a single, coherent word to say. *Get a grip, Miranda.*

"Miss Teeta invited us!" Ashley waved again. "Do you know where she is?"

"All over the place, usually."

"Did you see Gage and Parker? They got here way before we did."

"Then you musta been driving, yeah?"

"Don't make fun of me."

"What? I could never make fun of you," Etienne assured her, though his expression suggested otherwise. "They're probably all inside. Just go around front, door's in the middle."

He bent to retrieve his toolbelt. As Roo and Ashley walked on, Miranda started to follow, then suddenly stopped and turned.

Etienne was poised on a ledge, just below the third-story dormer, his back to an open window. Most of the glass had broken long ago, leaving nothing but a few jagged edges at the corners. No curtains hanging, no shades . . . only darkness.

But Miranda saw what was there.

She saw it, dimly, and she told herself that it was only the fading sunlight flickering through moss and leafy branches. Even though her skin went suddenly cold.

Because for one instant, she could swear she'd seen a hand.

A small, shadowy hand; fingers pressed flat against the air, as though pressed flat against a windowpane.

As if something—someone—were trying to get out.

Shadow Mirror

Richie Tankersley Cusick

speak
An Imprint of Penguin Group (USA) Inc.

SPEAK
Published by the Penguin Group
Penguin Group (USA) Inc., 345 Hudson Street, New York, New York 10014, U.S.A.
Penguin Group (Canada), 90 Eglinton Avenue East, Suite 700, Toronto, Ontario, Canada M4P 2Y3 (a division of Pearson Penguin Canada Inc.)
Penguin Books Ltd, 80 Strand, London WC2R 0RL, England
Penguin Ireland, 25 St Stephen's Green, Dublin 2, Ireland (a division of Penguin Books Ltd)
Penguin Group (Australia), 250 Camberwell Road, Camberwell, Victoria 3124, Australia (a division of Pearson Australia Group Pty Ltd)
Penguin Books India Pvt Ltd, 11 Community Centre, Panchsheel Park, New Delhi - 110 017, India
Penguin Group (NZ), 67 Apollo Drive, Rosedale, North Shore 0632, New Zealand (a division of Pearson New Zealand Ltd.)
Penguin Books (South Africa) (Pty) Ltd, 24 Sturdee Avenue, Rosebank, Johannesburg 2196, South Africa

Registered Offices: Penguin Books Ltd, 80 Strand, London WC2R 0RL, England

Published by Speak, an imprint of Penguin Group (USA) Inc., 2010

1 2 3 4 5 6 7 8 9 10

LIBRARY OF CONGRESS CATALOGING-IN-PUBLICATION DATA:
Cusick, Richie Tankersley.
Shadow mirror / by Richie Tankersley Cusick.
p. cm.
Summary: Seventeen-year-old Miranda Barnes' ability to communicate with spirits gets her in trouble when she crosses over to the "Other Side," and only love will bring her back.
ISBN: 978-0-14-241227-5 (pbk.)
[1. Ghosts—Fiction. 2. Space and time—Fiction. 3. Afterlife—Fiction. 4. Dating (Social customs)—Fiction. 5. Louisiana—Fiction. 6. Mystery and detective stories.]
I. Title.
PZ7.C9646Sh 2010
[Fic]—dc22 2009027240

Speak ISBN 978-0-14-241227-5

Printed in the United States of America

For Alex & Cathy . . .
my guardian angels . . .
for always being there with love and prayers,
friendship and faith,
and comfort from Cathy's Cupboard.

I love you,

Richie

1

SHE WANTED TO BELIEVE THAT IT WAS JUST AN ACCIDENT.

That the broken mirror lying in pieces at her feet was simply the result of carelessness, of trying to get ready too fast and not keeping her mind on what she was doing.

An accident, that's all. Don't be dumb, Miranda—everyone breaks mirrors. No big deal.

And yet . . . it didn't *feel* like an accident.

Standing there alone in the bathroom, Miranda was suddenly aware of her heart pounding, of sweat breaking out on her forehead. The air went sharply, unnaturally cold, and she could feel the walls closing in around her. *Not* the mirror, she told herself again firmly—*it's just me, some leftover symptoms from that stupid flu.*

Thinking about it now made her queasy all over again. Only two days after Walk of the Spirits—the ghost tour that she and her friends had created for their class project—she'd woken up with a raging fever, and then a week had passed without her. She couldn't recall much of that time—only the haziest memories of lying there aching and miserable in bed, while Mom and Aunt Teeta took turns off from work to give pills, take temperatures, force fluids, and coax down spoonfuls of Aunt Teeta's homemade chicken soup. In a faraway blur, Miranda had tossed, drifted, and slept the sleep of the dead.

But her mind had never rested. Hour after hour, images had scattered and flowed back and forth between her present and her past, her new life and her old. St. Yvette and the Falls, the phantoms of Nathan and Ellena Rose. Scenes of Florida and the hurricane, of Marge and Joanie and the best-friend things they'd done together. The vacant spot on the white sandy beach where her house had once stood, where she and Mom had been so happy. Hayes House and Aunt Teeta. The Walk of the Spirits and Grandpa. Parker and Ashley . . . Gage and Roo . . . Etienne . . .

And wouldn't it be weird, she'd sometimes wondered, floating through that senseless fog, *if I woke up in my old bed, in my old house, and no hurricane had ever come, and Mom and I had never moved here to St. Yvette, and all of this*—my life now—*was just a dream?*

But of course it wasn't a dream. Eventually she *did* wake up only to realize that she was still here in Hayes House, tucked safely beneath the eaves of her cozy third-floor bedroom, with its French doors open to the sun porch, and the scent of Aunt Teeta's chrysanthemums and late-blooming roses drifting up from the backyard. And eventually she'd felt well enough to go back to school—was even looking forward to it . . .

Until just a few minutes ago.

Until the mirror.

"Stupid," Miranda whispered. "Think you could be any clumsier?"

But it was Monday morning, already seven thirty, and she was in a rush.

She'd heard Parker's car pulling into the driveway and hadn't wanted to keep him and Ashley waiting. He'd blasted his horn. Twice. Three more times. Yelling her name while she'd scrambled to pull on clothes and find her shoes and run a comb through her hair.

"Hey, Miranda, move it!"

"I'm not deaf, Parker," she'd grumbled. "And neither are the neighbors." But she was all thumbs and trying to hurry, giving herself a quick frown in the bathroom mirror, disappointed with what she saw. Her slight, not-very-tall self; those natural-curl ends of short brown hair shoved carelessly behind her ears. The dark, sleepless smudges lingering beneath her hazel eyes; her heart-shaped face, still a little too pale, with a light sprinkling of freckles across her nose. She'd stuck out her tongue at the sorry image, then yanked Aunt Teeta's hand mirror from the vanity drawer while fumbling the cap off a tube of lip gloss.

She'd never expected that mirror to drop.

She'd watched as it slipped through her fingers and shattered across the floor, her fractured reflection staring up at her, Miranda-shards-and-slivers glittering in the harsh bathroom light.

Since then she hadn't even moved. Her gaze stayed fixed on those shiny splinters of glass, and she realized that her hands were trembling, that the sweat on her forehead was trickling down her cheeks. For one split second, she drowned in a wave of irrational sorrow. A surge of irrational fear.

And that's when the *other* feelings started.

The warning feelings, the caution feelings, the unwanted feelings she was beginning to recognize all too well. Those nagging, unnerving suspicions that she wasn't quite alone, that some invisible—but all too real—connection had been made. A connection meant only for her.

Stop it, Miranda. It's just a mirror, it doesn't mean anything.

Yet her heart was racing, and she didn't take time to be careful. She scooped up the glass with her bare hands, gasping in pain as one large fragment lodged in her palm, clenching her teeth as she pulled it out. Then she wrapped *all* the fragments in bloody, wadded-up tissues, ran to the kitchen, and buried them in the garbage can, beneath coffee grounds, rotten banana peels, and soggy paper towels. She didn't want Aunt Teeta finding any leftover traces of broken mirror anywhere. She didn't want to hear what Aunt Teeta was sure to say. *Seven years' bad luck.*

One thing Miranda had learned since moving here to St. Yvette was that most Southerners were just as superstitious as they were hospitable. And the last thing she needed in her life right now was more bad luck.

"Miranda!" The horn was blaring again from outside, Parker's voice even louder. "Don't make me come up there! Even though I know you want me to!"

Gathering her things, Miranda dashed for the front door. She grabbed another tissue for the cut on her hand. She took a deep breath and swallowed down a wave of nausea.

Just a mirror . . . a plain, old, ordinary, silly broken mirror . . .

Except that it *wasn't* silly. And it *did* mean something—though she couldn't possibly guess what that was right now, or even explain how she knew.

The answer's waiting for me.

At some unknown time . . . but soon.

In some unknown place . . . but close.

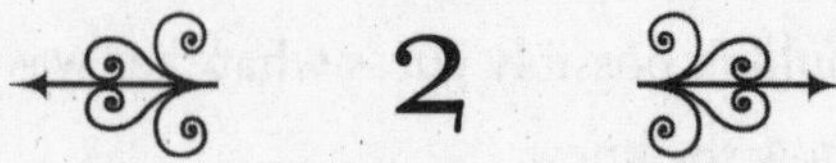

2

"**Miranda!**" Ashley squealed. "Oh my God, I'm so glad you're feeling better!"

Tightly squeezing her tissue, Miranda hurried toward the shiny red convertible idling alongside the curb. While Ashley jumped out to give her a hug, Parker lounged back, rested his left elbow on the door of his BMW, and pounded his right fist on the horn.

"Parker, for heaven's sake!" Whirling around, Ashley glared at him. "Stop that! It's so rude!"

"We're late!" he said, but eased off the steering wheel. "And you're the one who wanted to be there early for your fun . . . fun whatever the hell it is."

"*Fund*-raiser." Ashley's glare faded to mild annoyance. She was wearing one of her black-and-white cheerleader uniforms—one of the more *modest* ones, Miranda noted—which usually meant some in-school activity going on. Modest or not, the dress still managed to look sexy on Ashley's petite figure. Today her long blond hair was swept into a loose ponytail and tied back with black-and-white ribbons, a few stray curls falling softly around her face. Sometimes Miranda couldn't help wondering how it would feel, being that beautiful. Being one of those special, picture-perfect girls who would always be drooled over, sought after, and passionately admired.

"Fund-raiser," Ashley repeated, her attention back on Miranda. Like most everyone else in town, both Ashley and Parker had distinct Southern accents—but Ashley's was extra rich and ultra thick, like warm, melted honey. "We're sponsoring our Win-A-Date contest again this year. And we don't have to hurry *that* much; it's not like the cheerleading squad can't sell tickets without me. Oh, Miranda, we *all* missed you! I called to see how you were—but Parker wouldn't let me bring your homework by."

"You owe me for that." Parker smirked at Miranda. "Big-time."

As Ashley's arms went around her once more, Miranda realized that she was returning the hug just as tightly. "Aunt Teeta gave me your message," she whispered, and for just an instant there was a catch in her voice. "I missed you too, Ashley."

She hadn't expected this sudden depth of emotion. Not just for Ashley, and even Parker—but for the whole group that would be waiting at school. . . .

My friends.

"Where's Roo?" she asked quickly, not wanting to cry.

"Gage's mom gave them a ride. He still needs help, you know, with his cast and all."

"So Roo's still helping him?"

"Still making his life miserable, is more like it. But his cast comes off in a couple days, so that'll be great." Drawing back,

Ashley studied Miranda closely, put a cool hand to her forehead. "Maybe you're coming back too soon. Maybe you should give it another week. You have been *awfully* sick."

Miranda forced a laugh. "Forget it. If I have to spend even one more second in bed, I will *kill* myself."

"You're obviously not spending your seconds in bed with the right person," Parker advised her. "Trust me. That can make *all* the difference. In fact, I'd be more than happy to volun—"

"Parker, shush. Now listen to me, Miranda." Hands on hips, Ashley leveled her friend a no-nonsense stare. "You need to be really careful. You need to take things *really* slow, and take *really* good care of yourself. Or else you could get a relapse! And then I'd be missing you all over again! We'd *all* be missing you *all over again*!"

"No more hugging," Parker groaned. "Get in the car—no, wait! Have you been de-germed, Miranda? Absolutely no riding in my car unless you've been de-germed."

"*And* I missed you, too, Parker," Miranda teased as Ashley leaned in to swat Parker's shoulder.

"Ignore him, Miranda. He won't admit it, but he missed you terribly."

"Okay, I admit it." Parker sighed, "I missed you, Miranda. Terribly. I fantasized the whole time about you in your pajamas. With your runny nose and greasy hair, lying there in bed, all sweaty and breathing hard. Man, what a turn-on."

Though Ashley wasn't amused, Miranda found it impossible to resist that grin. Hard to resist almost *anything* about Parker, she had to admit. Parker Wilmington—most popular boy at St.

Yvette High School. Tall and blond, incredible sea-green eyes. Those gorgeous, unruly strands of hair framing his handsome face, no matter how many times he shook them back. Star quarterback, not a single game lost last season. Self-confident swagger and cocky smile. More money than he could spend in ten lifetimes. And—much to the disappointment of every female student—most definitely taken by Ashley.

"Oh, Parker, honestly," Ashley scolded, climbing in beside him. "Just be quiet and drive."

True to form, Parker managed to break all speed limits without getting caught. He skidded into the student lot, screeched to a halt in the last empty space, then the three of them hurried across campus. Even before they reached the main building, they could see a big crowd gathered outside. Several long tables had been set up; ribbons, streamers, and pom-poms seemed to be everywhere—all black and white, official colors of the St. Yvette Pirates. Banners and signs had been decorated in huge black-and-white letters: WIN A DATE WITH A CHEERLEADER! TICKETS ONLY $1.00! And while a few of St. Yvette High's cheerleaders handled sales and information, the rest were jumping, leaping, dancing, clapping, waving, cartwheeling, and rallying student onlookers with rousing chants.

Parker stopped in his tracks. He looked at Ashley. He let out another groan. "Tell me you're kidding."

"You know we do this date thing every year," Ashley said, half defensive, half apologetic. "I can't get out of it."

"Right. And the guy who wins a date with you—what does *he* get out of it?"

"Honestly, Parker, it's—oh, look, there's Roo and Gage!"

As Ashley rushed ahead and Parker followed, Miranda was content to trail behind. She could see Gage and Roo now, standing a safe distance from all the commotion—Gage's left leg in a cast, his lanky form balanced on crutches; and Roo beside him, munching solemnly on a limp wedge of pizza dripping with ketchup.

Looking at Gage, Miranda felt her heart warm. *God, I swear he's gotten cuter. . . .*

Tall like Parker, though a little more slender, his shoulders not as broad. Big brown eyes; long dark lashes; sensitive features. Soft brown hair, always a little long and shaggy over his ears and forehead. And those lips—perfect lips—though she'd never actually kissed them. As Miranda continued to watch, Roo gulped down some pizza, slid her hand beneath Gage's shirttail, and wiped her fingers on the seat of his jeans. Gage shot her an over-the-shoulder frown.

Next to Gage, Roo seemed even shorter than her barely-over-five-feet height. Her solid little body, more curvy than plump, was swathed in its usual blackness from head to toe—heavy black eye makeup; long black old-fashioned dress; high black combat boots. Dark purple beads dangled from her multi-pierced ears; thick bangs practically obscured her brows. And today she'd threaded more purple beads—the same shade of purple as her lip gloss—through at least a dozen strands of her overdyed black hair. Hard to believe that she and Ashley were stepsisters since the age of three—Miranda had been totally shocked when Roo told her.

Before she could call out, Gage spotted her in the crowd and began to smile. Casually he nudged Roo, who turned and waved her over.

"Miranda. Back among the living."

"And"—Parker looked Roo up and down—"the living dead."

"Did somebody speak?" Roo pointedly ignored him. "No? I didn't think so. By the way, Miranda, do us all a favor and never be gone this long again. Gage was inconsolable."

Gage smoothly deflected their teasing. "Just a *little* inconsolable."

"Come on, y'all *have* to buy some tickets," Ashley pleaded.

Glancing at Miranda, Gage winked. Parker let out his usual groan. Ashley kept right on talking.

"They only cost a dollar. And you could win a date with *any* of the cheerleaders. All you have to do is buy a ticket for the cheerleader you want, and it goes in a jar with her name on it. And then our coach draws a winner for each girl. Parker?"

"Huh?"

"You of *all* people can afford some tickets—how many do you want?"

"None."

"None?" Roo echoed, around another mouthful of pizza. Chewing, swallowing, she fixed Parker with a stare. "No tickets. No tickets at all to maybe win a date with your own girlfriend."

Parker grinned. "Hey. Why pay for something I get free?" Then, at the expression on Ashley's face, he added, "*Dates*, Ash. Come on, I was talking about *dates*."

"I'll buy some tickets," Gage offered swiftly. "I know Etienne will too."

At the mention of the name, Miranda's eyes did a quick sweep of the crowd. She hadn't seen Etienne since they'd gotten to school—she realized that she'd been looking for him all along.

"Thank you, Gage!" Ashley threw her arms around his neck, nearly knocking him over. "Look, y'all, I know we've got one more fund-raiser this year, but our squad needs money really, really bad. Like, for road trips. And competitions. And cheerleader camp. And we need new uniforms. And we need new pom-poms!"

Parker nodded at the front of her shirt. "Trust me, Ash. Your old pom-poms are just fine."

Though Gage choked back a laugh, he and Parker obviously found this hilarious. Now both of them received a withering glare from Ashley.

"Funny, guys, very funny. And I wouldn't say *anything* if I were you," she added, poking Gage in the ribs. "*I* know Babette LeBlanc wrote her measurements down on your cast."

"What!" Parker looked incredulous. "*Where?*"

"Right there." Ashley pointed while Parker crowded in to see. "Right next to her phone number."

"Damn! Yeah, with pom-poms that big, it's *got* to be Babette LeBlanc."

Rolling her eyes, Ashley began dragging Parker away. "Come on. You can help me sell tickets."

"I don't want to help you sell tickets."

"Parker, you're the star of the football team. You need to set a good example."

"I'm already a good example. In fact, I'm a *great* example."

"Yes, you are," Roo agreed. "But I don't think she was talking about stupidity." Hoisting her gargoyle backpack, Roo trudged for the entrance, leaving Gage and Miranda to follow.

It took Gage a few minutes to speak up.

"I'm glad you're better," he said at last. That soft-spoken voice . . . a half-shy smile. "It wasn't . . . the group wasn't the same without you."

Miranda turned to look at him, but his eyes were downward, intent on steering his crutches. "Yeah?"

"Cross my heart."

"That makes me feel really nice."

"It's the truth." His smile widened, showing a dimple in each cheek. Lifting his head, he regarded her with gentle curiosity. "So how are you?"

"Good."

"I mean, really."

"What do you mean, 'really'?" Playfully she bumped against him. "Don't I *look* good?"

"You look great. I just figured you might feel . . ."

"What?"

"You've been out of school awhile. Maybe you're feeling a little nervous about being back."

They'd reached the front steps. Without hesitation Gage started up—a slow but easy rhythm.

"Wow," Miranda said, holding the door, following him into the building. "You've gotten really talented at this."

"I should be; I've had six weeks to practice. And don't change the subject."

"Was I?"

"It'll be okay, Miranda."

Miranda didn't answer. All morning she'd been determined to hide her nervousness from everyone; she thought she'd managed to pull it off. *Leave it to Gage . . .*

Since their lockers were on different floors, Gage said goodbye at the next corner while Miranda watched him maneuver up the stairs. It always amused her, seeing the female attention he attracted—Gage, on the other hand, seemed oblivious that the flirting was meant exclusively for him. When he finally reached the landing, he paused, swiveled around on his crutches, and gave Miranda an encouraging thumbs-up. Laughing, she returned it.

Okay, Miranda. Keep telling yourself you belong here . . . keep telling yourself it feels good to be here. . . .

The weird thing was—it really *did* feel good to be here. Good to be out of bed and out of the house, good to be here at St. Yvette High. It was as though, for the very first time, she was allowing herself to feel a part of it all.

To *be* a part of it all.

The morning flew by. Parker was in her first class, complaining and cracking jokes, as usual; Ashley and Gage shared third period with her, teasing each other about some test question they'd both gotten wrong. To Miranda's relief, she hadn't missed as much work as she thought she had. A weekend maybe, with Ashley's help, and she'd be caught up again—but in the meantime there were new assignments to focus on, plus a whole range of upcoming activities to learn about. The Win a Date with a Cheerleader raffle. A Halloween dance. Assemblies, pep rallies, and football games. Something called the Harvest Festival. Volunteer projects, Homecoming events, and holiday bake sales. When it was announced that classes were canceled Friday because of teachers' meetings, a wild cheer resounded through the entire school.

But by the time noon rolled around, Miranda was dragging. She knew the others were expecting her to eat lunch with them, but she wasn't the least bit hungry—she wasn't sure she could even last the rest of the day. *Maybe I'm still sick. Maybe I came back too soon.*

Promising to meet them outside, she waved the group on without her. She couldn't remember the combination to her locker, and as she struggled to get it open, she kept glancing into the corridor. Still no sign of Etienne, though not so unusual, she kept reminding herself. With him working part-time and coming to school part-time, no one was ever quite sure of his schedule. *And not like I expect anything from him. Or that I should have heard from him by now. Or that I'm particularly important in his life, or that there's any sort of arrangement between us, or that we're anything more than friends—*

She bit hard on her bottom lip. What was she thinking? Etienne Boucher—elusive, alluring, and unattainable. *Get real, Miranda. The truth is, he promised Grandpa he'd look after you, that's all. Just friends.*

And yet . . . they *had* shared some close moments, she *couldn't* have imagined those—could she? Some really special moments, some private, more-than-friend moments? In spite of Etienne's busy life. In spite of the long hours he spent at all his different jobs. In spite of his silences, his solitude, his fiercely guarded secrets. *And in spite of the fact that he can have any girl in this whole town.*

God, Miranda, you are so pathetic.

Finally recalling the combination, she opened her locker, tossed in her books, and stared at the messy jumble. Not a bad locker, despite her own disorganized habits; in fact, Ashley had helped her with lots of personal touches. Some very cool magnets and stickers, hooks for hanging things, a message board, an extra shelf, and two mirrors—one at the rear, and one on the inside of the door. Miranda gave everything a good hard shove, then stepped back, taking a second to check herself in the mirror on the door.

My God . . . no wonder I'm dragging. Startled, she stared back at her shocking reflection—eyes too wide; shadows underneath, darker than ever; cheeks pinched tight; skin more pale. And that fine sheen of sweat was breaking out on her forehead again, just like this morning, dampening her hairline, even though she could feel another chill beginning to ache inside her.

What's going on?

It came to her then that something was horribly wrong, that her image in the glass wasn't natural—even for being sick. That everything about it seemed disjointed and frightening—her cheeks more sallow than white; eyes too hollow, too bruised, too vacant; the sweat too feverish; the chill too deep. *Something's not right . . . something . . .*

Trembling, Miranda lowered her head, took short, shallow breaths. *Don't freak out, there's a perfectly logical explanation, I just have to calm down and think . . .*

But instinct told her that it was happening again, just like it had happened weeks before. When she'd first become aware of her "gift." When she and the others had first become friends, first begun planning their Walk of the Spirits, when she'd first met the ghosts of Nathan and Ellena Rose. It had happened then, just like it had happened in the bathroom this morning when she'd dropped the mirror. Some message . . . some purpose . . . some connection . . . *except it's not the same—signs, signals, senses all twisted, all different—why isn't it the same—*

She fought down a wave of panic. She had to get out of here, go to the nurse, call Mom or Aunt Teeta to come pick her up. For a brief instant she wished Grandpa were still alive, wished Etienne would show up, wished Gage would find her—she was feeling worse and worse by the second. She'd just spent a whole week being miserable in bed, but none of that could even *begin* to compare with what she was feeling now. . . .

Sick . . . so frighteningly sick . . .

Lifting her head, Miranda stared once more into the mirror. And felt a slow, icy fist squeeze around her heart.

She saw her own face and the empty corridor behind her. No crowds, no activity, not a single student in any direction . . .

But *someone* was there.

Someone.

Watching her with a wide, fixed gaze—eyes so intense, so powerful, *so close*, that they missed nothing. Watching her from a place outside the mirror, but from *inside* the mirror, as well—looking back at her from within her own reflection . . .

Oh God . . .

The hairs prickled at the back of her neck. Miranda couldn't move or escape, could scarcely even breathe.

"Who are you?" she murmured. "*Where* are you? What do you want?"

Finally, fearfully, she was able to lift her hand.

She pressed it to the mirror and felt a scream catch instantly in her throat.

Another hand pressed back.

She could feel it, every detail, as though it were real—the firm pressure of it through the glass, distinct shape molded to hers, fingers lengthened against her fingers, alive but deathly cold.

And then a silent whisper. A plea she couldn't hear. Scared . . . sad . . . a noiseless sob.

"Who are you?" Miranda begged again. "What are you trying to tell me?"

But the hand, the voice, were gone now.

And the eyes that had watched her were closed.

3

"MIRANDA! Here you are!"

Numbly, Miranda turned to see Ashley hurrying up behind her. She took one last look at the mirror in her locker, then firmly shut the door.

"I thought you were coming to lunch and—"

Stopping abruptly, Ashley took in Miranda's condition at a glance—and obviously didn't like what she saw. "Are you okay? You're so pale."

"Am I?" Miranda opted for innocence.

"Extremely. Are you sick again? Do you need to go home?"

"I . . . maybe. Maybe I came back too soon."

"Oh, I knew it! Didn't I say that just this morning when we picked you up?" Ashley's arms went around her, hugging gently. "*Please* come eat something—I bet that's why you don't feel well. How do you expect to get better if you don't keep up your strength?"

"Maybe some crackers, then," Miranda agreed distractedly, knowing that Ashley wouldn't give up.

"Well . . . it's not great, but it's better than nothing." Taking Miranda's elbow, Ashley steered her firmly into the corridor. "The others are outside, our usual table. I have to go sell tickets now, though. And . . . you know . . . cheer. Oh, and I just saw your aunt Teeta on my way in."

"Here? You mean, at school?"

"By the principal's office. She said something about an appointment with Mr. Clark—I guess he's a client of hers?"

Not surprising, Miranda thought. Aunt Teeta's real estate agency was the most popular and dependable in St. Yvette; practically every family and business in town had been a client of hers at one time or another.

"I bet she's still there." Ashley's tone grew more anxious. "You could just leave with her. Come on, I'll walk with you."

It only took them a few minutes. And even before Miranda spotted her aunt, she could already hear that familiar laugh echoing down the corridor.

Giggling, Ashley shook her head. "I just love your aunt Teeta."

"Who doesn't? She's the best."

It was always that way with Aunt Teeta. The biggest heart in the world; an endless supply of comfort and hugs; and a warm, contagious laugh that made everyone within earshot laugh right along with her.

"Well, hey girls!" Waving some tickets in one plump hand, Aunt Teeta bustled toward them. "Now, isn't this a treat, I get to see both y'all in one visit!"

Miranda went straight into her aunt's open arms. It was one of the few places where she felt truly safe these days; now she wondered why that particular feeling of security seemed so important to her at this precise moment. She could tell at once that Aunt Teeta wasn't fooled. As the hug tightened around her, she heard genuine concern in her aunt's voice.

"What's up, darlin'? Miranda, are you—"

"Glad to see you," Miranda said quickly, pulling away, trying to tease. "Are those cheerleader tickets?"

For a second Aunt Teeta hesitated . . . then smoothly redirected her attention. "They most certainly are."

"So what cheerleader are you trying to win a date with?"

"Why, Ashley, of course! And if I win, I'm going to pay for her and that handsome boyfriend of hers to go out to some fine, fancy place for dinner."

This time Miranda had to smile. "Aunt Teeta, Parker could *buy* any of the fine, fancy dinner places in this town."

"Well then, I'll just have to cook them a special homemade dinner. My famous chicken pot pie and red velvet cake. Served by candlelight!" Laughing merrily, she glanced down at her watch. "Mercy, I didn't plan on being here this long. I've got me a whole afternoon free for a change, and I promised your poor mama I'd help her—she's gonna be wondering what on earth happened to me."

"Why?" Miranda frowned. "Where is she?"

"Out at the plantation. Buried under about ten million wallpaper samples, I imagine."

Ashley's face immediately lit up. "At Belle Chandelle? Oh, I can hardly stand it, I'm so jealous! That's like, my total dream house!"

"Well, honey, I'm afraid right now it's more like a total nightmare house. Although I shouldn't complain—I'm just thankful somebody finally bought it and decided to renovate. These new owners are rolling in money. They seem to know what they're in for, and they're committed for the long haul. So someday . . . God willing . . . the place will be beautiful again."

"I've *always* thought it was beautiful." Ashley's sigh was wistful. "I mean . . . it probably wasn't. But when I was little . . . and growing up . . . in my mind, it always was."

Aunt Teeta fixed Ashley with a long, thoughtful stare. "Would you like to see it?"

A moment of shocked, total silence. Ashley glanced at Miranda, then back to Aunt Teeta. Her eyes went saucer-wide.

"Really? *Oh, Miss Teeta, do you mean it?*"

"Well, of course I do—bring the whole group, if they want to come. In fact, why don't y'all drive on out this afternoon?"

"But you have practice, don't you, Ashley?" Miranda heard the urgency in her own voice, almost a plea. She hadn't meant to come up with excuses; the words just popped out. "And Parker . . . he has football practice, right?"

Before Ashley could respond, Aunt Teeta responded for her. "Don't worry if y'all are a little late. Miranda's mama has a meeting to go to later, but I've got lots to do out there. I won't be finishing up till at least six thirty or seven."

"Parker probably won't want to go anyway," Miranda tried again, still surprising herself. "And I don't have a car. And Gage, with his broken leg and all—"

"It's okay, Miranda." Ashley's face was growing more puzzled by the second. "Gage's mom is picking him and Roo up after school—if you don't want to wait around for Parker and me, you can catch a ride home with them. I'm pretty sure I can borrow Mom's car and come and get you after cheerleading. The guys are totally on their own, though. Oh, Miss Teeta, thank you so much!"

"You're entirely welcome, darlin'. I'll see y'all later."

Miranda waved as Ashley hurried off. All around her the hall was growing busy and more crowded, but the only thing she really noticed was the way Aunt Teeta was staring at her.

"*What?*" She didn't mean to sound so defensive. But Aunt Teeta only smiled and linked one arm through hers.

"Come walk with me, darlin'."

They went out the entrance, strolled slowly across the fenced grounds toward the visitors' parking lot. It was hot and humid, no trace of a breeze. Aunt Teeta smiled again . . . drew Miranda closer to her side.

"So how's your first day back?"

"Good."

"Glad to see your friends again? Think you can get caught up with homework pretty easy?"

Miranda nodded.

"Have you seen Gage?"

"You know I have, and stop making it more than it is."

"More than what is? It's a simple question. How about Etienne?"

"How *about* Etienne?"

"Uh-oh. I surely don't like the sound of *that* tone."

"I haven't seen him."

"No? Well, that's too bad."

"I've told you, Aunt Teeta, we're not . . ."

"What?"

"Anything." Miranda felt a quick stab of irritation. She wondered where it had come from. Then she felt even more irritated for wondering. "And stop playing matchmaker."

"Mercy, that would be like taking away the very air I breathe."

She wished Aunt Teeta would quit joking around—the last thing she felt like doing right now was laughing. School had started out so positive this morning, but things had gone steadily downhill. She was grumpy and exhausted, her hand was hurting again from the cut, and all she wanted to do was to go home and sleep. *And* not *go to Belle Chandelle.*

"You know," Aunt Teeta was talking again, "you still look a little under the weather."

"I'm fine. Just tired, is all."

"And I get the feeling you're not too happy about going out to the plantation today. Or maybe *any* day."

Miranda kept quiet. She concentrated on her sandals scuffing through the damp grass.

"The thing is, honey . . . your mama's been kind of wondering why you haven't shown more interest in her new job. She told me she's even offered to take you out there to Belle Chandelle a couple times."

Miranda nodded, half guilty, half resentful. Because deep

down she *knew* what was bothering her—and what could she say, really? To Aunt Teeta *or* to Mom? Neither of them was aware of what she'd been through these last few months, inheriting Grandpa's legacy, coming to terms with her newly discovered powers; neither of them had the slightest clue about the ways her life had changed, or the deep secrets she was forced to keep, or the fateful responsibilities that she carried on her shoulders, now that Grandpa was dead. *Souls and suffering . . . not of this world.* So how could she expect Mom and Aunt Teeta to understand how physically and emotionally vulnerable she was . . . how cautious she needed to be?

Old houses—especially an old, historic plantation like Belle Chandelle—meant lifetimes of memories. All those people who'd ever lived there—births and deaths and everything in between. Spirits who would ask her to open to their tragedies, open herself to places where the past could reach out and pull her in . . .

"Etienne's mama." Aunt Teeta's words startled Miranda back again.

"What about Miss Nell?"

"Darlin', have you been listenin' to a single thing I've said?" Laughing, Aunt Teeta gave her a quick, tight squeeze. "Those new owners of Belle Chandelle—they want to turn it into a bed and breakfast. Now, isn't that exciting? And they asked if I knew anybody to head up the kitchen. Well, I didn't even have to think. Nell Boucher's always been the best cook in this whole parish. And she and Etienne's daddy *did* have that restaurant in town once upon a time—why, people came from miles around just to eat there, it was so popular. And the food? Honey, I'm telling you, it was to die for."

"Really? What happened to it?"

"What always happened whenever Lazare Boucher got his mean, sneaky self involved with anything. Oh, there were plenty rumors—but the hard fact was, the restaurant shut down, and he blamed Nell for it. Not a soul believed him, of course. And Nell was heartbroken."

Miranda shot her aunt a sympathetic glance. "But don't she and Etienne have a tourist business now? Swamp boats or something?"

"Yes, but Etienne talked her into letting *him* do the tours from now on; he *wants* his mama to take the job at Belle Chandelle." Aunt Teeta's voice lowered, went thoughtful. "I know that boy worries about her all the time. Even though he never shows what he's feeling."

"But . . . her cancer's in remission, right?"

"Last I heard. And Nell never complains. Even when I've seen her right there on death's doorstep, I've never once heard her complain." Aunt Teeta clucked her tongue . . . rummaged deep in her purse . . . pulled out a set of keys. "Enough of this sad talk! I'll see you later at the plantation. Oh, and by the way—there *are* some pretty amazing sights out there. One in particular I think you'll enjoy."

"What is it?"

"You'll see." Giving her one last hug, Aunt Teeta pulled free. "Well, here's my car. Love you, baby girl."

"Love you too."

But long after Aunt Teeta left, Miranda stood there staring off across campus . . . the morning's strange events still clinging to her like a gloomy fog.

From some distant place, she felt something trickle down her fingertips, and she realized that her palm had started to bleed.

A pain much worse this time . . .

Aching from her hand . . . deep into her heart.

4

"Shouldn't we be getting close?" Chewing her bottom lip, Ashley strained forward to peer out the windshield. "You'd think there'd be signs or something, wouldn't you? It feels like we've been driving forever."

"We *have* been driving forever," Roo complained. "*Whenever* you drive, we end up driving forever."

"I'm ignoring that. I'm not even listening." Ashley settled back in her seat again. She shot Miranda a troubled glance. "Miranda, you haven't said a word since we picked you up. Maybe this wasn't such a good idea, you coming out here and—"

"No, I'm fine," Miranda answered, though she didn't feel fine at all.

She'd been glad to go home to an empty house after school; she'd gone straight to her room and crawled into bed and stayed there. She'd tried to nap, but couldn't. She'd tried not to think about the creepy experience at her locker, but wasn't able to think of anything else. Most of all, she'd tried to psych herself up for this little outing to Belle Chandelle—and hadn't done a very good job of it.

Now she leaned against the passenger door, determined to sound convincing. "I *wanted* to come. I'm just sort of . . . edgy, I guess."

"Global warming," Roo said solemnly.

"What?"

"Global warming. Halloween's in a couple days, Thanksgiving's only three weeks after that, and it's still almost a hundred degrees outside. I don't remember October ever being this hot before. It doesn't feel like the holidays, and it throws everything off."

Right, Miranda thought glumly. *If only it were that simple*.

"Oh, y'all, I'm just so *excited!*" Ashley burst out, inching the car around a pothole. "I've been in love with this plantation my whole *life*! Ever since I was a little girl, I used to dream I'd live there someday and fix it all up! And now—to actually see it! Inside! And in person!"

Roo was less than enthused. "We'll never see it at all if you don't go faster."

"I can't go faster—it's muddy. And deer and little animals might run out in front of the car."

"Ash, the only thing you could hit at this speed is road kill."

In spite of her mood, Miranda couldn't help smiling. She sat straighter, did her best to focus—on Ashley pouting beside her, on Roo lounging into one corner of the backseat, earbuds firmly in place, expression totally bored. Turning halfway around, she tapped Roo on the knee.

"Hey, what are you listening to?"

"My soul."

At some point since leaving school today, Roo had obviously attempted one of her spur-of-the-moment makeovers—with the usual startling results. The purple beads had vanished from her hair, replaced now with bright magenta streaks and several newly chopped, very uneven layers.

"And what's your soul telling you?" Miranda went along.

"That it will be fully evolved by the time this trip is over."

"Roo, you are *impossible*!" Indignant, Ashley frowned into the rearview mirror. "If Parker were driving, you'd be nagging him to slow down."

"That's because *Parker* drives like a maniac. *You* drive like Great-Grandma Fern."

"But . . . Great-Grandma Fern can't drive."

"I know."

"Well, it's not my fault—I *hate* using Mom's car, it always makes me so nervous! I mean . . . the radio's broken, I can't concentrate."

As Roo rolled her eyes, Miranda guided the conversation to safer ground.

"So you guys grew up here all these years, this close to Belle Chandelle, but you've never been inside?"

"No, it was always so spooky!" Ashley's blue eyes widened. "And dangerous, too. The place had been empty forever—the roof was caved in, and the galleries had fallen down, and most of the outbuildings were all rotted away. Our folks wouldn't let us go near it."

"And it's not that close to town." Rousing slightly, Roo took a long drag on her cigarette, flicked ashes out her half-open window. "Sometimes we'd ride our bikes out here, though. And sometimes when we'd be at Etienne's house, we'd all sneak over."

"On your bikes?" Miranda asked.

"We walked. When we got older, sometimes we took his boat—but mostly we walked. It didn't really seem that far then . . . even though it was."

"Etienne lives pretty close to Belle Chandelle," Ashley explained to Miranda. "How close, Roo? About a mile . . . mile and a half . . . down the bayou? Sort of between Belle Chandelle and the Falls?"

Roo's shrug seemed affirmative.

"So you'd be at Etienne's," Miranda prompted Ashley. "And then you'd come over here and sneak through the buildings?"

"The rest of us sneaked," Roo corrected. "Ashley was always too scared."

Ashley's voice raised in quick protest. "I was . . . careful."

"You cried and ran away."

"Well, Gage and Etienne always hid and jumped out at me!"

"You cried all the way back to Etienne's house. And you told on us."

"I did not!"

"Yes, you did. You were a little tattletale."

"I was not! I never told on y'all."

"You were the only one crying. Same thing."

Picturing the scene, Miranda chuckled. "So then what happened?" she asked Roo.

"Etienne got in trouble."

"Just Etienne? No one else?"

"He was always the instigator. He was always the one who

brought us over here, but then of course, we always *wanted* him to. Nobody would have known, if it hadn't been for Ashley."

"I don't remember him getting in any *real* trouble," Ashley defended herself. "Well . . . okay . . . I *sort* of remember him getting fussed at a couple times."

"Yeah, Miss Nell didn't usually do much more than fuss. Not that Etienne cared. And she *never* told Etienne's dad." Roo paused, her expression darkening. "She'd never have done that."

For a moment there was only silence. Miranda had seen the faded scars along Etienne's arms; she remembered Roo telling her about the regular beatings Etienne had received from his father. Now it was Ashley who changed topics.

"Miranda, your mom's so lucky—getting to work at the plantation every day! She must be really happy."

"At least she's in a good mood most of the time," Miranda admitted. "She's smiling a lot more. And we're not fighting like we used to. It's . . . you know . . . nice to see her smiling like that again."

"Okay, I know your mom's an interior designer, but explain it again, about her job." Clutching the steering wheel, Ashley slowed the car to a near crawl, slammed viciously on the brake, then lurched headlong into a wide, shallow puddle.

There was an awkward moment of silence. Roo took a long drag on her cigarette before she finally spoke.

"Now what?"

"I'm trying to miss all this water."

"It's a puddle, Ash. Not the Mississippi River."

Struggling not to laugh, Miranda resumed their discussion.

"Mom's in charge of all the decorating. And not just for the main house—for all the outbuildings, too. I think it's a pretty big deal."

"The whole plantation? That *is* a big deal. Can you imagine getting to pick out all that furniture? The rugs . . . the wallpaper . . . the curtains . . . the candlesticks . . ."

"The mosquito nets," Roo added blandly.

"Your mother must *love* going to work every day, Miranda." Ashley sounded wistful. "Who wouldn't want a perfect job like that! And I bet everybody's so excited to have her there."

"They seem to be." Miranda considered a moment. "Even Parker's mom thinks it's a good idea."

"Mrs. Wilmington? Really?"

"Mom and Aunt Teeta and Mrs. Wilmington are all on some renovation committee together. And Mrs. Wilmington actually told the members that putting Mom in charge of the decorating was the smartest decision they'd ever made."

"She's after something," Roo concluded.

"Get this. One day Mrs. Wilmington brought in a whole bunch of fabric samples she wanted Mom to use in the plantation house. And Mom turned them all down."

Ashley's voice was half shock, half awe. "Are you serious? She stood up to Mrs. Wilmington? And told her *no*? And didn't get *fired*?"

"Way to go, Miranda's mom," Roo murmured, impressed.

"Hazel," Miranda said. "Mom wants all my friends to start calling her Hazel, not Mrs. Barnes. Like how you call each other's moms. Not so formal."

"Then way to go, Miss Hazel." Roo blew out a slow, sinuous stream of smoke. "Parker must be ecstatic over *that* little confrontation. Anything that pisses off his mom *always* makes Parker ecstatic. Not that I blame him."

"Roo, don't," Ashley scolded. "Mrs. Wilmington can be really nice."

"Yeah—when she's *after* something. Listen, Miranda, you know she's just sucking up because she still wants your grandfather's War collection. She'd *love* to get her hands on all those artifacts."

Miranda looked thoughtful. "Hmmm . . . maybe. I know Mom's been after Aunt Teeta lately to get all that stuff appraised."

"That proves it. Your mom must suspect something too. I swear, just because Mrs. Wilmington runs the Historical Society, she thinks she can run the whole town."

"With all their money, they pretty much *do* run the whole town," Ashley confirmed. "And . . . pretty much *own* the whole town."

"It's weird, though." Once more, Miranda reflected. "For some reason, Mom really seems to like Mrs. Wilmington."

Roo made a sound of disgust. "That's because your mom doesn't really know her."

"Well, she knows Mrs. Wilmington's the authority on local history. She said—and I quote—'It only makes sense to include her expertise.' "

"Well, I'm glad *we're* being included," Ashley piped up. "This is so great of your aunt Teeta—letting us see the house before it's even finished!"

"Aunt Teeta's even more nuts about the place than my mom is—she's out there helping every chance she gets. Did you know she had the listing for Belle Chandelle ever since she's been a real estate agent? She said she never gave up on it—she knew somewhere, someday, there just had to be the right people willing to save it."

"Well, I can't believe you haven't been out there yet. If it were me, I'd be there every single day—I'd be *living* there if I could! Maybe you'll get to help decorate, Miranda. You're so lucky."

Right. Broken-mirror-seven-years'-bad-lucky.

Abruptly Miranda changed the subject. "So, are the guys coming, do you think?"

"They said they were. Well, Parker said he absolutely wouldn't come, but I sort of . . . bribed him."

"Do *not* elaborate," Roo ordered.

"Oh, honestly, Roo. I just promised I'd write his English essay for him."

"You write *all* his essays for him."

"I *help* write them. I don't *totally* write them. We'd get expelled if I *totally* wrote them."

Roo shook her head at Miranda. "She *totally* writes them. But she puts in a bunch of really ignorant parts, so the teacher will think it's Parker."

"So are they coming?" Miranda asked again, managing a straight face.

Ashley slowed down for a fallen branch. "Yes. Parker said he'd pick up Gage after football practice."

"Poor Gage. He's going to be so happy to finally get that cast off."

"In a few days, right?" Roo mulled this over. "Hmmm . . . I bet he'll still be really wobbly for a while."

Ashley shot her sister a frown. "Roo, shame on you. The whole time he's been in that awful thing, you've tormented him. And now it's finally coming off, and you've got a million *new* ways to torment him. Even before his leg can get strong again!"

"Not quite a million. I'm still deep in my creative process."

"You know he'll get you back," Ashley warned.

"No, he won't."

"He will eventually. He always does."

"Never. I have too many advantages."

"Such as?" Miranda asked her, amused.

"First, I've always got my guard up. Second, Gage is way too easy to embarrass."

"And so *cute* when he's embarrassed," Ashley insisted. "Don't forget that."

"Three major strikes against him."

"But then . . . Gage is cute when he's *not* embarrassed too."

"*No*. I'm going for embarrassment. Complete and total embarrassment, every chance I get."

As Miranda and Ashley laughed, Roo gave a satisfied smile and draped herself between the seats. Miranda shifted her eyes to the heavily wooded landscape.

"And what about Etienne?" she mentioned casually. "I didn't

see him at school today. Did anyone ask him if he wanted to meet us?"

"Didn't have to," Roo said.

"What do you mean?"

"He's on the construction crew out here."

"You're kidding." *Pretty amazing sights, huh? One I'd especially be interested in? Good one, Aunt Teeta.*

"You mean he never told you?"

Ashley sounded exasperated. "How could he tell her, Roo? She's been sick. And besides that, Etienne never tells anybody anything, you know that."

"Actually, it's sort of an on-again-off-again thing," Roo explained. "Whenever somebody decides to renovate Belle Chandelle, then Etienne gets hired."

"He worked there all last summer," Ashley added. "At least till the owner ran out of money and shut the place down. After that happened, he said Belle Chandelle was probably lost forever."

The information surprised Miranda. "I didn't realize anyone owned it before."

"Well, nobody ever kept it very long. They'd start to fix it up, they'd sell it. They'd start to fix it up again, they'd sell it again. Last Christmas, some people in New Orleans finally bought it. Etienne says they never come here, but they seem to know all the best experts to hire."

"Aunt Teeta said they're making it into a bed and breakfast."

"Seriously?" Bouncing in her seat, Ashley let out a squeal.

"That's so perfect! I *love* these new owners, whoever they are! And I'm so glad they want to protect Belle Chandelle."

Roo gave a vague nod. "They've made it a private road now—and fenced in a lot of the property. And they *really* don't want trespassers around."

"So do people ever sneak in?" Miranda wondered. "Or try to—"

As a cold shudder crept up her spine, she went rigid, her glance darting to the slowly passing scenery.

"Maybe we should turn around," she whispered. "Maybe we should go back."

Startled, Ashley let up on the gas pedal. "You mean, go home? But I thought—"

"I think maybe it *is* out here somewhere." For a split second, Miranda's thoughts scrambled, her mind went hazy, her words echoed hollowly through her brain. *Did I just say that out loud?*

She hadn't meant to, hadn't expected to—but the dark mood that had plagued her most of the day was suddenly unbearable. As though the very atmosphere were shifting and closing in . . . intrusive . . . oppressive . . . the way a room could feel when it held too many people. . . .

"*What's* out here somewhere?" Ashley asked, confused.

"I feel dizzy," Miranda mumbled. "I need some air."

Rolling down the window, she breathed deeply, felt her senses opening wide. Outside it smelled of swamp water and last night's rain; of creeping animals and the twisted underbrush that hid them. The earth here was rich and dark. A soggy breeze snaked its way through the weeds and tangled trees, bringing with it a heady confusion of moss and mold and remembrances. . . .

She felt Ashley squeezing her shoulder. With enormous effort, she pulled back inside, took another deep breath, and turned to face Roo's bold stare.

"The plantation's still two miles away." Without breaking eye contact, Roo tossed her cigarette butt out onto the muddy road. "And you're already picking up spirit vibes."

Ashley was instantly alarmed. "Are you really? Oh, Miranda, I wish you wouldn't. I don't think I want to go there if you're already picking up spirit vibes."

"It's nothing," *No worse than staring eyes and a disembodied hand in my locker.* Swallowing hard, Miranda tried to sound reassuring. "Look, even though I've been through it once, I'm still getting used to all this, you know? Weird stuff coming out of nowhere, hitting me when I'm not expecting it? It catches me off guard, it's like . . . like . . ." Her voice trailed off. She saw the guilt on Ashley's face, felt a second gentle squeeze on her shoulder.

"Don't worry, Ashley." Miranda forced an overly confident smile. "Honest. I'm okay."

Yet even though Ashley seemed relieved, Miranda sensed that she hadn't fooled Roo for a second.

"Uh-huh." One of Roo's eyebrows arched beneath her bangs. "Keep telling yourself that."

But they were driving closer every second, and Miranda's

head was filling with echoes and whispers and secrets and cries, all jumbled, all muffled, like wind rushing softly, like time spinning out of control . . .

I shouldn't have come. I should have stayed away, I knew *better . . .*

"Dammit," she murmured, so the others couldn't hear. "Why today?"

For she was certain now that this was all meant to be, all happening for a reason. A reason of grave importance that she'd become part of, but still couldn't figure out. Like the eerie connection she'd felt in the bathroom this morning when she'd broken Aunt Teeta's mirror . . . and the frightening events that she'd experienced at her locker . . . *and here I am, getting ready to walk right into that plantation, right into God knows what . . .*

She realized that Roo was watching her. There was both concern and understanding in that steady, black-ringed stare.

"Think you're ready?" Roo asked.

Hesitantly, Miranda nodded. Events were already in play; she had no choice but to see them through. And yet deep down she *wasn't* ready, not ready at all.

Not for memories . . .

Not for mysteries . . .

Not for what's waiting for me at Belle Chandelle.

5

"There's a car behind us," Ashley said. "Well, not *close* behind us. But it will be in a minute—it's coming really fast."

Grateful for the interruption, Miranda checked the side mirror, then once again craned her head out the window. The car was still at a distance, blocked from sight by drooping tree branches and long, gray strings of moss overhanging the road. But its engine was revving loud, bursts of rocks and shells and mud slinging wildly from beneath its tires. Annoyed, Miranda turned back to Ashley.

"I thought this road wasn't open to the public. Maybe it's some of the workers."

"Sure it's not Parker?" Roo asked, settling into her corner. "Whoever it is sure *drives* like Parker."

"That's not nice." Ashley frowned.

"It wasn't meant to be nice. It was meant to be true."

Miranda did another quick take in the mirror. "It's not a BMW. It's . . . I don't know. A station wagon? And it looks like maybe two people inside?"

"Ignore them, Ash." Digging through the pockets of her dress, Roo pulled out a matchbook and a crumpled pack of cigarettes. "Just keep driving."

"I can't keep driving," Ashley told her. "They're going to run me off the road."

"Pull over, then."

"There's no place to pull over."

"Sure there is. Just go between those trees."

"It's squishy over there. We might get stuck."

"We won't get stuck. Just do it."

"No. I'm stopping."

"You're what?"

"I'm going to stop here. They'll just have to go around me."

"Maybe Roo's right," Miranda echoed nervously. "Maybe you should pull over."

As Roo peered out the back windshield, Miranda heard the approaching car kick into high gear, accelerating rapidly, barreling down on them. The road was barely wide enough for two cars to pass, and Ashley had stopped in the middle. Thick stands of trees flanked each side, and both narrow shoulders were mucky with a week's buildup of rain.

"They'll stop." Ashley's eyes were glued to the rearview mirror. "When they see we're not moving, I'm pretty sure they'll stop."

"They're not stopping," Roo said.

The car burst into clear view. For a split second, it hurtled toward them at breakneck speed, then suddenly slammed on its brakes, fishtailing wildly, sliding to a stop beside them, angled half on, half off the road. Miranda didn't realize she'd been holding her breath. Not till the car's window rolled down and she saw the familiar face grinning out at them.

"What's this, Ash? A roadblock? Damsels in distress?"

Roo's stare was bland. "Roadblock. There's an idiot on the loose, but—oh. Never mind. I see we just caught him."

"Parker Wilmington!" Ashley exploded. "You scared me half to death! What on earth do you think you're doing?"

Despite their near collision, Parker obviously found the whole thing hilarious. And as Ashley continued to berate him, he only looked more and more amused.

"And why are you in that car?" Ashley demanded. "That's not your car!"

"No, it's Leo's."

"Leo's? You're driving your *gardener's car*?"

Parker started to answer, then stopped. His gaze redirected to Roo. "Hey. Your Gloominess. What the *hell* did you do to your hair?"

"Cut it."

"With what? A saw? A very dull meat cleaver?"

"I needed a change."

"Try a mask next time."

"You're driving your *gardener's car*?" Ashley asked again.

"Look, I got a flat tire; Leo told me I could use this. What's the big deal?"

"The big deal is, your family has a ton of brand-new cars, and you're driving this poor old car of Leo's, and you're totally trashing it in the process!"

"Hey, not to worry. I told him I'd fill the tank and wash it before I brought it back." Inclining his head, Parker's grin widened. "Hey, Miranda."

"Hi, Parker. And in case you didn't notice the speed limit back there—"

"I've got Gage," Parker interrupted quickly.

"Sounds contagious," Roo said. "Is it fatal?"

"Depends on where you touch it."

As Parker chuckled and glanced to his right, Miranda spotted Gage sitting next to him. The passenger seat had been pushed back to accommodate his cast, but he was leaning slightly toward Parker's window, staring out.

"Forget it," Gage informed Roo. "You're not touching me. I don't care where it is."

Parker made a dramatic show of checking the dashboard clock. "Ash, you left at *least* half an hour before I did. And then I *still* had to pick up Gage. I mean, even *I* figured you'd go over five miles an hour."

"She didn't go over *one* mile an hour," Roo grumbled. "I'm walking back."

"What's wrong with your broomstick?"

"You can ride with us," Gage offered, easing back into place.

"Excuse me?" Parker shot at Gage. "You can't invite her. It's not your car."

"It's not yours, either."

"Come on, y'all," Ashley scolded. "I just want to hurry so we can get there."

"Whoa, she's a speed demon!" Parker obligingly gunned the motor. "Christ, Ashley, the whole damn plantation will be rebuilt by the time you show up."

He left them behind within seconds. When Ashley finally

reached the turnoff to Belle Chandelle, the station wagon was nowhere to be seen.

"It shouldn't be too far now." Scooting to the edge of her seat, Miranda kept a sharp eye on their surroundings. "Aunt Teeta said there's a big gate and a barbwire fence. Maybe around this next curve?"

"I'm getting so excited again!" Ashley caught a quick breath. "Aren't you even the least bit excited, Roo?"

"Don't I look excited?"

"I can't wait to see—*oh my God!*"

"Now what?"

"Look, y'all! There it is!"

Magical. That's the first word that came to mind as Miranda stared at the scene ahead of them. Magical and make-believe, like something straight out of a movie. A perfect photograph, centuries old, caught in the fading glow of late afternoon, framed by those wild, tangled woods and the hazy aftermath of early rain.

Belle Chandelle.

"It's beautiful," Ashley murmured. "More beautiful than I even imagined."

"Except for the color." Miranda couldn't help making a face. "Why would anyone paint it such a horrible color?"

Set back among live oaks, cypress trees, and towering magnolias, the three-story plantation house rose majestically within deep, restful shadows and soft draperies of moss, where the full rays of the sun couldn't quite reach. Eight round columns adorned the front, rising all the way to the gabled roof. A row of tall, shuttered French doors lined the verandah and the wide, balustered gallery above it; a series of dormer windows marked the third floor. Higher still were the brick chimneys, while a railing-enclosed belvedere stood in silhouette against the sky, cresting the roof like a giant finial.

And all of it yellow. A dark, dull, nauseous yellow, with an ugly reddish tinge. Miranda's stomach instantly went queasy.

"It's not a horrible color!" Ashley objected. "It's *perfect*! Absolutely perfect. In fact, I can't imagine it being any better color than white."

"White? What are you talking about? It's—"

The words died in Miranda's throat. As she turned back toward the house, she could see all the creamy white walls, the tall white columns, the wide white galleries . . .

Not yellow—nothing *is yellow. It's all—*

"White," Roo finished. "What are *you* talking about?"

Flustered, Miranda tried to think, tried to concentrate, but the voices were whispering again, floating through her head telling secrets, and scenes were flowing, running together so fast, they were like one big blur that made no sense. . . .

"You're right," she mumbled, staring down at her hands, forcing herself to talk out loud. "I guess . . . the way the light was shining down, it just looked yellow to me." *Good . . . good . . . my head is clearing . . . the shadows are going.* "It must have been a reflection on something."

Yet deep down, though she *wanted* to believe that, she still wasn't sure. *It was too clear, too vivid, that hideous yellow.* And a cold, nagging dread had settled deeper in the pit of her stomach.

"Miranda, are you sure this is where we're supposed to be? It's all empty. I think we're the only ones here."

As Ashley's voice snapped her back to attention, Miranda realized they were still driving, that they'd come to an open gate at the end of the road. Beyond the high fence was a makeshift parking lot—a large, muddy tract of crushed oyster shells, potholes, and carelessly arranged lengths of plywood. *Pull yourself together, Miranda. Don't think about what just happened.*

"It's after five," she told Ashley now. "I don't imagine the work crews hang around."

Roo nodded toward the far corner of the lot, where two big pecan trees offered the only shade. "There's the station wagon. And Etienne's truck."

"I see Aunt Teeta's car."

"Do you want me to park next to them?" Brow furrowing, Ashley hesitated. "Because I need to warn you, I'm not very good at parking so—"

"No," Miranda said quickly, hoping she hadn't sounded too eager. "No, just stop the car right here. I think that's the path to the main house—over by the fence. This way we won't have so far to walk. Right, Roo?"

But Roo didn't take time to answer. She was already out of the car and onto the path, leaving Miranda and Ashley to trail behind.

It was obvious that this end of the property had been reserved strictly for construction—on all sides there were building materials, work vehicles, and heavy machinery. Deep tire tracks rutted the ground and seeped with water; any grass had been killed off long ago. The day was still warm and chokingly humid. Roo was right—even for south Louisiana, October had been unseasonably hot.

But as the girls walked farther, Miranda noticed the scenery begin to change. Despite more than a century of neglect, there were isolated spots of beauty here and there; colors peeking through the choked weeds and rambling vines; an overall park-like setting, tranquil beneath heavy layers of overgrown vegetation, dignified beneath the scars of blistering Southern weather.

"Miranda . . . do you know Kurt Fuller?" Ashley asked quietly.

Miranda threw her a glance. Ashley was frowning, eyes cast down, as if something important weighed heavily on her mind—but though Miranda was trying to listen, there were so many *other* things around her, tugging at her senses, demanding her attention. Wide-spreading trees dripping moss, some standing alone, some in thick groves, *cruelty happened here, beatings, hangings*—the promise of lush grass beneath heavy carpets of weeds, *duels were fought here, blood was spilled*—wildflowers springing up amidst piles of rotting boards, crumbling rocks and stones, *babies were buried here, mothers wept*—

"I . . ." Again Miranda tried to concentrate on Ashley. "He sits across from me in Spanish. He's on the football team, right?"

"He's our wide receiver."

"Don't they call him Sneak or something?"

"*Streak*, Miranda. Because he's so fast."

"Sorry."

Ashley's voice lowered even more. "He just broke up with his girlfriend Delphine. And after cheerleading practice today? He asked me to go out with him."

"Really?" Miranda glanced from Ashley's face . . . scanned the desolate surroundings. There were no buildings out here, only the trees and the empty sweep of land, *but the slave quarters were back there, two rows of cabins facing each other, raised up off the ground—and the cemetery, they had their own cemetery—almost like their own separate little neighborhood—the overseer's house—and sugarcane tall and ripe, growing for miles and miles in the scorching sun—*

"You can't tell Parker," Ashley said. With a start, Miranda realized that they'd stopped walking, that Ashley was waiting for her to talk. "And you can't tell Roo. She'd probably *want* me to go out with Kurt. Just to upset Parker."

"So . . ." *Focus, Miranda. Focus.* "What are you going to do?"

"I'm *not* going out with him," Ashley replied firmly. "Even though he *is* . . . you know. Handsome and godlike in every way. And he *knows* Parker and I are together. Why would he even ask me out? *Everybody* knows Parker and I are together."

"Maybe he just really likes you, Ashley."

"Or maybe he wants to make Delphine jealous."

"Or maybe he's liked you for a while, and he's been trying to get *out* of his other relationship, and now he's . . . you know . . . testing the waters."

"Or maybe he's trying to make Parker mad."

"Does he have something against Parker?"

"Well . . . they've always been really competitive on the field, but Coach won't put up with stuff like that."

"Hmmm. Sounds like they might be really competitive *off* the field too—especially now that Kurt's girlfriend's out of the picture. Did you tell him you wouldn't go out with him?"

"Of course!"

"And what happened?"

The girl's response was somewhat embarrassed. "He said he thinks I'm hot."

"What'd *you* say?"

"I told him it was because of the weather—you know, because I just finished practice, and I'm *always* hot when I finish practice. Oh Miranda, I don't *want* him to think I'm hot. Even though it *is* a really nice compliment. And he *is* a really nice guy. And charming. And he does things like send flowers and cards and candy, and he never forgets a special occasion, and—"

"How do you know all that?"

"All the girls know that—Delphine brags to everybody. In fact . . . Kurt's kind of obsessive about being wonderful."

"So . . . isn't that good?"

"I don't think he's going to leave me alone. I think he's going to keep asking me out, and I don't know what to do about it."

"Keep saying no?"

"I told you . . . the guy's obsessive."

"Then maybe you *should* tell Parker. If it bothers you that much, he might . . ."

Miranda's thoughts trailed away. As a soft warmth crept through her, her mind began to open . . . open . . . and for an instant she wasn't sure if she was actually turning around or only imagining it—peering off between long curtains of moss, far over the sweeping plantation grounds, back toward wild, overgrown fields. . . .

Magnolia blossoms, waxy cool fragrant trees—blazing sunshine, tall graceful green seas of sugarcane—low voices singing, work-weary chorus—meat curing billowing, thick black ribbons of smoke—sweet ripe orchards heavy with fruit—flies buzzing swarming, stinking outhouses on sweltering days—fresh herbs hot spices gumbo simmering in the fireplace, wafting from the open kitchen door—black rancid bayou water—sweat-soaked cotton shirts, dark oily grimy hands, bloody hands, hands thick with calluses, hands torn with scars—hammering chiseling sawdust underfoot, white hot sparks metal horseshoes—harvest wagons groaning, slow steady plodding of mules, whips cracking the air . . .

No. No . . . not *the air . . . something else . . . whips cracking, snapping, striking, like a snake striking—cutting skin bone raw tender flesh . . . wrists bound bodies trapped and tortured—*

"Parker would *not* handle it well." Ashley's reply jolted Miranda back again. "Sometimes he can get really jealous. And I don't want there to be any trouble between him and Kurt. I'd be so embarrassed, especially over something so stupid."

Miranda drew a deep breath. For a split second she felt shaky and light-headed—her usual transition between this world and another. Fortunately, Ashley didn't seem to notice. "Are you sure? It's not stupid if you're worried about it."

"Yes, I'm sure. I just . . . I guess I just needed to talk about it."

"You can always talk to me, Ashley."

"Look, Roo's waiting for us. Please don't say anything."

"I won't. And she still has her earbuds in anyway."

"Actually . . . I'm pretty sure they're not connected to anything. Sometimes she just sticks them in and walks around with the other end loose in her pocket. She thinks it's funny when people say rude things about her because they think she can't hear them."

"It doesn't hurt her feelings?"

"She says rude things back at them, just to see the looks on their faces."

Laughing, the girls continued walking. The sensations had stilled in Miranda's head; the sweeping images had faded. She felt stronger now and calmer, yet a tiny spark of wariness still flickered in the farthest corner of her mind. Instinctively she glanced in all directions. This place, this entire plantation property, was massive and overwhelming—over a century of human drama had played out within its boundaries. *And I'm only one person; it's too much, too much to take in. . . .*

She rubbed at her forehead, squinted down at the muddy edges of the path. *Stay focused, Miranda. Stay here, right in this moment. Don't look to the left or the right, don't let yourself think forward or backward, just stay focused and you'll be fine.* As she and Ashley caught up with Roo, she managed a smile and made an all-encompassing gesture with her arms.

"So what do you think, Roo? Anything familiar? Anything you remember from when you were little?"

Roo considered the question. Turning slowly, she scanned the landscape, then brought her gaze back again, full circle. "There were some buildings off that way, behind the house. Or at least what was *left* of some buildings. That's where we used to play. But they were already in such bad shape then, I didn't really expect anything to be left."

"Mom said they'll have to reconstruct most of the outbuildings. Hardly any of the originals survived."

"It's so tragic," Ashley sighed. "I bet this whole place was really happy and romantic once upon a time. Can't you imagine—just like in the movies? Full of hopes and dreams and love and charm and—"

"They had slaves here," Roo said flatly. "I don't imagine *they* thought it was very happy and romantic."

"Roo, don't spoil it! That's not what I meant."

"I'm just saying."

Still deep in conversation, the three started off again. Miranda hadn't realized how far they'd come, and as they passed through the last dense stand of trees, the plantation house rose suddenly before them—silent, imposing . . . and sad.

She was instantly disappointed. And though Ashley gasped in delight, Miranda felt only pity.

From this vantage point, they could see the entire west side of the house and most of the front. Her eyes swept the stately facade, the enormous round columns, the shaded galleries—and for one second, she actually wondered if this might be a *different* place from that magical, faraway image they'd admired earlier from the road. Because here, viewed up close and despite the evidence of work in progress, Belle Chandelle's flaws were all too evident, all too glaring. The countless years of abandonment, vandalism, and neglect; the ruthless encroachment of animals, water, weather, and time . . .

And sorrow, Miranda realized. *Terrible, terrible sorrow.*

Apparently, Ashley didn't notice. "Oh, it just goes deep inside me!" With a wistful sigh, she clasped her hands to her heart. "How perfectly *gorgeous* it is!"

Roo arched an eyebrow. "Are you talking about the house or *Etienne*?"

Etienne? Feeling her pulse quicken, Miranda was instantly annoyed with herself.

"*Where's* Etienne?" she heard Ashley ask, and Roo motioned vaguely upward.

"There. On top of the house."

Miranda followed the point of Roo's finger. And saw Etienne standing at the edge of the roof.

His shirt was off. His jeans fit low on his narrow hips, and his feet were planted wide apart, straddling a stack of shingles. Sweat glistened on his bare chest and across his shoulders, down the sinewy cords of muscles along his arms. His body was lean, easily six feet tall; his tan was natural, not dictated by any season. Though he'd dropped his tool belt to one side, he was still clutching a hammer in his left hand. A few stray waves of black hair clung damply to his cheeks and forehead; the rest had been tied carelessly back at the nape of his neck. Watching him now, Miranda remembered the very first time she'd ever seen him, how he'd reminded her of some wild gypsy.

Today—more than ever—he still did.

"Well." Roo nodded toward Etienne. "That's *one* good thing about global warming."

"Etienne!" Cupping her hands around her mouth, Ashley shouted, then began to wave. "Etienne! Hey! It's us!"

He saw them at once . . . lifted one arm in recognition . . . wiped it slowly over his dripping face. Even from that distance, Miranda felt the force of those swamp-black eyes.

"Hey, Boucher," Roo greeted him. "What are you doing up there? Showing off?"

Etienne propped a work boot on some shingles. Leaning forward, he draped an arm across his knee, while the faintest hint of a smile played at one corner of his mouth. "*Mais*, yeah. I been waiting up here all day just to impress you."

That unforgettable voice, deep and slightly husky. That thick Cajun accent mixed in with Southern charm. Before Etienne, Miranda had never heard a language like his before—that distinct strain of Acadian French combined so effortlessly with English. It was both musical and mysterious . . . and incredibly sexy.

"I'm impressed." Roo arched an eyebrow. "Especially with your big hammer."

"Will y'all two stop?" Ashley groaned at their usual banter, though Miranda couldn't help but laugh. "After listening to that for all these years, I can*not* understand why y'all still think you're funny."

"We're not funny." Roo sounded mildly indignant. "We're passionate about each other."

Expressionless, she winked at Etienne. Slyly, Etienne winked back.

"So where y'all goin' at?" he asked, but his gaze was on Miranda. She told herself that the rush of heat she felt was merely from the sultry air.

Answer him—you're being totally silly. The truth was, she'd thought about him all day long and had watched for him to show up. Now here he finally was, looking as only Etienne could look, staring as only Etienne could stare, and her heart was skipping a beat, and she couldn't come up with a single, coherent word to say. *Get a grip, Miranda.*

"Miss Teeta invited us!" Ashley waved again. "Do you know where she is?"

"All over the place, usually."

"Did you see Gage and Parker? They got here way before we did."

"Then you musta been driving, yeah?"

"Don't make fun of me."

"What? I could never make fun of you," Etienne assured her, though his expression suggested otherwise. "They're probably all inside. Just go around front, door's in the middle."

He bent to retrieve his tool belt. As Roo and Ashley walked on, Miranda started to follow, then suddenly stopped and turned.

Etienne was poised on a ledge, just below the third-story dormer, his back to an open window. Most of the glass had broken long ago, leaving nothing but a few jagged edges at the corners. No curtains hanging, no shades . . . only darkness.

But Miranda saw what was there.

She saw it, dimly, and she told herself that it was only the fading sunlight flickering through moss and leafy branches. Even though her skin went suddenly cold.

Because for one instant, she could swear she'd seen a hand.

A small, shadowy hand; fingers pressed flat against the air, as though pressed flat against a windowpane.

As if something—someone—were trying to get out.

6

"MIRANDA?"

Startled, Miranda's gaze shifted from the window to Etienne. He'd straightened up again, frowning, eyes narrowed down at her

"Miranda? What's wrong, *cher*?"

"I—I—"

But it was gone now. The window was empty and black; whatever she'd seen there had disappeared. If, in fact, she'd really seen anything at all.

"I—just—nothing." She was backing away, trying to smile, trying to act as if nothing had happened. And knowing she wasn't fooling Etienne for a second. "See you inside!"

Damn. She felt his eyes upon her till she rounded the corner of the house. Those black, black eyes that always seemed to see inside places she didn't want them to look and stir up emotions she wasn't sure she wanted to feel. Which didn't change the fact that she hadn't heard from him for a week, ever since she'd gotten sick. Even though she was *still* telling herself that it didn't matter . . .

Flustered, she hurried along the low brick verandah and caught up with Roo and Ashley just as they were entering the house.

"Hey, cancel that APB!" Parker called to Gage. Standing just inside the French doors, he grabbed Ashley around the waist and pulled her against him. "I guess they didn't die after all."

"I'm not *that* bad of a driver," Ashley said indignantly.

Roo shot her a look. "Yes. You are."

"It's not like I would have gotten us in a wreck."

"We weren't worried about you dying from a wreck," Gage assured her. "Just from old age."

As Ashley stuck her tongue out at him, he smiled and angled himself back into the corner beside Parker. Roo, walking several paces ahead, stopped to fuss with her earbuds while Miranda paused on the threshold and did a split-second appraisal of the room.

Emptiness, was her first impression—but so much *more* than emptiness, more than just no furniture or people, more somehow, than just a deserted house. A vast, *overwhelming* emptiness that distorted her friends' conversation around her, and swallowed the sound of their laughter, and stirred the air with echoes she didn't recognize.

Like being in some lost cavern, she thought. Dingy and bare, filled with nothing but shadows. Stale and musty and damp. Surprisingly cool, despite the lingering late-day heat.

The floors had been partially laid, their rich, cypress beauty scarcely recognizable beneath layers of ground-in dirt and plaster dust. The ceilings, at least thirteen feet high, showed various stages of carvings, moldings, and friezes. On the other three walls of the room, carved pocket doors stood halfway open, revealing another connecting room beyond each. Exterior rooms, Miranda guessed, from their rows of French doors, all tightly shuttered. Glancing off to her left, she noted a huge desk—Mom's, she was sure—surrounded by file cabinets and cardboard boxes, crates of dishes and glassware, and small items of antique furniture in various stages of disrepair.

"This is so amazing." There was no mistaking the awe in Ashley's voice. "I can't believe I'm actually inside this house."

Stay here, Miranda. Concentrate. Once again Miranda steeled herself, tried her best to pay attention to what was going on in the moment. Ashley, of course, was completely enamored, but what Miranda kept seeing was that empty third-story window; that small, shadowy hand pressed flat against the dark. . . .

"What'd you do to your hand?" a voice asked her.

Startled, she glanced up into concerned brown eyes. She hadn't noticed Gage moving close to her, but now he was lifting her injured palm and studying it.

"Just a cut," she stammered. "Some broken glass. No big deal."

"It's bleeding a little, though."

"Is it?" Parker, who'd been watching, reached out for Roo's back and grabbed the end of her long shawl. Before Miranda could protest, he swiped it over her hand, then dropped it again.

Roo instantly whirled to face them.

Parker pointed at Miranda. Miranda looked chidingly at Parker, who looked at Ashley, who looked at Gage, who gave Miranda a shrug.

"What?" they all chorused.

Roo frowned. Returned to her earbuds.

Ashley, however, had switched her focus to the room again—still taking it all in, still sounding slightly incredulous. "This house is so perfect. So *perfect*."

"It's a dump," Parker said, pulling her tighter. "It smells like mold."

"Let go—I want to explore. It was perfect once, and it'll be perfect again. You'll see."

"Yeah, perfect if you're *dead*." As Ashley pushed him away, Parker gave a mock shudder. "Am I the only one who sees the resemblance here? Or hasn't anybody else noticed how much this place looks like a tomb—inside *and* out?"

"Parker Wilmington, you are *not* going to scare me. So just stop it."

Though Miranda hadn't really thought of it, she realized that Parker was right. The house really *did* look like a tomb. *Inside and out . . .*

She'd heard Mom and Aunt Teeta explaining many times about how slow and tedious the work was, how early the stages of renovation—yet she'd certainly expected a whole lot more than what she was viewing now. Curious, she walked straight ahead, into the adjoining room. Ladders here, and scaffolding; sawdust and paint cans; drop cloths, tiles and grout; stacks of lumber. Enlarged blueprints on the wall, plumbing and electrical plans, landscape designs. Paint streaks, hundreds of different colors; wallpaper patterns, jig sawed and push-pinned with fabric swatches. And tables, straining beneath the weight of magazines, catalogs, bolts of material, binders, and sample books.

See, Miranda? Signs of progress and hope, signs that this house is trying to come alive again . . .

Then why did she still feel so sad?

Why did the *house* still feel so sad?

This area showed more damage, she noticed—holes pocking the walls and ceiling, glimpses of exposed bricks and lath strips, various stages of patchwork and plastering . . . *water seepage . . . rodents . . . rot . . .* Dust and debris had been carelessly swept aside, heaped against the French doors, pushed into corners and crevices, even stuffed inside the deep, massive cavity that had once been a glorious fireplace. Though obviously unused for years, the interior was still blackened—thick layers of smoke and soot—while from high up the chimney came the faint, far patter of bat wings.

"Great." Stepping back, Miranda kept wary eyes on the opening. Just her luck for some rabid bat to come swooping out and land right in her hair. The firebox was crammed with all kinds of garbage—no doubt the workmen threw their leftover lunches in here too; it was probably infested with mice and rats and roaches and God only knew what else. Not to mention all the centuries' worth of historical odds and ends that had most likely been swept up, then carelessly hauled off to landfills . . .

"Look," Roo said. She'd been pacing again, back and forth along the walls, but stopped now in front of the boys. As Miranda came back to join them, Roo lifted her arms wide. She held them up for a second, midair. She let them drop down again at her sides. "Look at this. This is weird."

Parker and Gage exchanged glances.

"I am looking," Parker agreed. "I am looking at you, and yes, you are weird."

Reaching out, Gage calmly pulled the plugs from Roo's ears and slipped them into his shirt pocket. "Stop talking to your soul. It's not polite when the rest of us aren't in on the conversation."

But Roo paid no attention. "I don't mean *me*. I mean being *here*. In this place. Who'd have thought?"

"Thought what?"

"We're connected."

"Who's connected?" Parker scowled. "Definitely not you and me in any way, shape, or form. *Ever*." Another glance at Gage. "Give those ear-things back. Maybe her soul can translate,"

Amused, Miranda watched from the threshold. A wet, sluggish breeze crept in through the French doors, bringing long shadows of early twilight and the promise of more rain. There was muffled thunder in the distance . . . leaves rustling . . . bayou sounds . . .

Laughter . . .

Immediately she turned, eyes scanning left to right. Verandah . . . outbuildings . . . overgrown lawn . . . mossy oaks . . . discarded piles of rubble. A rusty, wrought-iron bench. A headless marble statue. A wooden swing hanging by ropes from a tree branch, jerking restlessly in the wind . . .

Deserted. No one there.

Yet she was sure she'd heard it. Faint . . . fleeting . . . nothing more than that, nothing she could really describe, but laughter all the same.

Without warning, a flock of crows burst from the nearest

oak, making her jump. For several long moments there were only hoarse, mocking cries and wings beating furiously at the air—then just as suddenly, everything grew still.

"—I know what she means," Ashley was insisting.

Turning back again, Miranda did her best not to shiver. *Must have been those crows . . . that must have been what I heard—*

"I *do* know what Roo means!" Ashley went on loyally, hugging her sister, oblivious to the frown Roo gave her. "And it *is* weird! *We* had a past, and the *house* had a past. And *we* played here, and the *house* was here. And *we* grew up, and the *house* grew up—"

"And do I care?" Parker cut in. "And is there a bathroom around this place?"

Without a word, Gage pointed outside. Ashley, suddenly noting the four pairs of eyes on her, stopped talking. She lifted her nose at Gage and Parker. She turned loose of Roo.

"We all share a common bond with Belle Chandelle," Ashley finished indignantly. "We're connected."

Tilting his head back, Parker snorted a laugh. "Yeah. You and all the other gazillion people who've ever walked across this property since the beginning of time."

"It's more than that," Ashley argued. "More than just us. More than just the history and the land and the soil . . . and . . . It's our *heritage*."

"Uh-oh." Parker exchanged winces with Gage. "Is this where we get the Strong Southern Women lecture?"

"Yes!" Ashley declared. "Strong, brave, Southern women. And the strong, brave Southern . . . spirit . . . in . . . our blood!"

"Yep, there it is. I hear the background music playing. What is it with you girls, anyhow? All your stupid *Gone With the Wind* fantasies?"

Roo leveled Parker a look. She held out her palms, one at a time, weighing options. "Gosh, I don't know. Rhett Butler . . . Parker Wilmington. It's a total mystery."

"And it's the *romance*," Ashley scolded. "All that beautiful, old-fashioned romance. Girls love that."

Startled, Miranda felt a movement at her back. Before she could turn around, Etienne's hands settled firmly on her hips, easing her to one side of the doorway so he could slip through. Leaning close, his lips brushed lightly over her ear.

"You okay?" he murmured.

"Sure." Another shiver, only hot this time and not one bit controllable. Etienne must have felt it, though he gave no sign. Miranda was instantly annoyed with herself.

"Yeah?" he persisted.

"Yes. Why wouldn't I be?"

Reading the doubt in his eyes, she felt helplessly transparent. But Etienne simply focused on the others and asked, "So what y'all think?"

He'd put on a T-shirt—still wet with sweat, it clung to him like a second skin. And his hair was untied, so the damp, reckless waves tousled nearly to his shoulders. Roo offered a quick assessment.

"Of this place? Or you?"

That hint of a smile. "I already know what you think of me, *cher*."

"It's the most wonderful place I've ever seen." Ashley sighed. "When can we look around?"

Before Etienne could answer, there was rapid shuffling along the verandah, and the next second Aunt Teeta burst in, laughing, waving, and apologizing with every step.

"I am *so* sorry I'm late, y'all! The electricity just went out, and I don't have a clue what's going on! Why, Gage—you're lookin' better every time I see you, hon! And hey there, little Miss Ashley! And Roo—my goodness, just look how creative you've gone and done your hair! And Parker, I hear your shoulder's all healed up now—we're all countin' on you whuppin' that football team of yours into shape!"

Watching her aunt, Miranda couldn't help but marvel once again—the way moods always lifted whenever Aunt Teeta was around. Ashley, Roo, and Gage were laughing along with her; Etienne, as usual, looked amused. Even Parker couldn't hold back a grin.

"Etienne, darlin', is there anything you can do—" the woman began, but he was already walking toward her, brow creased in thought.

"It's been working fine, yeah? So what, it just quit, no reason?"

"Well, that's the darnedest thing! We've had power all day—then bam! Nothing! I'd say it was about . . . maybe twenty minutes ago? And everything died all at once."

Miranda caught Roo's stare, mildly accusing.

"When *you* got here?" Roo mouthed at her.

"No way," Miranda mouthed back.

Yet Etienne was staring at her now too, and so was Gage—till Etienne smoothly redirected everyone's attention.

"I'll go check it out," he promised Aunt Teeta.

Bestowing him a grateful smile, she turned back to the group. "Now, I know it's my fault we're runnin' behind—but Etienne, please tell me there's still time for a little tour?"

Etienne shrugged, ran one hand distractedly across his chest. "As long as we're outta here before it's too dark."

"Well, not all the house has power, anyway." Aunt Teeta reconciled herself. "So I think we can manage—it's not like there's a whole lot to see in those empty rooms. But I'm just wondering—if I give y'all a little bit of background first, would that help?"

There was a general chorus of assent. Motioning them to follow, Aunt Teeta moved toward the center of the room and began her speech.

"As y'all probably noticed from outside, the verandah and the galleries wrap completely around the building. We believe the *original* layout of the house was a typical Louisiana style—three rooms wide and two rooms deep, on both the first and second floors. Each room would have had at least one opening onto the galleries; some had more. And a few of the rooms connected to each other through interior doors—like these pocket doors y'all see here. There weren't any halls, and no central corridor, but there *was*—and still is—one sneak stairway at the back."

"Is that where the master sneaked in all his girlfriends?" Parker grinned wider, ignoring Ashley's jab in his side.

Aunt Teeta found this hilarious. It took several seconds till she caught her breath.

"Now Parker, I'm not saying it never served that particular purpose. But it got the name because it was hidden in the wall and used only by the servants. The rest of the family used the covered staircases at each end of the galleries."

"What about the third story?" Miranda asked quickly.

"That's the attic," Aunt Teeta replied. "And the access to the belvedere is from there."

Parker frowned. "The what?"

"Belvedere," Ashley repeated. "Honestly, Parker, will you please pay attention?"

"I am paying attention. What the hell's a belvedere?"

"It's a thing on top of the house."

"So are roofs and chimneys. And birds. Thanks, Ash. I feel completely enlightened."

"That little dome on the roof," Gage said, with a slight nod toward the ceiling. "People usually built them for the view. They could stand up there and see for miles in every direction."

"It was the perfect way to keep an eye on the plantation," Aunt Teeta echoed. "In the case of Belle Chandelle, they could see their whole property, plus the bayou and the road."

Miranda was trying hard to be patient. "The third floor, Aunt Teeta?" she pressed. "Was that all it was—just an attic?"

"Yes, darlin', used for storage. But on some plantations, that's where the house servants would have slept. And when guests came to stay, then *their* personal servants would have slept up there too."

Miranda gave a tight nod. She glanced up to see Etienne watching her.

"Oh, Miss Teeta," Ashley begged, "please tell us about all the rooms."

"Well, in a house like this, there might have been drawing rooms, sitting rooms, maybe double parlors, and most definitely a dining room on the main floor. Some houses had fancy ballrooms and music rooms and libraries. The kitchen was always separate, of course—to guard against fire."

She paused to survey her rapt audience. When no questions came, she smiled and continued on.

"Upstairs there were bedrooms and nurseries, naturally—and in some cases, there might have been little half rooms attached to the bedrooms. These would have been used for dressing rooms, or—if there weren't servants' quarters in the attic—this is where the guests' personal servants would have stayed."

Ashley's mouth opened, incredulous. "I can't believe they only had six bedrooms. I mean . . . there must have been so many people living here—how could they fit all their stuff in just six bedrooms?"

"Musta been plenty crowded, yeah?" Etienne kept a straight face. "All those big dresses and no closets?"

"They didn't have closets?"

He'd been propped on one shoulder, arms folded over his chest. Now he stretched himself away from the wall.

"These plantation houses, there were a lotta different designs. In some of them, people didn't even live on the main floor. Like where we are now, this woulda been an aboveground basement. And the rooms here woulda been used for stuff like wine cellars and laundry and storage."

"So then there would have been only six rooms total?" Again, Ashley was shocked. "Did they double up in their bedrooms? I can't even stand the thought of sharing a room with Roo."

Parker grimaced. "Who could?"

"But sons didn't usually live in the main house, did they?" Gage commented. "When they got older, they lived in garconnieres."

"In what?"

"Garconnieres."

"Gesundheit."

"That's true," Aunt Teeta smiled at Gage. "Garconnieres were small, separate buildings, often octagon-shaped, two stories high, and they usually stood at each end of the main house. A plantation this size would certainly have had at least one."

Parker was finally intrigued. "So . . . it was like a bachelor pad?"

"Something like that, yes. Boys were considered men at a much younger age back then. When they reached their teens, they'd move into the garconniere."

"Typical." Roo's disdain was obvious. "They had freedom. And privacy. And privileges. That the women didn't have—"

"But the real question is," Parker broke in, "did they have sneak stairs?"

"Sneak back doors," Etienne said.

"Sneak windows," Gage added.

Amused at their own cleverness, the guys continued to crack jokes, though Miranda was only half listening. Once more her eyes swept slowly up the walls, across the ceiling, back to her aunt's face.

"Aunt Teeta, you keep saying 'might have' or 'would have'—does that mean you don't actually *know* what was here?"

"We don't, darlin'." Aunt Teeta sighed. "The *miracle* of this place is that it finally has a future. The *tragedy* of this place is that it doesn't have a past."

"Oh, but it *does* have a past, Miss Teeta," Ashley insisted. "It has a past with us."

The guys had recovered themselves. Now Gage shifted his weight, realigned his crutches, and fixed Aunt Teeta with a slight frown. "So . . . you can't make this an *exact* replica of how it was. You don't even know what it looked like."

"Unfortunately, yes, that's what I'm saying." Pausing once more, Aunt Teeta made an all-inclusive gesture of the room. "Belle Chandelle sat empty for such a long, long time—way too long without anybody keeping track of it. When some buyers finally came along about twenty or so years ago, the house was nothing but a rotted shell—four crumbled walls and a collapsed ceiling. There wasn't really any interior to speak of; the place was pretty much gutted. From what little bit was salvaged back then, we know it went through floods and at least one fire—transients, probably, smoking or trying to keep warm. Or both."

"Smoking," Gage said, glancing pointedly at Roo.

Roo ignored him.

"We know there was a lot of vandalism—major parts of the original structure had been stripped and torn down. And for what wasn't stolen, time and Mother Nature did the rest."

"Oh, that's so sad." Ashley's voice faltered, teary. "This poor house has suffered so much."

As though some silent signal had been given, Parker, Gage, and Etienne all checked their watches. Smirking, Parker thrust his palm out toward the other guys.

"Pay up. I said twenty minutes; it took her nineteen."

Muttering good-naturedly, Etienne and Gage each dug into their jeans' pockets, relinquishing a five-dollar bill. The girls looked on in dismay.

"Parker Wilmington," Ashley demanded, "what on earth are you doing?"

Parker wasn't the least bit contrite. "We made bets on when you'd get all weepy about this house. And I won."

"Y'all are *not funny*!" Ashley protested, though the guys clearly thought they were. Roo looked at Miranda and rolled her eyes. And Aunt Teeta, trying desperately not to laugh, slipped a protective arm around Ashley.

"Shame on you, boys! Ashley, darlin', I feel the same way. My heart just *aches* for this sweet ole house."

Collecting the money, Parker jammed it into his shirt pocket, then winked at Gage and Etienne. "How well do I know my girl, huh?"

Roo shot him a dark-ringed glance. "How well do you know Kurt Fuller?"

Miranda saw the color change on Ashley's face. She felt her own expression freeze.

"Streak?" Parker asked, confused. "What the hell does he have to do with anything?"

But Roo was watching Ashley now, her expression genuinely puzzled. "What?" she mumbled. Then louder, "What'd I say?"

"You were saying about the house, Aunt Teeta," Miranda said quickly, while Gage and Etienne shrugged at Parker, the three of them completely lost. "What about those people who bought it? Did they do any renovation?"

Back on track again, Aunt Teeta shook her head. "Not that anybody could tell. They kept it awhile, then moved away and just let it sit there. And then some new folks bought it and worked on it a little bit, but they ended up selling, too. A place like this is overwhelming . . . time consuming—not to mention expensive. But the last owner *did* manage a partial reconstruction of the first and second floors—pretty much what you're seeing. You know, hon, I think they meant well, and I think they *tried* to base it all on facts, and I truly think they did their very best with what money they had—but it ended up being sort of a big ole hodgepodge. A *lot* of mistakes, and a lot of things *not* historically accurate."

"So the reconstruction you're doing now—don't you at least have pictures to go by?"

"One. Only one photograph of the original house, the exterior. Nothing at all of the inside. We're basing all the exterior and interior renovations purely on research—other plantation homes of that period."

"You'd think there'd be some sort of record," Gage mused. "A written description somewhere. A deed or a journal or something."

"What little information we have was discovered with a packet of notes and letters—and a few other personal belongings—written by a Yankee soldier. A scout, we think."

"Where'd you get it?"

"Parker's mama had it on file at the Historical Society."

Normally, Parker would have voiced a few negative comments at this. Instead, he was still staring at Ashley and Roo. "What about Streak?"

"The soldier's letter does mention a name," Aunt Teeta continued. "He talks about riding up to a sign on the road, that it's all overgrown with weeds and vines. The name on the sign is Belle Chandelle. And he thinks the plantation should be easy to take, because there doesn't seem to be anybody living there."

Ashley gave a visible shudder. "So . . . the whole place was just empty? Like . . . a ghost town?"

"Nobody knows, hon."

Frowning, Gage stroked a hand along his chin. "They would've known the Yankees were coming; they would've had some time to get out of there."

"What about slaves?" Roo asked. "Wouldn't there have been servants or workers around?"

"Maybe they were hiding and hoping the Yankees would go away," Ashley offered.

"I guess it's possible." Aunt Teeta's brow furrowed in thought. "Unfortunately, there's no more information on Belle Chandelle after that. And believe me, we've checked out every possible source."

But Gage wasn't ready to give up. "You said there's a picture?"

"Yes. It's taken from the bayou side. We know when the house was built. We think we know the name of the original owner. And we have a few items that were discovered on the property years ago. But other than that—"

"So . . . *what* about Streak?" Parker repeated, but Ashley gave a delighted little squeal.

"Miss Teeta, Miranda said Belle Chandelle's going to be a bed and breakfast! We're just thrilled to pieces, aren't we, y'all?"

Hardly, Miranda thought, surveying the group reaction. Parker couldn't have cared less. Gage didn't seem one bit surprised at the news. And while Roo at least nodded, Etienne just rubbed his eyes and looked tired.

"Gage," Ashley scolded, noting his reaction. "You already knew, didn't you. Etienne already told you—and you didn't tell me!"

Gage offered an apologetic shrug, the matter of bed and breakfasts clearly not high on his priority list. As Ashley aimed a punch at his stomach, he swiftly caught her hand in his while Etienne watched them, amused.

"But this isn't going to be just *any* bed and breakfast," Aunt Teeta emphasized, chuckling at Gage and Ashley. "The owners intend it to be *the* best bed and breakfast in this *entire* part of the South."

"With just twelve rooms?" Ashley fretted, pulling free from Gage. "I don't see how they can make it the *best* bed and breakfast with just twelve rooms."

"*Mon Dieu*, Ashley . . ." Mumbling, Etienne shook his head and walked past her, ruffling her hair on the way. The others followed him into the adjoining room, where he stopped beside the large set of blueprints, then began pointing things out as he talked.

"This layout here—what we think was the original—we're already taking those six rooms upstairs, breaking them down into smaller ones. Each guest room still has its own door out to the gallery. And each one has its own bathroom."

"Hey," Parker half raised his hand. "Speaking of bathrooms—"

Again Gage jerked his thumb toward outside.

"What about the main floor?" Miranda asked.

"Leaving it pretty much as-is." Etienne continued to slide his finger across the plans; he glanced back over his shoulder to see if the others had questions. "The entrance'll be here, in this middle room—pocket doors open on each side, closed at the rear. A nice big reception area, yeah? Sitting room, dining room, library, stuff like that. The rooms at the back are for extra—you got your ballroom, your space for banquets and weddings and whatever."

"What about storage?" Gage wanted to know.

"Outbuildings. And the kitchen, it stays separate—all the meals will be cooked there. Except for easy things—snacks, fast food, microwave."

"The owners are sure about what they want." Nodding at Etienne, Aunt Teeta received an affirmative nod in return. "Which is *great.* They're very specific. They want this place to be beautiful, top-quality, and completely authentic with modern conveniences. They want to attract tourists, not just from around the country, but from around the world. And they're even hoping to list it with the National Register of Historic Places."

Aunt Teeta stopped to take a breath. As her eyes moved from Etienne to the French doors at the front of the room, she let out a gasp.

"Oh mercy, it's getting dark, and I *swore* to myself I wouldn't rattle on! Why didn't y'all stop me? Etienne, do we have any flashlights around here, hon?"

Laughing at herself, Aunt Teeta grabbed Etienne's arm, playfully shook him, and shooed everyone out to the verandah. Etienne headed off in another direction, but the rest of the group turned left, making their way to the exterior stairs at the end, then up to the second-floor gallery, none of them even noticing when Miranda stepped aside and hung back.

She stood alone on the verandah now, listening to the strange and sudden quiet.

An unnerving quiet. *Unnatural quiet . . .*

The wind had died, not one hint of breeze. Thunderclouds hung low in the sky, bleeding dark into dusk; it was impossible to distinguish late day from early night. The thunder itself had silenced. Not a single sound drifted from the bayou. Miranda realized that she was holding her breath.

Calm before the storm. That's all it is. Just the calm before the storm . . .

She gazed off across the lawn, beneath the trees.

And saw the wooden swing . . . swinging.

It took her a moment to actually absorb what was happening . . . how the swing could be swinging without a breath of air to move it . . . and how it was moving so easily . . . not like a breeze might be stirring it, but a slow, deliberate rhythm, *up . . . back . . . up . . . back . . .*

She knew that the others were exploring the gallery above her—she knew that if she turned around, she would see them, she would hear them, all noisy and laughing and loud. . . .

But she didn't turn around.

Instead she began walking toward the swing.

Up . . . back . . . up . . . back . . . invisible legs pumping . . . invisible arms pushing . . . and if she squinted just right through the gloom, she could almost convince herself that there really *was* someone in that swing, a very *small* someone in that swing, even though she knew it was only shadows gathered there beneath the branches and leaves and moss, out there in the twilight. . . .

The swing stopped.

Stopped abruptly and hung perfectly still.

As Miranda stared at it, her heart froze. For she could see it now, that very small shadow drifting away from the swing, floating toward her, *deliberately* toward her, while all she could do was stand there and watch it, helpless, unable to move—

It was close now.

Close enough to touch.

"Oh God . . ."

A shadow—no, two shadows!*—silent footsteps on wet grass damp leaves soggy ground running straight at me two small quick busy feet—no,* four *feet!—*

Something took her hand.

Her body jerked at the sudden contact—*tiny fingers clutching mine shy curious fingers squeezing mine* . . .

So deathly cold now . . . quiet as the grave . . .

Miranda thought she might have called Etienne's name.

But the quiet was turning into a roar, and she fell deep . . . deep . . . down an endless spiral of centuries.

7

"MIRANDA."

She couldn't wake up.

"*Miranda.*"

Couldn't wake up, couldn't breathe, couldn't get warm—

"*Miranda, look at me, cher. Open your eyes.*"

Gasping, she tried to move. Her eyelids fluttered, lungs gulping air, but something was keeping her down—

"Breathe. That's right . . . nice and deep—"

"Etienne?"

"Try to focus. Here. On my face."

"What . . . happened?"

"I was kinda hoping you'd tell me."

Her eyes were wide now; his words calm and clear. She realized that she was lying on the ground and that he was kneeling over her, one arm cradling her head, his other hand patting her cheek. Full night was falling around them. The whole world teemed with shadows.

"I must have tripped," she murmured. "Can't . . . remember."

"Don't talk yet. Just keep breathing."

"No, I *have* to talk. What are you doing here? Did I yell or something?"

Etienne shook his head. "If you did, nobody heard you. They're pretty busy upstairs, taking the tour."

"Then how did you—"

"I just had me this . . . feeling."

"You came to find me? How long have you been here?"

"Not long. Just keep yourself quiet now, and—"

"And you didn't see anything? Not that you *could* have seen anything . . . and I don't even know how long I was—" She broke off, biting her lower lip. "What *was* I, anyway? Unconscious? Asleep?"

"I'm thinking you probably fainted. But you were trying to talk the whole time . . . somewhere way back in your head. Things I sure wasn't understanding."

Puzzled, Miranda considered a moment. "You couldn't make out *anything*?"

"Just . . . well . . . a couple times, you called for your mama."

"My *mom*?" she cringed. "That's so embarrassing."

"You seemed plenty scared. Only makes sense you'd be wanting your mama."

Miranda had no chance to respond. From out of nowhere, a chill stabbed through her, worming along her spine and into her limbs, leaving her trembling and light-headed. At once, Etienne eased her into a sitting position. He wrapped both arms around her and held her close.

"It's like summer out here," he mumbled, "and you're ice cold."

Darkness engulfed her. The darkness of nightfall, the darkness of Etienne. His eyes, his voice, his . . . *presence*. The smells that clung to him—dirt and sweat and windblown hair; worn leather and work-stained denim; blazing sunshine and autumn rain; moss and mud, wet grass and bayou breezes; the musky heat of his skin; his blisters, calluses, and scars. High cheekbones, chiseled features pressed close and hard . . . day-old stubble, rough against her forehead . . .

"So what do they want?" he finally asked. And then, when Miranda didn't answer, "The spirits, *cher*. The ones trying to reach you."

He ran his hands slowly down the length of her arms. Miranda tried to shut out the sound of him, the scent of him, the sight of him, but he only pulled her tighter.

"What are they needing, Miranda?"

Silence fell heavy between them. It was several long moments before Miranda could finally answer.

"How did you know?" she whispered.

"Hmmm . . . let's see. I get me this feeling something's wrong . . . I find you passed out here on the ground . . . you're half frozen and talking right outta your head . . ." Pausing, he gave an exaggerated shrug. "I'm just a lucky guesser."

"Etienne—"

"Listen, now. Your *grandpère* and me, we were friends for a long time. I saw what he went through; I understood him pretty well. And I understand *you* pretty well too. *Real* well, in fact. Probably even more than you want me to."

"No, you—"

"Yeah. I do. Your *grandpère*, he wanted to protect you from the tough things, the scary things. He never wanted you to be going through all that—but he knew you'd *have* to. 'Cause it's all part of the gift he passed you. The good and the bad of it."

"Well, I don't like the bad of it. But you're right—they are trying to reach me." In spite of herself, Miranda's voice trembled. "I think they've been trying to reach me all day, only I don't know what they want or who they are or—"

"Shh . . . calm yourself down. We'll just sit here awhile."

"But the others . . ."

"Your aunt Teeta, she's keeping them entertained. We got us a little bit of time."

Reluctantly, Miranda nodded. Everything was too fast, too mixed-up. She still wasn't sure what had happened by the swing; neither was she exactly sure what she was doing here in Etienne's arms. For a second, both situations seemed equally dangerous.

"So . . ." Etienne spoke at last. "You wanna start with the roof?"

"Roof?"

"What you were staring at on the roof earlier. When y'all first got here." Not getting any reply, he traced a fingertip slowly down her spine.

Another shiver went through her . . . but fluttery warm, not cold. "I just thought . . . I saw something," she admitted.

"Where?"

"In that window, right above where you were standing."

"What'd you see?"

"It could have been shadows, but—"

"It coulda been a *lotta* things, but—"

"It looked like a hand. A tiny hand . . . like a child, maybe . . . on the windowpane. Only there *wasn't* a windowpane. And it just made me feel . . ."

Etienne nodded. Waited for her to go on.

"Made me feel so *sad*. Like it was reaching for help, maybe . . . trying to get out." Frowning, Miranda pulled away a little, tilted her face to peer up at him. "Isn't this the part where you tell me there wasn't anyone inside?"

A not-quite-smile tugged at one corner of his mouth. "That's the attic you were seeing. The floor's not finished yet, and it's too dangerous to be walking around—so just the work crews go up there. And I'm the only crew here tonight. So . . . yeah. This is where I tell you there wasn't anybody inside." He paused, arched an eyebrow. "Nobody *alive*, anyhow."

"So you believe me."

"I always have. Always will. So . . . why don't you tell me what happened out here just now?" He stretched and shifted position. With knees drawn up and spread apart, he settled Miranda snugly between his thighs, drew her back against his chest. "Okay. From the beginning."

Miranda did so. From breaking the mirror in her bathroom that morning . . . to the vision at her locker . . . her uneasiness on the road to Belle Chandelle . . . her distorted view of the house . . . her glimpse of that shadowy hand at the attic window . . . the whisper of childish laughter on the lawn . . . the mysteriously moving swing . . . the ghostly feet running, the ghostly hands touching . . . till the moment she'd woken up, disoriented, on the ground.

Throughout every detail, Etienne said nothing, offered no comment. And though he did gently rock her from time to time, it wasn't till she'd finished that he finally spoke up, his voice tight.

"I'm sorry, *cher*. That's a hell of a lotta stuff to be dealing with—and especially in just one day. Whatever's going on—"

"*Wasn't* a dream," she insisted firmly. "*Or* a hallucination. It was powerful, and it was *real*. Like you said, someone—some spirit—is trying to reach me. And needs me to help them."

Etienne seemed to be pondering this. His eyes shifted to the oak tree, where the wooden swing hung, perfectly still.

"Listen to yourself," he said at last. "How far you've come in just a few weeks. Talking about all this, so natural—and how you fit into it."

"Well . . . do I have a choice?"

"You know you do. You can accept this gift of yours and do good things with it . . . or you can shut it out and pretend it doesn't exist."

"Honestly?" Miranda sounded almost wistful. "I don't think it's possible for me to shut it out. And I know Grandpa wouldn't want me pretending like it doesn't exist."

"I'm proud of you, *cher*."

"Don't be. This doesn't mean I'm still not scared out of my mind."

"Yeah, well that's why you got *me*, remember?"

She sensed his face lowering to her hair. Felt the light touch of his lips . . . the quickening of her pulse.

"Etienne?"

"Hmmm."

"I'm feeling too much in this place."

She was suddenly so aware of his heartbeat, hard against her back. Strong, solid, steady—not skipping like her own.

"This place?" he mumbled, his lips on the curve of her neck now, his arms tightening around her.

Instinctively, she tried to steel herself, but her insides were already beginning to melt, going weak and soft and helpless. She gathered her defenses . . . determined to stay focused on the matter at hand.

"This place?" Etienne asked again, his whisper warm and soft along her ear.

"Belle Chandelle," she murmured. "Etienne, are you listening to me?"

"Um-hmm."

Miranda caught her breath, steeled herself even more. "On the drive over . . . and when I got on the property . . . all these sensations started hitting me—sounds and smells and scenes in my mind, coming from every direction. But this place is so huge . . . and I'm only one person. I can't take it all in."

"And you shouldn't." Though he still held her close, Etienne finally lifted his head. His tone was thoughtful now; she had his full attention. "You shouldn't even be *trying* to take it all in."

"But—"

"Remember when we talked about this, me and you? When all this first started happening, when you first found out about your gift? Your *grandpère*, he had *years* of practice—you, you've only had a few weeks. You've hardly even *started* knowing what you need to know. It took him a lifetime to learn what to shut out, what to let in. You'll learn too."

A wave of emotions washed over her. Even though she knew it was just because of the crazy day she'd had . . . the things she'd been through . . . *Etienne* . . .

Get a grip, Miranda.

But she heard herself saying, "It's just that when things like this happen . . . I wish I could talk to Grandpa and get his advice. I wish he were still here."

"Your *grandpère*, he'll *always* be here with you. *Always.* And sure, you still miss him—you miss all those yesterdays you never had, all those tomorrows you got cheated out of. There's no rules about when you gotta stop missing somebody. Just talk to him, *cher*. Just think about him. Jonas, he'll help you. He'll show you the way."

Jonas Hayes. My grandfather. The reason all this got started in the first place . . .

Not wanting to cry, Miranda quickly changed the subject. "There's one more thing I need to tell you."

"Uh-oh. This sounds serious." His black eyes narrowed, teasing.

Shaking her head, Miranda laughed. "Please don't tell the others yet about . . ." She gestured vaguely toward the swing, the lawn, the house. "About . . . what's happened. I promise I'll tell them as soon as it's the right time. But not tonight, okay? I'm tired. I'm exhausted. It's been a long, awful day, and I just don't want to have to go through it all again."

Before Etienne could answer, there was a commotion from the gallery above.

"Hey!" Parker shouted. "Check out the action on the ground! I see you two rolling around down there!"

But Etienne was already standing, taking Miranda's hands, pulling her to her feet. There was an enthusiastic chorus of cheers and whistles as the others gathered at the upstairs railing, and Aunt Teeta roared with laughter.

"Etienne Boucher!" she called. "Hanky panky is most definitely *not* allowed till you take my niece out on a proper first date!"

Etienne feigned innocence. "But Miss Teeta, this *is* our first date."

More cheers, even louder. While Miranda concentrated on brushing herself off, Parker leaned over the baluster and shook his head.

"Perfect spot for that beautiful, old-fashioned romance, huh, Miranda? Mud . . . weeds . . . spiders . . . mosquitoes—"

"Trust me," Roo broke in, "she didn't notice."

The applause went wild; Miranda's cheeks went hot. Clearly unbothered by the teasing, Etienne steered her onto the verandah, where they waited for the others to join them.

"So . . . how was the tour?" Miranda asked, ignoring a sly nudge from Roo. "What did I miss?"

Parker did a droll rendition of enthusiasm. "Wow. Now, let me think. *Galleries.* All four of them. And . . . *French doors.* All . . . many of them. And *rooms.* All empty and boring and torn up. You should have been there, Miranda—the excitement was overwhelming."

"That's okay. I can explore another time."

"Okay, I guess we're done here!" Trailing Gage down the stairs, Aunt Teeta paused for a last backward glance. "We've seen all there is to see—for now, anyway. Etienne, did you find the problem with my electricity?"

"Yes ma'am, but I can't do much about it tonight."

"See there? That boy can fix anything." Aunt Teeta smiled at Ashley now, apologetic. "I just wish more of the house was finished, darlin'. And I wish there was more I could tell y'all about it."

"Me too." Ashley's sigh was wistful. "I'd love to know about the people who lived here . . . listen to their stories."

"Well, the only stories *I've* ever heard through the years are the spooky ones."

Miranda was instantly alert. "What do you mean? What spooky ones?"

"*No* spooky ones," Parker blurted, though Aunt Teeta kept chattering on.

"Oh mercy, you know—the ones we've all grown up hearing. Ghost stories and such like—"

"Stories!" This time Parker forced a laugh. "Yeah . . . but . . . see . . . that's just it. What *are* stories anyway? Just dumb rumors, right?"

Miranda ignored him. "What kinds of stories? What kinds of ghosts?" She was feeling cold again, colder by the second. No one was answering her questions, and Aunt Teeta was still talking.

"Well, Parker, I guess you're right about that. And we all know how small towns are. They need their own local haunted houses to talk about. And *brag* about!"

"People *always* think old houses are haunted if they've been abandoned for a while," Gage added smoothly. "And especially if they're in really bad shape."

But Parker's tone wasn't casual now. In fact, he was beginning to sound slightly panicked. "Hey . . . come on. No ghosts, okay? That ghost tour we did is *over*. We did our project, we all got A's. So no more ghosts. No more ghost *stories*, no more ghost *research*, no more ghost—*anything*. We're *all* done with ghosts. No more ghosts *ever*."

"Well, hon, I can't truly say if I believe in ghosts or not," Aunt Teeta conceded good-naturedly. "But I sure do love to hear tales about them. And I *do* know these new owners would be thrilled to *pieces* if there ended up being some nice, interesting ghosts here. Having a ghost or two on the premises is a major tourist attraction—and there's a whole lot of competition in this business. As a matter of fact, Miranda's mama and I were just talking about that this morning. Don't you think ghosts would be a good tourist draw, Miranda?"

"I . . ." Miranda's mouth had gone dry. She could feel her friends watching her, sympathy in every gaze but one. "Ghosts are sure . . . fascinating," she finished lamely.

"That's it." Spinning on his heel, Parker stepped off the verandah, his hands in the air. "I'm gone. Good night."

"Yeah, we better hit the road," Gage said quickly. "Thanks, Miss Teeta."

"Now, you boys wait a second." Aunt Teeta motioned them to stay put. "I don't want these girls walking back to their car by themselves."

"I'll lock up," Etienne offered, but she shook her head.

"Darlin', I've got plenty of good lanterns and lamps inside, and I need to look over a few more things before I leave. Now, y'all take these flashlights, and be careful where y'all step."

"Mom's frying chicken—she said everybody could come eat at our house!" Ashley announced, which brought hungry grunts of approval from the boys. "Miss Teeta, wouldn't you like to come too?"

"Bless your heart, hon, but when I finish up here, I'm heading home to a hot bath, some TV, and a nice, soft bed."

Linking arms, Miranda gave her aunt a hug. "I'll wait for you, okay? So you don't have to drive home alone."

The truth was, she didn't want to be with people tonight. Despite having talked with Etienne, been comforted by Etienne, suddenly she didn't feel reassured at all. And Aunt Teeta's idea of going home to a bath, TV, and a nice, soft bed seemed too tempting to pass up.

"Nonsense, darlin', I'm not one bit afraid to drive home by myself." Returning the hug, Aunt Teeta pushed Miranda toward the others. "Besides that, I'll be awhile. You just go on without me and have a good time. Can you get a ride home?"

"I'll bring her," Etienne promised. "It's a school night—we won't be late."

With Etienne and Parker holding flashlights, the six of them started back across the grounds to the parking lot. It was total dark out here now, that blacker-than-black-darkness found only in the countryside, made worse by thick canopies of moss overhead. A sluggish breeze blew off the bayou. Mist hung in the air, curling through the trees, glowing a fuzzy halo around the beams of the flashlights. While Ashley chattered to Gage and Parker, Roo lit up a cigarette, inhaled deeply, handed it to Etienne. Without breaking stride, he took a long drag and passed it back.

Shivering, Miranda couldn't help looking back over her shoulder. For one brief second, a breath of wind fluttered through the moss, sweeping it aside, offering her a view of the house. One small section of the roof . . . that dormer on the third floor . . .

And the pale glow of light moving past the window . . . flickering faintly beyond the broken glass . . .

"You sure your aunt's okay in there?"

Startled, she whirled around, saw that Parker had caught up with her. She didn't realize that she'd stopped walking or that he was staring in the same direction as she was, through those rippling curtains of moss.

"I'd be nervous about her being up in the attic like that." He frowned. "Especially now, with just that lantern or whatever it is she has. And all those sneaky stairs."

"Sneak stairs," Miranda whispered. "Parker . . . you *see* that?"

But the wind had died, and the moss was settling softly back into place.

And the attic window was empty and black as the night.

8

"MIRANDA, WHAT THE HELL WERE YOU THINKING?" Parker muttered.

He wasn't looking at the window anymore, he was scowling at her. Miranda realized that Gage and Ashley had caught up, and were practically on her heels.

"Thinking about what?" She didn't have a clue what Parker was talking about. Her thoughts were jumping back and forth between the house, the attic window, and what might possibly be inside. . . .

"I tried to save your ass back there about the whole ghost thing. *Which*, by the way, *Ashley* started with her stories-about-dead-people crap."

"I did," Ashley admitted guiltily. "I'm sorry, Miranda. Sometimes I forget to think."

Choked laughs all around. Ashley looked mildly offended.

"Well, I can't help it," she insisted. "It's not like I do it on purpose."

"We know," Gage managed a straight face. "We know you would never deliberately try to not think."

"It takes a lot of talent to do what you do, Ash," Roo added seriously.

Hesitating, Ashley smiled. "Well . . . thank you."

"So, as I was saying," Parker went on, "about saving Miranda's ass"—he broke off, pulled back a step, gave her rear end a quick once-over—"not that I minded so much, as it's a pretty nice ass, but all the same—"

Miranda walked faster. "I know you meant to help, Parker. But I *want* to hear about the ghost stories. I *should* hear about the ghost stories—"

"Why?" He still sounded slightly incredulous. "Haven't you heard enough about ghosts for a while? Or do you *enjoy* being terrorized on a regular basis?"

"It's not that, it's—"

"And did I mention that Gage *also* tried to save your ass?"

"Worth saving." Gage winked. "My pleasure."

Flustered, Miranda stammered on. "I know he did. I'm—I'm sorry, Gage. I just . . . look, you don't have to protect me. I appreciate it, I really do, but—"

"He's not trying to protect you," Roo said calmly. "He's scared of ghosts, and he still thinks we don't know."

Parker instantly snorted a laugh. "Right. Like I could be scared of *anything*, seeing you every day."

"I *appreciate* it," Miranda repeated, more firmly this time. "But I'm pretty sure ghosts are going to find me, even if you . . ."

Her mind was weaving back and forth. She could feel Etienne's eyes on her, and the silent message they were sending: *Tell the others what's going on.* But she wasn't ready, she had to think, sort things out, *and that light in the window, Parker saw it too, though he doesn't even realize what he saw. . . .*

"If we . . ." Parker prompted.

"Even if you"—Miranda snapped back to the present—"pretend ghosts aren't real."

Parker's expression went numb. "Oh my God. Listen to her. It's Ashley logic."

"What's that?" Ashley asked.

"Never mind. Miranda . . . you're trying to ruin my life."

For a long moment there was silence.

Then Parker drew a deep, slow breath.

"I'm throwing you in the bayou." Without warning, he lunged for her, catching her around the waist. Miranda never saw it coming. As Parker grabbed her, she jumped, let out a squeal, and twisted free from his grasp.

The minute it happened, Etienne swung the flashlight on them. Miranda saw the slow, sly dawn of surprise go across Parker's face. Her heart immediately sank.

"Why, Miranda Barnes!" He feigned shock. "Are you ticklish?"

"No," she said, a little too quickly. "No! Definitely not."

But Parker grabbed her again, before she could get away. Only this time he held on to her till she was helpless with laughter, "Why yes, I think you *are*! I most definitely think you are ticklish."

Everyone else seemed to be laughing now too, plus whistles and catcalls from the guys. It was Ashley who ran over to save the day.

"Parker, you let her go right this instant!"

Parker's hands flew up in the air while Miranda scurried out of reach. "Hey, it was an accident! All I wanted to do was throw her in the bayou—I didn't know she was going to be so *sensitive*." Then, cupping one hand around his mouth, he turned and gave an exaggerated stage whisper. "She's so little—*no contest*. Gage? Etienne? Have fun."

"Big bully," Ashley scolded, linking arms with Miranda. "You should be ashamed of yourself, Parker Wilmington."

But Parker couldn't resist one last taunt. "Surprise attack," he warned Miranda. Kung-fu style, he flung out his arms as though he might grab her again. "Perfect ambush. You'll never see it coming."

The group started moving again, getting near the parking lot. Miranda kept close to Ashley and as far as she could from Parker.

"Parker tried to tickle Roo once," Ashley recalled, "and she knocked him out."

"Knocked me out?" he blurted, indignant. "She almost *killed* me!"

Roo merely shrugged. "I didn't mean to. And I didn't knock you *all* the way out. Just stunned you."

"You hit me with a damn board!"

"It was lying there. How was I supposed to know how heavy it was?"

Grumbling, Parker joined ranks with Gage and Etienne while the girls brought up the rear.

"Oh, stop whining!" Ashley pointed her finger at Parker. "We'll just see y'all at the house."

Within minutes, everyone was on the road. Having flatly refused to let Ashley drive, Roo was behind the steering wheel this time, and Ashley in the backseat—while Miranda, resting her head against the window, felt numb, exhausted, and emotionally drained. She'd hoped for a quiet ride back to town, but Ashley's sudden outburst brought her up straight.

"Roo! I cannot *believe* you said what you did back there in front of Parker!"

The glance Roo flicked her was totally baffled. "And that would be . . ."

"Kurt Fuller!"

"You've been waiting all this time to yell at me about *that*?"

"What do you know, and how did you hear about it?"

"About him asking you out? It's no big secret, Ash. Your little cheerleader pals have been very busy spreading the news."

"Oh my God . . ."

"They saw you and Streak talking after practice." Lighting a cigarette, Roo held it out the open window. "They said he hung around for a long time, and he smiled a lot. And he was touching your thigh—"

"A bug! There was a bug on my leg, and he got it off!"

"And now that he's broken up with Delphine . . ."

"Oh . . . my . . . God . . ." Ashley covered her face with her hands. "Parker doesn't know, Roo."

"Well, he will by tomorrow. No, make that tonight."

"This is horrible."

"Why is it horrible? Did you tell Kurt you'd go out with him?"

"Of course not. But I suppose you want me to, right? Just to upset Parker?"

"Why, no. That would be shallow of me."

Ashley peeked out through her fingers. "I just don't want Parker to get mad and do something stupid." Even as Roo opened her mouth, Ashley cut her off. "Don't. Don't *even* say it."

Roo closed her mouth. Ashley lowered her hands again and looked miserable. And Miranda, thinking wishfully of her nice bed at home, resumed leaning on the windowpane, her gaze intent on the flowing darkness beyond.

Eventually the car swung into a wide, smooth curve . . . trundled over the old drawbridge . . . passed a moss-shrouded cemetery, bone-white tombs, a high-steepled stone church. Through the heavy downpour, buildings and streetlamps of St. Yvette came into bleary focus, and after several more turnoffs and a maze of quaint, crowded neighborhoods, Miranda realized that they had finally reached their destination.

She'd never been to Roo and Ashley's house before. Large and rambling, it stood on the very last lot—a double lot, at least—of a dead-end street, with curtains open and light streaming out from every window. Like so many homes in town, it looked old and well-kept—yet with a certain distinctiveness that set it apart from the others Miranda had seen. As though this eccentric, outdated, randomly-added-onto, four-story farmhouse had defiantly stood its ground while the rich land around it had continued to disappear and more modern houses had sprung up in place of cotton fields. A faded picket fence lined the front, where Parker's borrowed station wagon was angled onto the curb. And what might once have been a small barn—now rather lopsided and painted garishly orange—stood toward the back of an enormous tree-shaded yard, illuminated by strings of fairy lights dangling from its eaves.

A dog was barking close by; as Roo pulled into the driveway, Miranda turned to look. Next door, to the left of the house, stood a charming Victorian—pale blue with dark blue shutters, a wrap-around porch and gingerbread trim, fanciful gables and a three-story tower facing the street. Etienne's truck was parked at the side. Miranda could see a golden retriever racing back and forth behind the porch railing, and the silhouette of a woman in the front doorway, motioning the dog to come in.

Gage's house, she immediately thought, and couldn't help smiling. Soon after she'd met them, the girls had told her about being childhood neighbors with Gage. They'd also told her about Gage and Etienne being first cousins—another discovery that had surprised her.

"Etienne must have stopped for a shower," Roo said, indicating the pickup. Ashley, noting Miranda's curiosity, went on to explain.

"Yes, that's where Gage lives, if you're wondering. Oh, and that's Jazz on the porch—he's such a big goof—he adores everybody in the world. You'd *love* their house, Miranda. It's really old; they've done a whole lot of fixing up."

"I like the way *yours* looks," Miranda said truthfully. "It's old too, right?"

Roo slowed down, gestured vaguely toward the newly mowed lawn and the field of wildflowers that bordered it. "Older than Gage's. The story goes, that the farmer who lived here built the house next door as a wedding present for his daughter."

"I think that's so sweet," Ashley sighed.

"Yeah. If you want your parents spying on you for the rest of your life."

The garage was already open when they pulled around back. Feeling suddenly shy, Miranda got out of the car, then followed Roo and Ashley through a connecting door into a huge, country-style kitchen that was warm and fragrant and full of activity.

"Come on, Miranda." Ashley laughed. "Welcome to our zoo."

But Miranda stopped. She stopped just over the threshold and stood beside an antique pie safe that hid her from view.

There were dogs—*cocker spaniels, two; no, three*—running in and out of the room at breakneck speed; there was a mynah bird on top of a wooden hutch in the corner, yelling something that sounded suspiciously like "Roo's a bad girl!" Gage, minus crutches, had balanced himself against the sink and was rinsing silverware; Ashley immediately went over to help. A gang of cats—*five? you're kidding me . . . six?*—had surrounded Parker, rubbing against his legs while he muttered and swore and tried to maneuver his way to the refrigerator. And the two grown-ups in the room, cheerfully oblivious to the chaos around them, were Roo's and Ashley's parents.

Though Miranda knew that the two girls were stepsisters, she'd never been able to figure out who actually belonged to which biological mom or dad. As with the rest of the group's parents, Miranda had met Miss Voncile and Mr. Sonny at the hospital that night of Gage's accident—and her reaction now was the same as it had been then. She'd never seen such an odd couple—but odd in a cute and quirky way. Miss Voncile, an admired and respected artist. Crinkly eyes and smile; close-cropped spiky white hair; dangly feather earrings to her shoulders; tall, skinny body dressed tonight in jeans, raggedy moccasins, and an oversized work shirt—her clothes, face, hands, and hair streaked with all colors of paint. And Mr. Sonny, famous for his "Sonny Slim the Singin' Used Car Salesman" local dealership and commercials. Lanky as his wife; squinty blue eyes behind wire-rimmed spectacles; toothy grin and long handlebar mustache; and his customary Wild West attire—black snap-button Western shirt (this one with identical red stagecoaches across the chest and back), black jeans, black cowboy hat and boots. Right now Miss Voncile was at the stove, while Mr. Sonny—perched atop a tall stool—strummed a guitar and sang a country song.

"Oh, God, he's doing it." Roo groaned deep in her throat. "Somebody please shoot me."

Parker instantly brightened. "I volunteer."

"Is that a new song, Daddy?" Ashley asked.

Pausing mid-strum, Mr. Sonny touched a finger to his hat brim. "Just wrote it this afternoon, princess!"

"*This* is why I have no friends," Roo mumbled to herself, and walked past her dad while he winked at Ashley.

"He looks tired." Miss Voncile was fussing. "Gage, you look tired."

"I'm fine," Gage said.

"He's fine," Mr. Sonny echoed, breaking off the song. "Look at him, he's strong and healthy. Good exercise for that pitching arm—right, Gage? Hauling that crutch around for six weeks, working up those muscles for spring ball?"

Gage smiled, but Miss Voncile rushed on. "I don't care. His cast comes off soon, and I don't want to jinx it. I don't want him overdoing."

"If you're so worried about him overdoing, then why do you have him washing dishes?" Roo grumbled. "Does that even make sense?"

"Because *somebody* here didn't load the dishwasher before she left for school this morning, and we have no forks to eat potato salad. Does *that* make sense?"

"Where's Miranda?" Gage asked.

"And anyway, how can he overdo?" Roo grumbled again, heading straight for the refrigerator, bumping Parker out of the way so she could grab a soda. "He's got a whole harem around him every single minute of the day."

"What are you talking about?" Her mother held up a gigantic platter of golden fried chicken. "What is she talking about, Gage—this harem?"

"Nothing," Gage answered.

"Your entourage at school?" Roo mimicked a high, girlie voice: "Oh Gage, let me carry your books . . . oh Gage, let me open the door for you . . . oh Gage, let me help you up the stairs . . . oh Gage, that cast makes you look *so sexy*—"

"Oh Roo, you're just jealous," Parker mimicked back at her.

"Oh Gage, let me help you get dressed—"

"Nobody says that," Gage protested, flushing slightly.

Leaning over Gage's shoulder, Parker nudged him in the side

and did a falsetto of his own. “Oh Gage, let me help you get *un*dressed—”

Gage shook his head and continued rinsing.

“Exactly,” Roo echoed. “And they’re writing their *bra* sizes on his cast now.”

Mr. Sonny tried to keep a straight face. “Is that true, Gage? Their *bra* sizes? Hey, let’s see that cast. We might have us a good idea for a song there, buddy.”

Laughing, Ashley hugged Gage, yanked a dishtowel from the oven door, and began drying the forks that he handed her.

“It was so beautiful out at Belle Chandelle today, Mama. Just one of the most *beautiful* places I’ve ever seen!”

“I’m *sure* it was for *you*, Ashley,” Miss Voncile agreed, catching a bored glance from Roo.

“It was old and romantic and wonderful and just—just—in my heart, you know?”

“I’m sure, sweetie.”

“Where’s Miranda?” Gage asked again, louder this time. “I thought she was riding with you two.”

“Miranda? Oh, I’m so glad! Did you bring Miranda?” Miss Voncile looked in every direction. “Roo, what on earth have you done with Miranda?”

“Maybe she’s in the bathroom,” Roo suggested. “Gage, go see.”

Gage stayed where he was. “How can she be in the bathroom? We would’ve seen her go by.”

“And,” Ashley said solemnly, “she’s never been here before, so she doesn’t even know where it is.”

“Maybe she talks to dead plumbing, and it told her where

to find the toilets," Parker mumbled, then winced as Ashley punched him on the shoulder.

"She was right behind me." Ashley sounded puzzled now. "Miranda?"

But Miranda's head was spinning; she couldn't move. All this confusion and noise and commotion . . . *all this closeness and family and love.* Suddenly she felt completely overwhelmed—*too much to handle, too much for one day.* In a split-second glance, she spotted a door on the side wall of the garage; at the same time she saw Parker turn from the refrigerator and stare directly at her. He stood there a moment, Coke in hand, a half grin on his face. Then, to her surprise, he cleared his throat and went back to the others, leaving her undetected there on the threshold.

"Do you smell smoke?" Miss Voncile sounded distressed. "I smell smoke. Ashley, I hope Roo wasn't smoking in my car."

"Maybe something's burning," Ashley said smoothly, exchanging amused glances with Gage. "Maybe something's boiling over on the stove."

"There's nothing boiling, and it's not that kind of smoke."

Roo retreated to the walk-in pantry. Her mother, with a stern shake of her head, lifted her voice disapprovingly.

"Roo, I hope you weren't smoking in my car!"

"No," came the voice from the pantry.

"Roo's a bad girl!" cawed the mynah bird.

"Hey, what about that game on TV last night!" Mr. Sonny exclaimed.

The guys immediately lapsed into sports babble. Two kittens tumbled out of the pantry. A door slammed somewhere, and

Etienne walked into the kitchen from an adjoining room, his hair wet, his jeans and T-shirt changed and clean.

"Where's Miranda?" he asked.

"Here." Taking a deep breath, Miranda stepped forward, miserably conscious of every eye upon her. "Sorry. I had . . . mud on my shoes. I didn't want to track it in."

This brought a general round of laughter. Miss Voncile, obviously sensing Miranda's awkwardness, swept over to greet her with a big hug.

"Honey, bless your heart for being so polite—but there is nothing in the world you could do to mess up this house. It's made to live in and feel comfortable in—we don't worry about nasty little things like mud and dirt."

"Or Roo," Parker added, which brought an even bigger round of laughter. As Roo emerged indifferently from the pantry, he handed Miranda a Coke and used his foot to drag out a chair for her at the table, while the free-for-all resumed around them.

"Now, Dad and I already ate, so y'all kids fill up your plates and go on in the den—there's chicken and baked beans and potato salad and biscuits and—and Roo, I should *not* have to remind you about the dishwasher. How many times do I need to remind you about the dishwasher? Please tell me you'll remember next time."

"I'll remember next time."

"Good. Now, see that you do. By the way, Ashley, did you have any trouble with the car?"

"Don't ask her that, Mom," Roo answered. "And don't ever give her the keys again."

"Why? Did something happen? Etienne, come over here. How's your mama? Ashley, don't you dare give him that dishtowel to dry his hair! You know better than that—"

"I didn't give it to him, he just took it."

"Shame on you. Y'all act like you were raised in a barn."

"We were," Roo said under her breath, while Mr. Sonny started singing again.

Amidst much shoving, laughing, and teasing, Miranda soon found herself in the cozy den off the kitchen, seated on the sofa beside Gage, with a huge plate of food on her lap. Old, well-worn furniture cluttered the room. Covering the wall next to Gage was an eclectic assortment of artwork—Miss Voncile's, she guessed—sketches and paintings; woven tapestries; designs in feathers and beads, cloth and metal; a round mosaic of silvery glass; arrangements of dried leaves and pressed flowers.

"Hey, eat up." Gage nudged her gently. "Before Parker comes over here and steals it."

"I will, too," Parker insisted. "I'm starving."

Grinning, he took the easy chair across from her while Ashley perched on the armrest. Roo sat on the floor, leaning against Gage's cast. And Etienne, standing comfortably in one corner, nodded at Miranda over a spoonful of beans.

"Whatcha thinking so hard about, *cher*?"

It came out before she could stop it. "You guys said there were spooky stories about Belle Chandelle—"

"God, Miranda," Parker groaned. "You haven't even swallowed one bite yet, and you're already talking about that damn house! Gage—just grab her right now."

"Yeah, Gage, grab her," Roo echoed under her breath. "You know you want to."

Gage moved his leg. Roo fell backward into the coffee table.

"I'm serious," Miranda said firmly. "I want to hear them. So tell me."

But Parker kept scarfing down fried chicken. "There's nothing to tell. Haunted Houses 101. Flickering lights. Clanking chains. Screams and moans and . . . gosh, come to think of it . . . Belle Chandelle's ghosts are really boring. And not very original, either."

"Actually, he's right," Gage agreed. "Everything I've ever heard is general stuff, pretty much stereotyped. And it's usually from kids who sneak out there on a dare, either to get drunk or make out."

"Or *both*." Roo flicked Parker a meaningful glance. She sat up again. She frowned at Gage and rubbed the back of her head.

"Not exactly credible witnesses," Gage concluded, ignoring her.

"I'd like to see that photograph of the house," Miranda decided. "And read that letter."

Parker's eyes rolled back. He moaned dramatically and flopped sideways in his chair.

"I've seen the picture." Pulling himself from the corner, Etienne chewed . . . swallowed . . . wiped one hand absently on his T-shirt. "Miss Teeta, she's got a copy of it—so does your mama."

Miranda couldn't help but feel a quick stab of guilt. If she'd shown an interest sooner in Mom's job, she'd have already known something about the house.

"So what does it look like?" she asked him.

He pondered a second . . . frowned. "Like Miss Teeta said. The house, it's in the distance, at an angle—all that's showing is most of the front and part of one side. I'm thinking you *should* see it for yourself, *cher*. See what you get out of it."

"Anybody for seconds?" Eagerly, Parker raised his hand, but all attention was on Etienne.

"So what *do* we actually know about the house?" Gage spoke up.

Etienne rested his fork on his plate, dark eyes sweeping the group. "Like Miss Teeta said, not that much. The original house they figure was built sometime late eighteenth, early nineteenth century. Later on from that, it became one of the biggest sugarcane plantations around here."

"How big? I mean, what kind of operation are we talking about?"

"Around thirty outbuildings—maybe more—plus the slave cabins."

"Wow." Even Parker looked reluctantly impressed. "And with all those sugarcane fields? There must have been hundreds of acres. Thousands, even."

"That'd be my guess."

"Seems like a spread that size would have been pretty famous."

Gage gave a slight shrug. "A plantation that big would've been almost totally self-sufficient. Practically like its own little town. They wouldn't have needed much at all from the outside world."

"Wait, wait—" Ashley was so intrigued, she could hardly sit still. "But Parker's right—that doesn't make sense. If it was that big, then why wouldn't there be anything more written about it? There should be *tons* of history about Belle Chandelle."

"Maybe not so unusual," Gage said quietly. "I mean, think about it. So many plantations were looted and burned during the War—and never rebuilt. And when towns were occupied by Union armies, there were probably lots of records stolen or destroyed . . . or just plain lost. There's no telling how many local histories disappeared."

"And what you said about the plantation," Etienne nodded in Gage's direction. "If it really *was* that independent, then maybe it really *didn't* have that much contact with the outside world. At least not on any regular basis."

Scooting to the edge of the couch, Miranda set her plate of half-eaten food on the coffee table. "That makes sense. Remember when we were trying to find out about Hayes House—Aunt Teeta's house? Traveling was such a big deal back then . . . not like it is now. People in the country were pretty isolated; it took a long time to get from one place to another."

"And Belle Chandelle *is* kind of far from town—even today, by car," Ashley echoed. "And all those woods, and being hidden there on the bayou. Back then, it probably would have taken *forever* to get there."

"Especially if *you'd* been driving," Roo noted.

But Parker was still stuck on the outbuildings. "Thirty-plus outbuildings? So these new owners—they're not planning to rebuild every single one of them, are they?"

Etienne looked mildly pained. "That's what I'm hearing."

"Just for some storybook bed and breakfast? That's crazy!"

"Why is it crazy?" Gage asked, shrugging. "Miss Teeta said they want it to be authentic. You can't have an authentic plantation without all those other buildings that go with it. Otherwise, it's just a house."

"He's right," Etienne affirmed. "Lots of people, when they hear the word 'plantation,' they just think of a house. But a plantation, it was really the whole farm, the whole estate. So yeah, the new owners, they're wanting every single outbuilding just like it was back then."

"Ooh, I love it!" Clapping her hands, Ashley almost toppled her dinner into Parker's lap. "And it's so smart, too! This way the whole thing will be historically accurate *and* it'll last forever, because it'll be done right. Because . . . you know . . . today's building materials will hold up a whole lot longer."

Parker smacked his palm against his forehead. "You're right! Damn! If only they'd put seamless siding on all those castles over in England."

"I'm ignoring you. This chair is an empty chair."

Finishing his plate of food, Gage stacked it on Miranda's. Etienne set his own empty plate on top.

"Unbelievable." Parker muttered, leveling a frown at the group. "Can you even imagine how much this whole thing is going to *cost*? These new owners must be richer than God. Who the hell are they anyway?"

Etienne slowly shook his head. "*Mais*, I don't know, I've never met them. I don't think Miranda's mama has either. Miss Teeta, she's been driving over to New Orleans when they call her for meetings; they always stay at one of those fancy hotels in the French Quarter."

"Don't they ever come here?" Surprised, Ashley let this sink in. "I mean . . . don't they ever come to Belle Chandelle?"

"From what Miss Teeta says, they've never seen the place at all."

"Then maybe they're celebrities! Or . . . or a royal family from some rich foreign country! And they don't want anybody to know it's them, because then they'd be mobbed when they come to St. Yvette!"

"Right," Parker agreed dryly. "All those wild paparazzi hanging out at Hank's Hardware and the Snowball Shack."

"What about that stuff on the property?" Miranda remembered suddenly.

Conversation stopped. All stares shifted to her.

"You mean the outbuildings?" Etienne raised an eyebrow.

"No, I mean . . . didn't Aunt Teeta say there was some stuff found on the property years ago?"

"Miranda?" Parker warned. "Stop."

But Etienne was nodding at her, angling back against the wall again, folding his arms over his chest. "Yeah, I know what you're talking about. I'm thinking there were some things from the house . . . like, *parts* of the house . . . mantels . . . doorknobs . . . things like that. But I'm not sure what else. You'll have to ask her."

"I just . . . well, you never know. It wouldn't hurt to see those things from the house. I mean . . . as long as we're looking at the letter and the picture anyway."

"Hey. *We're* not looking at the letter and the picture, okay?" Frowning harder, Parker leaned forward in his chair. "Gage. Help me out here. Do something. *Anything* so she can't talk. This is war, man."

But before Gage could react, the pillow came out of nowhere. A ruffled throw pillow sailing past Miranda's head, bouncing off the back of the cushions, knocking over a lamp, and landing on the floor beside Gage's end of the couch. For a long moment, Parker stared at what he'd done. Then tried his best to look contrite.

"Oops."

"Parker, for heaven's sake!" Ashley scolded as the room erupted in laughter. "You could have hurt Miranda. What on earth is wrong with you?"

"If we could figure *that* out," Roo replied solemnly, "world peace would be no problem."

Gazing at Parker, Etienne kept a perfectly straight face. "What, is that some kinda secret pass you been workin' on? No wonder y'all nearly lost your last game—"

"Win 'Em All Wilmington," Gage broke in. "I hear he was *awesome* in his glory days."

A sheepish grin tugged at Parker's mouth. He pointed his finger at Gage. "Meet me outside, Hopalong. I'll race you."

Another round of laughter—Miranda included. As both Ashley and Etienne started toward the fallen lamp, Miranda shook her head at them, jumped up, and circled around the couch. Luckily, nothing was broken. It only took a minute to reattach the lampshade, untangle the cord, and toss the pillow back to Parker—but as she set the lamp on the end table, an unexpected chill shot through her.

Someone's watching me.

Miranda froze. With one hand clasping the lamp, she stood there in sudden, inexplicable terror while the laughter and chatter of her friends faded into a distant roar.

Of course someone's watching you, Miranda—you're in this room with five other people. . . .

Yet she knew that wasn't it. Deep down in her soul, she knew that this was different, *something wrong, something close, something* here. . . .

The hairs prickled at the back of her neck. Her chest squeezed tight, breath trapped in her lungs as she finally lifted her hand, as she raised her eyes to the wall. . . .

The beautiful handmade art on the wall . . . feathers and beads . . . leaves and flowers . . . metal and cloth and glass—*no, not glass!*—the round mosaic of silvery glass—*not glass at all!*—staring at herself in those shiny little sections of mirror . . .

Miranda's reflection began to fade . . . go dark. Flickered softly again, in and out of focus.

She saw the horrified expression . . .

The dark eyes, wide with pain . . .

And the pale, mournful face gazing back at her.

The face of a woman . . .

A stranger whom she had never seen before.

9

In that split second, Miranda couldn't be sure—sure if she'd dropped the lamp or tried to fling it against the wall. She only knew that one minute she was holding it; the next minute, Gage was stretching sideways over the arm of the couch, catching the lamp before it hit the floor a second time.

"You okay?" he asked, puzzled.

"Clumsy," she mumbled, then wondered if she'd spoken aloud or merely in her head. "Sorry."

But her hands were shaking, and she knew that Gage could see. And even though Etienne was across the room, she felt the piercing scrutiny of his eyes, glancing between her and the wall.

"I . . . here, Gage. I'll take it," she mumbled again.

"You sure?"

"Yeah. Thanks."

As he passed her the lamp, his long fingers closed around hers, strong and steady, warm against her ice-cold skin. For a moment she wanted to cling to him, never let go, never look up at that wall again, or into the silvery glass—*a woman's face there, a young woman who's not me, staring straight into my eyes with a terrible, silent desperation, as if I'm* her *reflection, as if* I'm *the stranger in the mirror—*

"Isn't that pretty, Miranda?" Having forcefully taken away Parker's plate, Ashley was snuggling back against him. "That's what you were looking at, right? The glass thingy?"

Surprised, Miranda managed a nod. Focused on Ashley, not on the wall. "It's . . . fascinating. I've never seen anything like it."

"They're mirrors. Little pieces of mirrors. Mama put each one in by hand. Oh, and when the sun hits it, it's beautiful. It sparkles and makes colors all over the room."

"That's . . . really nice." Miranda set the lamp on the table, fiddled nervously with the shade.

"You can take it down if you want . . . if you'd like to see it up close."

"No!"

Was everyone staring at her? She couldn't tell, she just couldn't look at that wall. *But you have to, Miranda. You know you can't leave here till you do—*

"Miranda?" Gage's voice, concerned; Gage's hand, stroking her arm. Helplessly her eyes shot to the round mosaic, the glass, the mirrors, the reflection—

Me.

Just me, staring at me.

No woman. No stranger. No . . . whatever—whoever—that I wish to God I imagined but deep down I know I didn't. . . .

"Miranda?" Etienne's voice now, drifting through her confusion. She forced a quick, tight smile; felt Gage's touch slide away.

"You know what?" She laughed. Not a very convincing laugh, but a laugh all the same. "With school today, and the plantation, and all this great food—I am *so tired* all of a sudden. I think . . . Etienne, would you mind taking me home?"

Etienne didn't hesitate. "Yeah, I gotta get myself home too. Much as I hate to leave this wild party."

"Hey, no helping," Ashley ordered as Miranda began gathering plates, cutlery, and soda cans. "That's Roo's job, to clean up tonight."

Secretly, Miranda was glad. The urge to get home was stronger than ever now; she wanted to be in her own room, in her own bed, where she felt safe. She followed the others to the kitchen, joined in the chorus of compliments, thank-yous, and good-nights. When Etienne closed the truck door behind her, the last of her reserve gave out. She was vaguely aware of his cell phone going off, his voice muffled in a brief one-way conversation while he stood on the curb. Her whole body was tense. She leaned stiffly against the window, but she was trembling again and couldn't stop. All she wanted was to forget. Forget about the woman in the mirror . . . forget about every creepy experience she'd had today . . .

There's a mirror in my bedroom . . . will I see something in that, too?

She jumped as the driver's door opened and Etienne climbed inside. He shoved the key in the ignition but didn't turn it; instead, he sat there regarding her with a long, pensive stare.

"That was Mama," he said at last, tapping his cell. "I'm picking her up at your house."

"My house? What's she doing there?"

"Went with your mama to some meeting tonight. Guess you heard she's got herself a job cooking at Belle Chandelle."

"Aunt Teeta told me this morning. I think it's great."

"Yeah . . ." His black eyes narrowed, intent on her face. "But *you're* not feeling too great . . . not since you looked at that thing on the wall back there."

Miranda propped her elbow on the window ledge. She pressed one hand to her forehead, rubbed at the ache along her brow. Quietly, Etienne kept on.

"What, you think I can't tell the difference between clumsy and scared?"

Of course he'd realized. She'd known right away that he hadn't missed a thing. "That obvious?" she murmured.

"I don't think anybody there caught it. Well . . . except for Gage." Etienne paused . . . frowned . . . angled back against his door. "What'd you see, *cher*?"

"A reflection." Drawing a deep, shaky breath, she focused on being calm. "When I looked in that mirror, I saw a reflection. Only it . . . wasn't me."

He'd been ready for just about anything—but not this, she could tell. And though there was only a brief hint of surprise on his face, she saw it all the same.

"Who was it?" he asked bluntly, but Miranda could only shake her head.

"I have no idea. A woman . . . no one I've ever seen before."

"Can't you remember anything about her?"

Shaking her head again, she closed her eyes. It had begun to rain again, a light drizzle pattering the roof and misting over the windshield. After a few more seconds, Etienne squeezed her hand, started the engine, and headed for Hayes House.

It never took long to get anywhere in St. Yvette—not even clear across town to Aunt Teeta's. They made the drive in silence, though Miranda's mind was in full turmoil. She didn't want to think about what she'd seen, yet that was impossible. The mirror-woman's face was still seared into her brain, and she couldn't get rid of it, couldn't shut it out, even though she was desperately trying to.

Hang on . . . you can do it . . . you're almost home. . . .

The pickup slowed to make a turn. They were starting onto the Brickway now—the quaint, brick-paved road that wound through the town's historical district—and when Miranda opened her eyes, her own street corner was just coming into view. In another couple minutes she could escape to her room, lock the door, and have a private little breakdown. *Except Miss Nell's going to be there, remember?* Miranda didn't know if she could hold it together that long. As Etienne stopped in the driveway, she sat for a moment, trying to compose herself.

"You never have to go back, *cher*." His voice lowered, unmistakably protective. "You never have to see that mirror again, if you don't want to."

Oh, why can't it be that simple?

But if Miranda had learned anything from her experiences, it was this one bitter truth—that even if she *didn't* ever see that mirror again, the haunting wouldn't stop. That woman—whoever she was—would find some other way to reach her. Again and again . . . till Miranda finally figured it out.

"You know that won't help," she whispered now, even as Etienne nodded.

"Yeah. I know."

Somewhat distantly, she heard her door open and felt his hand on her shoulder, coaxing her out; then his hand on her back, guiding her to the porch. The second they were inside, Aunt Teeta hurried from the kitchen to greet them.

"Here y'all are!" Throwing her arms around each of them in turn, Aunt Teeta couldn't have looked more delighted. "Come on in and have some carrot cake. Why, us three girls are just having ourselves the best visit!"

"I . . . I'm really tired, Aunt Teeta—" Miranda began, but the woman quickly cut her off.

"Just for a few minutes, hon—Nell's been waiting to see you, and your mama hasn't talked to you all day. And I'll put on some hot milk to help you sleep. Come on now."

There was no way out of it. Receiving a shrug from Etienne, Miranda reluctantly followed her aunt.

The kitchen, as usual, was a delicious haven—strong black coffee, sugar and cream, homemade cake, sweet tea, and stale cinnamon rolls left over from an early breakfast. Mom and Miss Nell were deep in conversation at the table, and from all the crumpled napkins, spilled crumbs, and used coffee filters heaped in the sink, it was obvious that the girl-talk had been going on for quite a while.

It was Miss Nell who looked up first. Miranda hadn't seen her since the night of Gage's accident—six weeks ago at the Falls—but she hadn't forgotten her. Small and delicate, almost frail; hair and eyes like Etienne's; dimples in her pale cheeks; and a brave smile that defied her most recent brush with cancer.

As Etienne winked at her and mumbled in French, she stood up, walked straight to Miranda, and gave her a hug.

Miranda didn't expect it. She barely managed to return the hug before Miss Nell stepped away, held Miranda at arm's length, and gave her a swift appraisal.

"I'm sorry you've been sick, Miranda." The woman's glance shot between Miranda and Etienne. "Maybe *some* people will be easier to get along with, now that you're back again."

Everyone laughed. Except for Etienne, who looked vaguely embarrassed and raked a hand back through his rain-damp hair.

"How are you, Etienne?" Miranda's mom spoke up cheerfully as Miss Nell returned to her chair. "You know, Teeta's been telling me how you used to come by here all the time to help out our dad."

Etienne paused, cleared his throat. "Yes ma'am. I helped out a little."

"Oh, don't be so modest!" Aunt Teeta fussed. "Listen to him! Why, he certainly helped out more than a little—he practically *rebuilt* this old house. And I *miss* having him around!"

"Well then," Mom smiled, "maybe he should start coming by more often."

"Maybe I should," Etienne agreed, nodding at the floor.

"Hon, you know there's always stuff around here that needs some special attention," Aunt Teeta reminded him sweetly.

Miranda shot daggers at both her mother and her aunt. Neither seemed to notice, though Miss Nell definitely seemed amused.

"But you know, it is so *funny* that y'all came in when you did—we were just talking about you two." Puttering at the counter, Aunt Teeta fixed Etienne and Miranda with an innocent smile. "Just look at y'all! I swear, y'all look so cute together! Don't you ladies think they just look so cute together?"

While the women laughed in agreement, Miranda cringed all the way to her toes. She couldn't even face Etienne; she had no idea how he was reacting. *I'm going to kill them. Mom and Aunt Teeta both.*

Luckily, Miss Nell stood up again and slung her purse over one shoulder. "Okay, Casanova, why don't you take your poor old mother home, hmm? I'm beat."

While the three women exchanged hugs and good-nights, Miranda walked with Etienne to the door.

"I'm so sorry," she mumbled, still flustered. "They just—Aunt Teeta—I didn't expect them to—"

His lips brushed hers with a kiss. She never saw it coming, never even saw him lean down.

"Don't be worrying tonight, *cher*. Get some sleep. We'll find the answers, yeah? We'll figure it out."

Slightly breathless, Miranda managed a nod. "I really want to believe that."

Amusement flickered in his eyes . . . faded slowly to genuine concern. Lightly he traced a fingertip over the spot where he'd kissed her. "Believe it."

"But—"

"Believe it 'cause I said so."

Miss Nell was there now, with Mom and Aunt Teeta behind her. And Etienne was already running to open the door of the truck. And her skin felt so warm, and her heart was pounding so hard, that she almost felt faint. . . .

Fear, of course. *Fear of the unknown.*

She watched till the pickup backed all the way down the driveway . . . honked its horn . . . disappeared into the pouring rain.

Fear of the unknown spirits, Miranda?

Or fear of the unknown Etienne?

10

SHE LAY AWAKE FOR HOURS.

Tossing . . . turning . . . trying not to remember, but remembering too much . . .

She didn't want to think of Belle Chandelle, yet the place kept pulling her back to an overwhelming sense of sorrow . . . a shadow at an empty window . . . a swing moving in motionless air. . . . She'd been so certain of those footsteps approaching, running straight toward her. . . .

And what about the mirror in my locker and the one on the wall at Roo and Ashley's house?

The shock, the terror when she'd looked up to see a stranger's face where her own should have been. The reflection of a woman she didn't know . . .

That woman . . .

And now, for the first time, Miranda began to separate the face from the fear. *That woman . . . a young woman.* She hadn't allowed herself to think about the mirror-woman before; all she really recalled were the eyes. But now, here in the calm and safety of her room . . . she slowly, reluctantly, let her mind open and her memory unfold. . . .

Blackness. Only blackness at first, deep and silent as death. But then . . . as the face of the woman began to materialize, small bits of color began to emerge with her . . . not bright or vivid, but faded . . . unnatural yellows and browns . . . like a distorted old photograph slowly being developed. . . .

A young woman, though she doesn't look it. Her skin is yellow, a picture yellowed with age—her face is worried and gaunt, making her seem older than she is, but she's no more than twenty-two. . . .

Miranda paused, stiff on her back, gazing sightlessly up at the ceiling. The images were coming faster now—soon she wouldn't be able to stop them. She pressed her hands over her eyes and drew a deep breath.

Dark hair pulled back, but messy, untended . . . a bun, maybe at the back of her neck, but strands hanging around her face, she's tired, so very tired, she hasn't brushed her hair in a while, hasn't fixed her hair in a while, she's tried many times to tuck it back but it keeps falling. And something on top . . . a cap?—a cap of dark lace and dark ribbons . . . and her collar is dark, too, the collar of her dress is dark, dark material and very dirty—

*But her eyes! What is it about her eyes? So scared, no—*more *than scared—terrified panicky desperate pleading praying but God isn't answering! And something else,* something else, *something's wrong with her eyes, the color, it's not natural, the color of her eyes—what's wrong with that woman's eyes—*

With a cry, Miranda bolted upright. She was shaking all over, and as she huddled back into her pillows, she could scarcely catch her breath. She knew that those details she'd seen just now—clothes, hair, even the woman's face—were far more than anyone could *possibly* see in a handmade design of tiny mirror fragments. Yet she *had* seen them—*known* them—with absolute certainty.

Were the things she'd experienced today all separate events? Or were they each somehow connected with Belle Chandelle?

"What does it mean, Grandpa?" she whispered into the darkness. "Can you hear me? Can you help me?"

God, how she wished she could talk to him again. Learn from him. Hear his wisdom and his guidance, face-to-face. And yet, here in the quiet of her room, she almost felt as if she *could* hear him, a little. And the promises he'd asked her to keep.

"Don't turn them away," he'd said. *"They'll come to you because they know you can see them. They'll speak to you because they know you'll hear."*

Jonas Hayes hadn't been afraid of the spirits. He'd spoken of them as if they were every bit as real as the living; he'd accepted them just as matter-of-factly as he'd accepted his own purpose of being their mediator.

"Don't turn them away. . . ."

And now, for whatever reason, desperate spirits had come to Miranda for help—had purposely sought her out, knowing that she'd be able to see and to hear. . . .

I can't turn my back on them. . . . I can't turn them away, these spirits who need me. . . .

A weight seemed to settle around her heart. Feeling more restless than ever, she flung back the covers, climbed out of bed, and went quickly down the stairs. On the second-floor landing, she could hear Aunt Teeta's faint snores and soft music playing behind the closed door of Mom's room. Good, they were both asleep. She didn't want either of them fussing over her right now, worrying about her being up at this hour. She needed to think but didn't want to . . . needed to calm her brain, but didn't know how. When she slipped out the front door, the warm, balmy air felt soothing against her skin, and she stood for a moment, breathing it in.

The rain was still falling, hard and steady, muffling out the world. From time to time it sprayed in beneath the eaves, but not onto the porch swing, where Miranda chose to sit. Curling up, she drew her knees to her chest, rested her chin on her knees. The swing rocked gently with every gust of wind. She let her eyes drift shut and her thoughts drift free. . . .

"Miranda?"

The voice was familiar and very close. As Miranda gasped and jerked upright, Etienne reached out for her, catching her shoulders and holding her in place.

"Whoa, take it easy—"

"Oh my God, you scared me to death!" All the strength rushed out of her. Shaking violently, she grabbed for his hands . . . started to shove them away . . . held on to them instead. "What are you doing here? Do you have any idea what time it is?"

"Around three in the morning, last I checked."

"Don't you have a curfew like normal people? Doesn't your mom ever wonder where you go?"

Both questions seemed to amuse him. As Miranda's grip finally loosened, he pulled free and stepped back. "I been parked over there for a while." He jerked his thumb toward the street. "Trying to decide if I should come up to your room. Just . . . wanting to check you're okay."

Miranda stared at him. Wet clothes clinging to his body . . .

Black eyes skimming over the porch . . . front door . . . swing . . . her. Shaking his head, shoving back his hair, lifting his T-shirt to mop off his face—unsuccessfully.

She looked down at her own T-shirt—last minute nightwear of choice. She'd forgotten about what she was wearing—just an oversized shirt and underwear, not much. Sitting up straight, she tried to yank her shirt down over her thighs, and nearly fell off the swing.

Etienne waited while she rearranged herself. Then he leaned casually against the porch railing. "So. Bad night, yeah?"

"I'm okay."

"Which is why you're sitting out here in the rain at three in the morning?"

Miranda almost smiled at that. "You could have come up," she said quietly. "Everyone's asleep."

"Hmmm. And how come you always got me sneaking up the back way?" Voice teasing, expression serious. "I'm starting to feel like a pervert."

In spite of herself, she laughed. "You're perfectly welcome at any door, day or night, and you know it. But then Aunt Teeta fusses over you—"

"Me, I like being fussed over—"

"And she embarrasses me—"

"That's always fun—"

"And you *know* I can't talk about ghosts and spirits and—and my *job*—in front of her and Mom and—"

"And you want me all to yourself, I get it."

Miranda tried to sound stern. "That is *not* what I meant—"

"Oh, I'm not complaining. It *is* a pretty small room. Not much space to outrun me."

More sternness—a look this time. He didn't seem at all intimidated.

"If you remember," Miranda scolded him, "the very *few* times you've been up there were emergencies. You talked me out of being terrified. You saved me from . . . from ghostly stalkers. You . . . you helped me figure out what to do. . . ."

Her words trailed off. All seriousness now, Etienne walked to the swing, nudged her over, and sat down.

"I *was* coming up. I was on my way to the back steps when I saw you walk out. And I was damn right to be checking on you." Again his eyes slid over her in cool, quick appraisal. "You haven't slept one minute tonight, I can tell. And you got that too-much-to-worry-about look on your face. Which means you been doing a lotta thinking and being scared since I left here with Mama."

Reality had returned, and Miranda said nothing. Seconds passed into minutes. Distractedly, she chewed on a fingernail but still didn't talk. When Etienne finally slipped his arms around her shoulders, she resisted at first, though her willpower didn't last long.

"You had yourself one hell of a day," he murmured. "You shouldn't be alone with it. And I'm staying right here—if you wanna talk, if you don't wanna talk—I'm staying till you tell me to leave."

She knew that he meant it. And that she didn't *really* want to be alone with it after all.

"I started remembering what she looked like," Miranda spoke so quietly that he had to bend closer. "But what I keep wondering is how she . . . *found* me. I didn't feel her anywhere at the plantation, and that mirror at Ashley's house doesn't even belong to me—I've never even seen it. This almost seems more personal than spirits I dealt with before. More . . . I don't know . . . intrusive. Like the barriers between me and them are getting thinner. Except I don't know how they *could* be getting thinner, because I haven't been doing it that long."

"So maybe they've always *been* thinner, and you didn't know," Etienne mused. "Maybe it's just you having to realize it on your own." Pausing, he gazed out at the rain. "So . . . what'd she look like, this woman?"

Miranda began to describe her. The yellowish overtones, like an old photograph; the woman's face and hair, the cap and collar; the inexplicable shock of those eyes; the feelings of panic and despair. Then, when she'd told Etienne all she could remember, she regarded him with a troubled frown.

"But I'm not getting it all," she murmured.

"What you mean, *cher*?"

"There's more. So much more she's trying to tell me—but I'm not getting it. Why can't it all just be simple? Why can't these . . . these ghosts, these spirits, follow a rule book? So I can be prepared when it happens? Not caught totally off guard?"

Etienne's voice softened. His gaze was firm, but not unkind. "It's life, *cher*. And whether it's *this* life or the *afterlife*—you can't be preparing yourself for every little thing that might come along. None of us have all the answers. And those people on the other side—they don't have the answers either, or they wouldn't be needing your help."

"Grandpa always knew what to do, didn't he?" She sighed, surprised when Etienne adamantly shook his head.

"No, your *grandpère*, he made *lotsa* mistakes. *Plenty* mistakes. What, you think he had everything perfect? Listen to me—he had to start over every single time. Feel his way, learn how to help them, trial and error. 'Cause each one was different—had a different problem, a different need. What worked for one didn't mean it worked for another one."

"You're making that up."

"Not me, I swear."

"How do you know that?"

"Your *grandpère*, he told me." Despite Miranda's obvious doubt, Etienne added an afterthought. "Maybe there's stuff you need to be learning about while you're helping them."

"Learning about what?"

"Yourself."

It was an answer she didn't expect—an answer she'd never considered. Puzzled, she reflected on Etienne's words, then relaxed a little and leaned into him.

"You know what's weird? Ever since I met Grandpa . . . and ever since he died . . . I've had this image in my mind of how perfect he was. Even if people *did* think he was crazy—I just knew that he *saw* things perfect, *did* things perfect, with his gift." She paused, her sigh almost wistful. "I hardly knew him . . . but I really miss him."

Etienne said nothing. His head was lowered, jaw clenched

tight, dark eyes fixed in a pensive stare—but Miranda wasn't fooled.

You miss him too, don't you, Etienne? That special bond you had with Grandpa, the one I still don't understand—you miss him too, even more than I do. . . .

"The thing is," she went on quietly, "when I found out I had his gift . . . *I* wanted to be perfect too. Just like him."

Etienne's eyes remained downward. "You don't need to be like anybody else. You're already perfect, *cher*. Just the way you are."

She smiled at that. Her fingers gently touched his shoulder . . . stroked down the strong, lean muscles of his arm. Though he was slouched back, she felt the slow tensing of his body, the ever-so-subtle catch of his breath, the heat of his skin, as she worked her hand beneath his wet T-shirt and over the tightness of his belly.

Scars here . . .

Without warning, her eyes filled with tears, and a surge of injustice shot through her. *Scars here and on your arms and God only knows where else your horrible father beat you—*

"Grandpa must have known, Etienne," she murmured, not even stopping to think. "Grandpa must have tried to protect you from him. . . ."

She knew at once that she'd crossed the line. Even before her words were out, even before the dark, steely look on Etienne's face, Miranda knew that she'd gone way too far.

"What the hell are you talking about?" His voice was deep, hoarse, almost threatening. His hand clamped hard around hers, making her wince before he pushed it aside. "I don't need anybody protecting me."

More startled than hurt, Miranda watched a whole range of emotions struggle over his face, while another range of emotions struggled through her heart.

"I'm sorry," she whispered. "I shouldn't have—"

"Don't ever ask me about that again."

He'd turned loose of her now . . . his body angled away, muscles so tense she could practically feel him quivering. Miranda realized that *she* was shaking. Shaking and sad and scared, all at once. For one crazy second she thought of wild animals—the ones people always try to tame—*only you can't ever trust those wild animals . . . their instincts, their true nature, always win out in the end.*

"I'm so sorry," she said again, choking through tears. "I didn't mean to hurt—"

"You didn't," he muttered, glancing down at one arm. "I've had these scars a long time. And believe me . . . they don't hurt."

Maybe not on the outside, Miranda longed to say, but didn't.

She couldn't see his face. He was still turned away from her, their bodies not even touching. Staring at his shadowy profile, she drew a deep breath and made an impulsive decision. Then pulled his arm slowly around her shoulders and nestled against him.

She was relieved—and a little surprised—that he didn't fight her.

"When I broke that mirror?" she went on, as if everything

were perfectly normal, "when I cut my hand on the broken glass? I think that's what started everything . . . you know, opened up some doorway. I had such a weird feeling about it, like I sensed something was about to happen. So maybe *that's* the connection."

"Could be, I guess." His tone was belligerent, his stare just as fierce, but at least he was looking at her again. "Did the mirror have anything to do with Belle Chandelle?"

"No. It was Aunt Teeta's."

"Then maybe it's something about *breaking* the mirror. Or cutting your *hand*."

"Or maybe they're all related. And I still have more pieces of the puzzle to find before I can put everything together." When he didn't respond, she made a show of yawning and rubbing wearily at her forehead. "We're not going to put it all together tonight. And you . . . you probably need to go home now."

"I told you, I'm not going anywhere till—"

"Till I tell you to leave, I know. Which is what I'm doing. Look"—Miranda was firm—"we're both really tired. We'll both think better after we get some sleep."

She could see the hesitation in his eyes and another silent battle of emotions. *You* want *to go, don't you, Etienne? You felt trapped and betrayed, and I caused it, and now you want to go. . . .*

At last he nodded. Releasing her, he slid to the edge of the swing.

"You sure?" A faint shrug, apathetic at best. "You sure you don't want me staying?"

"I'm sure." *Of course I want you to stay. Just as much as I know you should go, and as much as I want to know you, Etienne Boucher—all of you—the good and bad, the right and wrong, and all the places that hurt—*

"Last chance." Finally, a lame attempt at humor. Pretending—just like she was doing—that the whole unpleasant incident had never occurred.

As Miranda managed a weak smile, she noticed him reaching toward her lap. With all the other distractions to deal with, she'd completely forgotten about her T-shirt. Now, to her embarrassment, she saw that it had twisted up around her waist.

Cheeks flaming, she fumbled to untangle it, but Etienne was smoother. Grasping the bottom of her shirt, he eased it slowly down over her thighs while her whole body flushed hot.

He didn't seem to notice.

Instead he stood up and walked to the porch steps . . . paused there and gazed steadily out at the night.

"Just worry about your ghosts, *cher*. They're the ones you can help."

Miranda watched him disappear into the rain.

He didn't hurry, and he didn't say good-bye.

And he never once turned back to look at her.

11

"So what's happened since yesterday?" Mom teased. "Why the sudden interest in Belle Chandelle?"

Staring out the car window, Miranda was barely listening. Bad enough to have hauntings on her mind—now Etienne's visit had left her with a whole different set of questions and emotions that she'd grappled with till the alarm went off.

I should never have asked him about that stuff—about any *of that stuff—not Grandpa, or his father, or the scars. . . .*

Miranda gave an inward groan.

Could you have been any nosier? Brought up memories any more upsetting to him? He'd come by to check on her, and she'd blown it. She only hoped he'd forget about it and not hate her for the rest of her natural life.

"Miranda?" Mom asked gently.

But Miranda, deep in troubling thoughts, scarcely heard. Though some of Etienne's comments had stung, he *had* been right about one thing. It was the spirits—whoever they were—that she could help right now. Her own problems—including Etienne—would have to wait.

"Miranda?" Mom's voice again, more insistent this time. "You okay, honey?"

"Sorry, Mom. I was up late studying."

She'd been relieved when Mom offered to drive her to school. Usually Mom was gone when she got up, already at work on the grand resurrection of Belle Chandelle. *Things turn out weird sometimes,* she couldn't help thinking. *Now Mom and I are* both *connected to the plantation, but in totally different ways.*

Of course, Mom didn't know that. And even if she did, Miranda knew her mother would never understand. Ghosts and ghostly experiences just weren't in her mother's realm of believability.

"It's different seeing Belle Chandelle in person." Fumbling for an explanation, Miranda kept her tone casual. "I mean, once I was actually *there*, it really intrigued me."

"The *house* intrigued you? Or a certain *worker* out there intrigued you?" Mom teased.

His damp hair and warm skin . . . fingers gliding over my T-shirt . . . body tense . . .

"Come on, Mom," Miranda said quickly. "You're getting to be as bad as Aunt Teeta. I've told you before—Etienne and I are just friends. That's all."

Nodding, her mother laughed. "Well, *whatever* the reason, I'm really glad you like the place. Do you know, I remember it when I was a little girl? Going out there with Daddy, and how fascinated he always was with it? Of course, it was still in pretty bad shape then. And to think I'm going to have a part in bringing it back to life! It's . . ." Her face softened, nostalgic. "Well, it's . . . a *privilege*, really."

Smiling at her mother, Miranda felt an unexpected glow of happiness. It was rare these days for them to spend much time together, to have close and special talks. Not that she was complaining—Mom had a job she loved, and living with Aunt Teeta was a total joy, and Miranda was busy with her own life. But sometimes their schedules were so different that they seemed more like roommates coming and going. And Miranda forgot how nice it could be, she and Mom, just the two of them.

"Honey, you're always welcome to bring your friends out to the plantation," Mom offered. They were pulling up in front of school now, and once again, Miranda forced herself to pay attention. "Teeta and I don't even have to be there—I can give you an extra set of keys. And Etienne has a set, of course. Just don't go wandering around where it's dangerous."

The car was stopped, but Miranda made no move to get out. "Mom, Aunt Teeta said something about a picture of the house. And a letter written by a Yankee soldier. Any chance I could see them?"

"Sure, I know what you're talking about. The originals are in the museum at the Historical Society, but Mrs. Wilmington had some copies made for us. I can find those for you, if you like. Another school project?"

Miranda shrugged, evasive. "Maybe. Right now I'm . . . trying to decide on a topic."

"I'll be glad to help however I can. I just wish we knew more about the house. I keep thinking it probably has this whole dramatic saga going on that none of us will ever find out—or can even begin to imagine."

I'm sure it does too, Mom. Only I'm *going to find out what that saga is.*

"I'll pick you up here this afternoon. Have a great day, honey."

"Thanks, Mom. You too."

Hurrying up the front steps, Miranda wondered how she would ever keep her mind on school for the next seven hours. She wished she could just skip classes altogether, go out to Belle Chandelle instead, and start exploring the place in daylight. Things always seemed safer in daylight. More rational, less scary. Lots of construction workers would be around. Mom, too . . . maybe Aunt Teeta. Probably Etienne . . .

"You're perfect, cher. Just the way you are."

"Right," Miranda mumbled to herself, though her heart melted all over again. *And how many millions of girls have you said* that *to, Etienne Boucher? Danger signs, Miranda. Danger signs all over the place.*

Annoyed with herself, she maneuvered her way through the packed hallways. As she turned a corner, she saw Parker, Gage, and Roo in front of Ashley's locker—and even from a distance, she could tell that something was wrong.

"He asked you out, Ashley?" Parker was scowling when Miranda walked up. "He actually said that. He actually asked you out on a date."

For a minute, Ashley didn't answer, only met his accusation with a tight-lipped frown. Then she turned her back and shoved some notebooks into her locker. "It's no big deal."

"No big deal?"

"Maybe you two should talk louder." Glancing around, Roo defiantly met the stares of curious onlookers. "I hear people are putting big money on this fight."

"We're not fighting," Ashley said primly.

"One of you is."

Suspicious, Gage leaned close to Roo's ear. "Have you been taking *bets* on this?"

"No."

"I better not find out you're lying."

"You won't."

Ashley slammed her locker door. Parker's scowl deepened. "So what'd you say?" he demanded.

"What do you think I said?" Ashley's sigh was loud and impatient. "I said no."

"And you were going to tell me . . . *when*?"

"Oh, Parker, for heaven's sake. There's nothing to tell."

"Yeah? Then how come the whole school seems to know about it?"

"The whole school *does* know about it," Roo corrected.

Gage quickly stepped in. "Come on, you know how rumors spread around here. Streak's buddies are probably just trying to stir up some drama. And what do you care anyway?"

"Did you know about it?" Parker accused Miranda as she stopped beside Gage. But before she could respond, Parker turned his anger on Roo. "How did *you* know about it?"

"I am all-knowing," Roo replied solemnly. "I and God."

Gage elbowed her in the back.

"Plus the fact," Roo grudgingly relented, "that some of the cheerleaders heard Kurt talking to Ashley after practice. Apparently, he thinks she's hot."

Miranda caught Ashley's quick look of panic—and the angry

desperation that she shot at Roo. Thankfully, Parker didn't seem to notice.

"It's just what I heard." Relenting a little, Roo shrugged. "That definitely—"

"He thinks she's hot?" Parker broke in, incredulous. "He *said* that?"

"Definitely doesn't mean it's true," Gage finished diplomatically.

Roo stared at him "*What's* true? That Streak said it, or that Ashley's hot?"

"Everybody knows Ashley's hot!" Parker exploded. "That's the whole damn problem!"

"Okay. Hold that thought." Gage jerked his chin toward the classroom door. "Let's go, we're gonna be late."

"Parker, just drop it," Ashley said coldly. "It's stupid, and you're being silly."

"Oh. Now I'm silly. Do you think *Streak* is silly?"

"I'm not talking about this anymore."

"What's going on?" Etienne asked, sauntering up, books under one arm. His eyes slid over the group with lightning-speed perception.

"Well, look who decided to grace us with his sexiness," Roo greeted him. "What are you doing here?"

"Slumming." Nudging Roo with one shoulder, he held up a notebook. "Test."

"Did you study?" Ashley asked him, obviously concerned.

"Some."

"Come on, then, I can quiz you in study hall."

But Parker was still grumbling at Roo. "I suppose you're loving this. I suppose you think Ashley should go out with him."

"With me?" Etienne looked at Ashley. "*Mais*, yeah, I definitely think she should go out with me."

"No. Streak Fuller."

"You think Streak *Fuller* should go out with me?" Etienne raised an eyebrow. "He's not really my type, but . . ."

"Cut the jokes," Parker muttered. "He asked Ashley out."

"Streak asked *Ashley* out?"

"Oh, y'all!" With a cry of exasperation, Ashley spun and flounced off down the hall. Parker immediately glared at Roo.

"So *did* you? Come on, I want to know. Did you tell her to go out with him? Just to piss me off?"

"As much as I love pissing you off," Roo replied calmly, "I did *not* tell her to go out with Kurt. He's way too nice and polite and considerate. She wouldn't know how to act."

The bell rang before anyone could say more. Watching the rest of them leave, Miranda lingered a moment with Parker, falling into step beside him. Though he kept his eyes lowered, she could feel his anger and total frustration.

"Parker," she soothed gently, "you're the only one Ashley cares about. Don't you know that? Just trust her. Let it go."

Though obviously more confused than convinced, he managed a nod and walked with her to class.

By noon Miranda realized that this school wasn't so different from her old one when it came to gossip. In just those few hours, text-message rumors had it that Ashley had asked Kurt Fuller for a date, that Ashley was planning to break up with Parker, and that Parker had secretly been dating Delphine for months. When Ashley and Roo found Miranda in the library right before lunchtime, Ashley was visibly upset.

"You'll never guess what happened," she groaned.

Miranda immediately looked at Roo, who only shrugged. "Oh no, Ashley. What now?"

"You know I'm in the Tutor Group," Ashley reminded her.

Miranda nodded. She'd heard of it—a group of excellent students chosen by the faculty and appointed to help other kids with their studying. She knew that Ashley belonged, and as Ashley gazed at her miserably, she guessed what was coming next.

"You're . . . supposed to tutor Kurt Fuller?"

"I just found out. He has to pull up his grades, or he's off the football team."

"Well, first of all, do you *want* to? And second, can you get out of it?"

"No. And no. Everybody else is already working with somebody. And Mrs. Hayden specifically assigned me. I'm absolutely stuck. And anyway, how would it look if I said, 'I can't do this, my boyfriend won't like it.' I mean . . . it's for school. It's . . . business." She drew a long breath. "Parker will just have to understand."

"Good luck with that," Roo mumbled.

"Roo!"

"And don't be surprised if Kurt tries something."

"What would he try?"

"Hey. They don't call him Streak because he moves *slow*."

"Roo!"

"And I don't imagine you're very high on *Delphine's* popularity list right now either."

"Roo, stop it! Oh, this is just getting worse and worse. I don't even want to have lunch."

"Sure you do. You have to act like everything's normal. You haven't done anything wrong."

For a split second, Ashley's eyes misted. Her voice went sad and soft. "Parker thinks I have."

"Parker's a moron. A jealous moron. A jealous, insecure moron. A jealous, insecure, possessive—"

"Moron who loves her," Miranda broke in quickly.

Roo rolled her eyes. Ashley gave Miranda a grateful smile.

"I don't want people staring at me. Or talking about me." Ashley's sigh had gone miserable once more. "I wish Kurt had never said anything. I wish he'd never broken up with Delphine. I just want him to leave me alone."

The three headed outside to eat. While Ashley walked between them, Miranda scanned the lunch crowds scattered across campus, ignoring the occasional snickers and stares and whispered comments. Roo seemed oblivious. Linking her arm through Ashley's, she tilted her head back and squinted up into a warm, cloudy sky.

"Hey. It's getting cooler."

"Is it?" Miranda asked. "How can you tell?"

"I can feel it. Like a nip in the air."

"A very hidden nip."

"Maybe it'll be cold for Halloween tomorrow," Ashley said

halfheartedly. "That always used to ruin it for us, remember? It'd be so hot, and then suddenly it would get really cold, and then we'd have to wear coats over our costumes, and nobody could see them. After Mama and Daddy spent all that time making them for us."

Roo nodded. "Yeah, it was really hard duct-taping those sparkly little fairy wings to your jacket."

They'd reached their usual table now. Etienne was leaning comfortably against it, drinking a Coke, while Gage lounged back on one of the benches. Parker sat on the bench across from Gage, guzzling orange juice from a bottle. The three were obviously having an intense conversation, which abruptly broke off as the girls walked up. Miranda could only conclude that their guy-talk had been centered around Ashley and her new admirer.

"Hi, what's going on?" Miranda greeted them, but the three kept unusually quiet. Parker looked away. Gage slid over to make room for her. Ashley and Roo squeezed onto the bench beside Parker while Etienne, always casually detached, seemed even more distant than usual. Miranda had hoped to tell everyone about her latest ghostly experiences—but now was most definitely not a good time.

It was Parker who finally broke the awkward silence. Shouting a snap count, he aimed his empty bottle at the trash can and let it fly. The bottle hit . . . bounced—and unlike last night's pillow toss—landed perfectly on target. After a round of forced cheers, everyone relaxed a little and began talking again.

Teasing, Miranda bent to examine Gage's cast. "Any more intimate information since Babette LeBlanc?"

"Yeah, Gage." Parker kicked at him under the table. "I hope you're writing everything down for future reference."

"He's gonna need it," Etienne nodded. "Once that cast is off, all those girls feeling sorry for him are gonna forget who he is."

"No way!" Stretching over the table, Ashley pinched both of Gage's cheeks before he could dodge her attack. "How could any girl forget these dimples? These big brown eyes? This—"

Gage pulled free, scooted to the end of the bench, and resumed eating his sandwich. Laughing, Miranda scooted next to him and leaned against his side.

"This really cute blushing thing he does?"

Gage shook his head, a smile of good-natured surrender.

"Well, I won't forget you, Gage—cast or no cast. So it really comes off tomorrow, huh?"

"Tomorrow afternoon. I'll be free."

"And then what?"

"Rehab. Rehab. And . . . rehab."

Roo propped her elbows on the table . . . leveled him a solemn stare. "When they take off your cast, your leg will be all shriveled up. And totally pasty white. And rotten and smelly. And there won't be any hair on it."

Parker shrugged. "And she'll love you even more."

Shaking his head again, Gage took another bite of ham and Swiss. As Roo suddenly tugged at his arm, the sandwich dropped onto the table.

"Nice going," he began, but Roo was motioning across campus.

"Hey," she observed curiously, "is Kurt Fuller actually coming over here?"

Parker followed the direction of Roo's gaze. Etienne straightened up and narrowed his eyes. Miranda and Ashley looked at the same time. And then, as the six of them continued to watch, Kurt Fuller strolled past their table, taking his time, his handsome smile pinned on Ashley.

"Hey, Ashley," he said. "You look nice today."

"Hey. Thank you." Unnerved, Ashley nodded politely but kept eating her yogurt. Her cheeks went a ladylike pink. Kurt passed on by.

As Parker started to get up, Ashley's hand shot out to stop him. Roo pulled the ham from Gage's sandwich and popped it into her mouth.

"One thing you gotta say for him," Etienne mumbled. "He's got balls."

"Humongous ones," Roo said. "According to Delphine."

"*I* think you look nice," Parker blurted to Ashley. "I *always* think you look nice."

"Thanks." Gathering up her mostly uneaten lunch, Ashley paused to hand Etienne some notes. "Do you want to study a little bit more? I can quiz you on a few more things before that test."

"Ashley's tutoring Kurt in math," Roo announced.

"What?" This time Parker fairly sprang to his feet. His arms flew up in the air. "And when did *this* happen?"

"It's nothing," Ashley said tightly. "Roo, will you just keep quiet?"

"I'm helping you," Roo defended herself. "He's going to hear about it sooner or later—better he hears it from a friend."

"Since when have you and I been friends?" Parker shot back at her.

"Parker, I just found out last period," Ashley explained. "I hadn't even had a chance to tell you yet."

"So tell me now."

"And don't act like I'm trying to hide something from you. Mrs. Hayden assigned me to tutor him. If he doesn't get his grades up, he's off the team."

"No surprise there. The guy's dumb as a stump."

"But big as a tree," Roo added. "According to Delphine."

"I have an idea." Gage frowned at her, then at his two empty slices of bread. "Why don't you try making things worse?"

"Parker, it's nothing," Ashley insisted, but she was wringing her hands now, anger replacing embarrassment. "I'm helping him with schoolwork—that's *all.* As for that other thing, he broke up with his girlfriend, and he's looking for somebody to go out with—like *most* people do when they break up. Only *I'm not interested.* I told him *no, and he didn't push it*. There is *no drama here. End of story.*"

"Except that he's coming on to you," Parker snapped back at her. "And he knows you belong to *me*."

The silence that fell was icy cold. Parker gave a noticeable cringe and looked slightly ill.

"Oh, man." Etienne raised an eyebrow. "You must be tired of living, yeah?"

Taking a step toward Parker, Ashley clamped both hands on her hips. Her eyes were wide and seething, her voice like steel. "I do *not* belong to you, Parker Wilmington."

"That's not what I meant. I meant . . ." Parker glanced helplessly at Gage. "Tell her what I meant."

Gage opened his mouth. Closed it. Opened it. "What he meant was—"

Ashley cut him off. "I do not belong to *anybody*. This whole thing is stupid and ridiculous, and I'm *not* going to discuss it *anymore*. And if I want to go out with Kurt Fuller—then—then—I'll go *out* with him! And maybe I just *will*!"

Grabbing her things, she stuck her nose in the air and marched off toward the building, leaving Parker to stare morosely after her. Etienne regarded his study notes with a mixture of amusement and apprehension.

"I'm not sure if she's gonna be quizzing me or killing me. *Merde*, she's sure got a mad on."

Gage nodded and gave Parker a sympathetic shrug. "Not one of your brightest moves."

"No shit." Looking completely put out with himself, Parker reached over and shoved Roo, who nearly fell off the bench.

She caught herself just in time. Then glowered at him. "Excuse me?"

"Excuse my ass! See what you did?"

"What *I* did? You're just taking everything out on *me* because you know *Kurt* would pulverize you. And if you shove me again, *I'm* gonna pulverize you."

Etienne's chin jerked toward Roo. "My bet's on her."

"Forget Streak," Parker muttered. "I could take him in half a second."

"Do it then," Roo challenged. "Just let me get a shovel first, so we can scoop you up off the grass."

"Parker, it's not Ashley's fault." Once again Miranda tried to soothe him. "She doesn't even *want* to tutor Kurt. The teacher decides who Ashley gets stuck with—she doesn't have a choice."

But Parker didn't seem to be listening. "I need to stop by the gym," he muttered, and started off across the lawn. After only a few steps though, he turned and glared back at them.

"Gage!" he yelled irritably.

"Oookaay." Giving a low whistle, Gage hoisted himself up and grabbed his crutches. "Guess that's my cue for an exit."

Roo and Miranda got up as well, trailing the guys at a distance. Miranda was in no hurry to get back to class. She was worried about Ashley, frustrated about Etienne, and in a complete quandary over yesterday's supernatural happenings. From time to time she saw Roo casting her a sideways glance, but if the girl suspected what was going on—ghosts, Etienne, or otherwise—she didn't let on.

When Roo finally spoke, all she asked was, "What are you doing for Halloween?"

Miranda was glad for the distraction. "I haven't thought about it. Nothing, I guess. You?"

"What I always do. Make popcorn, sit in the dark, and have a horror-film marathon."

"Let me guess. And you can recite the entire dialogue from each one."

"Of course. Want to join me?"

"No, thanks. I think I just want a quiet night. What does everyone else do in this town?"

"We're pretty boring, actually. All the stores on the Brickway give out candy, but the sidewalks roll up before nine. Most of the kids from school go to parties."

Instantly Miranda's mind went back—to her life before, to her best friends. She and Marge and Joanie always went to at least one party on Halloween.

And I used to think Halloween was silly. I used to think that the supernatural was make-believe. I used to think that ghosts were just figments of crazy people's imaginations.

"Parties at their houses," Roo clarified. "Except Ashley always volunteers for some dumb Halloween program over at the preschool. And she's always totally worn out when she gets home."

"You mean she and Parker won't do something afterward?"

Roo shook her head. "Even if they *are* still speaking by then, there's a guys' night tomorrow." Then, when Miranda looked blank, Roo added, "At Belle Chandelle."

"What's that about?"

"The owners are nervous—with all the renovations going on, they think it's way more likely to be vandalized. So Etienne offered to keep an eye on the place. And he asked Gage and Parker to stay with him. I think they might be spending the night."

"How'd you find out?"

"I heard Gage and Etienne talking. Of course, they don't want *us* to know about it. They're probably afraid we'll go out there and crash their little get-together." Roo gave a sly half-smile. "Not that I haven't considered it. Sneaking out there. Giving them all heart attacks."

Picturing the scene, Miranda almost laughed. "I can't believe Parker's even going. Not after all his fuss about ghosts and Belle Chandelle."

"Point of honor, Miranda. He can't let the others know what a wimp he really is."

"Roo . . . he *did* save our lives at the Falls that night. Remember?"

Roo grimaced . . . gave a reluctant shrug. "Ugh. One night, then. I'll give him that, but absolutely no more."

They were going up the steps now, into the building. Roo paused on the threshold to scrape mud off the soles of her army boots.

"I wouldn't be surprised if something happens though," she added.

Miranda felt herself stiffen. "What do you mean?"

"Halloween night, Belle Chandelle—*any* night, Belle Chandelle." Another shrug, and a knowing glance at Miranda. "A place like that? That old, that much history? You know it must be swarming with all kinds of miserable spirits."

Roo planted both feet back on the floor. Her dark-ringed eyes pinned Miranda.

"But you know that better than anybody, right? Because you've probably already seen them."

12

"I DON'T KNOW WHAT'S HAPPENING OUT THERE." Mom frowned. As promised, she'd picked up Miranda after school, and now they were heading for Belle Chandelle. "Not a bit of trouble all this time, then suddenly this morning, four construction workers quit."

Miranda threw a quick glance at her mother's profile. A ripple of trepidation was already working its way up her spine.

"Did they say why?" she asked, trying to sound casual.

"Teeta was there; I wasn't. Oh, it was all nonsense. They said they felt weird. Like they were being watched. That the house has a funny feeling."

Miranda gave a vague nod.

"Now does that even make sense?" her mother asked irritably. "The house has sat there all these years. Renovation has started on it before. And nobody's ever had a problem with it."

"Well . . . I did hear rumors about it being the town's haunted house."

"Right. *Rumors*. Teeta and I were talking about it this morning. Rumors, but no actual proof. No reliable witnesses. It doesn't make sense. Why *now*?"

Growing quiet, Miranda redirected her gaze out the window. She didn't *want* to think what she was thinking, but it was there all the same. *Because of me? Because I went out to Belle Chandelle and disrupted something? Attracted someone?*

It was a frightening possibility—one she hated to even consider. That her mere presence somewhere could stir up spirits that had been quiet for hundreds of years . . .

"So what are you going to do?" she asked her mother.

"We found some replacements—that wasn't such a problem. I just hope these guys aren't as silly and superstitious as the others were."

It's not silly. Not superstitious. But again Miranda kept her eyes on the window and didn't answer. *You don't believe, Mom . . . and you're not helping.*

"Honey, I have a favor to ask," Mom went on, her mood lifting. "Would you mind taking some pictures for me at the plantation?"

Miranda winced, a new stab of dread shooting through her. "I don't know anything about taking pictures—"

"And I don't need anything professional. Just some before-and-after shots. Except these would be the *before* ones."

"Don't you and Aunt Teeta already spend enough time out there as it is? You need photos to remember it by?"

Mom obviously found this hilarious. "You know how Teeta and I are on that renovation committee? Well, the Harvest Festival's coming up, and the committee's decided to set up an information booth—right next to the Historical Society. People have been showing so much interest in Belle Chandelle, we thought this would be a good way to let the public know what's going on—along with some pictures to look at."

Miranda had learned about Harvest Festival just yesterday from the announcements in class. An annual November event when every business, organization, and club in town set up fun, tourist-friendly booths along the Brickway, and visitors came from miles around. Not to mention the local food and free samples, baking and cooking competitions, barbeques, picnics, and seafood boils—all of which St. Yvette was famous for.

Reluctantly, she nodded. "What kinds of pictures?"

"Details would be nice. Both insides and outsides of the buildings. It will certainly help with my research. We might even be able to use some later in a guidebook for the bed and breakfast."

"Okay. I'll give it a try."

"Honey, I really appreciate this; you have no idea how much time it will save me. The camera's right there in my tote bag—just go ahead and take it out."

Miranda did so, while trying to muster some enthusiasm. "Any new projects I should know about? And please don't tell me you're working till midnight."

"Well, I've got at least a million different decisions to make about the double parlors—but the main thing is, all the kitchen appliances are supposed to be delivered."

"Kitchen? You mean the one behind the house?"

"It's the first building we'll finish, and it's really starting to shape up."

"I thought none of the outbuildings were being renovated till after the house was done."

"They're not—but this one had a head start." Reaching over,

Mom rolled her window down and sniffed the air. "Is it my imagination, or is there a cool breeze out there? Anyway, the last owner rebuilt the kitchen so he could live in it while he was renovating the big house. Which is excellent for us."

"So it's a real kitchen? Or more like a cabin?"

"An authentic plantation kitchen. Walls, ceiling, floor, hearth, fireplace, the whole bit. What we've done is divide it so the old-fashioned part is what the tourists see. Then the other part—what the tourists *won't* see—is the actual working kitchen. And that's where all the cooking will be done for the bed and breakfast."

"Smart. Best of both worlds."

"Nell said she'd be here today too. Just to look things over . . . make sure they delivered the right orders."

Miranda couldn't help but smile. "I like her. I'm really glad she decided to take the job."

"From what Teeta's told me about her, she's a remarkable woman. And I guess Etienne is completely devoted to her."

"They've been through a lot together," Miranda said quietly, while her mother gave a sympathetic nod.

"Yes, honey. I believe they have."

A thoughtful silence fell between them. As the car began to slow down, Miranda recognized the turnoff to Belle Chandelle and knew they were getting close.

"So." Straightening in her seat, she tried to steel herself for the afternoon ahead. "Where should I start with the picture-taking?"

"Anywhere you like. Just don't wander off where you could get hurt."

"Which would be . . . ?"

"Didn't you get the whole tour yesterday? Including off-limits?"

Miranda thought fast. "Actually, I kind of got sidetracked. I started studying those blueprints and some of your sample catalogs—"

"Well, no wonder," Mom chuckled. "As for the house, there's still work that needs to be done on the roof and a few ceilings . . . and more plastering over the brick columns in front. Several wood floors still need to be put in, but the foundation is good and sound. All the rooms have pretty much been sectioned off, upstairs and down . . . but some of the windows—especially those dormers on the third floor—have to be replaced."

Just thinking about that dormer window, that shadowy hand, made Miranda shudder. She crossed her arms over her chest and hoped that Mom hadn't noticed.

"They still need to install all the ductwork for the central air and heat. And even though parts of the building have lights, not all the electricity or plumbing has been finished. Oh, and honey—the attic and the belvedere definitely aren't safe yet, so stay away from those."

On a whim, Miranda asked casually, "Mom . . . was the house yellow before you redid it?"

"Yellow?" Her mother looked perplexed. "No, I don't think so. Why?"

"I just . . . wondered."

"I can ask, but I've never heard that." Her mother thought a moment . . . gave a slight nod. "I guess it would make sense, though. 'Belle Chandelle' means beautiful candle . . . yellow for a candle flame?"

There was a half-empty delivery truck parked in the lot when they got there. While more appliances were being unloaded, Miranda grabbed the camera, then helped her mother carry boxes and shopping bags to the main house. She didn't see Etienne, but workers were crawling over the roof and moving along the galleries, filling the air with loud shouts, the noise of drills, hammers, and nail guns. As she and Mom neared the front entrance, a wild shriek stopped them in their tracks. Whirling around, they saw two little girls running at breakneck speed across the side lawn.

"Oh dear." Mom sighed. "I wish she wouldn't bring those kids here."

Miranda regarded her in surprise. "Who are they?"

"They belong to Coralee . . . she comes out here to help us clean," she explained as they went inside and deposited their stuff. "She's a single mom, and when she can't find a babysitter, she brings her little girls with her."

"They look . . . lively."

"Don't get me wrong, I love kids, and I admire a responsible parent—especially one on her own. But she can't watch them every minute, and there's just too much going on around here, too much for them to get into. I worry they'll get hurt."

Even as she spoke, the little girls ran to the doorway, peered in and waved, then took off again, squealing. Mom shook her head and looked distressed.

"Just do whatever you want, honey." Sighing again, she handed

Miranda a large metal ring full of keys. "Room angles would be helpful—locations of windows and doors—even though most of the upstairs bedrooms are all the same. Some long shots of the galleries. Some nice views of the grounds in front, with all those trees leading up. And any little details you notice? Like carvings or moldings . . . some of the ceilings have friezes . . . anything that looks really old . . . I'd love to have pictures of those. Oh, and take these keys. You can keep them—I made you a set."

"Aunt Teeta said there were a few things that probably came from the original house." Instinctively, Miranda glanced around the room, but saw nothing. "What are those, do you know?"

"I have a list of them . . . somewhere . . ." Rifling back and forth through a file folder, Mom paused, then frowned. "Honestly, even with my main office in town, I could sure use a *real* office here. Don't worry, I'll find it for you. Oh—and those other things you wanted. The house photo and the letter. I'm sure I'll remember where I put them by the time you come back. Right now I've got to go check on the kitchen."

"Okay, Mom. See you in a while."

"And be careful. Stay away from those dangerous spots."

"I will."

Taking the digital camera, she roamed leisurely through the downstairs, exploring rooms that she hadn't explored before. She still didn't see Etienne—she guessed he was probably helping his mom with the appliance deliveries—but from time to time various workmen strolled past, stopping to examine walls or floors or ceilings, greeting her with friendly smiles. This main level was even larger than it had appeared last night. As she wandered in and out of connecting doorways, she began to snap pictures and keep a sharp eye out for . . . *what?* She wasn't sure; she had only her instincts to guide her. She suddenly realized that she'd been guarding herself, holding herself in, ever since she and Mom had driven onto the property. But now . . . cautiously . . . she allowed her senses to open.

Anything. Anything that might give me some clue about this house . . .

The sadness was still here—that part hadn't changed. Hanging thick in every room, like a wet, black fog. *Wet with tears . . . black for death . . .* Closing her eyes, Miranda focused harder . . . reached farther. From some distant place, she could almost hear laughter—faint and tinny, like an old music box—fading even as she listened. *Joyful laughter, childish laughter*. Weaving its way through the mournful fog . . .

The present came back to her, veiled in past sorrow. Rubbing a chill from her arms, she went out to the verandah and stood for a moment, gazing off through the oak-lined alleyway, toward the bayou. She could see the swing hanging motionless from the tree limb. She snapped some photographs, then followed the verandah around the entire first story of the house, not finding much more of interest along the way. Massive, empty rooms, practically identical, bare of much décor . . . a chandelier here and there . . . wooden doors, banisters, and fireplace mantels in various stages of polishing, refinishing, and repair . . . Mom's requested friezes and crown moldings covered in layers of dust . . . one area rug, rolled up in canvas. Nothing that touched her, called to her. No whisper of long-dead secrets.

Frustrated, Miranda moved on. Up the staircase at one end of the verandah, up to the gallery above. She wasn't ready to tour all the bedrooms yet; she leaned on the baluster and tilted her face into the air. A breeze blew off the bayou, through the moss-laced trees, cooling her cheeks. It was bittersweet, standing where they must have stood, gazing where they must have gazed, those people who lived here once upon a time. *You could see for miles from up here. Past the driveway under the oaks, beyond the formal gardens, up and down the dirt road leading to town, over all your acres of land, clear across the bayou . . .*

You were happy once. Blessed.

What happened to you, Belle Chandelle? How could anyone have abandoned you?

So perfect, this spot, for some reason. This sheltered spot of calm and beauty, even though power tools hummed in the background and bulldozers crushed through the fields on all sides. The air grew thick around her. Thick and hot and suffocating, shutting out every sound of renovation . . . every sound of progress . . . *every sound of today . . .*

"Wait," Miranda whispered, "please wait . . ."

But she could already feel it happening—that strange but not unpleasant sensation of being removed to some different place. Some close but hidden place where she could watch herself frozen there, helpless on the gallery.

Where she could watch the tragic woman reaching out to her . . . a pale, misty hand passing cold through Miranda's heart, as if Miranda herself didn't even exist . . .

Dark hair pulled back, messy . . . strands limp around her haggard face; she's exhausted, empty, she hasn't slept in days, many days and nights, not for a very, very long time. The dark lace cap on top of her hair . . . and her dark collar, dark dress, black, smells sharp strong metallic rotted sour—

Eyes! Eyes full of horror, desperation—panicky pleading praying but still no one hears—unnatural eyes, brittle-yellow-photograph eyes, brittle-yellow-photograph skin, but the eyes are cloudy, foggy with despair—red coming through showing through red blurring her beautiful eyes, murky beautiful bloodshot eyes—

Miranda's breath came faster; she couldn't cry out, but she couldn't turn away. In a hazy rush, she heard carriage wheels trundling up the road—*why aren't they stopping?*—glass shaking, rattling, breaking—*look! For God's sake, look at the window!*—*and feet stumbling, walls smeared red—creaking, creaking, slow steady rhythm monotonous creaking on and on and on . . .* I'm here—I'll always be here—*soft muffled crying, innocent laughter, the high-pitched laughter of children—*

"*Stop!*"

Miranda brought herself back. As the present came sharply into focus, she felt the breeze on her face, saw her knuckles clutched white on the railing. A sick swirl of helplessness rose up from her heart, filling her head, bringing tears to her eyes. *I can't do it right now. . . . I can't figure it out.* She felt drained and unsteady. Holding tighter, she peered down onto the lawn below and suddenly realized that a small part of reality must have penetrated her vision.

Coralee's little girls were running across the lawn, laughing and squealing, playing hide-and-seek among the trees. As

Miranda watched, they turned and ran off, disappearing around the corner of the house.

Her knees were still shaking, her stomach still queasy. Every sense told her that the woman wasn't here anymore, yet her eyes scanned the wide gallery, the row of tall French doors along one side, the delicate tendrils of moss cascading onto the balusters. *Was this your favorite place to stand, where I'm standing now? On the original gallery, of the original house?* Miranda's grip slowly loosened. *Who are you? How am I supposed to find out about you? And what awful tragedy happened to you here?*

For a brief second, she could almost swear that she was being watched. By invisible eyes, from some invisible place. And that a faint glimmer of music drifted past her, carried gently on the breeze.

No, not music. Laughter.

Soft, giggling laughter. Children's laughter.

"Come and find us!"

Of course. Not ghostly laughter . . . Coralee's girls. With a sigh of relief, Miranda started walking to the far side of the gallery.

"Okay, you two! I hear you playing!"

The giggles came again, louder this time and more delighted.

"Come and *find* us!"

"How about I find you downstairs, okay? It's not safe to be running around up here."

They must have come up another stairway, she reasoned. There were four different sets of exterior stairs, one at each corner of the house—it would have been easy for the girls to slip up here unnoticed. *Especially in the zoned-out state I was in.*

But as she approached the end of the gallery, she saw no sign of the girls. She noticed only a pair of French doors standing halfway open, showing the dark, vacant room beyond.

"Girls?" Miranda called. A stab of uneasiness went through her. She was sure the voices had come from this direction, but maybe the kids had already retreated back to the first floor.

And then she heard the giggling again. Inside the empty room.

"Come on, I mean it." Hands on hips, Miranda planted herself in the doorway. Heavy shadows hung like black crepe, and dust motes thickened the stale, still air. "I mean it—it's not safe up here. Come out *now*, or I'm calling your mom."

The giggling stopped. Abruptly, chillingly. Miranda could hear time passing . . . could hear the wary beat of her own heart . . .

And the small, choked, frightened sob . . .

"Mama?"

"Is that you?" her voice asked, but it seemed to come from somewhere outside her, a voice in slow motion. "Girls, is that you? Tell me where you are."

The child was afraid—she could feel it in that cry, coming from somewhere inside the room, coming from somewhere inside the shadows, *somewhere no child should ever be—*

"Oh, God." Springing to action, Miranda began combing the guestroom—the walls, the floor, the fireplace—any area the girls might have gotten trapped. Because it *was* Coralee's girls, she kept telling herself, it *had* to be Coralee's girls, who else could it possibly be . . . ?

"Where are you?" she cried, half angry, half afraid. "Listen to me, girls—tell me where you are; I'm going to get you out of there!"

The cry came again. Muffled . . . just as frightened. And they were *both* crying now, she could hear their voices, two terrified little cries, only where *were* they, why couldn't she see them, there was nowhere else to search—

"Mama! Mama! Look at us!"

Miranda froze and stared. Impossible, she knew—yet the cries seemed to be coming from a spot against the wall, the back wall of the bedroom. Very slowly she ran her eyes over the surface, then noticed something she hadn't seen before. A wooden panel—a narrow door—concealed so cleverly in the woodwork that it was practically invisible. Hurrying over, she pounded on it and tried to pry it open.

"Hey!" she shouted. "Girls? Can you push from the other side? Just push the door if you can, okay?"

The crying grew worse. Heartbreaking sobs and whimpers. Pleas for their mother to save them. Despite her growing frustration, Miranda couldn't bear to hear those anguished cries.

"I'm here!" she reassured them. "Don't cry, I'm right here, I'm going to get you out!"

The panel moved a little. Putting her shoulder to the door, Miranda heard a groan of warped, damp wood giving way. And as the panel finally opened, she saw the narrow flight of stairs recessed in the wall behind it.

The sneak stairway.

The one Aunt Teeta had talked about, that ran from the main level all the way to the attic—

Oh my God. The attic.

It was obvious now, what had happened. The two little girls must have discovered the sneak stairs on the first floor, climbed inside to play, and then panicked when they couldn't get out again. And now they were still climbing . . . on their way to the attic and belvedere and certain danger.

Miranda wasted no time. Despite the close, winding passage, she raced up, shouting as she went. "Don't be scared, girls! I'm going to take you to your mom, okay?"

But it was so quiet. *Too* quiet. With a surge of panic, she reached the final step and the hidden door at the top of the stairwell.

A horrible stench washed over her. *Choking—suffocating—* dropping her to her knees while she gagged and fought desperately to breathe—*sweat urine vomit feces blood infection flies oozing sores rotting flesh baking heat festering heat—*

Miranda dragged herself to her feet. She pounded the door with her fists, but it wouldn't budge.

"Damn!" Even shoving as hard as she could, Miranda had no luck. It was as if the weight of the world were on the other side of that door, and her own strength couldn't begin to break it down. *What have those kids wedged up against that door?*

"Come out of there, you two! Open up!"

She remembered the keys. Yanking them from her pocket, she tried each of them in the lock, but to no avail. It was clear to her now that she wasn't going to get in this way. That the attic could mean only serious accidents; the belvedere, fatal falls. Not knowing what else to try, Miranda dashed back down the stairs all the way to the first floor, where she shoved open the camouflaged panel and fell out into one of the parlors, nearly scaring her mother to death.

"Good Lord, Miranda! What on earth are you doing—"

"Mom, Coralee's daughters, they were upstairs playing hide-and-seek—and I heard them in the stairwell—"

"Miranda—"

"And I tried to get them out, but they couldn't open the door, and I think an animal must have died up there—"

"Honey—"

"Is there another key or something? Or maybe we could use one of the ladders—"

"Stop." Squeezing Miranda's shoulders, Mom gave her a little shake. "Honey, stop. Calm down . . . take it easy."

"But Mom—"

"Miranda, I don't know what you heard, but it wasn't Coralee's girls."

"Yes! Mom, it was! Please, we have to hurry and get them—"

"Look. Just look."

Before Miranda could answer, her mother led her firmly across the room. Then, stopping at the open French doors, she pointed outside.

One of the little girls was on Etienne's shoulders; the other he was swinging around and around, by her hands, in a circle.

"But . . ." Miranda's throat closed up. She took a step back, suddenly weak. "They couldn't have gotten past me. It's impossible. They must have come down some other way."

"I guess they must have." Mom gave a puzzled smile. "Because they've been right out here all this time, playing with Etienne."

13

"MIRANDA, ARE YOU ALL RIGHT?"

"I . . ." Miranda's mind was racing. She braced herself against the wall, hugged herself tightly, tried to think.

"Honey, you're white as a sheet. Sit down; let me get you some water."

"I'm . . ." *Careful, Miranda. Pull yourself together; don't give anything away.* "I was just so scared, you know . . . that those kids might get to the attic."

"Well, of course you were. That attic is supposed to be kept locked, but you just never know."

"Mom, have you been here in the house the whole time?"

"I just got back here. I've been out in the kitchen."

"So . . ." It *could* be possible, she supposed. Panic, terror, a cramped, dark stairwell—time might easily have a way of getting distorted. And she *had* zoned out earlier, hadn't she? Those two little girls *could* have been playing hide-and-seek, playing a trick on her. *Yes, it* could *be possible.* Anything's *possible. . . .*

"Don't you want to sit down?" Mom worried. She forced a cup of water into Miranda's hand. "Drink this. I want to make sure you don't faint."

"I won't faint." Sipping her water, Miranda continued to gaze at Etienne. Coralee's girls were playing a new game now—

clinging to him, one on each side, squealing and trying to pull him in opposite directions. He was grubby and disheveled from work; his hair fell stubbornly over his cheeks and into his eyes. For several long minutes, he patiently endured the tug-of-war, then without warning, grabbed both girls in his arms and gave them a fierce tickling. Laughing and screaming at the top of their lungs, the two of them took off on a merry chase across the lawn and down the alleyway of oak trees.

Stretching, Etienne shoved his hair back from his face, and saw Miranda watching him.

"How long have you children been having fun out here?" she asked him. Though the matter was serious, she couldn't resist teasing him a little.

Etienne seemed faintly embarrassed. "Why? You gonna dock my pay?"

"I was just wondering." Pausing, she could sense his swift, keen appraisal. "When you started playing with the kids . . . did they come out of the house?"

"*Mais*, I don't know. They ambushed me behind those trees over there."

She wanted so much to believe it—that the little girls had somehow tricked her and run back down the sneak stairway. That the pitiful crying that she'd heard had come from real, live, flesh-and-blood children . . .

But she knew it wasn't true.

Deep down inside, she knew it wasn't true. And in that terrible, dark place where no child should ever go, two lost children were waiting for her to find them.

"Why you so interested in those kids, *cher*?"

Miranda wiped quickly at a blur of tears. "No reason."

"Don't be lying to me now. You got that look on your face."

"What look?"

"The one that says you just saw or heard something nobody else can see or hear."

He stepped close, strong fingers gripping her elbows, body brushing lightly against hers. No hint of awkwardness now, their argument apparently forgotten. Miranda stared at the front of his T-shirt; the damp trails of sweat; the long, dirty streaks where he'd carelessly wiped his hands.

"I saw the woman again," she told him softly. "On the gallery this time, not in a mirror. And I heard some children. Laughing at first, then scared and crying. I thought it was Coralee's girls, that they'd gotten lost on the sneak stairs."

Listening intently, Etienne gave her an encouraging nod. Then shot a curious, sidelong glance at the house.

"But maybe," Miranda went on, "maybe they're connected somehow—the woman and the children. And maybe those poor kids are lost in a different place. A dark, empty place where they're all alone."

"And you think something mighta happened to them here? Something bad happened to the kids?"

Miranda shook her head. "I don't know. The feelings I had . . . those heartbreaking cries . . . it was all really, really intense. And the smell—"

"What smell?"

"I almost threw up, it was so awful. Like something died in the attic—"

"No smell, *cher*," he murmured. "No smell—"

"Are you absolutely sure?"

"I was up there just a while ago. I think I woulda smelled something that bad, yeah?"

Miranda gave a reluctant nod. "I was *sure* Coralee's girls were trapped behind that wall . . . that they were headed straight for trouble in the attic."

"You actually heard them going up there?"

"I followed them. Well . . . I followed the *voices*. But I couldn't get the panel open. I couldn't figure out how they'd managed to drag something so heavy up against the door."

"But you were hearing them *inside* the attic?"

Frowning, Miranda thought back. A flicker of uncertainty went across her face. "No. When I got to the attic, it was totally quiet. Which scared me even more. That's when I figured they'd come back downstairs . . . except there's no way they could have gotten past me."

For a long moment neither of them spoke. Then Etienne broke the silence.

"So what about the woman? Why you thinking she's connected with those kids?"

"I don't know. It's just . . ." Miranda gave him a wry smile. "I *feel* it."

"Can't argue with that."

"If you'd seen the expression on her face—how frantic she

was. It's obvious she's begging for help." As thoroughly as she could, Miranda recalled the details of her vision. "She's worn out by something, Etienne . . . beaten down by something. I can feel her panic, but I can feel her helplessness, too. It's like she doesn't have any strength left. No . . . no will. Nothing left inside her."

"Maybe that's how come she couldn't touch you, *cher*—why her hand passed on through."

"What do you mean?"

"Maybe it's more than just being a ghost. Maybe her spirit died a long time before *she* died."

Miranda blinked away fresh tears. "After that, is when I heard the children playing."

"Well, yeah, that does seem connected."

"But also—when I first heard the kids' voices—they were saying, 'Come and find us.' And I didn't think about it then, because I just assumed it was Coralee's girls playing hide-and-seek, you know? But now . . ."

"Now," Etienne said quietly, "you're thinking maybe those kids were calling for *you*? *You* specifically . . . for help?"

"I think . . . they were terrified and needed their mother. And they couldn't find her. And . . . maybe they were trying to get *my* attention because—"

"'Cause they knew they could."

"Yes. Because—somehow—they knew they could."

"So . . . maybe they got something to do with that swing yesterday?"

Miranda nodded. His hands, still resting on her arms, began

a slow ascent to her shoulders . . . slid reassuringly over her back. A warm, shivery feeling went through her.

"Damn." Tilting his head, Etienne gazed up thoughtfully through the trees. "You been busy, *cher*."

In spite of everything, Miranda had to laugh. "Yes. Welcome to my wild, busy, exciting life." Then, solemn once more, she tugged on his shirt, forcing his attention back. "I've been thinking about something else, too."

"Me?"

She frowned him a look.

"Uh-oh." He winced. "Not Gage, I hope."

"I'm serious."

"So am I."

"Mom said some workers quit this morning."

"Yeah, I heard that—"

"Because they had a weird feeling about the house. And Mom said that's never really happened before. And I can't help thinking it's because of me. That because I came out here, other spirits who've never . . . I don't know . . . had a way out for all these years, have sort of . . . woken up."

"What I keep telling you, *cher*? You're not even *close* to tapping those powers of yours—you're gonna be *way* stronger than your *grandpère* ever was."

"Hey. Even though I'm all into helping unhappy spirits, I do *not* like the idea of walking around being a constant ghost magnet."

He stared down at her. The flicker of amusement in his eyes narrowed to shrewd intensity. "How many more times I gotta say it, then? That's why you got *me*. And no, before you even start thinking it, *not* just 'cause I promised your *grandpère*—"

"Hey, you two!" As her mom shouted from the open doorway, Miranda stumbled back out of Etienne's reach. "Sorry to interrupt, but I could sure use some help taking stuff to my car! And I'm talking *heavy* stuff!"

"I'm on it!" Lifting one hand in acknowledgment, Etienne winked at Miranda and strode off toward the house. Miranda started to follow, then suddenly remembered her mom's camera. At some point during her panicky experience on the gallery, she'd dropped it and left it behind. Now she wasn't at all sure that she wanted to go up there again and retrieve it.

She needn't have worried. The camera was lying just where she thought it would be, right where she'd had her vision. Still unsettled, she glanced nervously down the length of the gallery, then beat a hasty retreat and headed off behind the house to the kitchen.

Apparently, all the deliveries had been made. There wasn't a soul around that Miranda could see, but as she walked across the old tiles; around the long, functional trestle table; beside the wide brick hearth and big iron cooking pots, she heard an awful clanging and clattering from behind the rear wall.

"Miss Nell?" she called, though now there was only silence. "Miss Nell, are you here?"

Miranda peered through the connecting doorway. At once she spotted Miss Nell leaning forward against the counter, pots and pans scattered around her feet.

"Oh my God—Miss Nell, are you—"

"Fine." Instantly the woman turned, coming to greet her, taking Miranda's hands, squeezing them tightly in her own. "I'm just fine, honey. You know, I've had so much caffeine today, and then I skipped lunch—I *know* better. Made me totally light-headed for a second."

"Are you sure?"

"Yes! Of course."

But Miranda wasn't convinced. The woman's face was totally drained of color, her forehead shone with sweat. Her touch was too cold, and though she always appeared frail when Miranda saw her, she seemed even frailer now, her dark eyes unusually bright.

"Miranda, I'm so glad you stopped by." Miss Nell was pulling her gently, guiding her to a tall wooden stool in the corner. "Sit down, honey, while I clean up this mess I made—"

"Miss Nell, do you want some water—"

"No, don't you budge. It'll only take me a second."

Quickly, she gathered the pots and pans. After stacking them at the end of the counter, she reached down into a cooler on the floor, took out two soft drinks, and handed one to Miranda.

"No air-conditioning in here yet—Etienne swears it'll be in by the weekend. But isn't this wonderful? All these pretty things?" The woman spread her arms, indicating the shiny, new appliances surrounding them. Despite her wan appearance, her voice was excited and happy. "By tomorrow, we'll have cold drinks in the fridge. And hot food in the oven and on the stove."

"That's great," Miranda agreed. Despite her concern, she began to relax a little; at least Miss Nell didn't seem quite so shaky as she had a few minutes ago. "But I especially like that other part of the kitchen—the reproduction. It looks real. Like the servants are going to walk in any second and start fixing dinner."

"That's exactly what we're hoping guests will think too. Once it's finished, we'd like to do cooking demonstrations out there. Fix recipes that would have been served back then. Show how to cook in the fireplace. Bake in the brick ovens. How to grow herbs and use a real kitchen garden."

Miranda couldn't help but be fascinated; Miss Nell's quiet enthusiasm was contagious.

"What about recipes?" Miranda prompted, and was glad when the woman smiled. *A sweet smile, a determined smile—determined to be brave, to be happy—but sad, too . . . old beyond her years . . . very, very tired . . .*

You're scared of something, Miss Nell. Something you've hidden very well but not quite deep enough, because I can sense it, right down here—

"My own recipes, when we had our restaurant," Miss Nell was saying, and Miranda snapped back to attention.

"Aunt Teeta told me about that. You had a really great restaurant here in St. Yvette—a long time ago, right?"

"It was pretty popular, and customers had their own personal favorites. I need to get back in shape, though." Pulling up another stool, Miss Nell sank down and perched on the edge. She gave an exaggerated shudder. "It's been a long time since I cooked for that many people. Though come to think of it, that's probably not so different from cooking for two teenage boys."

"You mean Gage and Etienne," Miranda said, and the

woman's smile widened. "You and Gage's mom are really close, aren't you? I mean, being sisters and all."

"Extremely close. Jules and I are twins, though we don't look alike." Miss Nell paused, went thoughtful. "That's one reason Jules and Frank decided to move here, you know. When the boys were small. We wanted them to have each other . . . to grow up together and experience some of that closeness."

Miranda considered this. "Gage told me once that Etienne's not close to anyone . . . but that if he were, he'd probably be closest to Gage. And I know—we *all* know—he's close to you."

"Close to making me crazy, is what you mean." Chuckling, she slowly shook her head. "Etienne *is* closest to Gage, and vice versa. Even when they were little, they always had each other's backs."

The image made Miranda smile. "So how old was Gage when he came to St. Yvette?"

"They moved here from Natchez when Gage was five. And Etienne was six."

"Really?" Miranda was only mildly surprised. "I didn't know that . . . but Etienne *always* seems older to me."

"He got held back a grade. He . . ." A quick, dark cloud passed over Miss Nell's face. "He missed too much school. He was . . . sick a lot."

Because of those scars on his arms . . . those beatings from his father . . .

"So," Miranda redirected, "I guess it's like Gage and Etienne have always had two families?"

"Absolutely. And it's good for them. Keeps them both in line."

Miranda found the concept hilarious. The thought of this tiny woman keeping Gage and Etienne in line. Though she had no doubt that Miss Nell could do it—and did it often.

"When our boys were little, if Etienne needed a firm hand, Jules and Frank had my full cooperation—not to mention my blessing. And the same went for Gage, when *he* needed correcting." Miss Nell paused, raised an eyebrow. "Though I don't recall Gage needing *nearly* as much correcting as Etienne."

"Those big, brown eyes," Miranda stated.

"Dimples!" They both laughed.

"Or," Miss Nell speculated, "maybe he was just sneakier at not getting caught."

"I don't know . . . Etienne's pretty sneaky, if you ask me."

Miss Nell was clearly amused. "And you seem to know him pretty well."

Miranda could feel her cheeks warming. "Not that well," she said quickly—too quickly. "Just . . . just a little well. Like I know Gage. Just sort of . . . well." *Great, Miranda. Nothing like being obvious.*

Miss Nell hadn't missed it, of course. She was still trying to keep a straight face. "So you think a lot of our boys, do you?"

"Gage and Etienne?" Miranda fumbled. "What I think of them?"

Again Miss Nell burst out laughing. "Not such a hard question, Miranda. One or two words will do."

"They . . . they . . ."

"They sure think a lot of you." A secret twinkled in the woman's eyes. "And *about* you."

Miranda didn't know what to say. For a split second, two distinct images flashed through her mind—Etienne's night-black stare, Gage's melt-your-heart smile. The two equally irresistible, just in different ways.

"And I could be all wrong about this," Miss Nell went on casually, getting up from her chair. "But my guess is, you like *them*, too." Pausing, she shot Miranda a knowing glance. "Both of them."

Blushing again, Miranda was at a loss. She watched silently as Miss Nell picked up a damp sponge, ran it over the countertop, then tossed it into the sink.

"Quite the catch, our boys." A dimple flashed in Miss Nell's cheek. "Either one of them."

"What, is this all girl talk going on in here?" As Etienne appeared in the doorway, Miranda avoided his eyes. She had no idea how long he'd been in the building, no idea how much of the conversation he'd heard. His face, of course, told her nothing. His mother only shrugged at him and dug down into the cooler for another soda.

"That's for us to know," she replied. Handing him the can, she pulled back and stared hard into his face. "And don't look so smug. You don't have a clue what important matters Miranda and I have been discussing."

She reached up to wipe dirt from his cheek. Clearly amused, Etienne ducked out of reach.

"Your mama, she's ready to leave," he informed Miranda. "Or I can bring you on home later, if you want."

"No, I better leave now." *Too much to think over . . . too much to sort out*. "Thanks, Miss Nell. I love your kitchen. And I hope I see you again soon."

"You can count on it." The woman gave her a quick hug. "I'm sure we'll find lots to talk about."

Etienne's eyes narrowed suspiciously. "Like what?"

"Like it doesn't concern you." Miss Nell turned back to her new refrigerator. Muttering under his breath, Etienne shepherded Miranda outside.

"I love your mom," Miranda told him. "I'm so glad she's going to be here."

Nodding, he squatted down to retie one of his boots. "Yeah, this is gonna be good for her. It's making her happy. She's just loving to be busy in the kitchen again."

"Listen . . . will you do me a favor?"

"Sure, I'll come up to your room tonight."

"I'm serious."

"So am I."

"That's *not* what I was going to ask you."

She swung at him as he stood up. Catching her fist, he jerked her against him and steadied her in his arms.

"I mean it!" she scolded, though she couldn't help laughing. "I need to tell the others what's going on. And I've really been trying to, but it's never been a good time."

For just a moment, she surrendered. Let herself relax against him; her body fit with his.

"Miranda?" a voice called.

Jumping, she tried to disentangle herself while Etienne

deliberately held her closer. Miss Nell was standing right outside the kitchen door, assessing things with a split-second glance.

"Honey, why don't you come for Sunday dinner?" Miss Nell asked, expression perfectly composed.

"I—I—" Miranda twisted, but to no avail. Etienne glanced from her to his mother with a carefully hidden smile.

"Etienne can pick you up," Miss Nell went on smoothly. "How about six? Okay, good."

She raised an eyebrow at Etienne. Shook her finger. He replied with an innocent shrug.

"I can't believe you just did that to me!" Miranda railed, though he only held her tighter.

"You were saying . . . about the meeting, *cher*," he reminded her, all business.

Miranda made an exasperated sound in her throat. "Just be there. Be there with me when I tell them."

"And where is this gonna be happening?"

"A public place," Miranda grimaced. "So Parker can't kill me."

14

"MIRANDA, I'M GOING TO KILL YOU," PARKER SAID. Rising halfway from the bench, he made a sweeping gesture of the schoolyard. "It doesn't even matter if there are people around. No sane jury in the world would convict me."

Miranda had the grace to look sheepish. "Sorry, Parker. It's not like I have a choice."

Sometime during the night, autumn had finally arrived, gusting all the hot weather away. The air was cool now, and fresh—the mood across campus, noticeably lighter. A few kids had thrown on ridiculous Halloween costumes. A few more were running and laughing, tossing candy. As a shower of candy corn rained down on Parker's head, he yelled out his opinion and plopped back down on the bench.

"So how come you waited to tell us?" Roo asked Miranda. Opening a small plastic container, she peered down at the wet glob of food inside. "It just makes sense to tell us from the beginning. That way, we don't miss any good stuff. Or waste any time."

"I tried to," Miranda assured her. "I wanted to. But there were too many other things going on."

As Roo placed her lunch on the table, Parker instantly recoiled. "What the *hell* is that?"

Roo tipped the container on edge. Set it back down again. "Some kind of casserole, I think."

"You think? Don't you know?"

Leaning sideways, Gage gave the meal a cursory glance. "How long has that been in your refrigerator? It's black."

"So?" Roo's stare was mildly irritated. "What are you, a food critic?"

"No, and I'm not a paramedic, either. So don't eat it."

"Oh, Miranda, you should always tell us," Ashley insisted, reaching across the table, squeezing Miranda's hand. "You should always tell us *anything!* And . . . *everything*!"

Despite Parker, Miranda felt that her announcement had gone well. She'd waited till they were all gathered outside for lunch. She'd waited for a lull in the conversation. And then, after an encouraging nod from Etienne, she'd dropped her bombshell.

The reactions had been varied. And predictable.

Ashley had gotten emotional over the children on the stairs; Gage had once again volunteered his time and research skills. Parker, looking stubborn, had pulled back and not offered anything at all. Roo's comment had been wise and matter-of-fact—"See? I knew you were picking up spirit vibes that day in the car." And Etienne, silently observing, had seemed amused.

"Please don't do this again, Miranda," Ashley pleaded. "You don't have to go through these things by yourself. It's too hard, and we want to help you. In fact, we *like* helping you."

Parker's reply was muffled by a large bite of taco. Gage offered Miranda a heartening smile.

"She's right, you know. We all have different ideas, different perspectives—"

"Different talents," Etienne broke in.

Roo leveled him a stare. "I like *your* talent best. I hear you win first prize in every contest you enter."

Etienne winked. Roo smiled slyly and turned back to her lunch.

"Different information about stuff," Gage went on, as though he'd never been interrupted.

"Thanks, you guys." Miranda smiled at each of them in turn. "*Thank you*, Parker."

Parker's snort was derisive. "Don't thank *me*, *I'm* not helping. Did you even *hear* me say I'm helping? Because . . . you know . . . I'm *not*."

"So the woman you saw in the mirror," Gage prompted Miranda, "do you think she's connected to the children somehow?"

"I don't know," Miranda answered truthfully. "But that look on her face . . . in her eyes . . . it's so intense. It goes right through me. I think that's the kind of desperation only a mother would feel for her kids."

Ashley was starting to look weepy again. "You said they were calling for their mom. And they sounded scared."

"At first they didn't." Miranda frowned, thinking back. "At first they were just playing . . . well, it *sounded* like playing. Like some game—"

"Like the swing that night," Etienne broke in. "Little kids having fun, not being scared."

Again, Miranda let her mind go back. "Whatever—whoever—it was, didn't *seem* scared. The footsteps were light and quick, definitely not grown-up. And they came right to me."

"Maybe you surprised them," Roo suggested. "And they ran into you because they didn't realize you were there."

"Or maybe they *did* realize," Gage added quietly. "When they first saw you . . . or sensed you . . . maybe that's when they realized you could help them."

Remembering the ghostly touch on her hand, Miranda shivered. "It's like they're leaving me this weird trail of clues, you know? First the games . . . and then afterwards on the stairs—that's when they sounded so lost. Really frightened and sad."

"And calling for their mother," Ashley whispered, still upset.

Parker kept a straight face. "Maybe they got stuck in the wall and died."

"Parker Wilmington, that is a terrible thing to say!"

"Why is that terrible? Miranda just got through saying she heard them hollering in the wall—"

"They were crying," Miranda corrected. "And calling for her, but not loud. They sounded . . . faraway."

"Afterlife far enough away for you?"

Ashley clapped her hand over his mouth. Parker pulled it away, grinned, and kissed her fingers. It seemed that Ashley had forgiven him for his behavior the day before.

"Even if they *had* gotten stuck inside the wall"—Miranda gave Parker a scolding look—"which seems *very* unlikely—someone would have found them."

"Maybe not." Parker shrugged. "If nobody else was there."

"Well, of course someone else was there—someone else was *always* there. The house servants used those stairs all the time. And their mother probably knew all their hiding places."

"They were rich," Roo pointed out. "They would have had a nanny."

Parker's reaction was immediate—and disdainful. "Then trust me. Their mom was totally clueless about what they did each day."

An uncomfortable silence fell. As knowing glances crisscrossed the table—*Parker's childhood, Parker's too-busy-to-be-bothered parents*—Ashley tried to keep the discussion going.

"Maybe it's just that they were happy there . . . and then they *weren't* happy there. I mean . . . something happened to make them *not* happy there."

"Ashley logic." Parker patted her head. "That's my girl."

Amused, Gage twirled his soft drink can between his fingers. "It sort of . . . makes sense. If the kids were really happy, the house would've held on to that happiness. But if they were also really sad . . . the house would've held on to that, too."

"Two major reasons for ghosts to be hanging around, yeah?" Etienne shot a glance at Miranda. "Deep happiness and deep sadness."

Ashley squirmed excitedly in her seat. "So maybe it's just their emotions you're supposed to pay attention to! And the game on the stairs is more like a . . . a symbol! Just a symbol of their happiness, not an honest-to-goodness clue!"

"I'm not sure." Miranda mulled this over. "The way they kept calling for me to come and find them, while Coralee's girls were outside playing hide-and-seek. It just seems like too much of a coincidence. But I also don't see how a game—even if they *did* get lost for a while—has anything to do with their mother and how frantic she looked."

"Tell us about her again," Roo said, and Miranda did so. Listening intently, Roo was so focused on Parker's last taco that he nervously moved it to the far edge of the table. "Her eyes," Roo stated, when Miranda had finished. "You said her eyes were red?"

"Forget it, Roo," Etienne teased. "I'm sure she wasn't a vampire."

Miranda almost smiled at that. "Bloodshot. They looked really bloodshot. I kept thinking how exhausted she was. Just . . . if I could have seen her move, I'm sure she'd have been weak and staggering around—"

"Dead on her feet?" Parker looked pleased with himself while everyone else groaned.

"I think you're right," Roo assured Miranda. "From the description, it sounds like she was sick. And that cap on her head . . . with her hair pulled back . . . she was probably married. Single girls wore their hair down."

"Where do you get this stuff?" Parker asked, both curious and annoyed.

"Louisiana History, eighth grade. Gage and I had the mother of all term papers."

"Which *Gage and I* wrote," Ashley couldn't help reminding her.

Roo merely shrugged. Nibbling halfheartedly on a pretzel,

Miranda watched dead leaves and stray bits of litter somersault over the grass.

"Her clothes," Miranda mumbled. "When I saw the woman this time, her clothes were a lot more real somehow. A lot more detailed."

Parker offered a sage nod. "Right. Real clothes on a not-real person. Makes sense to me."

"Parker, if you don't shush—" Ashley warned.

Miranda tried to concentrate. "They were all so black . . . *more* than black. Her dress, her collar, her cap, every button and piece of lace—I know this sounds weird, but it's like her clothes were a color . . . and a *feeling*."

Miranda didn't realize that she was shivering. Not till Gage leaned toward her and began to gently rub the chill from her arms. And then . . .

"Those are funeral clothes," Miranda murmured, the truth slowly dawning. "She's in mourning."

An uneasy quiet settled over the table. Almost at once, Parker began attacking his lunch, rustling paper, rattling plastic cutlery.

"Oh, Miranda." Ashley seemed dangerously close to tears again. "Do you think her children died? And she wants you to find them?"

"But they're all in the same place, yeah?" Etienne frowned. "The mama, her kids—Miranda's seen all of them at the house already."

"But the first time she saw the woman wasn't at Belle Chandelle, right Miranda? It was on the wall in our den!"

"And what's that about, anyway?" Parker unexpectedly spoke

up. "If she belongs out there at the plantation, what the hell's she doing at Ashley's?"

Ashley's face instantly lost color. "You don't think she's coming to our house again, do you? Looking for Miranda or—"

"She was in that mosaic," Roo cut in dryly. "She could have been anywhere, so why there?"

"The mirrors." Satisfied that Miranda had stopped shaking, Gage settled back in place. "It's made of all those little mirror pieces—"

"But what does that have to do with anything?" Miranda frowned, even as Etienne gestured toward the school.

"You had that weird thing going at your locker, remember?"

"But that wasn't her. I mean, I didn't actually *see* anyone."

"Then it *coulda* been. You can't be sure."

"There just doesn't seem to be any connection. This whole mirror thing doesn't make sense."

"You broke a mirror that morning," Roo said ominously.

Gage pointed at Miranda's palm. "And cut your hand."

"People cut their hands every day," Miranda grumbled, but Gage only smiled.

"Maybe you're not supposed to know any significance yet, Miranda. Maybe right now, it's just the way your ghost got in. The . . . open door between you and her."

"And what about that little ghost hand you felt by the swing?" Ashley piped up. "Maybe *that's* what connected you with those children."

"It . . . sort of makes sense, I guess," Miranda admitted grudgingly. "Even though I wish it didn't."

Lounging back against the edge of the table, Etienne crossed his arms, stretched out his legs, and focused on Roo. "You're looking awful serious, *cher*."

"Forget serious," Parker corrected. "She just looks awful. As usual."

Roo grazed him with a stare. Then nodded at Etienne. "So we're pretty sure the ghost woman's in mourning. And she's also sick. With those shadows under her eyes, and the way her cheeks are kind of sunken—"

"I look like that when I've had too much beer," Parker scoffed. "Maybe she's really drunk."

"Maybe you're really dead."

Before Parker could respond, Miranda intervened. "My feeling was so strong about her being sick. And that maybe she'd been sick for a while. You know how sometimes when people are sick for a long time, you can see it in their faces? They have this certain look. Like . . ."

As she caught sight of Etienne's stoic face, her voice trailed away. She'd been thinking about her own bout with the flu; she hadn't meant to bring up any reminders of Miss Nell's cancer. *Oh my God . . . first Etienne's scars, and now this.* Horrified at her slip of the tongue, she sat there, miserably aware of everyone else trying to ignore what she'd done.

"Like . . . when you had the flu," Gage suddenly announced, way too casual. "You probably had bed hair."

"Yeah!" Parker jumped right on it. "Did the woman in the mirror have bed hair? Or maybe . . . bed cap?"

"Pillow face," Roo added, and Ashley burst out laughing.

Miranda shot Gage a grateful smile. Etienne, seeming all too aware of her discomfort, shrugged and shook his head: no big deal.

Not sure *what* to say now, Miranda chose her words more carefully. "And even though she *looked* sick, how could I know for sure? That first time, she was more like an old photograph. The way old photographs are shaded."

"That's right," Ashley recalled. "You said she looked more like an old *picture* than an actual *reflection*."

"Those old-fashioned tints, like old photographs have . . . and the way papery things always turn yellow and sort of brittle with age? It made her skin look yellow. So . . . maybe in a different light, *true* light . . . she wouldn't look so unhealthy."

"But still scared?"

"Yes, still scared. No colors could *ever* hide how panicky she was."

Frowning slightly, Gage shifted his leg to a more comfortable position. "Speaking of photographs," he reminded Miranda. "What about that letter and photograph your aunt Teeta was talking about? Have you seen them yet?"

"Mom made copies for me. I looked at them last night, but they seem pretty obvious—just like Aunt Teeta told us."

Roo jabbed a fork at her mystery lunch. "Refresh me on the letter and photo."

"The letter's written by a Yankee soldier—he talks about the Battle of St. Yvette and how his scouts have spotted this big plantation about a mile away, and they're going to see if there's anything left to raid. But they're not going to burn the house, they're going to stay in it instead."

"So how do you know it's the same place?" Parker stole Ashley's napkin, wiped salsa from his upper lip. "How do you know he's even talking about Belle Chandelle?"

"Because he says something about a sign, they see a sign on the property . . . you know, quite a ways from the house."

"Well, they probably would have had a beautiful sign," Ashley imagined. "Or maybe one of those big arbor things curved over the driveway to the house." Resting her head on Parker's shoulder, she lapsed into dreaminess. "It probably would have been close to the road, don't you think? Right at the front of the property. To welcome everybody who passed by. And let everybody know the name of the plantation."

"They find the name Belle Chandelle written on the sign—but the soldier says it's all overgrown with weeds and stuff. That the sign is so camouflaged, they almost missed it."

"Maybe the plantation had already fallen on hard times." Parker's shrug was dismissive. "Slaves off fighting or run away . . . no crops . . . no money . . ."

"Maybe. The soldier *does* say the whole place looks quiet and deserted, that they shouldn't have much trouble taking it."

"That wouldn't be so unusual," Gage noted. "Some families took off when they heard the Yankees were coming. Just left everything behind."

"But some of them didn't have anywhere else to go." Ashley's tone went sad. "Just think of all the ones who stayed. And tried to hang on to their homes. And be there when their husbands came back. And their sons came back. And their brothers came back. And their uncles—"

"We get it, Ash." Parker finished his taco. Wadded his napkin. Tossed it into Roo's half-empty container. "So did you bring these great pieces of history with you today?" he grumbled at Miranda, seeming resigned to his fate.

"They're in my locker."

"Could I borrow them?" Pushing aside his unfinished lunch, Gage reached for his crutches, hoisted himself to his feet. "I've got to leave early for the doctor . . . but I'm always in the waiting room forever. And I'm really tired of those twenty-year-old magazines."

"Sure. I'll grab them when we go in."

"What about the pictures?" Roo asked suddenly.

Everyone looked at her, puzzled. Roo looked back at them, unfazed.

"The camera you used yesterday," she told Miranda. "At the plantation. What about the pictures you took?"

Miranda still didn't get it. "Mom said she was going to get them printed after she brought me to school this morning."

"There could be something on that memory card, you know. Ghosts. Some kind of spirit activity."

"Are you kidding?"

"You could have photographed a ghost and not even realized. You could have surprised him . . . caught him off guard."

"I hope he wasn't naked." Parker shot Miranda a reproachful glance. "Shame on you, Miranda. Taking porno shots of ghosts—"

"Parker," Ashley broke in sternly, "this is serious."

"Hey, we could start our own website. The Paranormal Peeping Tom. Or would that be Peeping Miranda—"

"*Parker!*"

But Miranda's attention had stayed on Roo. "There wasn't anything weird about the pictures I was taking. It's a digital camera—I saw all the images while I was shooting. And there wasn't anything there that shouldn't have been there."

"That's just it." Roo solemnly returned her gaze. "Just because you didn't see anything weird *then*—or any ghosts *then*—doesn't mean they won't show up when the pictures get printed. God, Miranda, don't you ever watch that stuff on TV?"

"Roo's right," Gage agreed. "As intense as your visions were yesterday, there's no telling *what* you might've picked up on camera."

"I do *not* want to hear this." Fidgeting anxiously in her seat, Miranda appealed to Etienne. "If there really *is* something there, I don't want Mom seeing—"

"I'll take care of it," Etienne assured her. "Where'd she drop off the memory card?"

"I . . . the drugstore, I think."

Etienne nodded. Shoving off from the table, he gave a long, leisurely stretch. "Just call and tell her I was stopping off there on my way to work. If we're lucky, she hasn't been by to get them yet."

"She's picking me up at two thirty. She wants me to have one last check-up at the doctor."

"Me, I'll be gone by then, *cher*. No problem."

"I just wonder what kinds of great pictures you could take out there after dark." Roo seemed slightly stunned at the prospect. "Can you imagine? Or during a storm? The conditions would be a million times better."

Parker reared back, regarded her with cool disbelief. "You'd actually go out there to that big dead house. And wander around with a camera. And go into those pitch-black rooms to take pictures. Of nothing."

"Oh, don't worry—we know y'all are having your fun little guys' sleepover out there tonight. We wouldn't *dream* of crashing your party."

"They are?" Ashley asked, surprised. "Is this like, a celebrate-Gage's-leg party or something?"

"Okay. Who's the spy? As if I didn't know." Parker frowned at Roo. "And yeah, Ash. We're honoring Gage's leg. With a special welcome-home celebration."

"But don't say anything," Gage echoed, managing a straight face. "It's a surprise. My leg doesn't know."

"There's a cake with its name on it," Etienne added. "And balloons."

"And *no girls allowed*," Parker finished.

"And like we'd even want to." Roo's tone was as patronizing as her stare. "But as long as you're there, why don't you big brave heroes do some serious investigating on your own?"

"Maybe we will," Parker threw back at her. "In fact, maybe we'll solve the whole Belle Chandelle mystery tonight."

The three girls exchanged glances. And began to laugh.

"Right." Roo nodded. "And maybe I'll be wearing a bikini to school tomorrow."

Parker immediately grimaced. "Jesus, Roo. That's even scarier than Halloween."

Miranda was glad to be staying home that night.

While Mom worked late at the office, Aunt Teeta made a big batch of blueberry pancakes, country ham, and buttery grits for the two of them, then they ate together in the kitchen, talking and laughing and enjoying each other's company. Afterward, Miranda gave out candy to a steady stream of little trick-or-treaters while Aunt Teeta watched her favorite TV shows. Etienne called around nine to confirm that he'd picked up the photos—and that they were perfectly normal. Relieved, Miranda headed upstairs to her room to finish up the small bit of homework she had.

She was surprised when Aunt Teeta knocked on her door about eleven o'clock; even more surprised when Aunt Teeta asked if she could run an errand.

"Now?" Miranda was puzzled. "Does Mom need something?"

"No, but Etienne does."

"Etienne?"

Laughing heartily, Aunt Teeta nearly shook the curlers off her head. She already had on her nightgown and robe and favorite kitty slippers.

"Those boys, bless their hearts! You know, darlin', I asked Etienne to go out to Belle Chandelle tonight and kind of keep an eye on the place? With it being Halloween and all, and you just never know about kids playing pranks. Well, I just called his cell phone to check on him, and guess what? Gage and Parker offered to go out there too, and keep him company! Now, wasn't that sweet?"

Miranda didn't think *sweet* quite described it. God only knew what sort of stupid guy-things the three of them were doing out there. But she humored Aunt Teeta with a smile. Then tried to focus back on her studying.

"I just feel so sorry for them." Aunt Teeta clucked her tongue sympathetically. "I told them the least I could do was bring them some food."

Uh-oh, this can't be good. And though Aunt Teeta didn't say anything for several long seconds, Miranda had a sneaking suspicion where this was headed.

"Now, I know this is an imposition, darlin'—and I wouldn't ask you to do it otherwise—it's just that I can't see worth a darn to drive at night, and that ole road out there is so dark . . ."

"Just have it delivered," Miranda interrupted. "Just call some pizza place and have it delivered."

"It's almost midnight—this is St. Yvette, hon. There's nothing open this late on a weeknight. But I've got all kinds of fixin's for po-boys and there's plenty of that carrot cake left over. Oh, and what about the macaroni salad—"

"Aunt Teeta, Miss Nell probably left them tons of stuff in the fridge. I really don't think you need to worry—"

"Well, actually." Cupping one hand around her mouth, Aunt Teeta gave an exaggerated whisper, "I wouldn't be a bit surprised if those hungry, growin' boys already ate everything in Nell's fridge *and* pantry. Now . . . I really hate to ask, but . . ."

Oh no, Aunt Teeta—do not *do this to me.* "Why can't one of the guys just come here and pick it up?"

"Because I just don't feel right, asking them to drive all the way back *here*, when they're out *there* doing me a favor! That wouldn't be polite. Now, you're still dressed—I'll hurry with those sandwiches, and you take my car. And put on a jacket. It's actually feeling cold out there!"

Miranda couldn't believe it. Here she was, tucked in all safe and warm and happy, and of all the places she *didn't* want to go, it was Belle Chandelle. She wished she had the nerve to just refuse—but what could she say? By the time the food was ready, she was more agitated than ever. She grabbed a jacket and Aunt Teeta's keys, and stood there frowning with an overloaded picnic basket in her arms.

"Now, be sure and hold it from the bottom," Aunt Teeta instructed her. "It's mighty heavy. And I boxed up a couple big jugs of tea in the trunk—and a couple thermoses of hot cocoa. And some cider. Oh, and a few other little things I thought the boys would like. That should just about cover it, I think."

"Why don't I just take the whole kitchen?'

"Darlin', this is such a nice thing the boys are doing for us."

Miranda grunted. "Will the gate be locked? You better show me which key to use."

"I'll call the boys as soon as you leave, so they can be waiting for you in the parking lot. And take a flashlight—there's one in the backseat!"

Miranda was still grumbling to herself when she drove off.

The country road seemed even longer tonight, even blacker—a bottomless-well black that pressed too close around her. The sky was starless, and the chilly breeze that had finally blown in whipped ragged clouds across the moon, keeping it mostly hidden, snuffing out its pale gray light . . . Miranda turned on the heater, but still shivered. It was silly, she kept telling herself—but there was a sad sense of foreboding hanging over her. *No, not hanging over me . . . deep inside my bones . . .*

At last she reached the parking lot and pulled inside. Twisted shadows writhed across the ground, macabre distortions of empty construction equipment. The sky seemed to shrink into itself . . . grow darker. The wind felt raw. Where were the guys? Why weren't they out here to meet her?

She sat there for a while, trying to decide what to do. *Wait till someone comes? Turn around and go home? She wished Aunt Teeta hadn't crammed so much food into the car;* the smells were making her sick. I'm going to kill those guys! It would serve them right if she left, but Aunt Teeta would be so disappointed. And anyway, she couldn't very well drive all the way back in a reeking car, could she? Great, Miranda. Won't this be fun, lugging a two-ton basket and a big flashlight, and trying to keep an eye out for . . .

For what?

She was beginning to learn that the people who stalked her were invisible and silent. Protected from flashlights and the sharpest of ears. *So what do you expect could be out here tonight? The woman in the mirror? The children on the stairs?*

Countless other spirits trapped there in the house, in the fields, in the memories of Belle Chandelle?

"Well, I haven't got all night," she muttered, and got out of the car. Fumbling with the basket, she balanced it in her arms and clutched the flashlight in her right hand. It was awkward, but manageable. *If something scares me, I'll attack it with macaroni salad and run.*

That made her smile, a little. But *damn* that Etienne. And *Gage*! She'd expected at least *one* of them to show up. She made her way from the empty lot to the pathway. And started walking.

This world was shrouded in darkness and moss. As Miranda kept cautiously to the path, she could almost believe that the house didn't exist at all . . . perhaps had *never* existed. Or if it did, if it had . . . it was now faded helplessly into a fragile netherworld. Caught between the living and the dead . . . rooms empty and silent . . . longing to be filled with hope.

Stop. Quit scaring yourself.

She could feel herself getting annoyed again—angry, even. Good. That was a lot better than being scared.

She kept her eyes deliberately focused, gazing straight ahead over the heavy basket. She knew that if she glanced to either the left or the right, she might see things she didn't want to see, things she didn't want to know about. Because from the corner of her left eye, she could *already* make out the image of flames sputtering from outdoor fires, cooking fires outside the slave quarters, and long curls of smoke, black against black, from the chimneys of their cabins. And from the corner of her right eye, more images danced in light—lanterns bobbing through the shadows of the bayou; carriage lamps bouncing along the road, turning into the long driveway, sparkling through the oak trees, up the alley to the house . . .

And the house!

At last Miranda saw it; she was there.

And the sight was so spectacular that she stopped in her tracks and let out a cry of wonder.

The whole house was ablaze with light. Like one magnificent candle, as lovely as its name—*Belle Chandelle, Beautiful Candle*—every window glowing, every gallery flickering like stars, golden warmth and hospitality flowing from every welcome-wide French door . . .

Oh my God . . .

Tears filled her eyes.

Her heart ached; she couldn't breathe—

None of you knew, none of you realized that these were your last bright moments of happiness here—

And then it was gone.

One last sputter. One desperate burst of radiance. Fading . . . fading . . . to a deep, eternal sorrow . . .

Miranda's picnic basket was on the ground.

The flashlight shook in her hand.

Completely unnerved, she stood there on the path, probing the dark with her senses, hoping for one more spark of light.

But Belle Chandelle was glorious no longer . . .

Barely even a memory in the shadows.

15

Miranda was furious by the time she reached the main house.

Still badly shaken from her vision and angry that no one had met her in the parking lot, she lugged the basket as quickly as she could, muttering the entire way. She could see doors standing open off the verandah; light glowed out across the threshold, while voices laughed and argued from the room beyond.

Slipping to the doorway, Miranda peered in.

An intense poker game seemed to be in progress, the three contenders slouched in folding chairs around one of Mom's cleared-off worktables. Parker was laughing, elbows propped on the table edge, drinking a beer and holding a fan of cards. Etienne was hunched forward, one eyebrow raised as he slid a stack of chips toward the center pile. And Gage, minus his cast, was balanced comfortably in a tipped-back chair, baseball cap turned backward, shaggy hair tucked behind his ears.

In spite of her anger, Miranda couldn't resist watching them. *The past-five-o'clock shadow on Gage's jaw and upper lip . . . the chiseled angles of Etienne's face . . . the cocky charm of Parker's grin.* Music was blaring from an iPod and portable speakers. There were coolers scattered around, along with bags and boxes of snacks, and a growing heap of trash in one corner.

Without warning, Etienne let loose with something in French; Gage answered back in kind. Parker was immediately indignant.

"Hey, if y'all are going to cheat, at least cheat so I can understand you!"

An amused response from Gage; laughter and swearing from the other two. Miranda, doing her best to look intimidating, cleared her throat and stepped in.

"Where have you been?" she demanded.

The three boys nearly fell off their chairs.

"Christ, Miranda!" Parker yelped. "Why don't you warn a guy when you're sneaking up on him?"

"You were supposed to meet me!"

"*I* was?" Parker looked mystified.

"I was waiting in the parking lot!"

"*You* were? Are we having an affair?"

Miranda shoved the basket out in front of her. "You were supposed to come and get all this food! And don't bother hiding that beer—I've already seen it. Wait. You're *all* drinking beer?"

Quick, covert looks passed one to another—too late to hide the evidence. Parker offered a sheepish grin; Gage, a reluctant but guilty shrug. Etienne, gulping the mouthful he'd just taken, was on his feet and moving toward her, but Miranda wasn't ready to be appeased.

"Does Aunt Teeta know you're drinking out here?"

"Well—we—it's just—"

"Does my mom?"

"Aw, come on now—it's not like we're hurting any—"

"Does the renovation committee?"

"You mean the prohibition committee?" Beer aloft, Parker gave her a toast.

"Look, *cher*," Etienne insisted, "I can explain."

But Miranda was finding immense pleasure in this. "Hmm. Looks like grounds for blackmail to me."

"Wait now. You're not even supposed to be out here, yeah? So how come—"

"Macaroni salad." Again she shoved out the basket. "I'm pretty sure the lid came off, so you'll have to scrape it all back together."

"And I'm still not understanding this . . . what about macaroni salad?"

"Aunt Teeta sent food, Etienne. Didn't she call?"

A quick flinch went over his face. "*Mais* no. The last time I talked to her, she told me she was going to bed—so I turned off my phone. I'm really sorry—"

Miranda's sound of exasperation said it all. She started to leave, but he reached out and caught her arm.

"Why don't you sit yourself down and eat with us."

"No thanks."

"At least take something to drink."

"We've got Cokes!" Parker announced, yanking open a cooler. "See? Ice cold and ready for fun. Cokes for the little lady."

Miranda gave him a scowl. "No, I want to go home. You guys just enjoy your little slumber party."

"At least have a look at Gage's leg."

"It looks just like my other leg." Gage quickly assured her. "When you've seen one of my legs, you've seen them all."

As tempting as it was to embarrass Gage, Miranda kept her eyes on Etienne.

"So you're supposed to be guarding this place tonight?"

"That's the plan, yeah."

"Uh-huh. And you do realize the gate was open when I got here?"

Another round of glances, sheepish this time.

"Kind of defeats the purpose, don't you think?" Miranda couldn't help adding, but now Etienne was starting to look amused.

"Kids are gonna be climbing the fence whether that gate's locked or not. And folks don't usually try to steal bulldozers, *cher*. They'd rather be sneaking around up here by the house."

"Yeah," Parker frowned at her. "Like you."

"Pretty quiet tonight, though," Etienne went on. "Nothing much going on."

"See, Miranda?" Parker shrugged. "No big bad ghosts. Or . . . should I say . . . no little bitty kiddie ghosts."

She considered slamming the basket over his head. Instead she suggested, "Well . . . maybe you haven't been looking in the right places."

It was hard to tell who actually caught on first—Gage or Etienne. Both their expressions changed simultaneously, furtive glances sweeping the shadows, then returning to Miranda's face. Parker either didn't notice—or didn't want to.

"Something happened, didn't it?" Gage asked her quietly. "After you got here. And we weren't with you."

He sounded so sorry for it that a little of her anger began to fade. Etienne was gazing down at her with a half-stern, half-apologetic frown.

"Mon Dieu, *cher*," he mumbled. "Tell us. What happened?"

"Yeah, tell us," Parker echoed. "This will be perfect entertainment, right guys? Halloween stories while we eat." He was rummaging through the basket, unwrapping po-boys, examining containers. He pulled out a lidless one, turned it upside down, then scowled. "Hey, Miranda. This one's empty. And there's . . . like . . . slimy shit everywhere."

Miranda glared. Parker, oblivious, began picking out macaroni, piece by piece, and popping them into his mouth.

"It's good, you know? But it's stuck to everything. You should be more careful next time."

As Miranda stepped toward him, Etienne blocked her path and put both hands on her shoulders. "That contest at school." He was speaking so low, from one side of his mouth, that she could barely make out what he was saying. "That Win a Date with a Cheerleader thing?"

Miranda was completely in the dark. "So?"

"Streak, he won a date with Ashley."

"*What?*" Miranda actually felt her jaw drop. "Are you . . . are you *sure*?"

Etienne nodded. Glancing around him, Miranda saw Gage give another shrug, sympathetic this time.

"How do you know that?" She was whispering now too,

though Parker, still searching for macaroni, didn't seem aware of their discussion.

"They had the drawing at the end of the day," Etienne explained.

"When you and I weren't there? Oh, poor . . ." She hesitated, gave Etienne a bewildered frown. "Actually, I don't know *who* to feel worse for. Parker or Ashley."

Etienne jerked his chin in Parker's direction. "He's got a game tomorrow night. He can't be drinking."

"Oh, no. And he's been doing so much better about that. I was hoping—"

"Yeah, I know. He was pretty bad off when he got here. But me and Gage, we been watering everything down, pouring everything out as much as we can. Keeping him distracted."

"Trust me," Gage added. "It's been easy. He hasn't noticed."

Miranda hadn't heard Gage approaching. Turning, she saw him standing close behind her, while Parker continued to dig through the food.

"What about Ashley?" she asked softly. "How did she take the news?"

"Ashley's fine with it." Lifting his head, Parker chewed thoughtfully on a slice of roast beef. He considered a moment, glanced at the three of them, then gave a philosophical shrug. "It's all for a good cause. She's doing it as a . . . *business* arrangement. I don't have *anything* to worry about. In fact, I'm being *stupid* for worrying."

"Parker," Miranda said seriously, "listen to Ashley. She's telling you the truth."

"I didn't try hard enough," he sighed.

As the others watched, he sat down on the floor, unwrapped a wedge of cake, and gazed morosely at a clump of icing on his finger. Miranda, Gage, and Etienne exchanged hidden smiles.

"Didn't try hard enough," he sighed again. "Should have tried harder."

"At what?" Gage asked.

"I bought a hundred tickets."

Gage's eyes flew wide. Etienne snorted a laugh.

"*Merde*, a hundred damn tickets?"

"And I lost," Parker grumbled. "What does that tell you?"

"It tells me the drawing could've been rigged," Gage concluded, while Miranda nodded agreement.

"So is it fate?" Parker sighed. "Should we really be together?"

Etienne could no longer take the drama. Squatting down beside Parker, he clapped a hand on his shoulder and gave him a shove. "Hey. Ashley, she's been crazy for you all these years, yeah? But when she finds out you spent a hundred dollars just to win a date—"

"No, no. *Hell* no. She can't find out."

"How come?"

"Hey!" Indignantly, Parker drew himself up. "I've got my pride, haven't I?"

Another silent exchange of amusement among the other three; Parker, fumbling for a fresh beer, didn't catch on.

As Miranda watched Parker lift the can to his lips, Gage mouthed, "I'll get that one. I hope."

"Look, there's more stuff in the car," she informed them.

"Aunt Teeta sent tea and cocoa and cider and another whole box of food. I just couldn't carry it all."

Squeezing her shoulder, Gage nodded. "We can handle that. But first, you need to tell us what happened tonight."

Miranda really didn't want to talk about it now. What she really wanted to do was go home—but she realized that neither of them would ever consent to that. Gage pulled out his chair for her to sit. Etienne stood pensively by, eyes narrowed. And even Parker, who was doing his best to look uninterested, sat down and leaned over the table, resting his chin on folded arms.

Miranda described her experience in detail—the ghostly splendor of Belle Chandelle. By the time she was finished, Etienne was doing his usual pacing, and Gage had lowered himself into the seat beside her, his gaze thoughtful.

"So," Gage mused, "you don't really know if what you saw has anything to do with those children. Or the woman in the mirror."

Miranda's reply was weary. "That's just it. I've been getting hit with so many images since I first stepped on the property, I don't know how to sort it all out. This place has way too much history going on."

No one seemed to have any ideas. As the silence stretched out, Parker buried his face in his arms, and Etienne finally motioned to the door. "I'm gonna get that stuff from your car, *cher*. You got the keys?"

"I left it unlocked."

"I'll be right back."

Nodding, she and Gage watched him go. Then after several quiet moments, Miranda sighed and leaned back in her chair.

"So how's your leg?" she asked Gage. "I really did mean to ask you when I got here. I was just . . . upset."

"Understandable. It's good."

"I noticed you're still limping."

"Just a little. The doctor says it'll go away eventually. Especially once I start rehab."

Miranda couldn't help herself. "So I guess the girls at school are still going to feel sorry for you after all, with that limp."

"Stop."

"And you still won't be able to outrun Babette LeBlanc and her bra size for a while."

"Okay, that's enough."

Hiding a smile, Miranda reached over and lightly touched his thigh. "I bet your leg's really cute."

"Not as cute as yours," he mumbled, glancing away.

Parker's head instantly came up. "Rehab," he announced, having missed their last few seconds of talking. "You have to be ready for spring ball, hotshot."

A little flushed herself now, Miranda pulled back from Gage. "What about spring ball?" she asked innocently.

"He's starting pitcher for our baseball team," Parker explained. "Pitcher. That's what you were saying, right? 'Pitcher'? Or 'pictures'?"

Miranda looked at Gage. He was leaning sideways, elbow propped on the table, cheek resting against his palm. He shrugged, smiling.

"Speaking of pictures," he said agreeably, "those things you loaned me? The picture and the letter? I was looking at them this afternoon."

"And?" Intrigued, Miranda straightened in her seat, senses sharpening.

"Something . . . I don't know, exactly. *Maybe* something."

But Miranda had seen Gage's instincts in action before. And trusted them. "Tell me."

"In the letter—which he dated—the Yankee soldier says they're going to seize Belle Chandelle. That they don't anticipate trouble, because it already looks deserted—in fact, he says it looks like a place where only the dead would stay."

Nodding, Miranda recalled those words from the letter. Words that hadn't affected her till now, listening to Gage repeat them. "Go on."

"He says they're going to use the house for their headquarters. They know there's going to be heavy fighting, there's already been some pretty bloody skirmishes. Now . . . we know the date of the Battle of St. Yvette, and we know when the town was occupied. And it's been pretty well documented—a timeline of less important battles—raiding parties and smaller attacks around the area."

Miranda didn't have a clue where this was headed. But she nodded encouragement anyway.

"When you look at the photograph," Gage's voice dropped, more intense now. "You see Belle Chandelle at a distance, in the background. And you can tell just by the landscape that at least one battle's already been fought there. I mean . . . everything's burned and bloody and torn up. But . . . the house still looks the same."

Again she didn't get it. Staring at Gage, she frowned and shook her head. "Sorry, but I—"

"It doesn't look like there's anybody there. It's after the time of the letter, but there's nobody around the house. No horses, no officers. There's no flag. The house still looks totally empty and deserted. Like the Yankees never even stayed there."

"But . . . why wouldn't they?"

"That's just it—*why wouldn't they*? It was free and clear; they didn't have to fight anybody for it. That whole, big house, and they planned to stay there, but I don't think they did. It just doesn't make sense."

But something was stirring in Miranda's brain. Something deep inside . . . something gnawing and nagging, just at the edge of her consciousness. Gage, noting her sudden restlessness, gave a concerned frown.

"What?" he asked. "What is it?"

"What the soldier said about the house."

"You mean, a place where only the dead would stay?"

"Hey, maybe the Yankees were afraid of ghosts." More alert now, Parker allowed himself a stretch, then swigged from his beer. "They didn't have Miranda around back then—they were probably afraid of the ghosts in Belle Chandelle."

"Oh my God." Miranda's eyes widened. Leaning across the table, she grabbed Parker's arm and shook it so hard that the beer can went sailing to the floor. "That's it! Parker, honestly, sometimes when I least expect it, your genius still amazes me."

"Me too," he grumbled, wiping a spill off the front of his shirt. "What the hell did I do?"

"Maybe it was the *ghosts*," she said excitedly to Gage. "Maybe Belle Chandelle was *already haunted* when the Yankees got there. Maybe they were afraid—maybe there was a bad feeling they got, or maybe something happened, they saw something, heard something, that scared them off."

Gage straightened slowly in his chair. Pushed his cap higher up his forehead. "Wow. You never think about there being a haunting back *then*. You always think of back *then* as being what caused the haunting. But . . . it makes sense. Which means—"

"Which means, whatever happened here—to the woman and the children—must have happened before the War."

"And sometime between then and the siege of St. Yvette, the plantation was totally abandoned?"

"Or . . . what if the thing that happened, and the plantation being abandoned, took place at the same time?"

"Jesus," Parker mumbled, and lowered his head onto his arms once more.

"When the Yankee soldiers came, Belle Chandelle could have been sitting empty for years." Gage lounged back more comfortably in his chair. "Still . . . you'd think somebody would've bought it in the meantime."

"Not if it was haunted," Parker's voice was muffled *and* annoyed. "How many times do I have to say it?"

Gage and Miranda shrugged.

"He's right," Miranda conceded. "Definitely a possibility."

"So what about the woman and the little kids?" Gage asked.

Frustrated, she let out a sigh. "*That* I haven't figured out yet."

"Figured *what* out yet?" Etienne stood in the doorway, boxes clutched in both arms, expression curious. "What'd I miss?"

"These two playing touchy-feely under the table." Parker didn't even bother to look up. "Other than that, not much."

Etienne's glance slid between Miranda and Gage. Miranda looked innocent; Gage motioned dismissively in Parker's direction.

"He's been asleep," Gage said.

"No, I haven't," Parker replied.

Shaking his head, Etienne jerked his chin toward the verandah. "I'm gonna go put this stuff in the kitchen. And for sure, we need to be making some coffee."

"Do you even know how to use the coffee maker?" Miranda spoke up, relieved to change the subject.

Three pairs of eyes aimed in her direction.

"Guys don't make coffee." Parker stated. "It's a law."

"I think I can figure it out, *cher*," Etienne assured her. "You need to be going on home. Your aunt Teeta, she just called me . . . worrying about you."

"Oh. So your phone's back on."

"And gonna stay on till morning. Who knows? Maybe we'll get us another nice surprise like you."

"Doubtful," Gage said, matter-of-fact.

Etienne nodded agreement. "I'll walk you to your car. And you can be filling me in on all those theories y'all came up with while I was gone."

"Well . . . how about *Parker* walks me to my car?" she asked, surprising all of them—especially Parker. Then, lowering her voice, she added, "Nice fresh air. Might make him feel better."

"Ah. Good idea."

"And actually . . . I can even drive him home, if you want."

Blocking Parker's view, Etienne dangled a set of BMW keys between his fingers. "I think we can keep us a better eye on him here, yeah? Thanks, though."

Miranda had to laugh. "Come on, Parker." Standing up, she tugged on him, ignoring his moans of protest, forcing him to his feet. "Be a gentleman and walk me to my car."

"I'll tell you one thing," Parker grumbled, following her to the door. "I'm never buying this kind of beer again. I swear to God, it tastes like Coke."

"If he's not back in a little while, you better come look for him," Miranda warned.

"No way," Gage deadpanned.

"He sleeps where he falls," Etienne insisted.

Smiling, Miranda turned on her flashlight and led Parker away from the house, still hearing Gage and Etienne in the background, their voices back and forth.

"So you gonna tell me what was happening while I was gone?" *Etienne.*

"We talked." *Gage.* "We came up with some great theories."

"I mean, everything."

"That is everything."

"Even the touchy-feely parts?"

"Stop."

"I can't even be trusting you for a few damn minutes. . . ."

Their voices faded into the night. A stark, stygian night that swallowed the house and all its secrets, like a curtain drawing shut between worlds. Miranda was thankful that Parker was with her. To her relief, he seemed to have no trouble maneuvering the path.

"Here," he said, and unexpectedly reached for the flashlight, aiming the beam higher and farther. "You . . . you're okay about driving home alone?"

Surprised, she glanced at him, but his eyes were fixed straight ahead. "Sure. Small town, right? Even the hitchhikers are safe?"

"That's not what I meant. I meant . . ." In typical Parker fashion, he grew irritated at his own show of concern. "Driving on this road. Kind of a long stretch till you hit town."

Miranda's heart softened. "You mean . . . because of the visions and things?"

"I heard you tonight. Watched you tonight." The flashlight bobbed and weaved, vague patterns over moss-shrouded trees. Parker's voice lowered, mumbling. "You could give it up. You could *turn your back* on it. You could . . . *ignore* it."

"Ignore it?" An ironic smile worked over her lips. "Right. I've got visions coming out of nowhere, like miniseries inside my head, till I don't even know what world I'm living in. I've got invisible strangers talking to me about their problems and expecting me to solve them. It's like . . . like the worst sort of intrusion. Like I'm being . . . violated." She paused, drew a deep breath. "So no, even though I really *want* to and I really *wish* I could—no, I don't think it's possible to just ignore it."

"Yeah, well. I guess some people think it's totally great, what you do." Though Parker's tone was neutral, Miranda heard the underlying disdain. "Helping spirits. Wow. Big, noble calling. But I don't see it that way. As a matter of fact, it doesn't make sense to me at all. Putting yourself through fear and pain. Opening yourself up to every weird, creepy, dangerous thing floating around out there."

Jokingly, he clawed the air with his hands. Moaned a spooky sound . . . held the flashlight beneath his chin, made a spooky face. Then glanced at her and shrugged his shoulders.

"To me, that's just . . . *hell*. And a whole hell of a lot . . . *unfair*. But hey . . . what do I know about noble callings, anyway." Waving the flashlight, he curved a great arc over their heads through the sky. "You're a weird kid, Miranda Barnes."

"How's that?"

"Dead people don't scare you. But you were hiding behind the pie safe in Ashley's kitchen the other night."

As her mind scrambled to refocus, Parker leaned over and snapped his fingers in front of her face.

"Hey, listen up. Pie safe. Ashley's kitchen. Ring a bell?"

Annoyed, she grabbed his fingers and held on. "I was . . . I told you. Wiping mud off my shoes."

"Lie. You looked like a deer in headlights. You were scared shitless."

"Oh, all right," she conceded grudgingly. "I was . . . observing."

"You were overwhelmed. Just like I was, the first time I went to their house."

"*You* were?"

"It took me a long time to get used to that crazy family. And by the way, if you want to hold on to me, I have lots of other parts you'd like better."

Miranda turned loose his fingers. As Parker gave her a suggestive half-grin, she ignored it and kept talking.

"I wanted to go in," she admitted. "It was just so wonderful, and everyone was so comfortable with each other. Like one big happy family. And I wanted to be part of it, but . . ."

Her excuse trailed off. This was getting too personal, and she didn't understand why she was feeling so anxious all of a sudden, so edgy and sentimental. Besides that, she knew Parker would just make fun of her if she said any more.

"But I'm *not* part of it." The words were out before she could stop them. "Not really. I mean, I actually *had* those things in my old life, but they're gone now. Like they never even happened. And I hear you all talking about when you were kids, and I hear all the memories you share with each other. The five of you have a history together. You have all these private jokes and little rituals. You know each other better than anyone else ever will. Who wouldn't want that? To be a part of that?"

But Parker didn't joke. For a split instant, Miranda sensed a heaviness about him—a deep, sudden plunge into troubling thoughts. And when he finally *did* speak again, his voice was low and very serious.

"My family was never like Ashley's," he explained hesitantly. "No jokes . . . no pets . . . forget the noise and laughing. No happy, old-fashioned family dinners . . . though Imogene—our cook—*does* make some pretty great jambalaya once in a while. And God forbid anybody should ever hug." He gave a mock shudder. "The first time I went home with Ashley, I wanted to turn and run like hell, just like you wanted to. It was, like, totally foreign to me. I thought they were all insane. Almost made me not want to ask her out."

"You never went over there till you asked Ashley out? Never in all those years?"

"I wasn't here all those years, Miranda. My folks lived in St. Yvette, but I was stuck away in boarding schools. Which I consistently got thrown out of." He paused, looking proud of himself. "I didn't start school here till eighth grade."

"So when did you get together with Ashley?"

"Two years ago." Another wink, more sly this time. Back to his usual self. "She wanted me. Bad."

"Uh-huh."

"Yeah," he insisted, puffing out his chest, "she did. She chased me for months, but I kept playing hard to get. Finally, I felt sorry for her and let her catch me."

As Miranda reached over and shoved him, a wide grin spread across his face. "Yeah, she's lucky, all right. But *major* pressure on *me*."

"What do you mean?"

"Are you kidding? If I ever hurt Ashley, don't you think Gage and Etienne would come after me and hunt me down? Hell, they'd cut me up in little pieces and throw me in the bayou. And that's not even *half* the suffering Roo would put me through."

A look of extreme horror before his grin began to fade.

And then unexpectedly, his features went still once more, and thoughtful, and he gazed full into Miranda's face.

"It's this thing between them, you know. The four of them. This bond they have. Growing up together like they did . . . that history you were talking about."

For a while, both of them were quiet. And a question was forming in Miranda's mind—a possibility that she'd never even considered before now.

"Parker," she mumbled at last, "are you saying that *you* still feel like an outsider sometimes?"

He stopped abruptly. In the drawn-out silence, Miranda felt his embarrassed discomfort, those defensive walls going up again, that cocky irreverence slamming back into place. He leaned toward her with deliberate slowness, his eyes narrowed, his face perfectly deadpan.

"I'm saying that if you tell Ashley *one word* about the beers I had tonight, there will be *no* place in the universe you can hide from me. Got it? Now, where's your damn car?"

It *did* seem like they'd been walking quite a distance. . . that they should have reached the parking lot by now. Unconsciously, Miranda sped up, trying to match Parker's long strides. He was going faster, and she began to have the oddest feeling that the two of them had passed this way already, just moments ago. Nervously, she scanned the edges of the pathway, where thick shadows drew back from the light. If she didn't know better, she could almost swear that even those shadows looked familiar. . . .

That's stupid . . . doesn't even make sense. . . .

A ripple of fear crept up her spine.

"What the hell . . ." Parker muttered under his breath, then sliced the darkness right to left with his flashlight beam.

Miranda hadn't noticed any fog out here before—yet a thin, gray mist had materialized out of nowhere . . . swirling softly, seductively, along the path . . . enclosing them all around.

The fear inside her was turning cold. Instinctively, she reached out and touched Parker's arm. "Are we lost?"

"Lost? Of course we're not lost, how the hell could we be lost? Come on."

But the forced confidence in his voice wasn't convincing, and once more Miranda hurried to keep up with him. *He's right—there's absolutely no way we could be lost—the path only goes in one direction, between the parking lot and the house; there's no possible way we could have wandered off track without knowing—*

And yet she had the distinct sensation of going in circles . . . winding back and forth . . . retracing their own steps over and over again. An endless loop outside of time and space and—

"Shit!" Parker stopped so abruptly that Miranda ran into him from behind. She didn't even notice when he reached back to steady her, then drew her quickly, protectively to his side. "No way," he croaked. "That's impossible."

She could see now what he was gawking at. Through the rapidly vanishing fog, through the swiftly opening curtains of moss—*oh my God, we're right back where we started!*—Belle Chandelle looming high above them, silent and watchful, cold and black as the night . . .

No . . . not *quite* black.

That window . . . that window in the attic . . .

It should have been empty, Miranda told herself. That third-story dormer window should have been empty, as empty as the room locked up tight on the other side of it. And yet something was moving beyond it. Something flickering beyond it . . . gliding slowly, deliberately from side to side . . . a candle carried by an unseen hand . . .

"You see that," Miranda whispered. "My God, Parker . . ."

For one brief instant, the movement stopped. And then . . . without warning . . . a vague silhouette appeared within the window frame. Invisible eyes watching them from the dark. Invisible eyes, brimming with purpose and pain and terror . . .

As Parker squeezed her shoulders, Miranda clutched tightly at his hand.

The window went blank.

The moss settled softly back into place . . . the night went eerily still.

"Parker," she whispered again. "She knows. She knows we're here—"

Her words broke off as he grabbed her. As he grabbed her arm and began dragging her down the path, even while Miranda stubbornly kept talking.

"Parker, you saw her too—"

"You're crazy," he grumbled, yanking her harder, though Miranda tried to twist free.

"Don't pretend you didn't just see that! Just like you saw something out here the other night—in the very same window! Except you thought Aunt Teeta was up there, you thought she had a lantern, but it wasn't her at all—"

"Knock it off, Miranda. You don't know what I saw or didn't see—what, are you communicating with my eyeballs now?"

"I *asked* her, Parker. *Aunt Teeta wasn't up there.* Nobody goes up there except the workmen; it's too dangerous—"

"Christ, what's with this stupid path? If you hadn't been babbling forever, and if that damn fog hadn't come—"

"Well, do you see any fog now? No! Admit it, you can't explain what we just experienced! So tell me what's going on with you—"

"Nothing's going on with me. Besides the fact that I can't *think* because *you* won't shut *up*!"

"You know I won't say anything to anyone. And—"

"Holy crap—look." As Parker halted midstride, Miranda was finally able to break loose. She saw the lurch of his flashlight beam and the roof of Aunt Teeta's car illuminated beneath it.

"The parking lot," she murmured. "We're back at the parking lot."

"Get in the car."

"But—"

"Get in your damn car, Miranda."

He had her elbow in a viselike grip. He snatched her keys from her hand, then opened the door and thrust her behind the steering wheel.

"Go on." Reaching in, he started the engine. He slammed the door and jerked his thumb at the gate. "Go home."

But Miranda couldn't give up now—she had to know. Before he could back completely away, she got the window down and clamped her fingers around his wrist.

"Please, Parker," she begged him. "I know you're upset about what just happened—"

"Upset? I'm not upset. There's nothing to be upset about, because nothing happened, so I'm definitely not upset—"

"You're the only one who sees some of the things I see. I need to know why—don't you understand how much it would help me? How much it would help both of us—"

"I don't need help. *You're* the one who needs help. I don't even know why we're arguing—"

"Parker, please talk about this with me, please tell me what's going on!"

Silence plunged between them. For an endless moment, Parker's eyes lowered, his features tense, his body rigid. And then he looked at her again. And slowly, methodically, began to uncurl each of her fingers from his arm.

"Jesus, Miranda, you ever consider pro wrestling? You got a hell of a grip there—"

"Parker—"

"I'm drunk tonight, remember? And the whole world is beer." Backing away, he made a mock bow, swept his arm in a grand gesture toward the road. "That's what I saw, Miranda. And by morning, it'll be just another hangover."

16

FOR THE SECOND TIME THAT WEEK, MIRANDA OVERSLEPT—which meant catching a ride with Aunt Teeta and being late for school. The whole campus was abuzz with the news of Ashley and Kurt Fuller's date. Once again, there were underground wagers being made on Parker's temper, but when Miranda saw him in first period, he seemed resigned, almost quiet. Though a few jokes were tossed his way, he deflected them with his usual wit, and—best of all, Miranda noted—he also seemed completely sober. Maybe he and Ashley had discussed the whole Win-a-Date matter earlier. She certainly hoped so.

At lunchtime—and with Gage's help—she filled the others in on the latest happenings and theories regarding Belle Chandelle. Etienne wasn't at school, and Parker offered no comments about visions, speculations, or anything else. Roo listened intently while pinching the batter off her French-fried onion rings. And Ashley, despite her usual enthusiasm for the plantation, had a hint of sadness in her smile.

"Is Ashley upset about the contest?" Miranda asked Roo on their way back to class.

"Kind of. She wouldn't talk to anybody yesterday after she found out."

"Not even you?"

Roo shook her head. "She locked herself in her room after cheerleading practice. I think she really dreads this stupid date, but she doesn't want to upset Parker. So she's trying to make the best of it."

"And Parker's trying to make the best of it for her?"

"Since when do I know what Parker's trying to do?"

"What about the game tonight? Do you think there's going to be trouble?"

"I'm sure the coach knows exactly what's going on. He'll probably threaten Parker and Kurt at practice."

Sighing, Miranda shifted her books to her other arm. "So when's the date, do you know?"

"Tomorrow night. He's taking her to an outdoor concert." Then, when Miranda drew a blank, Roo added, "Not here. In Moss Bridge—it's about an hour away."

"Well, that seems pretty platonic, doesn't it? Music, fresh air, lots of people around?"

Roo's tone was flat. "Hello? An hour away? If she wants to come home in a hurry, she can't."

"Why would you even say that? Are you *expecting* she'll want to come home in a hurry?"

"Look. Everybody says how nice Streak is. And nice guys are usually really boring on dates. Would you want to be stuck for hours and hours with some totally nice, boring guy, and you can't escape?"

"*Gage* is nice. And *he's* not boring."

A knowing glance from Roo. "So you'd like to be stuck with Gage for hours and hours, and you can't escape?"

"Roo, that is *not* what I said, and you know it."

"Gage might surprise you, Miranda. You might not *want* to escape."

Flustered, Miranda steered the conversation back on track. "Well, I hope you're right about Kurt being boring. The situation's already tense enough without him making macho moves on Ashley."

"He won't," Roo assured her. "Not if he wants to live long enough to graduate."

The afternoon seemed to drag forever; Miranda couldn't wait for the day to be over with. By last period, she was so tired, she could hardly keep her eyes open, and she could hardly talk without yawning. Luckily, Miss Dupree's class always seemed to fly—mainly because the others were there with her.

She saw Roo come in and walk over to her place near the middle row, just opposite Gage's seat. Ashley sat directly across from Miranda, Parker closer to the front of the room. As Gage maneuvered toward his desk by the window, he tossed a small packet casually on top of Miranda's book.

"Etienne forgot to give you these."

"Oh, thanks. The stuff Mom asked me to take pictures of."

"Ghosts?" Roo asked loudly while Miranda tried to ignore a few curious glances. Gage smacked Roo on the head with his notebook.

"He said not," Miranda murmured.

Ashley peered over her shoulder. "That's disappointing," she whispered. "I was really hoping something would show up in there to help us."

Before Miranda could answer, Miss Dupree clapped her hands for attention.

"Okay, people, let's get started. Well, Gage, this is certainly wonderful—I see you've finally got that cast off."

Gage dropped into his seat as all eyes turned to him. He nodded politely and mumbled a reply.

"And how does it feel?" Miss Dupree asked.

"That's what we'd all like to know," Roo declared. "Let's all line up and touch it."

"Oh, me first!" Ashley waved her hand, winking at him.

The room exploded in laughter as Gage slid lower in his seat. Miss Dupree struggled to hold back a smile.

"All right, class, tempting as it is, Gage and his leg will *not* be the focus of our discussion today."

Boos from the girls now, cheers and insults from the guys. Looking relieved, Gage immediately opened his notebook.

Luckily, everyone's focus quickly switched to Miss Dupree and the handing out of study guides. But Miranda couldn't concentrate—just like the night before, her mind kept going back over the strange occurrences at Belle Chandelle. She tried her best to block it; she couldn't afford to fall further behind in class. The woman in the mirror . . . the children on the stairs . . . the faded glory of that long-ago house . . . *go away . . . leave me alone. . . .*

It was happening more and more, these intrusive images and questions. She could hardly think about anything else. She chewed on her pen, scribbled patterns through her notes. She glanced up to see Gage watching her. *He knows . . . he knows where my mind is.* She doubled her efforts to concentrate, but it didn't do any good. *Thank God it's Friday. Maybe this weekend I'll figure something out, find the right clues, end this once and for all.*

Growing more agitated, she shielded the photographs with her textbook and began flipping through them again. *Boring. Really boring. Boring to me, but just what Mom wanted—mantels, ceilings, tiles, floors, marks on walls, carvings, doors and windows, and—*

Miranda heard herself gasp.

A loud, audible sound, a sharp wheeze of cold air catching hard in her throat.

Her hand fluttered to her neck as though she might dislodge that gasp, push it back down. She wondered if anyone else had noticed, but then she saw Gage. Gage straightening in his desk, clear across the room, but stretching, as though he were trying to reach her. And the others, too: Ashley, face worried, hand already touching Miranda's arm; Parker frowning, puzzled; Roo swiveling around in her chair, that dark stare, not surprised—

"Oh God . . ." Miranda choked. "Oh my God . . ."

But how could they have known, she wondered—none of the other students seemed to have heard her, or seemed to have seen—just the group, just her friends, frozen in their places, while she gazed down at the photo that was trembling in her hand.

"You said no ghosts," she whispered, even though Etienne wasn't there to hear her. "That was what you said. *No ghosts.*"

But there *was* a ghost.

A ghost standing by the fireplace.

His body nearly transparent, part of the shadows, part of the fireplace he was next to, part of the wall above it, features pale and hazy and half-formed, yet she could see them all the same . . . and she *knew* that face, that spectral face, with eyes looking straight into the camera, and out of the photograph, and into her own—

"Grandpa . . ."

"I'm sorry, Miranda." Ashley was genuinely distressed. "I can't see him."

Gathered outside their classroom door, the others peered over Miranda's shoulder, scrutinizing the ghostly photograph.

Gage touched it lightly with his fingertip, sounding almost apologetic. "And he's here by the mantel?"

"Yes," Miranda insisted. "He's looking straight at the camera. He's standing right in front of the fireplace."

Roo's frown was puzzled. "Where in the house *is* that fireplace?"

"I don't know. I mean, there are so many rooms, and I went into all of them. I think each one had its own fireplace, and some of those bigger rooms had two or three. I'll have to go through the whole house and look again."

Ashley gave her a consoling hug. "Maybe Etienne will recognize it. Or your mom or aunt Teeta."

"Yeah, maybe." But even to herself, Miranda wasn't convincing. Once more she stared down at the photo; once more she racked her brain, trying to recall where that fireplace might be. "I need to find it. I *have* to find it. He's trying to tell me something, I know. Either about that mantel, or about the room it was in."

"He wanted you to see him, Miranda," Ashley said quietly. "Even if we can't."

"But think about what this means," Roo said matter-of-factly, taking the picture from Miranda, squinting at it through her bangs. "The intelligence this shows. The awareness—not just of *his* world, but *yours*. Your grandfather knew you were there, knew you were taking the picture. He knew the exact second you shot the photo."

"And that ability to transpose," Gage murmured. "Stepping back and forth between his world and ours . . . with no effort at all."

In spite of herself, Miranda teared up. "Ever since he died, I've wondered. I mean, I know he helped me before with the spirits of Nathan and Ellena, but I hadn't felt him around me since then. And now . . . with this . . . I do think maybe he's watching over me."

"He is," Gage's hand slid to her shoulder, gently squeezed. "Sure, he is."

"See?" Catching Parker off guard, Ashley, jabbed him in the stomach. Parker woofed out a startled breath.

"See what? Damn, Ashley!"

"There is *no* way you can deny now that ghosts exist, Parker Wilmington. After *not* seeing Miranda's grandpa in this picture."

As Parker's brow furrowed, he shot a bewildered look at Gage. Gage hid a smile and shrugged.

"So there," Gage told him.

"Perfect logic, as usual," Roo mumbled.

"Thank you," Ashley said. "I have to go to practice."

"Yeah, me, too." Still looking slightly befuddled, Parker followed Ashley down the corridor, while Miranda turned back to Roo.

"Are you going to the football game tonight?" Miranda asked her.

Roo's tone was derisive. "I don't do football games." Then pausing, she considered. "Though it might actually be worth it to see Parker and Kurt annihilate each other."

"Are you kidding, they'll be on their best behavior," Gage assured them.

"How do you know?"

"First, Coach will be watching them like a hawk. And second—if I know Parker, he's saving up everything till *after* Ashley's date."

"Good point. So where are you off to now?"

"Locker. Meet you outside."

As Gage went in the opposite direction, the two girls headed for the exit. There weren't many students lingering this afternoon; with no school tomorrow, the hallways and campus had already cleared out. Digging into the top of her boot, Roo immediately withdrew a crumpled pack of cigarettes and an even more crumpled book of matches. She shifted her backpack to her other shoulder, barely breaking stride.

"Miss Nell invited me for Sunday dinner," Miranda blurted. She hadn't planned to; it just popped out before she realized.

Roo, however, looked anything but surprised. "Wow. I can't believe you kept it in this long."

"You knew?"

Rolling her eyes, the girl shot Miranda a sidelong glance. "Don't be nervous. She'll make you feel right at home."

"I'm not nervous—"

"And this is a really good thing you're doing, by the way. Seeing where he lives . . . where he grew up . . . what he's all about." She pursed her lips, seemed to be carefully choosing her words. "I'm not sure I can even explain it—Etienne's world. But I think you'll realize, once you're out there. I think you'll get it."

"You mean . . . sort of like Etienne's territory?"

Roo gave a snort of amusement. "Wherever Etienne happens to *be*, that's his territory. Don't worry, you'll figure it out. Oh . . . and did I happen to mention—don't be nervous?"

"Yes, you did, and I'm not."

"If you say so."

"Just . . . kind of surprised, that's all."

"Miss Nell likes you, Miranda."

"She doesn't even know me. I've only talked to her three times in my whole life." Then, when Roo didn't answer, Miranda added softly, "I like *her*, too."

"Yeah, she's special." A smile played over Roo's mouth. "I remember the very first time I ever met her. She'd brought Etienne over to Gage's house, and we were all out playing in the wading pool, and she sprayed us with the hose. Etienne tried to drown Gage, and then she took us to get ice cream."

"Etienne tried to drown Gage?" Miranda chuckled.

"No . . . wait. I think that was *me* trying to drown Gage."

"That sounds a lot more accurate."

Roo shrugged, clearly untroubled by her homicidal past. "We must have been about five. That's when Gage moved in next door."

"Really? I thought you and Etienne were friends way before then."

"No, he never went to preschool or kindergarten—Ashley and I didn't even know him. But after Gage moved here from Mississippi, Etienne started coming over to their house, so that's when we really got to be friends. Ash and I were so excited to have this new kid next door to play with—and then it was even better, because his cousin would be there too. We had so much fun . . . all of us running and screaming and rolling around in the backyard."

Miranda lapsed into silence. It was easy to picture younger versions of Roo and Ashley and Gage—the three of them roughhousing, teasing, playing games. But not Etienne . . . *so hard to envision Etienne as a carefree child . . .*

"Was he ever happy?" she asked Roo now. "Etienne, I mean. I've never even seen him smile. And I certainly can't imagine him laughing."

"He used to laugh. He still does sometimes."

"I bet it's a nice laugh."

"Deep . . . sexy . . . kind of hoarse. Definitely worth waiting for." Slowing down, Roo pulled out the very last cigarette, stuffed the empty packet in her boot. "I remember I got this detective kit once for my birthday—it had these very cool handcuffs, strong for a toy, you know? They looked really authentic."

"Uh-oh." Miranda braced herself. "Do I even want to hear this?"

But Roo kept right on, her expression perfectly composed. "So I put the handcuffs on Etienne, and he could *not* get out of those things. Gage and Ash and I tickled him till he was totally exhausted. He couldn't move. He couldn't even *breathe*."

"Etienne playing, laughing, *and* ticklish? No way, you're making it up."

"Ash thought Etienne was dead. She started crying and ran in the house to get Mom." Despite her solemn tone, Roo's dark eyes had begun to sparkle. "Naturally, I figured I'd get in trouble, so I told Mom I'd lost the key. That made Etienne mad, and he swung at me, so I punched him and tickled him harder."

Miranda burst out laughing. As Roo paused to light up, there was a sly hint of mischief on her face.

"Mom was fussing, Gage and Ashley were trying to pull me off, and Etienne was cursing in French at the top of his lungs."

"Poor Etienne! What happened to him?"

"Dad finally ended up cutting those handcuffs off."

"So did you ever figure out where you lost the key?"

"I didn't lose it." Roo took a long drag on her cigarette. "I put it down the front of Etienne's pants."

"You didn't!"

"Yeah." Roo was looking more and more smug at the memory. "Etienne's ticklish, all right. And in some really . . . *fun* . . . places."

"Roo!"

"I sure wish I still had those handcuffs."

Both girls dissolved into laughter. As they neared the gate by the parking lot, Roo plopped down on a wooden bench, crossed her legs, and seemed immensely pleased with herself. Groaning, Miranda leaned against the fence and tried to catch her breath.

"You'll see him," Roo said suddenly, seriously, as Miranda regarded her in confusion.

"See who?"

"Etienne. You're worried about him being happy. He's happy sometimes. One of these days you'll see it."

The mood had changed so quickly that Miranda was caught off guard. Roo took another deep puff on her cigarette, held it in the V of her fingers, studied it thoughtfully.

"I watch them sometimes, him and Gage. I can see them from my bedroom window, when they don't know I'm there. Just hanging out, the two of them. Shooting hoops or playing with Jazz . . . working on Etienne's truck. They're so cute, you know? Laughing and goofing around like two kids."

Another long drag. Another moment of reflection.

"Etienne's relaxed then, just being himself. His guard's down. Like . . . he's free."

Miranda's eyes stung with tears. Surprised at Roo's sentimentality. Surprised at her own reaction.

"It's nice," Roo said quietly.

"What's nice?"

Startled, the girls saw Gage approaching, just a few feet away. Neither had noticed him coming. As Miranda straightened and waved, Roo drew herself up, bland expression resumed.

"You," she informed him, "when you loan me money for cigarettes."

"Forget it."

"We were just talking about childhood," Miranda said quickly. "Well . . . your childhood."

"Mine?"

"Ours," Roo clarified. "When we were all little. Miranda thinks it's hilarious, for some weird reason."

The girls exchanged glances, hid smiles.

"Just dumb stuff," Miranda added.

Shrugging, Gage lifted his can of root beer and took a swig. "Dumb stuff, huh? Then it must have been about Roo."

"Actually, we were talking about games." Roo looked up at him, innocent. "Why don't you tell Miranda how we all used to hold you down and—"

"There's Etienne." Whatever memory Roo had triggered, it was clearly not one that Gage wanted to share. "Come on."

"Why don't you tell her how we *still* hold you down and—"

Roo's words gasped off. As Miranda watched in stunned silence, Gage poured a slow stream of root beer over the top of Roo's head.

"Hurry up," Gage said, his tone now as innocent as Roo's. "Etienne's waiting." Crumpling the can in his fist, he pitched it into the exact center of the trash barrel, then left through the gate. "See you, Miranda."

Roo blinked a few times. Ran her palm slowly across her forehead . . . shoved her wet bangs from her eyes. As Gage climbed into the truck, Etienne leaned out the window and shook his head at Roo, a smile tugging one corner of his mouth.

"Be sure and get yourself cleaned up, *cher*. I don't want you dripping all over my fancy seats in here."

The sound of Gage's laughter. The radio turning up loud.

"Oh, Roo." Trying desperately to be sympathetic, Miranda was already digging in her bag. "I think I have some tissues in here somewhere—"

"I don't need tissues. Tissues would be admitting defeat." Shaking her head, Roo gazed at her fizzled cigarette. With complete dignity, she got to her feet, then stomped her cigarette under her boot. "I will track him down. Slowly and methodically. He will never see me coming; the ambush will be swift, silent, and complete. I am . . . *Anaconda Woman*."

Try as she might, Miranda could no longer keep from grinning. She could see Aunt Teeta's car now, pulling up in the driveway, so she followed Roo out to the parking lot.

"By the way," she called, before Roo quite reached the truck. "About that handcuffs thing."

It worked, obviously—just the distraction Roo needed. Even from where she stood, Miranda saw her friend's shoulders move with stifled laughter.

"What about it?" Roo called back.

"I was just wondering . . . have you ever tortured him since?"

"In my deepest, darkest fantasies."

"Only there?"

Roo stared at her. Arched an eyebrow. Gave a slow, catlike smile. "Wouldn't you like to know."

17

Miranda hadn't told anyone that she was going out to Belle Chandelle again after school. She planned to go through the house with a fine-tooth comb, if necessary—and discover the truth about the photograph. All this time, the mysterious and frightening things that had happened to her had left her feeling confused and frustrated and helpless. But now, thanks to Grandpa, she felt strengthened. She hadn't been sure where to start before, she'd felt sabotaged by dead ends—but now she had hope. Direction. Jonas Hayes, her grandfather, had shown up in the photograph with wisdom in his eyes, *conviction* in his eyes, looking straight into her mind and her heart. Miranda *knew* that he had a message for her. Something crucial, something that would help *her* help those poor, tormented *others.*

Remember this, Miranda. The next time you doubt that Grandpa is with you, remember this—how he's contacting you, how he's guiding you.

It gave her a new sense of purpose. Even on the boring trip, while Aunt Teeta drove and chatted the entire way, Miranda was deep in her own thoughts, trying to tune in to her grandfather's message. *What is it, Grandpa? What are you trying to tell me?* When they finally got to the house, she cautiously showed the photo to Mom and Aunt Teeta, asking them if there was anything about it that they recognized. Luckily, neither of them noticed the spirit of Jonas Hayes—*unluckily*, neither of them could quite remember the fireplace.

"I'm sorry, honey," Mom told her. "There are so many around here, and memorizing them all just hasn't been high on my priority list. Is this one important for some reason?"

"I just . . . really like the carving along the top."

"That's odd," Lifting her glasses, Aunt Teeta peered more closely at the picture. "I can't recall a single mantelpiece around here being this clean. Everything we've seen so far is in terrible shape. Layers and layers of gunk to scrape through."

"All these photos you took are great." Mom was sincerely delighted. As she pulled them from Miranda's hand, Miranda grabbed the one photo back again.

"Okay if I hang onto this awhile? I'd like to find that fireplace, if I can."

"Well, you really captured those details I wanted, honey. While you're going back through the house, maybe you'll notice something else interesting . . . take some more pictures for me."

Yes, I might find something interesting, Mom—but I doubt if you'd want to see it. . . .

"I'm leaving pretty soon, darlin'." Aunt Teeta gave Miranda a hug. "So be sure and catch a ride home with your mama. Or Etienne, if you can find him. I don't think he's working here today, but Nell is, so he might be around somewhere. And take a flashlight when you go off exploring. The sun's setting earlier now—when dark comes, it comes fast."

Miranda had no desire to be crawling through Belle

Chandelle after sunset. For the next few hours, she worked her way along the upstairs galleries as quickly as she could, checking every room, trying to finish before nightfall. Like the changing weather outside, the rooms felt damp and wind-chilled. She soon realized that Aunt Teeta's observation was true—the details of the fireplace in the photograph were sharp and clear, while the other fireplaces in the house were sadly inconspicuous due to years of neglect. Mantels lay shrouded in dust, their intricate carvings plastered over with grime. Many had been damaged, chipped, gouged, worn down, burnt by careless fires and flying embers. Inspecting each one, comparing it to her photograph, was a slow and painstaking process. When she finally stopped long enough to check her watch, she couldn't believe how late it was.

Tired, thirsty, and covered with dirt, she decided to make a trip to the kitchen. The place was empty when she arrived, though it looked as if Miss Nell had been there most of the day. Curious, Miranda decided to explore—she found sweet tea in the fridge, poured herself a big glass, and started looking around, poking through cupboards and drawers, examining bins and canisters and cabinets, flipping through the growing stack of cookbooks that Miss Nell must have brought. On one wall was a neatly camouflaged walk-in freezer that she hadn't noticed before; on another wall, the door to a pantry stood open, revealing row upon row of shelves and extra storage space. Miranda stepped into the pantry. And as she heard the door swinging shut behind her, she also heard voices coming into the kitchen.

She realized at once who it was—Miss Nell, Gage, and

Etienne. The boys had probably come to take Miss Nell home, Miranda figured—and they were obviously giving her a hard time about something. Miss Nell was fussing at them and laughing. The refrigerator opened and closed. Ice was dispensed, drinks were poured, food was unwrapped. More teasing then, more fussing.

Very cautiously, Miranda inched the door forward and peered out through the crack. She felt silly hiding in here, but she felt even more awkward announcing herself to the little group out there. From this vantage point, she could see one wide angle of the kitchen—Miss Nell busy at the sink; Gage sitting on the counter, legs dangling, hands tucked beneath his thighs; Etienne lazily straddling backward on a chair. There was a plate of cookies on the table behind him, a huge bowl of chips beside Gage.

"How many times I gotta tell you, Mama," Etienne was saying. "Me and Gage, we got everything under control."

"He's right, Aunt Nell," Gage insisted. "I've done those swamp tours a million times—I can do them in my sleep. I can do them anytime y'all need me to. So stop worrying."

"These aren't good months for business anyway. Not like the phone's ringing off the hook."

"And when tourist season rolls around again, we'll both be out of school."

"Let it go, Mama. You got all this new fun stuff going on in your life—you should be enjoying it."

For the first time, his mother turned slightly, shot him a mild frown over her shoulder. "I just don't think my being here is fair.

You work way too much as it is. You won't cook for yourself, you hardly eat . . . just look at you."

Etienne angled back, spread his arms wide, ran his eyes down to his feet. "I'm looking. Damn, it's a pretty sight."

"Pretty unimpressive," Gage said.

"Oh, yeah? I hear you were almost Miss Dupree's special class project today."

"What's that?" Miss Nell asked.

But before Gage could protest, Etienne quickly cut him off. "All the girls, they're still fussing over that leg of his. 'Oh, poor Gage . . . here, let me make it all better.' "

Gage shook his head. Tossed some chips into his mouth. Spoke around a mouthful of crunch. "When did Roo tell you that?"

"How you know it was Roo?"

"Who else would it be?"

"Maybe it was Miranda." Standing in one smooth motion, Etienne sidled up close to his cousin, leaned down to speak into his ear. "Umm, and I bet she could make it feel all better."

Gage reached out to shove him. As Etienne neatly sidestepped, he bumped into Miss Nell, who good-naturedly pushed him off and resumed adding sudsy water to her dishpan. Even with her back turned, the woman wasn't missing anything, Miranda suspected. Not a single movement or facial expression or under-breath comment from either of her two boys.

"See, Mama, he always goes ten shades of red when I talk about Miranda. I'm thinking he's in love."

"You don't know anything," Gage grumbled.

"Me, I know everything. Why you getting so defensive on me, anyhow?"

"You're the one who's always coming on to her. You and all your 'Me, I'm this big hot stud, yeah' bullshit."

Etienne was all innocence. He planted his feet wide apart, then once more swept his arms out to his sides. "Me, I'm just proud of my heritage, yeah?"

"Yeah." With a derisive snort, Gage nodded at the front of Etienne's jeans. "Proud of your heritage. Right."

Etienne aimed a punch at Gage's abdomen; Gage blocked it with his elbow. Miss Nell, moving back and forth around them to wipe the countertops, looked amused and acted as if this sort of behavior happened on a regular basis.

"Just tell her, Gage," Etienne persisted.

"Tell who what?"

"Miranda." Casually, Etienne wandered back to the table . . . studied the plateful of cookies. He chose the biggest one and stuffed it in his mouth, chewing thoughtfully. "Just tell her how you're feeling. Get it off your . . . chest. And . . . other places."

"Shut up."

"You boys better mind the way you treat Miranda," Miss Nell said. Her admonishment was firm—and obviously unexpected—judging from the guys' startled reactions.

Etienne was the first to recover. "Aw, Mama, we're just kidding—"

"I'm not kidding. I'm serious. She's a sweet girl. And she has a tender heart."

"But—"

"No buts. I don't want her hurt, you understand? She deserves . . . gentleness and . . . respect."

Gage and Etienne grew sober now . . . exchanged puzzled glances.

"Miranda's special. She—" Breaking off, Miss Nell stared down at her hands, at her fingers clasped tightly in front of her, twisted in the folds of the dishtowel.

"Mama . . ." Etienne murmured, but the woman quickly shook her head.

"Nothing." Lifting her eyes, Miss Nell stared at each of the boys in turn. Then her voice went quiet . . . almost sad. "She just reminds me of someone, that's all."

"Who, Mama?"

The awkward moment was gone. Miss Nell drew herself up, gave her dishtowel a dismissive flap. "Just someone I used to know—it doesn't matter."

"Aunt Nell—"

"The point is, and as I was saying," she continued, forcing a laugh, "I can just tell that Miranda is a very special girl. And that she deserves the very best. Like the two of you, God help me."

Tears burned in Miranda's eyes. All the while she'd been eavesdropping, her feelings had been in turmoil—surprise and embarrassment, excitement and happiness, shyness and confusion—from the things Gage and Etienne had said about her, to their gentle reprimand from Miss Nell. Miranda had never expected to hear herself being talked about; she didn't understand why Miss Nell had even brought it up. She only knew that the woman's emotions were sincere, and that Gage and Etienne had listened. And that she was deeply touched by what she'd just overheard.

With Miss Nell's lecture concluded, the mood lightened once again. Good-natured banter, jokes flying, cousins doing their best to one-up the other. The next time Miranda peeped out, both guys were leaning against the counter, propped back on their elbows, long legs stretched out and crossed. With Miss Nell wedged in between them, they slyly squeezed in tighter, exchanging winks over the top of her head.

Startling, the two boys' resemblance—it never failed to amaze Miranda when she saw them up close, side by side. Those high cheekbones, lanky frames, and dark good looks. Yet what was even more apparent was the stark contrast in their eyes—one soulful and sensitive, the other suspicious and blatantly defiant. Two different childhoods . . . two different worlds . . . As their bodies finally nudged Miss Nell out of place, the woman gave Etienne a playful swat on his backside; she lay one hand gently on Gage's hair. And watching them, Miranda could almost swear that Etienne's expression grew troubled.

"You feel okay, Mama?" he said seriously. "You're looking kinda tired."

"I'm no such thing." Stepping back, his mother motioned vaguely toward the outside door. "I need to run in the house for a second. Honey, are y'all in a hurry to leave?"

Gage shook his head. "Take your time."

"I won't be long, I promise. Why don't y'all take a walk or something." A suggestive wink. "Go and find Miranda."

The boys shrugged at each other, mock dismay. And stayed where they were.

The change in Etienne was almost immediate when Miss Nell left the room. Gage, staring solemnly at him, seemed to already know what he was going to say.

"Mama keeps saying she likes it," Etienne began. "She keeps on saying she's really liking it here—"

"She does," Gage assured him. "I heard her talking to Mom. She has energy. She feels good. She's doing something she really loves. Truth? I think she's happier than she's been in a long time."

"I don't know, Gage . . . I just . . ."

Gage pushed himself away from the counter. Stood in front of Etienne and peered intently into his face.

"Are you worried you're doing something wrong by letting her work here? It's a hell of a lot better than the tours . . . and so what if she spends long hours on her feet or at the stove? It's something she's passionate about. And you . . ." Gage paused, thought a moment, chose his words carefully. "You've got to let her live some kind of life. You've got to . . . let her have some kind of purpose to it . . . while . . ."

While she can. The words hung silent between them, so palpable that Miranda felt them too. *While she can . . . while there's time . . .*

What happened that day, Miss Nell? When I came in here to the kitchen, when you looked so sick and pretended like nothing was wrong?

"She's in remission," Etienne mumbled, averting his eyes. Gage gave an agreeable shrug.

"I know that."

"She's feeling okay. She's doing really well."

"I know."

But Etienne's brow was creased in thought, and he seemed to be studying something on the kitchen floor.

"Hey, you're taking good care of her," Gage told him firmly. "Nobody could take better care of her than you do. Than you've always done. She knows that. We all know that."

The long silence was almost painful. At last Etienne ran a hand back through his hair; Gage jerked his chin in an "okay?" nod. Then the two of them turned and left the room.

Miranda waited awhile to make sure they weren't coming back. As touching as that first overheard conversation had been, this one between Gage and Etienne had affected her even more, reaching deep, deep into her heart. She felt strangely troubled by it, both moved and depressed, as she slipped from the pantry and went outside, systematically moving along the rear verandah, searching what rooms she could. Dusk had already fallen; she was glad she'd examined the upstairs first. Since some of the rooms were still without power, she knew it would be even harder to explore by flashlight—but she couldn't wait for tomorrow, she had to know now.

It's got to be the answer, Grandpa. The answer to what the spirits need. It must be, or you wouldn't have tried to show me.

But her luck down here was no better. Room by room, inspecting each fireplace, scraping away more grime, comparing it to the photograph. Feeling more frustrated by the minute, more lost and more bewildered. *Surely it's in this house—it has to be in this house, Grandpa's standing right here, right beside it, clear as day—damn, why can't I find it?*

But the house was shrouded in darkness now. She'd looked everywhere that she could think of; there were no more rooms to search.

Except . . .

Except for the attic.

She'd forgotten about the attic. Never even considered it. Because she hadn't taken pictures up there . . . because of the dangerous conditions . . . because of the locked door . . .

But it's the only room left. The only room where that fireplace could possibly be.

Miranda paused, thoughts racing. She'd come full circle on her search, returning to one of the front parlors. Through the half-open pocket doors she could hear a radio playing, papers rustling, and the soft humming of her mother's voice. *I'm almost sure this is where I came out that day, out of the hidden staircase.*

She moved as quietly as she could. But as she tried to sneak past the doorway, her mother's head came up, and the volume came down.

"Oh, Miranda, you scared me! I wondered where you were."

"Sorry, Mom. Still . . . exploring."

"Well, I'm trying to finish up here, so we can go home."

"Great." Forcing a smile, Miranda moved on past the threshold and out of sight, straight to the back of the room. "Let me know when you're ready."

"Oh—Gage and Etienne were here earlier. Picking up Nell. They were looking for you."

"Really?" *Over on this wall, I think . . . a hidden panel . . .*

"Nell certainly seems to like you a lot."

"She does?" *Right about here, if I remember . . .* "I like her a lot, too."

"What are you doing in there?"

"Just . . . finding more stuff to take pictures of."

"Wonderful! I can't wait to see everything!"

"Uh-huh." *Yes . . . here it is.*

Miranda's fingers worked quickly at the panel. After waiting for Mom's radio to turn up again, she opened the door and slipped cautiously inside.

Instant blackness. The passageway was so narrow that she stood for a moment, gathering her resolve. She switched on her flashlight, played it over the walls . . . steps . . . ceiling. Dust and cobwebs. Spiders. Water stains and wood rot and mildew. Mice had been here recently . . . and rats.

She hadn't remembered it being this bad before . . . *But I was trying to save those children and didn't notice . . .*

Shuddering violently, she started up.

Up and up the close, cramped stairwell . . . up to the very top floor. Her hand slid into her pocket, pulled out her set of keys. Her mouth had gone dry, and her heart was racing—she had no idea what she'd find on the other side of that attic door.

So far, so good. No children laughing . . . no awful smells . . .

Yet it looked just like it had the last time she'd seen it, was locked just as tight. She had to fumble through half a dozen keys before she finally found the right one. Then, hand trembling, she heard the latch click free and the door creaking inward . . . inch by painstaking inch . . .

Just an attic.

As the flashlight made another thorough sweep, she felt a wave of disappointment.

Nothing special . . . just a plain old attic.

And nothing in here at all.

She wasn't sure what she'd expected, exactly—certainly more than this enormous space; low-sloped ceilings; gaping holes in sections of the floor; broken windows covered with boards and tarps; more spiderwebs and animal droppings; trash and dampness and years of dirt. Tools lay everywhere; a set of unpainted French doors leaned against one wall. But no keepsakes or memories, no trunks or boxes or furniture left behind, not a single clue from a long-forgotten past.

And no fireplace.

Miranda felt a curious mixture of disappointment and relief.

She'd been so hopeful that she'd find that mantel in here, but instead there were only shadows and emptiness and strange echoes. . . .

Soft, distant echoes . . . my breathing . . . my heartbeat . . .

The attic was so hot. Too hot for the season, too hot for this time of night. *It wasn't this hot when I came in, I would have noticed.* She suddenly realized that she was moving across the floor. Her hands had begun to tremble, yet the beam from her flashlight held steady, fixed on those carelessly propped French doors. She set her flashlight down on the floorboards. She dragged the doors away from the wall. And when she saw what was there, it was hardly even visible, shrouded so thickly in dust and webs and mold, and just beyond reach of the light.

But Miranda recognized it.

She would have known it anywhere.

Pulse racing, she stood in front of the fireplace, running her hands gently across the mantel, over the stains and scars and soot, along the carved edges and intricate designs.

Reaching up . . . reaching higher . . .

Hands pressed flat now against the wall—*no, not a wall!*

Her fingers dragged through mats of cobwebs, thick as moss, tearing them down . . . and something moving there—*moving like I'm moving*—like a shadow-person, not real . . .

A silent scream froze on her lips. With shocked eyes, she gazed at herself in a dingy mirror and saw a pale light glowing behind her, though she knew the room was dark.

The smell came out of nowhere. Thick and foul, washing over her, drowning her, the swarming of flies, the stifling heat. In the mirror Miranda saw an iron bedstead against the wall, shadows licking across two little faces—terrified! so terrified!—tearstained, dark eyes dark hair so much the same, holding hands, soiled nightgowns, sweat-drenched covers—and the eyes of the woman, staring eyes, imploring eyes—*I know those eyes*—black dress black hair black cap . . . back and forth, in and out of flickering candlelight, in and out of shadows creaking, so quiet in her rocking chair, back and forth creaking, back and forth on the floorboards creaking, slower and slower and silent.

Oh God! bloodshot eyes, yellow skin—the stench of sickness, the stench of decay—

"*Mama*"—the little ones weeping, the little ones pleading—"*Mama, look at us. . . .*"

And the whole time, the mantel in the sickroom, the mirror over the mantelpiece, she could see herself, Miranda could see herself there, her own reflection, staring back at herself in horror—

But the smell was too much now, smothering her, choking deep in her throat. She couldn't breathe, couldn't move, couldn't even cry out—"*Mama, Mama,*" the children sobbing, barely above a whisper now, baby cries, dying cries . . . "*Look at us, Mama, we're right here—*"

Miranda fell to her knees.

She watched her own reflection reach for the two little children . . .

But the candle went out . . .

And the crying stopped.

18

"MIRANDA!" *Mom's voice.* "Miranda, honey, can you hear me?"

"What happened?" *Etienne?*

"I don't know! Honey, are you all right? Please answer me!" *Mom distraught.* "Maybe we should call 911—"

"No 911," Miranda mumbled. Opening her eyes, she immediately closed them again and turned her head away. "I thought there weren't any lights up here."

"What's she talking about?" *Mom.*

"I saw the fireplace . . . but they were all so sick."

"Oh my God. She's delirious."

"She's probably just confused." *Gage?* "I'll get some water."

"Yes, yes, in there. On my desk, there's some."

"Good idea," Etienne murmured.

No, bad *idea.* Miranda felt totally sick. Sick at heart, sick to her stomach, sick in her thoughts. She was afraid that if she opened her eyes again, she'd throw up—so she decided to lie there and keep them closed.

"I'm okay," she said at last, so they wouldn't think she'd died.

"You don't look okay." Etienne's tone was half teasing, half concerned. "Do you know where you are, *cher*?"

"The . . . attic?"

"The parlor. Do you know what happened?"

Yes . . . yes . . . I know, but it was so horrible, I don't want *to think about it. . . .*

"Here," Gage said gently. His hand on the back of her neck, the rim of a cup at her lips, cool liquid in her parched throat. She prayed that the water would stay down.

But Mom wasn't ready to be reassured. "Do you remember anything? Did you feel sick all of a sudden? Are you in pain anywhere?"

"No . . . I . . ." *What do you want me to say, Mom? Certainly not the truth, not when the truth is so unbelievable.* "I must have passed out or something." *But how did I end up in the parlor? And how did I get downstairs?*

This time Miranda did open her eyes. Embarrassed, she saw Gage and Etienne staring down at her. A look passed among the three of them, which her mother didn't catch and wouldn't have understood if she had.

"Tell her I'm okay," Miranda begged them.

"She's okay," the guys echoed.

Miranda promptly sat up, Gage holding one arm, Etienne the other. "See, Mom? Nothing to worry about. I was standing over by this wall and . . . and I . . . sort of felt dizzy and then . . . you know what? I bet it was the paint fumes."

"That's odd. I didn't notice any paint fumes." Shaking her head, Mom's expression grew tender. "Well, thank God you weren't in that stairwell. What if you'd passed out and fallen down all those steps? What if—"

"The steps aren't even straight, Mom. I'd have to be a stuntwoman to roll all the way down."

Again Miranda was embarrassed that the guys were watching all this. Etienne was standing to one side now, arms folded, left hand stroking the stubble on his chin. Gage was still squatting on the floor beside her, one arm draped across his knee, holding the cup just in case. Neither of them looked particularly eager to surrender her to Mom.

"No more work," Mom insisted firmly. "I'm taking you home."

"We can take her, if you like," Gage offered, but Mom was already heading for her makeshift office.

"No, I think I better take her. But maybe you two could help me get her to the car."

"Mom, for God's sake, I don't need any help," Miranda declared, face reddening. "I'm fine. Just let me sit here for a second."

Pausing, her mother let out a sigh of relief. "Thank you so much, boys. I can't believe you were here when this happened. Wasn't that lucky!"

"Aunt Nell forgot her purse," Gage explained. "We came back to get it."

"Now, honey, don't get up too fast," Mom warned, as Gage and Etienne reached down and hauled Miranda to her feet. "Don't want you passing out again."

Miranda was getting annoyed with all the fuss. She tried to push the guys away, but both of them held on to her till they were convinced that she could walk.

They knew, of course.

She could see it on their faces, read it in their eyes—both of them knew what had happened to her, and that it didn't have the slightest thing to do with dizziness or paint fumes. That she had just gone somewhere, heard things, seen people, that none of the rest of them could ever experience or begin to comprehend.

They all said good night in the parking lot. Miranda managed to hold it together during the ride back to town, and even keep up appearances after she and Mom got home. It wasn't till after she went upstairs and closed the door to her room that she finally broke down.

The tragic memory still clung to her. The memory of that awful room, the stink of sweat and urine and vomit and blood . . . the endlessly creaking rocking chair . . . the plaintive sobs of the two little girls, clinging to each other in their bed . . .

Over and over, she tried to shut them out, force them away. Over and over, they crept stealthily back, into the dark, shadowy recesses of her mind, into the raw, tender places of her heart. . . .

Is this really what you wanted me to see, Grandpa? For this scene was so horrific that she almost felt betrayed. *You're supposed to be protecting me. Looking after me. Why did you let me walk into that?*

The pain of it was too deep, too overwhelming. The helplessness she felt, the outrage—even though she still didn't know the story behind what she'd witnessed, even though she still didn't know the truth. *Or what I'm supposed to do about it*, she reminded herself grudgingly.

She lay facedown on her pillows and cried. Unaware when she drifted . . . unaware when the stealthy figure slipped across the sunporch and through the door . . . pausing beside her bed . . . standing there to watch her. From some faraway realm of slumber, she felt the bedsprings give as he sat down . . . felt his hand, strong and protective, on her back.

"Etienne?" she murmured.

He whispered to her. Words in his soft, magical language that she didn't understand but loved hearing, *needed* hearing. His hands moved in slow, calming circles over her back. After her first trembling intake of breath, she felt herself warm and relax beneath his touch.

"So why didn't you wait for us, *cher*?" he finally asked. "Why didn't you wait for me or Gage to be with you?"

"Because I didn't know it was going to happen," she said truthfully. She paused as his hands slid gently to her waist. "And I certainly didn't *plan* for it to happen. I mean . . . I thought of the attic, I thought maybe the fireplace might be there, but the woman and—" Breaking off, she gave a humorless laugh. "You don't even know what I'm talking about, do you?"

"You'd be surprised what I know." A smile in his voice, as gentle tonight as his touch. "Gage, he told me about the picture. So your *grandpère*, he's looking after you, yeah? You can't be doubting that now."

"Looking after me? By making me go into the hell where I went tonight?"

"Guiding you, then. So you can be looking after all those other ones . . . all those spirits depending on you."

Miranda made a sound of disgust deep in her throat. She shifted slightly beneath his fingertips. "Why can't any of the scenarios be nice ones?"

"'Cause I'm guessing if they were nice, those spirits wouldn't be stuck here, needing your help."

"I guess not." Then, after a long silence, she murmured, "I knew you'd come tonight."

"Yeah? Guess I'll have to work on that, then—I'm getting a little too predictable."

"Can you . . . will you . . . hold me?"

"That's what I'm here for."

He stretched out beside her, wrapping her in his arms, his touch cautious, his body still. No intensity tonight—none of the longing that he could so effortlessly make her feel. Instead, he knew instinctively what she needed. The two of them lay silently side-by-side, pressed close. Miranda rested her cheek against him, traced her fingertips back and forth across his chest. His heart beat strong and slow. From time to time he reached over and smoothed her hair back from her face . . . lingered a kiss on her forehead. Miranda snuggled closer.

They stayed like that for a long time while the TV blared from downstairs and the sound of Aunt Teeta's snoring drifted up from the second floor. And gradually Miranda told him everything about the experience she'd had tonight, the horrifying scene she'd witnessed in the attic. Etienne stayed quiet, thinking, listening, staring at the ceiling. Then at last he turned his head and frowned at her.

"But it didn't happen right away, yeah? Just when you looked in the mirror?"

Hesitating, Miranda tried to remember. "That's right. After I found the fireplace and the mirror."

"And you were right there with them . . . in the room with them?"

"Not exactly. I was in the room, but I was seeing a *reflection* of the room. Like everything was happening behind me. You know . . . backward."

"And you didn't find out what they need? What you're supposed to do for them?"

"No. Or how I ended up downstairs again from the attic."

Another thoughtful pause. Then, "Maybe next time you will."

"Next time?" When she shuddered, he pulled her tighter, rubbed her arms, tried to warm her up. "Well, obviously I'm supposed to do *something*. So as much as I even hate to think about it, I'm pretty sure there *has* to be a next time."

"But not when your mama's around." Another hint of a smile. "You're scaring her way too much."

In spite of herself, Miranda chuckled. "Poor Mom. Totally clueless."

"That's good. Better keep her that way."

"Well, it's not like I passed out for the fun of it." And then, as the humor suddenly faded again, Miranda's mood went dark. "The children were dying, Etienne."

He didn't say anything this time, though his expression turned grim.

"Crying for their mother, but I knew they wouldn't live long. And she was in the rocking chair, not going to them. Staring at the room, but not going to them."

"Too painful, maybe? 'Cause she knew she couldn't help them?"

"Worn out? Remember I told you how worn out she looked in the mirror? Just exhausted . . . nothing left to give."

"And she'd have been plenty sad, yeah? Knowing she couldn't help them, that no matter what she did, they were gonna die anyway."

"But the room was a pigsty. I could smell blood and urine and vomit . . . it was hot, there were flies. Even if she knew they were going to die, she'd have kept the room clean for them."

Etienne considered this. "Unless she couldn't. Maybe she didn't have anybody to help her."

"She had the whole house. Servants."

"Maybe not. Maybe all the slaves were gone. Sold? Run away?"

"But why? That doesn't make sense—if the servants were gone, then why weren't she and the children gone too?"

Too sad, too depressing to think about. Closing her eyes, Miranda burrowed against Etienne, yet the unanswered questions kept nagging at her. They both heard the shrill ring of the telephone. As her mother called from the kitchen, Etienne jumped to his feet and prepared to flee.

"She won't come up," Miranda assured him. "Just stay here; I'll be right back."

She took the phone on the landing. She was all too aware of

Mom watching from the bottom of the steps, clutching a cup of coffee, and giving her a curious once-over.

"Look at you, honey—you should get your pajamas on. You look like you've been tossing and turning in those clothes."

"Good idea, Mom." Grimacing, Miranda picked up the phone. "Hello?"

"Hey, Miranda, it's Gage. Hope I wasn't interrupting anything."

"No. Of course not." Her face instantly flamed. Gage *couldn't* know Etienne was here—*could he*?

But Gage, as usual, was concerned and sincere. "I just wanted to make sure you're okay."

"I'm fine. Totally embarrassed, but fine."

"Come on, don't be. I think it's called an occupational hazard." He laughed softly, teasing her. Then his voice went serious once more. "Well . . . if you need anything. Anything at all. You've still got my number, right—and Etienne's?"

A twinge of guilt. No . . . *more* than a twinge of guilt, though she didn't want to address it at the moment. "Yes. Both."

"And whatever happened tonight . . . you're probably tired of hearing this by now, but you really *don't* need to go through it alone. I'm . . . you know . . . here. Always here."

Super guilt, and Miranda instantly melted. "I know. Thanks, Gage."

A brief pause before he cleared his throat. "Look, Roo and I were thinking, maybe breakfast Sunday morning? We can all meet and put our heads together—see what six great minds can come up with about Belle Chandelle."

"Where and what time?"

"The Tavern, as usual? Roo says she'll think a lot better with waffles."

"I love it there." Miranda chuckled. "And Roo's right—perfect food, perfect ideas."

"Okay if I come by for you about nine?"

"I'll be ready."

"Great. See you."

She hung up, imagining those soft brown eyes, that shy smile. *Not fair. Why do Gage and Etienne both have to be so perfect? And what the hell are you doing, Miranda?*

Hurrying upstairs, she slipped into her room and shut the door behind her.

"Etienne?"

But the bed was empty, and Etienne had gone.

Saturday was blissfully slow . . . wonderfully normal. Miranda declined her mom's offer to go out to the plantation—instead she stuck close to home. Caught up on all her missed schoolwork. Watched TV and ate a whole pan of brownies. Made a run to the grocery store, helped Aunt Teeta in the yard. She wondered about Ashley's date with Kurt. She wondered what she'd wear to Miss Nell's for Sunday dinner.

Ordinary things . . . routine things . . . *distracting things.*

Knowing the whole time that she needed to solve the mystery of Belle Chandelle, but not quite ready to face it yet.

Better to wait for the others' input . . . get the consensus of the whole group. Give her mind time to clear and calm down. Give her senses time to gear up again.

And stay away from mirrors. . . .

By evening she felt much better. Mom got home early, and they rented movies—the three of them in their jammies, sprawled comfortably around the den, having popcorn fights and laughing their heads off at old comedies. Miranda loved the being-togetherness of it all. She finally called it a night when both Mom and Aunt Teeta fell asleep—on the couch and easy chair respectively—and the last movie credits scrolled to the very end.

The phone rang on her way upstairs. Surprised, Miranda grabbed it, then glanced at the hallway clock. Midnight. *No, please . . . I can't take any more bad news. . . .*

But to her relief, it was Ashley. Sounding quiet and secretive and mildly upset.

"What happened?" Miranda immediately asked. Hurrying to her room, she shut the door and curled up in her bed. "You don't sound happy—did something happen on your date?"

A long silence. Miranda realized that she was holding her breath . . . fearing the worst. *Oh God, if Kurt tried something with Ashley, the guys are going to murder him.*

"Ashley? Tell me . . . what's wrong?"

"Nothing!" Ashley burst out. "That's just it! Nothing's wrong!"

"I . . . I don't—"

"It was *wonderful*, Miranda. I had a wonderful time . . . he was wonderful to me . . . it was just a wonderful, wonderful date."

Miranda groaned. Fell back into her pillows. "Tell me. Everything. Don't leave out a single detail."

"Can you hear me?" Ashley's voice had lowered again, nearly to a whisper. "I don't want Roo listening in."

"I thought you had separate rooms."

"We do. But you know how Roo is—she *knows* things. I don't want her hearing *any* of this."

"My lips are sealed. And I've got on my hearing aid."

Satisfied, Ashley recounted her entire evening. Kurt picking her up, bringing her flowers. Kurt opening her car door, helping her in. The nice things Kurt already knew about her, and Kurt wanting to know even *more* about her—showing interest and asking considerate questions. The things they both liked and didn't like, and "*Can you believe it, Miranda, we have so much in common!*" The outdoor concert, Kurt finding the perfect spot, Kurt bringing a blanket and picnic, Kurt so attentive, so smart, so sweet, so funny, so . . .

Miranda lay there with her eyes closed, letting it all sink in. And not missing the miserable confusion in Ashley's voice.

"Wow, Ashley. You really like him, don't you?" she finally said.

"I—I don't know. I don't think so." A long pause. A groan, even more miserable. "Yes, Miranda. I *like* him. I really like him a *lot*."

"Well . . . it's . . ." Miranda fumbled to console her. "It's all new, you know? A whole new person, a whole new experience. It's normal to feel . . . interested . . . in a brand-new experience. And person." Then, when Ashley didn't respond, "Are you planning on . . . having more new experiences with Kurt?"

This time the silence seemed to last forever.

"Ashley? You there?"

"I'm here. I want to go out with him again."

"You do?" Miranda flung one arm across her eyes. *Oh God . . . poor Parker.* "Well . . . did he ask you?"

"Yes."

"What'd you say?"

"I said . . . no."

A surge of relief shot through Miranda. Though she wasn't exactly sure why she felt so defensive about Parker all of a sudden.

"And then I said yes," Ashley added.

"You . . . you said yes?"

"Yes. I said yes."

"Ashley—what in the world are you—?"

"I don't know." Ashley's voice rose, genuinely distraught. "That's just it, Miranda—I don't *know* what in the world I'm going to do. I can't go out with Kurt while I'm with Parker. And I don't want to hurt Parker. I just want to . . . you know . . . go out with Kurt. *And* Parker. Is that horrible of me?"

You're asking me *that?* Miranda's head was reeling. *You're asking* me *that, when I'm madly in love with both Gage and Etienne?*

"Okay," Miranda took a deep breath. "Okay . . . so . . . how did this end, exactly? *Are* you going out with Kurt again?"

"I told him yes, I wanted to go out with him again. But that I couldn't. Well . . . not like a *date* date. More like . . . I could . . ."

"Ashley?" Miranda did her best to sound stern.

"Like I could maybe tutor him at the coffee shop sometime.

Or the . . . you know . . . park. Nothing romantic. Just science, plain and simple."

"Yeah . . . right. And which science are you tutoring him in?"

"Well . . . biology. Well . . . human anatomy."

"Very smart, Ashley. Tutoring him in a crowded public place."

"Oh, Miranda. I had such a good time tonight. He treated me like I was . . . special."

Miranda's heart gave a curious ache. *None of your business; stay out of it.* Yet Ashley hadn't seen Parker's face the other night, hadn't seen how dejected he was after learning about Kurt winning the date. And Ashley didn't know how Parker had bought a hundred tickets—spent a hundred whole dollars on her—just so he could win the raffle. *And why am I still sticking up for Parker anyway? Parker can be a jerk. And Parker can take care of himself. . . .*

"I'll have to lie," Ashley sighed, snapping Miranda back to attention.

"You will?"

"Of course. When everyone asks me about my date, I'll have to lie and be very polite. I'll have to say it was nice and I enjoyed it, but thank goodness it's over and done with." Another sigh, more dramatic this time. "A sacrifice I had to make for the cheerleading squad."

Miranda held back a laugh. "So . . . is he a good kisser?"

"Shh . . . I have to go."

"Ashley! Hold on! You can't just hang up without telling me how he—"

"I know Roo's listening—I can *feel* her listening. I'll have to tell you later. Bye!"

Dial tone.

And the soft, still night sounds settling comfortably over the house.

Miranda stretched under the covers. Plumped her pillows. Rested her head on folded arms and gazed thoughtfully up at the ceiling.

Ashley would be dreaming sweet dreams tonight . . . about Kurt . . . and concerts . . . and probably passionate kisses.

Not dreams about attics and mirrors and children about to die . . .

I used to be like that . . . have dreams like that . . .

Normal . . . simple . . . innocent . . .

She suddenly realized that her pillow was damp.

She suddenly realized that she was crying.

Crying for that normal, simple, innocent Miranda . . . who would never be like that again.

19

SHE WAS WAITING OUT ON THE VERANDAH WHEN GAGE came by the next morning. The air was brisk, a definite touch of fall in the air, and some of Aunt Teeta's trees in the front yard had begun shedding leaves overnight. Miranda had put on jeans and a sweatshirt, opted for pockets instead of a purse. As Gage started up the walkway, she hurried to meet him.

"You look a lot better," he greeted her, and she immediately felt better. It was always that way with Gage—just seeing his face, hearing his voice, could lift her spirits like nothing else could. Today his jersey was the same chocolate brown as his eyes and hair. He was—to put it mildly—drop-dead gorgeous. "No scary visitors last night, I hope."

She flicked him a look of uncertainty. *Maybe he really* does *know Etienne was here last night, and maybe he knows about all the other times too*. It was naïve of her to think otherwise, she told herself grimly—but Gage merely stared at her, all innocence. Ducking his head, half smiling, he led the way back to the sidewalk, where they ambled up the street and turned onto the Brickway, following its loop to the top of the hill.

He didn't press her about what had happened Friday at Belle Chandelle—didn't even mention it. As they made their way past

St. Yvette's historic homes and buildings, Miranda was the one who suddenly found herself opening to him, naturally, easily, the way she always seemed to do with Gage. She took him through the whole experience, her reflection in the mirror and into the past. Gage listened intently, breaking in with a question from time to time, giving her his undivided attention.

"It was just so real," she finished. "Like actually being there, but watching a movie at the same time."

Considering a second, he shot her a sidelong glance. "And you're sure it's the same fireplace. The one where your grandpa was standing in the picture?"

"Positive. The thing is, I was never in the attic before. I never took that picture."

"But you said you dropped your camera on the gallery that day. And you didn't go back for it till later, right?"

Miranda couldn't suppress a shudder. "Grandpa wanted me to find that fireplace."

"And the mirror, too, obviously."

"And I think he must have guided me back downstairs, because I don't remember how I got there." Another shiver worked through her. "And I wish I couldn't remember anything about that attic, either. Their faces . . . that smell. Oh, Gage, what happened to those poor people?"

Still lost in thought, Gage absently shook his hair back from his forehead.

"Maybe this will help you," he said quietly. His voice had gone somber now, his dark eyes genuinely concerned. "I did some research last night. In 1853, there was a yellow fever epidemic here. Well . . . not just here, but all around here. Hundreds of people died. And a lot of places were quarantined."

Miranda stopped walking. As something suddenly struck her, she reached out and caught Gage's arm. "The woman's face . . . not just an old yellowed photograph? But maybe the real color of her skin?"

"It starts with an infected mosquito," Gage explained. "Once a person's bitten, symptoms usually develop in three to six days."

Miranda nodded, stunned. "And the vision of Belle Chandelle I saw that day. The house was yellow. . . ."

"The disease goes through three stages. In the first stage, her skin would've been jaundiced—that lemon-yellow color. She ached all over . . . fever, vomiting. She couldn't eat." Gage paused, clearly disturbed by his own narrative. "And you talked about her eyes, remember? You thought they were bloodshot from being so tired. But other symptoms were red eyes . . . even a red face or tongue."

Again she nodded. Turned loose of Gage's arm. "Yes. That all makes sense. The horrible smells in there . . ."

"It gets worse, though. After about three or four days, sometimes there's a remission. And a lot of people actually recover at this stage, but others go into a *third* stage, the most *dangerous* stage." Thrusting his hands in his pockets, Gage stared off into the distance with a troubled frown. "Liver and kidney failure. Hemorrhage. Delirium and seizures. Then coma . . . shock . . . and death."

For a long moment, neither of them spoke. Feeling weak, Miranda stopped abruptly on the pavement, and Gage stopped with her.

"Gage . . . they *all* must have died of yellow fever. And nobody came to help them. That's why I sensed prayers that weren't answered . . . the terrible panic and desperation . . . they all died, and nobody came."

Such tragic imaginings on such a beautiful morning. Depressed and angry, Miranda kicked at some rocks, swallowed a cry, forced back helpless tears. *Dying there, alone, the three of them, without anyone to help* . . . Her whole body was shaking now. She felt Gage's hands on her shoulders and looked up.

"Come here," he murmured, arms going around her, drawing her close. "I'm sorry, Miranda. I'm sorry you had to go through that the other night."

Her tears spilled over. She realized that she was hugging him back, hugging him tighter and tighter, her face to his chest—and she could feel the lean curves and ridges and muscles of his body. He was surprisingly strong, and there was nothing the least bit shy about the way he was holding her. . . .

"I'll always have to go through it." Her voice caught. "For the rest of my life, I'll always have to go through it—and what if it always gets worse—"

"You'll never have to go through it by yourself. I promise I'll never let that happen."

"Gage–"

"Shh. Don't cry."

She wasn't sure how long they stood there on the Brickway,

pressed together without speaking, while she struggled to get herself under control. That night in the attic had been bad enough—but now, knowing about the yellow fever and what the three victims in that room must have suffered was too painful to even think about.

"No wonder she was so desperate," Miranda whispered at last. Slowly, reluctantly, she pulled back from Gage and stared up into his warm, gentle eyes. "Knowing her children were sick, and there wasn't anything she could do for them."

"So what can *you* do for them?" he asked softly.

"God, I wish I knew. Right now I'm not even sure I can go back there."

"And I'm not even sure you *should* go back there. But . . . there's also the thing with your grandfather. Do you have any idea yet what he wants?"

"I found the fireplace that was in his picture, so at least I know *that's* right. From there, I don't have a clue. Only . . . I'm supposed to help somehow."

Hesitating, Gage seemed to be carefully choosing his words. And seemed to already know what Miranda's response would be. "Are you upset with him? Because of this?"

Oh Gage . . . you always understand. "Yes," she replied truthfully. "More than upset. Hurt, too, I think."

"It's a normal way to feel, Miranda."

"It's just that . . . why would he show me such a tragedy? These are . . . little girls. Sweet little girls crying for their mother. Can't you just imagine how she must have felt, hearing them cry and not being able to make them better? And having to watch them die?"

"No, I can't imagine. It's got to be a mother's worst nightmare." Shaking his head at the prospect, he only grew more serious. "Miranda . . . I don't know what plans your grandfather has for you. And I don't know if what I'm going to say will help. But some spirits are always going to be stuck because they're unhappy. Because they're suffering, because they were part of some terrible tragedy . . ."

He ran a hand back slowly through his hair. A slight frown settled between his brows.

"It's okay," Miranda encouraged. "You can tell me."

"And I know this doesn't seem fair, but . . ." He drew a deep breath. "Maybe so you can empathize with why they're here, *you* have to feel it yourself. Maybe when you take on some of their pain, it allows them to let go and move on."

Again Miranda stared into his eyes. Those liquid brown eyes so full of compassion, of wisdom beyond their years. Cautiously, he reached out and brushed a lingering tear from her lashes.

"Your grandfather wouldn't have given you that responsibility—as painful as it is—if he didn't think you could do it," Gage assured her. "Because . . . you know . . . not just anybody could."

Miranda hadn't taken her gaze from his face. His hand was resting on her forehead now; she laid her own hand on his and pressed it to her cheek.

"Gage?

"Yeah?"

"You know what I love about you?"

A brief flash of dimples as he smiled. "Everything?"

"Yes. Everything." Playfully, she touched a fingertip to each side of his mouth. "Especially this . . . and this."

Color rose in his cheeks. Before she could pull away, he caught her wrist and once more pulled her against him. They were both laughing now, playfully wrestling, and as Gage's arms locked around her, a horn blared loudly, close by.

"Hey, y'all need a ride?"

Heads jerking up, they saw Etienne's truck idling at the curb. He was leaning out his window, and as his glance flicked from Gage to Miranda, she could swear that one corner of his mouth twitched.

"No, thanks," she said, embarrassed. "We . . . need the exercise."

"Yeah." Etienne gave a solemn nod. "It sure looks like y'all are exercising. I swear to God, Gage—what is it about those dimples of yours?"

Gage's flush deepened. As he turned away, Miranda latched on to his arm and steered him up the sidewalk.

"Come on," she said, wanting to laugh, knowing it would only make things worse. "We should probably hurry."

Gage cast a frown back over his shoulder; Etienne, driving slowly past them, responded with an innocent shrug.

Always a favorite hangout, the Tavern was crowded when they got there, but Miranda spotted the others at their regular table near the back. Ashley looked uncharacteristically subdued—Parker, seated next to her, seemed edgy. Whether the two had discussed Ashley's date last night Miranda could only guess, but neither looked particularly happy. Roo slumped in her chair, glancing between Ashley and Parker, then shifting to Gage and Miranda as they made their way over. When Etienne walked in a few minutes later, they all got down to business.

Once again Miranda related the events of Friday night, her discovery of the fireplace, her tragic observation in the mirror. She recounted everything, described everything—sights, smells, sounds—and when she was done, Gage filled them in on his research about the yellow fever epidemic. Between her narrative, general comments, curious questions, and emotional exclamations, they all scanned their menus, ordered their food, and started in on their coffees, juices, cappuccinos, and—in Roo's case—peanut butter milkshake. Parker, sitting next to her, looked seriously close to gagging.

"I can't stand it," Ashley choked, dabbing a napkin at her eyes. "Having to watch your children die. Knowing there's nothing you can do. And that nobody's coming to help."

"And listening to them call for you." Miranda couldn't shake the memory. "It was like she was in shock. Completely empty. Just sitting there, rocking and rocking in her chair."

"And there wasn't anybody else there? Not even any servants?"

"All I saw were the two little girls. They were huddled on the bed, absolutely scared to death and holding on to each other."

Again Ashley's eyes brimmed. "Tell us again, what they looked like."

Miranda didn't need to think back—their faces were engraved on her memory. *Engraved there forever, probably.* "They looked alike, but one was older. I'm not sure how I know that . . . just an impression I had. They both had dark hair and dark eyes; the younger one had a softer, sweeter, more babyish face; the older one was holding her hand. They were crying so hard. And . . . and *pleading*. And their little nightgowns . . ."

Her voice trailed away. *Just a dream, it's not real, just a glimpse through time, it's not real—*

"Their little nightgowns were filthy, soiled. Their hair was matted, their little faces were wet, streaked with tears . . ." Like Ashley, Miranda grabbed for her napkin, wished she could escape, from the table, the restaurant, her purpose, and the past. "Sorry," she whispered, "I know it's not real—"

"Yes, it is." Roo gave Miranda a somber frown "It *is* real, it *was* real. Look, I know the whole thing sucks, but that's why they're here. And why you're here. And why you have to help them."

"Don't sugarcoat it," Parker said coolly. "Tell us what you really think."

"It *does* suck." Keeping her stare on Parker, Roo demonstrated, sucking noisily on her straw. Parker groaned and turned away.

But Miranda was together now; taking a deep breath, she willed herself to continue. "They were practically babies. Both of them just little kids. And Roo *is* right. I've got to help them. But how?"

Their meals arrived. There was a short break while everyone passed around syrup, jam, hot sauce, ketchup, butter, salt and pepper, sugar and cream. Cups were refilled; water glasses refreshed. Then, enjoying their breakfasts, they all picked up the conversation.

"Okay," Gage began, "we know they were alone there . . .

abandoned there for some reason. And we know they had yellow fever. That the mother couldn't save her kids, and they died—"

"Quarantined," Roo announced flatly. "Or . . . the doctor just wouldn't come."

"A lot of doctors died during those epidemics. Slaves, too, if they stayed."

"And the plantation *was* pretty isolated."

Nodding, Gage rested his knife and fork on his plate. "So . . . what's the actual point?"

"Main objective: free the spirits so they can move on." Finishing off her milkshake, Roo started in on peanut-butter-whipped-cream waffles. Parker immediately stood up.

"Somebody trade places with me? Please? I'll give you my car."

In grave unison, everyone shook their heads. Parker groaned again and sat back down.

"Okay . . . so . . . why are they not free?" Miranda asked, still trying to focus. "What's holding them back?"

"Something about that room," Roo answered.

"But Miranda heard the children outside," Ashley reminded Roo. "And on the stairs—"

"Maybe the stairs and the swing were just ways to get my attention," Miranda guessed.

"Gotta be the room," Etienne agreed, splashing hot sauce over his biscuits. "That's where Jonas was standing—by the fireplace—so that's where he wanted Miranda to look."

Exchanging glances, Gage nodded at his cousin. "I think so too. That seems to be the source of the tragedy."

"Death usually *is* the source of the tragedy." Parker stated. "Hello? No death? No ghosts?"

"It's more than the room," Miranda insisted stubbornly. "With all the weird experiences I've had, there's got to be something about the mirror, too."

Ashley pondered a moment . . . picked listlessly at her fruit plate. "Maybe just a reflection of the past. Like I said before . . . a symbol."

"Everything happened with the mirror, yeah?" Etienne offered. "That was pretty intense stuff, what Miranda was seeing. Like everything was coming together, when she looked in that mirror."

"Eww." Ashley shivered. "Y'all make it sound like it was alive or something."

Miranda's senses honed in. "But it *did* seem almost alive. I can't explain it . . . it was just a mirror, like any mirror. But then—when I looked into it—there were . . . people and . . . sounds . . . and emotions and smells . . . and it was like . . . it really *did* come to life."

"Miranda, that's so scary. I would have died of fright right then and there." As Ashley's voice sank to a whisper, she pressed against Parker's side. Instinctively he reached for her, then stopped, paused, and leaned slightly away.

Roo didn't miss it. And neither did anyone else.

"There's a connection," Gage said quickly. "Only we're not getting it."

"Try again, *cher*," Etienne urged, dark eyes fixed on Miranda. "Everything you can remember about that room—and that mirror. I know how hard this must be, reliving it over and over again—but maybe there's something else, yeah? Some tiny little detail you missed."

"I don't think so." Miranda sighed. "But . . . okay."

She squared her shoulders. Wiped her hands nervously on the napkin in her lap. Took a deep breath . . . coaxed her mind to that different, distant place . . . "The awful smells of sickness . . . and the flies . . . the heat. The little girls crying . . . their mother in the rocking chair . . . rocking back and forth . . . that awful creaking sound, back and forth and—"

A frown brushed her lips.

"What is it, *cher*?"

"The creaking," she realized. "It was so loud and annoying, so *irritating*, back and forth, the rhythm of it, the sound of it. And then"—clutching her napkin, Miranda wiped her damp palms—"the creaking stopped."

"You're sure?"

"Yes." Eagerly she bobbed her head. "It stopped. That awful sound, and then suddenly it *stopped*. And the silence, when it stopped, the silence was so much louder than the creaking."

"So . . ."

"Her face." Miranda choked now, fingertips at her own cheeks. "Her face, in the candlelight, back and forth in the candlelight . . . and the way her eyes were so big and staring."

"Miranda, don't do any more," Ashley begged, alarmed. "If it's too much, you don't have to do any more—"

"You said she was in shock," Gage prompted gently. "About her children."

"No. I was wrong." Miranda could hardly speak. "I think . . . I think she was dead."

"What?" Ashley burst out, close to tears herself. "Their mother was dead?"

Miranda was thoroughly shaken now. She could sense customers glancing over, curious stares, even from the servers; and Ashley making soft, whimpering sounds in her throat; and her own tears welling up and running over . . .

"She was dead. Oh, God, she was dead, and . . . and her little girls were still alive."

It was as if the restaurant receded around her, the noise, the activity, the crowds, even the smell of food vanished into the past. For one brief second, she was there again, standing at the mirror, watching that pathetic scene, the children crying for their mother, their mother dead in the rocking chair. . . .

"They were there alone," Miranda murmured. "They cried for her, but they were there alone. Sick and alone. Dying and alone."

The restaurant was back. Every fork at their table had lowered, every head lowered as well. Ashley was crying. Gage's eyes were endlessly sad. A muscle tightened in Etienne's jaw. Roo gazed solemnly at her plate. Even Parker looked grim and upset.

"She must have known," Miranda said at last. "She must have known she was dying. And that her children would be there alone."

"Oh my God." Ashley covered her face with her hands. "I can't even stand to think about it. It's too much for a mother to bear."

"Not bad enough that she suffered from yellow fever," Gage reflected quietly. "Then she had to suffer even more, knowing her kids would die all alone."

"How can life be that cruel?" Ashley whispered. Again she leaned toward Parker; this time he slid his arm around her shoulders.

Roo, glancing around at curious onlookers, boldly stared them down.

"Their mama, maybe she never knew till the end." Etienne sounded hopeful. "I mean . . . she woulda known her kids were dying—but maybe she really thought she'd live long enough to be there for them."

Ashley, however, was practically inconsolable. "But there *had* to come a point when she realized. When she realized what was happening. And then that anguish she must have gone through."

None of them had expected it to be this tragic. None of them wanted to imagine what those last days, those last hours had been like for that desperate mother. Trying to nurse and protect her children. Knowing that despite her love and best efforts, she couldn't save them from dying. And then—after all that heartbreak—to realize that she would die before them and leave them totally alone.

"And what the children went through," Ashley couldn't stop agonizing. "What they must have thought. Crying for their mother . . . seeing her in that rocking chair . . . wondering why she didn't come to them or comfort them—"

"Do we really have to talk about this now?" Parker, growing

irritated, began to fidget. "Can't we just eat our breakfast and talk about something nice and normal for a change? Which, of course, means we can't talk about Roo."

"It would have been a bad way to die, too," Roo said philosophically. "A horrible way to die."

More silence around the table. Though everyone toyed with their food, there wasn't much interest in eating anymore. Except for Roo, who kept digging away at her gooey layers of waffles.

Frustrated, Miranda glanced at each of them in turn. "But . . . that still doesn't tell me what I'm supposed to do."

"No, it doesn't." Ashley's sniffles had eased a bit. "So let's all put on our thinking caps."

Parker viciously attacked his steak and eggs.

"It's there, I know it is," Miranda persisted. "Right in front of us. Something I should be tuning in to, but I'm not. In fact, it's probably so obvious that's why we're missing it."

Gage answered with a distrait nod. Picked up his hot coffee . . . blew carefully over the rim of his cup. "What about you?" he asked Etienne.

"What *about* me?" Etienne met the stare, unflinching.

"You've been working in the attic, right?"

"Sometimes, yeah."

"Did you ever notice any weird stuff going on up there?"

"Me, I didn't even notice the mirror." Etienne seemed genuinely annoyed with himself. "I didn't even know that fireplace was there."

"Are you serious? How could you not have—"

"It was covered up," Miranda explained, before Etienne had

the chance. "It had stuff leaned against it—some big French doors. I wouldn't have found it either if I hadn't . . . you know . . . sensed something."

"As in *good* sense?" Parker did mock surprise. "Oh . . . no. My mistake."

Aiming him a fierce kick, Ashley scooted forward and propped both elbows on her placemat. "So you pulled all that stuff away, and the fireplace was just there? And you realized it was the same one in the photograph?"

"Not right away." In her mind, Miranda could see the whole scene again, clearer than any movie. "I had to scrape all the dust and spiderwebs off—they were hanging everywhere, like big sheets of them. On the mirror, too. It was totally covered, and—"

Breaking off, she looked over at Gage. She could see him straightening slowly in his chair, his lips moving ever so slightly, the strange expression on his face as he set his cup down on the table and pointed vaguely to some invisible revelation in the air.

"Covered," he mumbled.

"Right." Parker pointed back at him. "You got me covered; I got you covered, amigo."

But Gage wasn't in the mood for jokes. Instead he fixed Miranda with a calm, troubled gaze. "The mirror in the attic, Miranda. It was covered when you found it—but what if it *wasn't* covered when they died?"

Perplexed glances passed from Miranda to Etienne to Parker. "Meaning? . . ."

"He's right," Ashley echoed, almost reverently. "Back then, when somebody passed, all the mirrors in the house were covered. Draped with some sort of cloth."

"My *grandmère*, I think I remember her talking about that," Etienne admitted. "She heard stories from *her grandmère*." Pausing a moment, he frowned. "I never really thought about it though . . . she had herself a lotta superstitions like that."

"Which obviously are *not* superstitions." Roo couldn't help sounding smug. "People believed if they didn't cover up the mirrors, then the dead souls would be trapped inside there forever. And wouldn't be able to move on."

Miranda's heart was beginning to race. As a sense of expectancy stirred through the group, she leaned forward, her voice tight.

"So, Roo . . . if the mirrors weren't covered . . ."

"She and her little girls are trapped there. Inside the mirror."

Once more the room seemed to fade, the present swirling into the past, the past beckoning through a sorrowful, gray haze. Miranda could only sit there and try to focus, dimly aware of voices speaking around her, the faint smell of restaurant food, the way she was clamping her fingers together, a vague, alarming awareness of where she had been two nights ago—and where she was destined to return. . . .

"I have to go back," she murmured. "I have to go back there and get them out."

Roo was touching her arm. Frowning at her, mildly incredulous. "Miranda, do you even realize what you're saying?"

“Yes, I’ll have to go into the mirror.”

“And *then* what?”

“Cover it. From the other side.”

Silence descended, heavy and charged with emotions. Miranda felt the weight of five grave stares.

It was Parker who finally broke the stillness, though his laugh was forced and loud. “That’s insane! Listen to yourselves—mirrors and walking through glass and covering up dead—what?”

“Parker, stop.” Ashley’s tone was no-nonsense. “I know you don’t want those little girls to be in torment forever, do you?”

“No. Shit no, of course not. You mean, the little girls—*ghosts*—whatever—that *aren’t real*?”

“You always do this when you’re nervous. You always do this when you’re scared.”

“Scared? Oh, right, Ash. That’s a good one.” Indignant now, he started talking faster. “If it was worth being scared over, well, okay, great. But since it’s *not* real, then I’m not *scared*. And I’m certainly not *nervous*. In fact, I’m not even halfway—”

“Intelligent?” Roo finished.

But Ashley persisted. “What is wrong with you, Parker? You don’t have to do anything about *anything* at Belle Chandelle. Everybody knows how you feel—and nobody needs your help.”

“So what do you want from me, Ash?” Parker snapped back at her. “You’ve been on my case all morning—maybe I should take you over to Streak’s house, huh? Maybe you should have breakfast with *him*.”

“Now, now, children,” Roo began, wagging her finger, “if you two can’t get along, we’ll have to separate you.”

Gage jabbed her sharply in the ribs. "Great choice of words. See? They look happier already."

For a brief moment Etienne observed the furious couple—Ashley close to tears again, Parker hurt and sullen. Then, clearing his throat, Etienne smoothly stepped in.

"But *something's* really bothering you." he confronted Parker. "Something besides Kurt Fuller, yeah?"

Parker's outburst was sudden, angry, and completely unexpected. "Hey—fine if y'all don't need my help. Like I could give a crap. But if Miranda covers the damn mirror—then how is she going to come *out* again?"

Shocked, everyone stared. Parker, flustered at having given himself away, ravaged his leftovers with a vengeance. He kept his eyes on his plate. He refused to look at any of them. His whole body was practically quivering.

For an endless moment, Miranda watched him hacking away at his steak. Then, trying to break the tension, she caught his eyes and gave him a wink. "Hey, are you actually worried about me, Parker? Just a little?"

"No." A quick glower in her direction. "I'm worried about my food. Why the hell did we come this morning anyway? Nobody's eating. Everybody's too *grossed out* to eat—yellow fever and vomit and blood coming out of people's eyes, for Christ's sake. Oh, excuse me. Everybody's too grossed out to eat *except* for Miss Weird Cuisine here. And why the hell do my eggs taste like peanut butter?"

The strain began to ease a bit . . . into amusement . . . relief . . . yet lingering concern.

"Is that possible, what Parker said?" Ashley's glance flicked nervously from Gage to Etienne. "Could Miranda not come out again?"

"I'll be fine, Ashley," Miranda soothed her before the two boys could answer. She hadn't missed the looks passed between them—thoughts unspoken but obviously understood. "The spirits want my help, they don't want to hurt me."

"But . . . what about the mirror?"

"I can't get trapped in the mirror. I'm not dead." *And listen to yourself, Miranda Barnes—you might as well be discussing the weather.* She was startled by her own show of confidence. Startled and somewhat reassured, though the fear was definitely still there. *I wouldn't have sounded nearly this positive two months ago. . . . I just hope I know what I'm talking about now.*

"So when will you do it, Miranda?" Ashley broke cautiously into her thoughts. "When are you going into the mirror?"

Eyes downcast, Miranda shook her head. To be honest, a part of her wished that she could put it off forever. Not because she *didn't* want to help them—but because of what she'd have to face *before* she could help them. That foul room again . . . the incessant creaking of that rocking chair . . . the dead woman . . . the terrified faces and pleading sobs of those dying children. *So maybe I* have *made great strides in accepting and using my gift. That still doesn't make my job any less painful or heartbreaking.*

"So when, Miranda?" Ashley asked again, more quietly.

"No rush," Parker quipped. "Once you've been in torment for eternity, a few more days won't matter."

Ashley landed another kick under the table. Yet Parker's words were just what Miranda needed to hear. The thought of those children being in torment for even *one* more day—no matter how much she longed to put it off—was suddenly unbearable.

"Now," Miranda decided. "The sooner the—"

"Hold on now, *cher*," Quickly Etienne stopped her. "I know you're wanting to take care of this right away, but your mama needs that electricity fixed—she's got an emergency crew working out there all afternoon." He paused . . . frowned . . . checked his watch. "Damn, and I'm late. You're gonna have to put it off a little, yeah? At least till tomorrow."

He hadn't said anything about dinner at his mom's. Miranda glanced at Roo. Roo glanced back, then shot a shrewd look between Etienne and Gage. Both boys glanced at Roo but not at each other.

"Etienne's right." Noting Miranda's disappointment, Ashley tried to bolster her with a smile. "You can't concentrate on helping those spirits with people coming in and out, and all that mess and noise."

Miranda knew her friend was right—there was no way she could reach those spirits again without some privacy and uninterrupted time. Distantly, she felt a comforting touch . . . realized that Gage's hand was resting on her shoulder.

"Tomorrow, then?" he asked, scanning each face in the group. "I know y'all have stuff after school—and there's no way Mom's gonna let me miss physical therapy. So later's better anyway. Everything—and everybody—will be a whole lot calmer."

Ashley was the first to nod. "And we *all* go. Miranda, you do *not* go by yourself."

"That's an order." Etienne's expression was as unrelenting as his tone. "Don't even be thinking about it."

Pinning Miranda with a stare, Roo joined the consensus. "It's for your own good—and theirs. Think about it. If anything happens to you, then who else is going to get those kids out of the attic?"

They were all standing now, pushing back chairs, tossing money onto the table, turning to leave. Throughout their final discussion, Parker had kept silent, turned away from the conversation, seemingly lost in thought. Not looking at anyone—not even Ashley—as they headed for the front of the restaurant and out the door.

Miranda was the last in line. She saw Gage step aside to hold the door open, but Parker grabbed it first. He caught her arm before she could walk through; he leaned down quickly and put his mouth close to her ear.

"Don't do it," he whispered tightly.

"Parker, I—what?"

"This whole mirror thing. Just . . . don't do it."

She couldn't ask him anything else.

One second he had a hold of her . . .

Then next second, he had a hold of Ashley, walking rapidly away down the street.

20

She spent the afternoon worrying. About Belle Chandelle, the long-ago tragedy in the attic . . . Parker's warning . . . and what she was going to wear for dinner.

Come on, Miranda, it's just dinner, don't be so paranoid. It's not like you've never had dinner at someone's house before.

"True," she muttered to herself, digging through her clothes, systematically tossing them on the bed. She'd had dinner at hundreds of people's houses before. *Just not Etienne's.*

It didn't even count as a real date. After all, Etienne hadn't invited her to come, his *mom* had. Not that she had ever *considered* it a date to begin with. *And why can't I stop thinking about Gage?*

Miranda, you are completely hopeless. You are so *going to get your heart broken.*

In the end, she decided on her favorite jeans, her blue flats, her favorite knit top—also blue—with the tapered sleeves and tiny buttons down the front. She'd always liked this outfit; it was flattering but not showy; it was comfortable, but made her feel confident. When she saw Etienne's truck pull into the driveway, she thanked God that Mom and Aunt Teeta weren't home to embarrass her.

She climbed into the passenger side before Etienne even

had time to get out. He looked as if he'd come straight from work—hadn't even stopped to change—torn jeans and work boots all grimy, ripped T-shirt all stained. His thick, black hair was straighter than usual, hanging longer in back, falling limply over his cheeks and brow. Telltale furrows there, Miranda noted, where his long fingers had raked back through it many times. There was a light trace of windburn on his narrow cheeks. The day was pale sunshine and turning more chilly, but his skin was deep summer, and he wasn't wearing a jacket.

"You thinking how handsome I am?" he asked suddenly as they headed out of town.

"No, I'm thinking how smelly you are." She couldn't resist picking on him. "Are there any more windows we can open?"

He reached over and grabbed her. Hooked his arm around her side and dragged her against him, never once taking his eyes from the road.

"Now . . . what was it Parker was saying about you being so little and so much fun to—oh yeah, now I remember."

Miranda squealed as his fingers dug into her ribs. Laughing helplessly she twisted in his grasp but couldn't get away. Etienne was obviously enjoying himself—though he did ease up for a few seconds to let her catch her breath.

"That Parker, he sure knows what he's talking about." Etienne's shrug was innocent. "Especially with that cute little laugh you got going on there, and—"

"Stop! It's not funny!"

"And *damn*, you're looking good today, *cher*."

"No, I'm not," she insisted, trying to sound stern despite the flush on her cheeks. "And even if I *did*, then I certainly don't *now*—not with all your dirt and sweat on me."

Once more his fingers threatened lightly against her ribs. Renewing her efforts to escape, she glimpsed a hidden smile teasing at one corner of his mouth, and she realized that struggling was useless.

"You're going to run us off the road," she warned, opting for a different approach.

"Me? No, I'm a good driver."

"I'll tell your mom," she threw back at him.

That not-quite smile grew more amused, though he gave a dramatic groan.

"Uh-oh, now I *really* gotta be on my best behavior."

Finally relenting, he let her scramble into the safety of her corner. Then he glanced at her and winked.

Not a date, she thought firmly. *Just a visit, Sunday dinner, not a real date . . .*

And what *would* a real date with Etienne be like, anyway, she wondered—she couldn't even imagine such a thing. The kind of normal, typical, boring high-school date like everyone else went on? No, Etienne was . . . *beyond* that somehow. *Above* that somehow. A whole, secret, mysterious world away from everything and everyone else . . .

"Miranda?"

How long had he been watching her? She'd been so deep in thought that she hadn't even noticed, but now she jumped and met his eyes.

"Hey," he said casually, "I didn't mean to upset you—"

"No. You didn't. It's not you."

"What, then?"

Yes—what *then, Miranda?* She'd been halfway confident earlier, getting ready in the security of her room—but now she was starting to feel nervous and uncertain. Being here in the truck with him, and his closeness and his touch and the playing around, and staying in the Boucher house for an entire evening with no Roo or Ashley for backup—

God, Miranda, you're embarrassing yourself.

Her stomach fluttered; she ran the tip of her tongue slowly between her lips.

Could you possibly act any more immature?

"You thinking about the plantation, *cher*?"

Miranda nodded, though she could tell that Etienne didn't believe her. "Did you get the electricity fixed?"

"No. And one of the guys got himself hurt pretty bad, so that didn't help any."

"You mean electrocuted? Is he okay?"

"Gonna be. But they're shutting down work for a few days. Till they can figure out what's going on."

Good, Miranda thought. *Easier for me to do what I need to do*. Then she instantly felt guilty because of the injured worker.

"What you looking so upset for?" Noting her frown, Etienne tried to reassure her. "I told you, the guys's gonna be okay."

"Do Mom and Aunt Teeta know?"

"I already called Miss Teeta. She said they're driving to New Orleans tomorrow. Meeting with the owners."

"Oh. Right. Mom told me, I think. But I'd forgotten."

She could feel his stare, his suspicion, his concern—but he didn't press her.

"Hey." He shrugged, gaze back on the windshield. "Try and forget about Belle Chandelle for just one night. Try to have yourself a good time for a change."

"I will."

"And don't be nervous about coming to my house."

"Why would I be nervous?"

"I can't think of a single reason."

He shot a quick glance at the rearview mirror . . . shifted gears . . . veered off the main route. With St. Yvette far behind them now, Miranda turned her attention to the open window and the bayou country beyond.

Almost immediately, the woods closed ranks around them. Trees crowded tight in all directions, leaving practically no space between one massive trunk and the next. From both sides of the road, branches arched and knotted together, weaving an overhead canopy, obliterating the sky. She couldn't even see the ground anymore—just an unbroken tangle of leaves and vines and snaking roots, layered in shadows. Like long gray tears, moss wept from every limb. And the farther they drove, the darker it grew.

Miranda shivered. She didn't even realize that she'd reached for Etienne's hand . . . not till his strong fingers closed tightly around her own.

"The bayou's that way," he said, gesturing vaguely toward his window. "If we keep ourselves here on this road, we'll end up at the office, where we run the tours."

But he didn't stay; he took yet another turnoff, onto yet another track of crushed oyster shells. The forest was denser then ever, squeezing the road to half its width. And though the day had been cool back in town, the air here hung warm and still and perpetually damp.

Despite her best intentions, she was still uneasy. *More* uneasy, she realized, with every mile and minute that passed. She had no idea how far they'd come or how long they'd been traveling; she had absolutely no idea how Etienne or anyone else could *ever* find their way around this godforsaken place—

"This is it," Etienne announced, though Miranda saw only wilderness in every direction. "I told you not to be nervous, yeah?"

"I'm—I'm not, but—"

"What, you think I was kidnapping you? Or maybe I forgot where I live?"

Just ahead of them, the trees were finally thinning, the road widening again and straightening out. To Miranda's surprise, the branches suddenly parted to reveal a clearing on the other side, and as the pickup drove in and rolled to a stop, she sat forward and stared.

And instantly fell in love with the place.

Built mostly of wood, the Boucher house perched modestly on raised concrete blocks, protected against the floodwaters of the bayou. A red front door—the same cheery shade as the trim and shutters—stood open in welcome, and birds sang noisily atop a chimney of faded red bricks. Bordered by flowers, a neat picket fence enclosed the small front yard while even more flowers lined the path to the steps. There was a wide front porch and a screened one in back on the bayou side, its view overlooking a large wooden pier at the water's edge. The driveway angled off to the right, toward a big garage and several wooden sheds. And though everything was surrounded by moss-drenched trees, soft patches of afternoon sunlight still managed to break through, dappling the rooftops and roses and recently mowed grass.

"It's beautiful," Miranda murmured, and realized that Etienne had been watching her again. Quickly he turned his eyes away and cut the engine.

"Maybe you'd like to see the bayou while you're here?" He shrugged. "I could take you on the tour, if you want."

Before she could answer, Miss Nell was already down the front steps, coming toward her, waving.

"Miranda! Come on in, honey, you need something cold to drink!"

Miranda got out before Etienne could help her. The nervousness was back again, but a sort-of-nice nervousness, she decided, not the sick-to-your-stomach kind. As Miss Nell greeted her with a hug, she suddenly felt shy, and caught Etienne's knowing glance from over his mom's shoulder.

"And my, my, just look at you." Turning Miranda loose, Miss Nell scrutinized Etienne with an unconvincing frown. "So glad you dressed for dinner."

Etienne was completely unfazed. "Miranda likes me in these clothes, Mama."

"Why, yes, I'm sure. She *looks* like the kind of girl who likes dirty laundry and a complete lack of personal hygiene."

"Manly smells, Mama." Etienne leaned down and kissed her on the cheek.

She jerked her thumb toward the house. "Go. Wash. Change clothes. I'm sure Miranda and I can find lots to talk about."

"Me, probably."

"Go. And use plenty of soap!"

Hiding a smile, he bounded easily up onto the porch, then turned back to face them.

"I thought I'd take her on the tour, Mama. We got time before dinner?"

Before Miranda could object, Miss Nell instantly brightened. "That's a wonderful idea—and yes, y'all should go now, while it's still light out."

"Oh. Hey. Listen," Miranda assured her, "really, I don't have to do that today. I can do it next time. *Anytime*, actually, so please don't go to any trouble—"

"Honey, it's no trouble at all—in fact, I think you'll really enjoy it. Lots of our tourists write back to us, saying how much fun they had and how they want to come back again. And—as much as I hate to admit it—you won't find a better guide *anywhere* than that one."

A hint of pride in Miss Nell's tone as she indicated her son. A fresh spark of apprehension in the pit of Miranda's stomach as she glanced toward the water. She'd already had a realistic glimpse of this wild bayou world, and that had been from the relative safety of the truck. But the thought of being thrust out there in the very middle of it, in a boat where anything could climb in—

"I think something might be wrong with the motor, though." Miss Nell's voice snapped her back. They were walking into the house, and Etienne stood aside, holding the door, allowing them to pass. "I tried it this morning, and it's acting up again. And none of the usual remedies seemed to work."

"How many times I gotta tell you, Mama. Let me be the one worrying about all that. Or call Gage or Uncle Frank."

His mother feigned indignation. "In case you've forgotten, I've been repairing boats and motors and cars and trucks for longer than you've been alive."

"Yeah, yeah, I know. I'll go have a look."

"And don't worry," Miranda assured him quickly. "Don't worry if you can't fix it."

"Jesus, *cher*, how many times I gotta tell you—I can fix anything."

He was right, of course; Miranda knew she was stuck. *No way I'm getting out of this stupid swamp tour if anyone here can help it.*

Yet it didn't take long for her nervousness to disappear. Enveloped by Miss Nell's hospitality and the genuine warmth of the house, Miranda soon started relaxing and enjoying herself. From the very beginning, she and Etienne's mother found dozens of things to talk about, sharing memories and experiences, personal feelings they had in common, like two longtime friends. Miranda adored the small, homey rooms; the old wooden floors and lace curtains and fresh flowers; the oversize brick fireplace and worn, comfortable furniture that she guessed was handmade.

"Etienne's father," Miss Nell admitted, when Miranda asked. Miranda could swear that the woman's voice tightened—a mixture of anger and sorrow—though her face was as kind as ever. "He built this house for me when we first married... but of course, it's been added on to through the years. Frank—Gage's dad—did some of it. But Etienne did the most."

A million questions yearned to be asked, but Miranda knew that this was neither the time nor place.

"The house and the fireplace and a lot of this furniture... all Lazare's work," Miss Nell volunteered. "He... he was the one who taught Etienne how to build things. How to work with his hands."

"He's great at that," Miranda agreed. "Working with his hands." Then, blushing, she stammered, "Building things and... making things, I mean."

Obviously amused, Miss Nell seemed to appreciate the distraction. "Lazare's side of the family is pretty traditional—somehow they've managed to hang on to their culture in this crazy modern world." A brief pause, her voice hardening once again. "I'm not close to them anymore, but Etienne stays in touch... sees them when he can. They care about him so... that's good."

They had settled in the kitchen at a large wooden table. Though the other rooms lacked nothing in coziness, this one was more spacious and clearly the heart of their family—shelves filled with cookbooks, dishes and teapots on display, pots and pans hanging from the rafters, potted plants and herbs crowded along the window ledges. A huge pot bubbled on the stove; the promise of stewed chicken and shrimp and peppery spices filled the air. Homemade bread was baking in the oven. Two sweet-potato pies cooled side-by-side on the countertop. As Miss Nell and Miranda refreshed their glasses from a pitcher of sweet tea, the girl talk continued.

Miss Nell's childhood in Natchez. Life with her twin sister, Jules. Her favorite grandmother, who had inspired her love of cooking. At one point, Miranda worried about being too nosy, but the woman quickly laughed and dismissed it. She was enjoying herself, she assured Miranda—and in turn began asking about Miranda's years in Florida, her friends, her school, and how the hurricane had changed her life. When Miranda teared up at one point, Miss Nell reached over and squeezed her hand.

"But you're here now," she insisted sweetly. "Everything happens for a reason, you know. And I'm so very glad you're here with us now."

"Thanks, Mama," Etienne broke in. "I knew y'all would be missing me."

Startled, Miranda got herself under control. Miss Nell simply stared at Etienne, who was propped lazily against the doorframe, barefoot. He cleaned his hands on a rag, then wiped his face on the sleeve of his T shirt, leaving a trail of grease across his left cheek. Miranda couldn't believe how sexy he looked, even with all the grime.

"There you are," his mom fussed. "Worse than ever."

"Here I am," Etienne responded. "Fixing that motor you told me to."

Miss Nell burst out laughing. Rising from the table, she nudged Miranda in his direction. "She's all yours, Etienne—I've monopolized her long enough. You two have fun. And *be careful.* We'll eat when you get back."

A hundred excuses whirled through Miranda's brain, but Etienne had her by the elbow, steering her outside. She remembered him mentioning some office where the tours were launched, but they obviously weren't taking his pickup to get there. Instead he guided her down a wide, crushed-shell path that led away from the house, a route winding scenically between bayou and woods.

They walked close, side-by-side, without speaking. The humor had faded from his expression, and his pace was leisurely, hands in pockets, eyes straight ahead. Miranda could feel her emotions stirring again—that subtle mix of excitement and shyness that she found so confusing . . . and annoying. A tentative silence hung between them, yet she didn't know what to say. Trying not to be obvious, she stole a swift glance at his profile. Startled, she saw him watching her.

"Here," she said. Impulsively, she grabbed his elbow and stopped him. Then she took the rag he was holding, found a clean spot at one edge, and gingerly rubbed at his cheek.

He hadn't expected it, she could tell. For a brief instant, something like surprise flickered in the black depths of his stare. She could almost swear that he was a little embarrassed.

"Guess I coulda cleaned up a little," he mumbled, and immediately ran his arm across that same dirty cheek, smudging it all over again. "But then we woulda had less time for the boat and—"

"You don't need to clean up. I like the way you look."

"*Mais*, yeah? Sweat and all?"

"Sweat and . . . and *everything* and all—"

Oh my God. Out before she could stop it, just like that. *And how many* more *ways are you going to humiliate yourself today, Miranda?* She could feel her cheeks turning pink, she could see the muscle moving in his jaw and that maddening almost-smile playing at the corners of his mouth. She waited for him to tease her, but he didn't. Instead, he jerked his chin at the pathway, a signal to keep walking. It was several more minutes till he spoke again.

"I could hear Mama laughing when I came back to the house earlier. You and her musta been having a pretty good time? Going on and on about stuff?"

Miranda smiled . . . nodded. But before she could elaborate, Etienne kept on with his thoughts.

"That's just about the best sound—when she's happy like that. She . . . she really likes you."

Self-consciously, Miranda brushed it off. "Come on. I'm sure she really likes *all* the girls you bring home."

"I don't bring girls home."

This time he walked on without her, not even waiting while she hurried to catch up.

It didn't take long to get there. As a small wooden building came into view, Miranda noticed a wide covered deck in front, a dock and ramp and wooden posts on the bayou side. There was a large painted sign—BOUCHER SWAMP TOURS—some sheds, a workshop, a garage, and a boathouse. And tied to one of the posts, floating all by itself in the water, was what must be the—

"Tour boat?" Miranda stopped and stared. "I thought you said it was a tour boat!"

Etienne, already halfway along the dock, sounded amused. "This *is* our tour boat, *cher*. A Cajun fishing boat."

"It's . . . no, it's not. It's too small."

"I can go places in this boat where other boats can't even get to. And the motor's real quiet, so you can still hear the birds."

But Miranda was growing more and more skeptical. "And it's . . . open."

"Open? What, you mean like those Disney World kinda boats—"

"There's no top on it. Isn't it supposed to have a top?"

"What the hell you need a top for?"

"Snakes. They can fall out of the trees onto your head."

"Not my head."

"Etienne, I swear. I saw it on TV—"

"*Bon Dieu*, just get yourself in here."

Jumping into the boat, he reached for her hand. Miranda held her breath, stepped down to the wide, flat bottom, and glanced longingly at the shore.

"Don't we need lifejackets?"

"Naw. If we turn over, the gators'll have us before we got time to drown."

"That's not funny."

Yet despite her misgivings, Miranda reluctantly began to sightsee. And within minutes she was just like any other tourist, drawn with curious fascination to the wild, primal beauty of her surroundings.

"There won't be quite as much going on now, this time of year," Etienne explained, following the sluggish curve of the thickly wooded embankments. "Once fall and winter come, things start slowing down around here."

Leisurely, expertly, he began pointing out various highlights of nature along the way—rare plants and foliage, animals and birds, reptiles and insects and fish. The birdcalls were almost deafening—the chatter and singing, the patter of wings—Miranda guessed there had to be hundreds, maybe even thousands of different species. A nutria swam past them, totally uninterested; turtles basked on fallen logs in the last warm rays of sunlight. When Etienne's keen eyes honed in on a deer and a fox in the woods, Miranda couldn't see a thing; when he spotted an owl, a water snake, and a giant spider, too, she accused him of making it up.

"Be careful, now," he warned her. "I just saw about a hundred snakes up in those trees there. Better cover up your head."

Despite his teasing, she shuddered and made a face at him. He'd insisted she sit up front while he handled the motor, but she couldn't help glancing back from time to time. He was poised so confidently at the stern, lean silhouette against the backdrop of the sky, eyes narrowed, hair streaming back from his chiseled face. Yet his face grew hard when he talked about losing the bayou, the modern threats to its survival, the possible extinction of its wildlife. And though his voice went cold, his eyes burned with rage.

They turned down another, narrower waterway. More shadows here . . . more isolated. As Miranda gazed at some fallen trees near the shoreline, she could swear that one of them was moving. . . .

"You *were* kidding about the alligators, right?" she asked suddenly, suspiciously, and wondered why Etienne seemed to be steering them toward that one weird log. "Oh my God—"

"Now, don't be getting all Ashley on me, *cher*."

"Oh my God," Miranda choked, frantically gauging the shallow sides of her seat. *No escape. None.* "It's a real alligator, isn't it—it's going to crawl in the boat—"

"Not in my boat. Watch, now."

There was no other choice *but* to watch. As Etienne reached down into a tackle box and scooped something into his hand, the massive alligator lifted its head, slid into the water, and glided toward them, invisible except for its eyes.

Miranda couldn't move.

With one smooth motion, Etienne flung what he'd been holding—a shower of little white pellets. The alligator immediately went to retrieve them and began to eat.

"You got yourself a real treat today," Etienne assured her, sounding almost proud. "It's still kinda warm outside, otherwise you mighta missed him."

But she still couldn't talk. All she could manage was a reproachful glare.

"Marshmallows," he explained, as though this were the

most natural thing in the world. "I'm telling you, he *loves* marshmallows."

"And is this the *only* alligator out here in this entire swamp?" she accused him.

Etienne feigned innocence. "Well . . . you *see* any more?"

"They're watching us, aren't they? Probably millions of them—"

"Aw, now don't be getting upset with me. You're from Florida—I thought you'd be plenty used to gators."

"Oh. Silly me. I forgot about all those alligators who used to lay out on the beach to get a tan."

Straight-faced, Etienne stretched over, ruffled her hair. "That gator there, he's old and blind in one eye—he's lost a whole lotta teeth. But me and him, we've grown up together, since I was a kid. Bubba, he's a good boy. And he sure does love the tourists."

"Really? For main course or dessert?"

Again the boat turned, a different inlet, shores even wilder and overgrown, a soft and fading quiet. The water lay still and shallow here; a golden-green mist hovered lightly in the air. Etienne guided their boat easily around an obstacle course of ancient trees, some rising ghostlike from the water, others shattered or fallen or half submerged, practically everything shrouded in moss. Only a few birdcalls now . . . echoing hollow . . . sounding sad . . . like phantoms lost and trapped in time. From the clotted underbrush of the banksides came the swift rustling of predator and prey, the sudden, sharp scream of inescapable death. . . .

"Miranda. You okay?"

She spun around, startled. He'd come up behind her, and

the boat wasn't moving—she couldn't tell if the motor was idling or simply stopped.

"Talk to me, now. What is it?"

But Miranda turned back, to the camouflaged patterns of the forest—foliage rotting, never quite dry; air like a wet sponge, never quite squeezed. As though no sunlight could ever break through to illuminate ancient secrets, to heal nature's wounds and battle scars; as though no breeze could ever penetrate deep enough to sweep away perpetual dampness, wild territorial scents, and the struggles of death.

"That animal crying," Etienne tried once more. "I know it's hard to listen to."

Miranda paused . . . nodded. Refocusing on him, she noted the flash of sympathy in his eyes, though his tone remained matter-of-fact.

"Survival, *cher*. The swamp here, it's got its own laws, its own way of doing things. It's cruel sometimes . . . but—"

"But that animal didn't want to die. It wanted to live."

"And some of them *don't* die. Some of them *do* live. Some of them get scars that make them stronger—"

"But not *that* animal, the one we heard. Not that one."

A long silence fell between them. When Etienne spoke again, his expression had softened.

"No. Not that one."

"And sometimes *people* try really hard to survive," she insisted stubbornly. "They fight and they hope and they pray and they do *all* the right things, and *they* don't deserve for bad things to happen to them, and they *don't* deserve to die. . . ."

Her voice trailed off, uncertain. She had no idea where that unexpected outburst had come from or why that sudden surge of emotions. She was feeling all mixed-up—she didn't want to be out here anymore, so far away from her own reality where she felt safer and more in control of things. She wanted to leave this untamable world—this unforgiving and unpredictable world—yet she felt helplessly, inexplicably drawn to it, stirred and strangely aroused by it, threatened and thrilled and terrified all at the same time. . . .

"Come here." Slipping his arms around her, Etienne pulled Miranda firmly back against him. "You can't save everybody and everything, *cher*. Alive *or* dead. You can only keep doing what you do best. Which is more than most people *ever* do."

Tears welled up in her throat. She managed to choke them back down. *If only things could always be like this*, she found herself thinking—*Etienne's warmth, Etienne's wisdom, whenever the world was too much to bear* . . .

"You really do love this place, don't you?" she murmured.

For one split second, his embrace seemed to tighten. "What's not to love?" he returned quietly.

His fingers stroked her sleeve. Taking his hand in hers, she found his wrist . . . lightly kissed his pulse. Two scars there beneath the ground-in dirt, jagged lines coursing past his elbow. Cautiously, she touched one of the narrow welts . . . traced its length slowly along a hard ridge of vein.

His body tensed. That same trapped reaction as he tried to pull free—only this time she clasped him more tightly.

"Stop it, Miranda."

Miranda kept going. "I don't care about your scars . . . you don't have to be afraid to show me—"

"I mean it—"

"You said scars make us stronger, and you're right. You're the strongest person I've ever known—"

"Don't!"

Etienne jerked away. Before Miranda realized what was happening, he climbed over the seat and stood there in front of her, feet planted wide apart, eyes stormy. On his face was a look she'd never seen before—a fierce struggle of embarrassment, shame, and defiance. He yanked his T-shirt off over his head. Shook back his hair. Fixed her with a cold, hard, unrelenting gaze.

"So look," he muttered. "Look at me."

She'd seen him without a shirt before, but never this close, in this much light. Now here were the marks of his childhood—the badly healed burns and welts, the faded cross-cuts and creases and furrows—all the sad, permanent memories etched deeply into his arms and shoulders, his back and chest. She observed them with no emotion; she kept her tears and her horror inside. She slid to her knees in the bottom of the boat. Strained and silent, Etienne followed, squatting back on his heels to watch her.

She knew he was watching, and she took her time—caressing these scars . . . kissing these scars. His skin was burning salt. His breath was raspy in the back of his throat. She could feel him trembling, though every muscle was locked in place. Without warning, he grabbed her wrists. Eased her onto her back. Gently . . . gently . . . she drew him down.

He was lying on top of her now. His black eyes narrowed, his jaw clenched. Miranda traced the angles of his cheekbones, the faint stubble of beard along his upper lip, down each side of his mouth, across the strong line of his chin. His piercing stare never wavered. His head began to lower . . . lips brushing lips . . . and as she closed her eyes, he covered her mouth with a deep, slow kiss.

They pressed tighter. Etienne's heart beat wildly against her own, strong and solid and sure. She was lost in him, consumed by him—*his heat and scent, the feel of him, body and voice, lips and touch, the irresistible need to surrender—*

His kisses grew more passionate. As she whispered his name, he caught her face between his hands . . . gazed endlessly into her soul.

"*Belle* Miranda," he murmured. "So beautiful, *ma cher*."

And then he smiled . . .

And there was no other time but this one perfect moment . . .

No other world but this bayou and Etienne.

21

"**Merde.** Shit, Miranda, wake up."

As Miranda's eyelids fluttered open, she peered around in total bewilderment. Shadows lay thick as far as she could see, and for one split second, she had absolutely no clue where she was. *A boat?* Trees and moss and water and . . . *Etienne's bare skin beneath my cheek, Etienne's strong arms around me . . .*

"*Allons,*" he said, pulling free, instantly on his feet. "Get yourself dressed, *cher*. We need to go back."

Etienne's body, tall and lean in the last golden rays of sunset . . .

Reality slammed full force. As he threw on his jeans and T-shirt, Miranda's brain scrambled to make sense of what was happening. *Miss Nell's for dinner . . . we talked and drank tea . . . and then the bayou tour . . . and then . . .*

With lightning speed, Etienne gathered her clothes, helping her into them, fastening buttons, jerking everything into place, giving her hair a quick smooth-down. He was very good at it, she noted—he'd obviously done this sort of thing many times before.

Considering this, she began to feel paranoid.

"Your mom's going to know, isn't she?" Miranda asked suddenly. Drawing back from her, Etienne seemed half perplexed, half amused.

"What you talking about?"

"Coming back late like this . . . and I'm all wrinkled—"

"You're not wrinkled, you look fine. And Mama, she won't be thinking anything about it—she knows we got ourselves a late start. And folks, they always get themselves a little bit wrinkled when they ride in a boat, yeah?"

She knew he was teasing her, but she wanted to believe him. The day had been so perfect, what they'd shared had been so perfect—she'd expected a different follow-up, not the rush and panic going on now. She wished they could have drifted forever. But Etienne was busy with the motor, and she was feeling more agitated by the second.

Do I look different? Besides my rumpled clothes and messed up hair, do I look different? Is it obvious somehow, what just happened? Will everyone be able to tell?

God, Miranda, you are so lame.

Nervously, she smoothed her sweater. Smoothed it twice more. Adjusted the sleeves, noticed a smear of grease down the front. *Oh, great. Just great.* The boat was moving again, and Etienne was intent on their surroundings—thickening mist . . . murky water . . . shifting, distorted shadows . . .

Still huddled on the floor of the bow, Miranda tried not to watch. "How long were we asleep?" she asked him.

"Not long—we just dozed off. But Mama, she's gonna be plenty upset with me if dinner gets ruined."

"Are . . . are you sure you know where you're going?"

"What, you think I can't get around here with both eyes shut?"

Whether he was teasing again or not, Miranda soon realized that he was right. Swiftly now, just as expertly, he guided the boat all the way back, whistling softly, completely unconcerned about the encroaching night. She was almost limp with relief by the time they landed. After tying the boat, Etienne draped his arm around her shoulders and guided her along the pathway to the house. She could see bright lights glowing ahead of them—floodlights, she guessed—and right before they entered the clearing, he suddenly stopped, turned her to face him, and held her in a long, leisurely kiss.

Miranda's emotions went spinning. As Etienne finally released her, he stepped back, cocked his head, and regarded her with a frown.

"You got your buttons all wrong there," he mumbled.

"What!"

"No big deal. Here—let me help. . . ."

He was already solving the problem—long fingers opening her sweater, realigning buttons and holes, closing them up again.

Miranda's cheeks flamed crimson. "Wonderful. Just one look at my clothes and . . . and your mom's going to figure it out."

Though she tried to hang back, he nudged her forward, pushing her toward the yard.

"She's going to *know*," Miranda persisted.

"She's not gonna know."

"I bet *you'd* know."

"Well, yeah, if you and Gage did it, I'd know."

"See? Then Gage might know too."

Etienne groaned. "Okay, if Gage were here, then he might know. But Gage isn't here."

They could see the house now. A minivan was parked near the gate, and without any warning, Etienne froze midstride.

"What is it?" Miranda asked, stopping beside him.

"What the hell's Gage doing here?"

"Gage? Oh my God—"

"Hey." Before either of them could move, Gage appeared from the rear of the van, arms loaded with grocery sacks. "Hey, Miranda."

"What are you doing here?" Etienne frowned. And then, as his mother hurried past him to lend a hand, "What's Gage doing here?"

Miss Nell seemed genuinely puzzled. "What do you mean, 'What's Gage doing here'? He always comes for dinner when I fix gumbo. It's his favorite, you know that."

"I just didn't know you were inviting him, is all," Etienne grumbled.

Still pulling bags from the van, Gage shot his cousin a quick sidelong glance—definitely suspicious. Miranda's heart sank.

"I didn't invite him," Miss Nell scolded. "He's your cousin, he doesn't have to be invited. And I needed some things from the store, and he was sweet enough to pick them up on his way. As a matter of fact, I tried to call *you*, but your cell went straight to voice mail."

"I . . ." Frowning, Etienne ran a hand through his hair. "Wonder how that happened."

"Maybe you left it in your truck," Gage commented dryly.

“Yeah, maybe. Probably. Thanks for reminding me.”

But there was no helpfulness on Gage’s face, no humor in his expression. He’d walked away from the van, Miranda realized, and was only a few feet from her now. Miss Nell, oblivious to the sudden tension, took the last load of groceries into the house. And while Etienne wrestled the van door shut, Gage simply stood there and looked at her.

He knew, of course.

Those soft brown eyes sweeping over her, and in one split second he knew.

And it didn’t really matter what gave it away—her clothes, her hair, the flush on her cheeks, though she did her best to hide it. She even crossed her arms tight over her chest, but it wasn’t enough to keep him out.

That one instant glance of total awareness . . .

And hurt.

“You went out in the boat?” Gage asked, as though he already knew the answer.

“Yeah.” Sauntering over, Etienne kept his voice casual . . . almost indifferent. “Showing her all the sights.”

“I bet.”

Miranda blushed to the roots of her hair. She tried to look away, *wanted* to look away, but all she could see was the wounded expression on Gage’s face. A thousand regrets coursed through her. She knew she was being irrational, and she also knew that Etienne was watching her, just as intently as Gage.

“Y’all come eat!” Miss Nell called, breaking the mood, the awkward silence. But Gage turned and walked back to his van.

"I can't stay, Aunt Nell."

"What?" Standing on the porch, Miss Nell peered down at them, clearly disappointed. "But it's your favorite, honey. I thought—"

"Sorry. I have . . . I forgot I have to take Mom somewhere."

"Tonight? She never said anything to me—"

"Yeah, it . . . just came up. She just called on my cell."

"But I hung up with her about ten minutes ago. Etienne, why is he leaving?"

"You heard him, Mama," Etienne said crossly. "He's got stuff to do."

"What's going on? Something, I know."

There was a screech of tires, an explosion of gravel as Gage sped away.

Etienne promptly scowled. "Let's just eat, yeah?"

Miranda didn't know how she ever survived the evening. The whole mood, her state of mind, her entire life had done a complete one-eighty since Etienne had picked her up that afternoon. It took every ounce of effort to be a good guest—eating amazing food that she had no appetite for . . . making conversation that she couldn't concentrate on . . . forcing herself to smile and laugh when all she wanted to do was cry.

It's not supposed to be like this. Etienne and I were together today and it was so wonderful, more than wonderful. . . .

But Etienne was more quiet than usual—and it was obvious that his mother really *did* know that something was wrong, though she never once asked. Several times she covered Miranda's hand with her own, giving it a gentle squeeze. And several times Miranda caught Miss Nell staring at her—brief glimpses of sympathy and kindness and understanding—but she couldn't really be certain, and she was too embarrassed to meet the woman's eyes. When Etienne put her in his truck to take her home, Miss Nell called him back to the porch, and Miranda could hear their politely muffled voices, angry and arguing.

There was no talking on the way to town. Once they'd pulled up at the house, however, Etienne drew her into his arms and held her close, his chin resting lightly on top of her head.

"I'm sorry, *cher*," he murmured. "I'm sorry you were embarrassed tonight."

So maybe he *did* realize, maybe he *did* understand. Yet instead of feeling comforted, she only felt more unhappy.

"Gage knows, doesn't he?" she asked, and saw him nod. "And your mom?"

"Maybe. After tonight . . . probably, yeah."

Miranda blinked back tears, gazed out the windshield at the moonlit sky.

"It's just that . . . it's private, you know? It's like this really private, sacred thing, and I waited because I wanted to . . . and . . ."

Pulling away, she got out and slammed the door. And then, before Etienne could stop her, she hurried up the front porch steps and went inside.

Miranda was relieved to have the house to herself.

She took a shower and washed her hair and had a good, long cry. Luckily, Mom and Aunt Teeta were still out—and by the time they came home, she was already in bed, faking sleep and avoiding eager questions about her Sunday dinner experience. She knew they'd corner her eventually; in the meantime she needed to sort out her emotions. Practice looking innocent. The Mom Test would be the worst. Even as preoccupied as Mom was these days, this just might be major enough for her to pick up on.

Etienne didn't come back that night, and he didn't call her either. Not that she'd really expected him to—or even wanted him to. Still, a little confirmation would have been nice. A considerate follow-up to their evening together. *What did you expect, Miranda—for Etienne to show up on the sunporch with roses?*

I bet Gage would have brought roses.

Which had depressed her to tears all over again. Because she couldn't stop thinking about Gage.

She didn't even know why it upset her so much. They didn't have a commitment; Gage had never suggested it or made any kind of move. Yet she kept seeing him over and over in her mind—the way he'd looked at her with that sad sort of accusation, the betrayal and disappointment in his eyes. It killed her to think that she'd hurt him.

She dreaded going to school the next day. Though she was almost certain that Gage hadn't said anything, the group *always* seemed to know when something was going on. She'd have to face him sooner or later, get that first awkward moment over with. Still, that wouldn't be half as awkward as Etienne being there, watching her and acting as if nothing had ever happened.

She purposely dawdled the next morning—by the time she was finally ready, Mom and Aunt Teeta were too stressed about their business trip to spend much time being nosy. When they dropped her off, a pop quiz was already under way in first period. Parker barely acknowledged her as she walked in. Intent on his paper, he kept his head lowered while she sat down—though he did grin from time to time, trying to read her answers. To her relief, no rumors seemed to be circulating around school—not about her *or* Etienne—no gossip in the hallways, no smirks or whispered comments. Miranda's paranoia began to fade. In third period, Ashley subtly motioned to her, a secret "we need to talk" signal—then silently mouthed, "Kurt." Gage, sitting next to Ashley, was preoccupied with a book and a marking pen; he had nothing to say, and he kept his back turned for the entire hour. Deserved or not, it still hurt Miranda's feelings. And made her more determined than ever to patch things up with him.

She found her chance at lunchtime. As usual, the group was congregated around Ashley's locker before heading outside to eat, and when Miranda paused at the end of the corridor, Ashley gave her a halfhearted wave.

"Hey, Miranda. We were just talking about you."

Instant panic. *Cool, Miranda, stay cool.* "You were?"

"You and Belle Chandelle. Gage said it might not be a good idea to go out there tonight—something about the power being out? And somebody getting shocked?"

No answer from Gage, who was hidden behind the open door of his locker. *Okay, Gage—but you must have heard that from Etienne—which means he must be trying to talk to you, even if you're not talking back.*

"No goblins tonight, what a shame." Parker sighed.

Not looking particularly upset about it, he backed casually into the hall, bouncing a tennis ball off his bicep. Roo watched him, low tolerance level. No sign of Etienne.

"What do you think, Miranda?" Ashley persisted. "*I* really don't think we should go if it's dangerous; do you?"

But Miranda's attention had focused now, three lockers down from Ashley's. She could see Gage there, frustrated with an avalanche of papers and notebooks that kept sliding out as quickly as he stuffed them back in. She took one step, then halted. She thought about turning around and leaving, but mustered her courage instead.

"Hi, Gage."

It would have been better if he'd ignored her completely. So much kinder than the careless glance he shot her, the dismissive shrug of his shoulders.

"Uh-oh." Switching the ball to his other arm, Parker sidled closer to where Gage was standing. "Somebody got up on the wrong side of a wet dream this morning."

"Shut up," Gage grumbled.

"Well, you're certainly a Mr. Mopey," Ashley scolded him, shaking her finger. "He's never like this, Miranda—he's always so *sweet*. But he's been a Mr. Mopey *all morning long.*"

"Maybe Mr. Mopey needs more sex," Parker suggested.

But Ashley was still in fuss mode. "What are you mad about, Gage? Whatever it is, there's no reason to take it out on Miranda."

Roo's shrewd glance went from Gage to Miranda, assessing

the tension in between. When it finally settled on Gage again, it had changed to a knowing stare.

"Actually," Roo offered, "there might be one very *good* reason. Who just happens not to be here today."

"Ah," Parker caught on at once. "*That* reason."

Ashley was completely bewildered. Miranda stood there miserably while Gage ignored Roo's innuendoes.

"Okay, I'm starved!" Parker announced, a little too loudly. "Anybody for lunch?"

But before anyone could move, Miranda walked past them, directly over to Gage. He'd finished reloading his locker now; he gave the contents one last shove. His eyes were lowered, avoiding hers—and his body was tense, muscles clenched tightly on both sides of his jaw.

"Gage," she whispered, and gently touched his arm. "Gage . . . I . . . I just—"

"Hey, I'm not your boyfriend, Miranda." Shrugging, he stepped back and slammed the door of his locker. "You can go screw whoever you want."

Silence plunged around them—a cold, shocked silence of disbelief. Tears rolled down Miranda's cheeks. Ashley gasped, and Roo's eyes widened in dark reproach. Parker froze where he stood, tennis ball dropping to the floor.

"Jesus, Gage," Parker muttered.

As Gage turned, he met Parker's stare head-on. "What the hell are you looking at?"

"Uh . . . an asshole?"

The four of them watched him go. Numbly, Miranda felt herself being hugged, then suddenly realized it was Parker.

"Hey, he's in a crappy mood," Parker shrugged, one arm clumsy around her shoulders. "Don't take it personally."

"Don't take it *personally*?" Ashley was horrified. "Didn't you hear what Gage just *said* to her?"

"I'm just glad the whole *school* didn't hear what Gage just said to her." Hesitating, Parker considered. "At least he was pretty quiet about it."

Roo seemed deep in thought. Sliding her hand to her forehead, she pushed distractedly at her bangs . . . cleared them away from her eyes. "I'll go," she said flatly.

Before anyone could react, she marched off along the corridor in the same direction that Gage had taken.

"Look at her." Parker grimaced. "A troll on a mission."

"No, it's good," Ashley insisted, brightening just a little. "Gage listens to Roo. Wait, Miranda . . . you'll see."

"Yeah," Parker agreed, hug ended. "In some . . . weird . . . creepy . . . Roo way, I'm sure she'll . . . do . . . whatever."

But Miranda didn't wait. She didn't wait, and she didn't care about figuring things out. She heard Ashley calling her, but she didn't stop or look back. Instead she hurried down the hallway and the stairs, through the side door and across the grounds, hoping that no one would see her, or report her, or get her suspended for leaving campus. Then she started to run, out the back gates and into the parking lot, and past shops and quiet neighborhoods, all the way home.

Aunt Teeta's hatchback was in the garage, keys in the ignition, as usual. She and Mom had driven Mom's car to New Orleans and wouldn't be back till late. The group would be in classes for the next few hours. Ashley and Parker had practices; Gage had rehab; Etienne was off working somewhere. And if Roo wasn't walking dogs at the animal shelter, then she'd probably be spending the rest of the day trying to cool Gage down.

And no work crews at Belle Chandelle.

The plantation would be deserted.

The rooms would be dark.

The afternoon, quiet and undisturbed.

Perfect for me, Miranda thought. *Perfect for what I need to do.*

She wasn't even afraid, she realized.

For the afterlife wasn't nearly as scary as her own life had become. . . .

And the dead were far less trouble than the living.

Belle Chandelle welcomed her like an old and dear friend.

Miranda felt strangely at home.

She made her way directly to the hidden staircase, her footsteps echoing endlessly through the dark, empty house. When she reached the third story, she hesitated only a moment before thrusting her key in the lock . . . turning the knob . . . and slowly pushing the door. Her heart began to beat faster. Standing there on the threshold, she swept her flashlight beam over the floors and rafters and walls. . . .

Don't wait. You know what you have to do.

The attic was cold . . . only blackness around her, thick and musty. A tarp flapped at one of the broken windows, sucking in and out through the broken glass, as if the room were breathing.

Do it now.

Unsteadily, the glow of her flashlight slid across the mantelpiece and up to the mirror—catching its own image in a sudden burst of brightness. For one instant, Miranda saw the room reflected there—the *past* reflected there—and her face in the midst of it, ghostly pale but resolved.

Get it over with. Before you lose your nerve.

Almost dreamlike, she moved to the fireplace and stopped directly in front of it. Stared into the depths of the mirror, into her own solemn eyes. As she pressed her hand to the dingy glass, she could feel her instincts begin to stir, a curious though not unpleasant detachment. What she needed now was to distance herself. To focus. To find that place within where she could open her mind and her senses . . . reach out in all directions . . . surrender . . .

And pass through to the Other Side . . .

The room was just as she remembered.

The smell washing over her in waves . . . the terrified sobbing from the shadows.

Same fireplace, same mantel, same mirror, and her eyes gazing steadily back at herself across an eternity of sorrow . . .

It's okay, Miranda. You're here . . . but you're not *here. . . .*

Flies rose up around her, swarms of flies, and the heat, she was already choking, suffocating, *can't breathe, need air can't breathe . . . little faces—terrified! So terrified! Tear-stained, dark eyes dark hair so much the same, holding hands, soiled nightgowns, sweat-drenched covers—and the eyes of the woman, staring eyes, imploring eyes—black dress black hair black cap with lace—back and forth, in and out of flickering candlelight, in and out of shadows creaking, so quiet in her rocking chair, back and forth creaking, back and forth on the floorboards creaking, slower and slower and silent* Oh God! *bloodshot eyes, yellow skin—the stink of sickness, the stench of decay—*

"Mama," the little ones weeping, the little ones pleading . . . Mama, look at us . . .

And the smell was too much, much worse than last time, smothering, choking deep in her throat—*can't breathe—can't move—"Mama, Mama," the children sobbing, barely above a whisper now, baby cries, dying cries . . . "Help us, Mama, it hurts—"*

"Shh," Miranda soothed. "Hush, now."

She was moving toward them across the threshold, across the filthy floor, pools of urine and blood, gagging, trying not to, moving around the woman with the sightless, staring eyes, eyes frozen in desperate mother love. "Shh," Miranda murmured, "don't be afraid."

Lifting the babies one by one, jaundiced little faces and red eyes, red from sick, red from crying . . . gently, tenderly, "I've got you, my darlings, I've got you . . ." Two little girls squeezed tight against her, tight against her heart . . .

Miranda held them as they sobbed. Smoothed their damp, stringy hair, rocked them, comforted them, hummed them childhood lullabies. And all the while, "Your mama loves you," she promised them, over and over again, tears streaming down her cheeks, silent sobs aching in her chest, "Shh . . . your mama's here, your mama loves you so very much."

And when at last they were quiet and still, even then, *even then*, she chose to believe that they were sleeping instead of dead. Even while she laid them in their mother's arms and tucked their mother's worn black shawl around them, binding them close to her, keeping them safe. *Sweet little girls . . . sweet little—*

Puzzled, Miranda drew back.

She traced a fingertip over each clammy forehead . . . each nose . . . each tiny chin . . .

No . . . not girls—

Feeling in some weird, distant way that they were almost familiar somehow—*dark hair, dark eyes so much the same*— that she might have seen them somewhere, long, long ago, in another place, in another world . . .

No! Not little girls, she suddenly realized, *but little boys!* And she should have known it sooner, thought of it before—their nightgowns, long nightgowns that little boys wore back then, their hair, long curls that little boys wore back then . . .

Motherless boys . . . little boys lost . . .

But you're not lost now . . . not now, not ever again.

For one last time, she kissed them.

Sleep angels . . . sleep loved in your mother's arms . . .

Through timeless shadows, Miranda walked to the mirror. She pulled some covers from the bed, then stood for a moment, clutching a blanket in her hands and staring deep into the murky glass.

The room pulsed softly, low burning candles. From far across a century, the mother gazed back at her, tears of gratitude in her tragic eyes, beloved sons held close. . . .

Understanding, Miranda nodded.

She carefully lifted the blanket and draped it over the mirror.

Your own time now, Miranda . . . your own world. This isn't your place anymore.

Centering herself, she drew a calming breath. Emptied her mind . . . opened her senses . . . willed herself to follow . . .

Something's wrong.

She knew it at once, that catching of her breath, that quickening of her heartbeat, that sudden terrible fear inside as every candle flame sputtered . . . dimmed . . . began to go out. She groped for her flashlight, but couldn't find it; she whirled around and stared at the room while a scream clawed silently at her throat.

The room was still there—walls, floors, furniture, everything just the same—just as before, nothing any different, nothing changed. Nothing except . . .

Oh God . . . God no—

The sickroom all around her—heat and filth . . . death and decay . . . pain and suffering . . . hopelessness, anguish, despair . . .

This can't be happening, it's not supposed to happen like this—

Because something *was* different, she realized. Something

that struck her just as the very last candle faded, and the room went completely black.

They're gone. . . .

The mother . . . her children . . . all of them vanished . . .

I'm the only one here.

22

Don't panic, Miranda. *Stay right where you are, and be calm.*

It would be worse, she knew—*much* worse—if she panicked. She had to stay focused, had to gather her thoughts into some semblance of order. If she started screaming, she'd never stop. If she gave in to hysteria, every emotion would be exposed, and her senses would completely shut down, and she'd never get out. . . .

But you're not *really here, remember? You're only thinking this, it's only in your mind.*

Yet this room wasn't a dream or a thought—this room was *real,* just as the smell was real, as her terror was real, a primal terror, a childhood fear of the dark, *and things in the dark I can't see—*

"They're gone," Miranda kept telling herself, "The ghosts are gone now, there's nothing else in the dark, nothing else but me. . . ."

But there *were* things here, she could sense them. Other spirits suffering . . . and waiting . . . and watching . . . sizing her up, gauging her skills, waiting to make themselves known to her.

She couldn't breathe. So hot—so weak—so dizzy—her legs

wouldn't hold her, and she crumpled forward, hands clutching at the mantelpiece, tearing at the folds of the blanket, ripping it from the mirror—

No reflection there—no attic—no me—

"Help me!" she screamed. "Somebody please help me, I'm in here!"

But how could they help her, how could anybody help her? When this place she was trapped in was a world unknown to the living?

Yet over and over she tried. Clearing her mind, redirecting her focus, reaching out with her instincts. Over and over, determined and hopeful, till she was sick and shaking and utterly exhausted. With every failure, she grew more desperate. She'd been so confident, so sure of her abilities—she'd slipped through to this side so easily, it had never occurred to her that she might not be able to slip back.

Parker knew. Parker warned me. Parker, who hid his abilities from everyone, even Ashley, and most of all himself. *Why didn't I listen to him?* The very fact that he'd come to her with his warning should have been clue enough that something bad was going to happen.

"Oh, God, what am I going to do?"

Her panic was steadily mounting. No one knew she was here. They all had things to do this afternoon. After her confrontation with Gage, they'd all think she'd just run off to hide somewhere at school or maybe gone home. They'd made her promise not to come out here without them—why hadn't she waited? She didn't even know how long she'd been gone—there was no concept of time in this lost place. *Hours? Days? A hundred years or more?*

None of this is real, Miranda, just will yourself back again, back the way you came, it's a dream, a fantasy, you're still in the attic, you're standing here at the mirror, and you're imagining all this, in your mind, in your thoughts, just open your eyes, and it will all vanish like the worst kind of nightmare. . . .

But the voice of reason was a voice she no longer recognized. And the darkness was growing steadily darker, and the silence even more silent . . .

"I'm here! I'm trapped, and I'm here!"

Her screams, soundless in the air. Her fingers sliding slowly down the mirror where nothing at all was reflected.

"I'm in the attic! Can anyone hear me?"

But no one heard, and no one came.

Only shadows and sorrowful memories.

"*—body!*"

Parker was dozing.

"*—ease . . . some . . .*"

Dozing just the way he always did in the library. It had the most comfortable chairs in the whole school, it was the only time all day he could do any real relaxing around here, and besides, Miss Callaway the librarian thought he was cute and let him do pretty much whatever he wanted, as long as he didn't snore.

"*—elp . . . please . . .*"

"Huh?" he mumbled. "What?"

A kid at the shelves gave him a funny look. Parker gave him the finger and settled back in the cushy, oversized chair.

"*—in here!*"

"What?" Parker asked, and realized once again that nobody was talking.

Dammit, what's going on? He was trying to sleep, he had important things to think about, like the game Friday and making sure Ashley got his English paper done on time and keeping an eye on that jerk Streak Fuller . . .

He wanted to believe that things were okay with Ashley.

After all the agonizing he'd done, and the money he'd spent on those stupid cheerleader tickets. And even if he did still think the raffle had been fixed.

And Ashley *had* been open about the whole date thing; she'd told him about her night at the concert—so he couldn't complain about that. She'd had fun, though, he could tell—so he sure as hell *could* complain about *that*. . . . And sometimes lately she had that weird look on her face—the look girls always got when they were thinking about some guy. Except suddenly he wasn't quite sure if *he* was the guy Ashley was thinking about, so there was one *more* thing he could complain—

"*Parker!*"

"Who is that?" he demanded, and got to his feet, turning in a slow, suspicious circle.

Miss Callaway was at her desk, politely frowning. So it didn't really make sense that somebody was playing a joke on him, rigging up voices, watching to see what he'd do so they could laugh. And Miss Callaway would never allow that in her library, anyway.

Maybe he'd fallen asleep, he reasoned—gone into one of those deep, eye-twitchy levels people always talked about. Whatever it was, it was really starting to piss him off. He looked forward to these little catnaps. And it creeped him out when things played with his head.

Parker sat again, slid down in his chair. Folded his arms over his chest. Lowered his chin . . . closed his eyes . . .

"*Parker, please hear me!*"

"Miranda?"

This time he bolted upright, brain spinning wildly. Not a dream, he was sure of it—he'd know her voice anywhere.

But where was it?

And how come he was the only one in the whole library who seemed to be picking it up?

She'd run away earlier, after Gage had acted like a total prick. Ashley had tried to stop her, but Miranda had been so upset, and actually he couldn't blame her. Damn that Gage. And Etienne, too, since it was pretty obvious what had happened. Parker hated seeing girls with hurt feelings, but especially girls he knew . . . and liked. Miranda was cool. She had balls. He didn't want to see her heart broken.

So what's going on?

He walked outside to the water fountain. Trying to calm himself down, trying to think. He'd assumed Miranda had gone home; under the circumstances, he'd have gone home. He would have gone after her too—but he couldn't afford a suspension for leaving school grounds. Luckily, Ash knew that chick in the office. After Miranda left, Ashley had told the girl that Miranda was sick, and so she'd marked it down, all legal. Ashley was upset for Miranda, and Parker didn't blame her. It had surprised him, how fast Miranda and Ashley became friends.

"*—help . . . in here—*"

Goosebumps shivered up his spine. He was totally freaked, hearing Miranda like that, being so sure it was her stuck up in his head with nowhere else to go. He gulped some water, then began to pace. Maybe she was just bored at home right now, testing out her stupid powers, using him for a guinea pig.

Damn you, Miranda. Damn you for making me face this—

"*Parker!*" Shit, was she crying? It sure *sounded* like she was crying—"*Parker, please find me!*"

"Jesus Christ . . ."

What's happening, Miranda? Can you hear my thoughts like I can hear yours? Can you tell me where you are?

"*Help me. . . .*"

There was terror in her voice . . . a sense of loss and emptiness . . . like a voice at the bottom of a well. A lonely place . . . a dark place . . .

And she was scared . . . and alone . . . and . . .

Trapped.

Parker bolted for the exit, fished his cell phone from his pocket, punched in an all-too-familiar number.

It rang once, twice, and then—

"Etienne? You need to find Miranda—*now*."

* * *

Gage knew immediately that something was wrong.

The way Etienne's tires screeched right up next to the fence, the way he was out of the truck before it even had time to stop. From the top row of bleachers, Gage watched his cousin slip through the back gate, hurry toward him across one end of the playing field, then stop in front of him with a frown.

"Gage, Miranda's gone."

"Gone? What are you talking about?"

"Nobody can get a hold of her, they've all been trying to call. I'm thinking maybe she got herself in some kinda trouble over at Belle Chandelle. Parker said she was upset earlier—ran outta school in a hurry—"

"Well, you know Belle Chandelle better than anybody," Gage cut him off. "You should be able to handle it."

"And that mirror? The one she was talking about going into? I'm having a real bad feeling about that. You need to come."

For a long awkward moment, neither said a word. Then finally, unapologetically, Etienne sighed. "Look, Miranda and me—it just happened."

"It always just happens."

"I'm not gonna hurt her. I could never do that."

"You'll do it. This one won't be any different."

"Look, Gage, we can be having ourselves a pissing contest all day long . . . or we can go find Miranda. What's it gonna be?"

Etienne turned and headed back to his truck.

Gage silently watched him go.

* * *

Help . . . somebody . . . the attic . . . the mirror . . .

Miranda couldn't scream anymore. Not with her voice and not with her mind. Her throat felt raw, as raw as her hands felt from pounding on the mirror, from prying at the hidden-panel door. *But maybe there really is no pain, no screaming, no pounding or prying. Just this nightmare where I'm trapped, this imaginary place that I can't come back from.*

Reality had no meaning here; time had ceased to exist. She'd fought so desperately to hold out, but the fear and the dark and the sickroom smells had eventually worn her down—drifting her in and out of consciousness. After a while, she hadn't even tried to struggle anymore. She'd shut off her senses, her thoughts, her emotions—to block out the horrible truth. *To survive.*

Not real . . . not real . . . not real . . .

And then the shadows began to come.

Comforting her, caressing her, in soft, seductive whispers. *Stay, Miranda, stay here with us . . . stay at Belle Chandelle . . .*

She wondered if she really might be dying. And realized that she was already in her tomb.

She thought of Mom and Aunt Teeta. Of Roo and Ashley . . . Parker and Gage. Etienne.

She imagined him on the boat, in those last golden rays of sunlight, and his hands making her feel safe, and his heart beating strong against hers, and his voice calling her name, *Miranda . . .*

"Miranda!"

So sweet this imagining, so perfect in her memory, that she could almost believe it had happened once. . . .

"Miranda!"

But it never happened, and it's not real, and it's only in my head—

"Miranda, can you hear me? Wake up!"

Etienne?

The room began to grow smaller. Shadows stirred restlessly on every side. Shadows content to sleep, not wanting to be disturbed by intruders. *Stay with us, Miranda . . . no fears . . . no problems . . . no running away . . . nothing to cry over, ever again . . .*

"Miranda, where are you?"

Gage? "Oh, Gage, yes! Yes, I'm here!"

The room had disappeared now. Smothered in shadows, and only this mantelpiece remaining. Only this mantelpiece and mirror left behind.

Miranda reached out cautiously toward the glass . . . saw a faint shadow move on the other side. *A silhouette of a hand . . . the low murmur of voices . . . voices that I recognize . . .*

And then, like a fog slowly lifting, the mirror began to clear . . . lighten . . . and reflect.

An image of another attic . . . another time . . . another Miranda . . .

She could see herself lying there on the cold, dusty floor. Darkness lit eerily by lanterns and flashlights, friends gathered closely around. Gage and Etienne kneeling over her, one on each side, Etienne holding her hand. Ashley sobbing in the circle of Parker's arms. Roo standing somberly behind Gage.

Like dream people. Like people in a play.

No . . . no . . . I'm the dream person . . . and I'm trying so hard to wake up. . . .

"Wake up, Miranda," Etienne mumbled. "Come on, *cher*. Open your eyes."

"Is she dead?" Ashley sobbed, while Parker held her closer. "She looks dead, are you sure she's not—"

"She's not dead." Gage insisted quietly. "She's . . . just . . ."

"In another place," Roo finished. "An in-between place." Collecting jackets from everyone, she leaned over, covered Miranda, then lightly touched Etienne's shoulder. "Does she even know us? Does she even know we're here?"

Etienne frowned, his face half light, half shadow. "She can't stay like this. Not for much longer. She's hardly even breathing."

"Well, we can't take her to a hospital," Parker argued. "They sure as hell won't know what to do with her."

"Oh, and like, you do?" Roo challenged him.

Ashley held up her hands for peace. "We don't even know how long she's been like this. She's never done this before . . . this hasn't ever happened. Not *supposed* to happen."

"It's my fault," Gage said unhappily. "If I hadn't said what I did—"

"Your fault?" Etienne scowled. "I'm the one who got her all upset—"

"Does it even friggin' matter?" Parker was pacing, back and forth, the width of the room. "Just figure out a way to get her here. You can settle this other shit later."

Reaching out, Ashley stopped him midstride. "Parker's right. How do we get her back?"

"Same way she went in," Gage replied softly, "would be my guess."

"But she went in through her mind."

"But her mind went through the mirror."

Miranda could see Gage standing, moving toward the mirror. His face leaning in, his eyes and fingertips carefully scrutinizing every inch of the glass. He was so close, she could have touched him. He pressed his hand flat against the mirror; she placed hers against it. He stared at her, almost as if he sensed her presence, but obviously seeing nothing.

"Gage, I'm here. Please see me."

But instead, Gage turned on his heel and gazed at Etienne. "You'll have to bring her back."

A quick glance, startled. Etienne's hand tightened around Miranda's limp hand. "Me? How?"

"You're the one with the strongest connection. You're the one her spirit will be most drawn to. Especially if she's lost . . . or doesn't have the strength . . ."

"I'm not leaving her." Again his grip tightened on the unconscious Miranda's hand.

Gage took a step toward him. "Look. Suppose she *is* stuck in some alternate world. And because she went in through the mirror, that world is . . . backward. Everything reversed. I mean . . . it makes sense. The attic there would be switched around, opposite to this attic. We have the living on this side, they have the dead. And just because we can't see Miranda doesn't mean she can't see us. Right now. She could be watching us right now, even though our side of the mirror looks empty."

The attic was silent for several moments. It was Etienne who finally spoke.

"Look at her." His voice was rough, barely a whisper. "What if she's *not* over there, on the other side of that mirror? What if she's really in *here*? Really still in *here*, and she's not coming back, no matter what?"

Tears rolled down Ashley's face. Roo's eyes shone with undisguised emotion; Parker choked down a sudden lump in his throat.

"Miranda's not in there." Walking over to Etienne, Gage put a hand on his shoulder. "Etienne, it's not her lying here on the floor. Trust me. Let go of her hand . . . so you can get her back."

But mirror-Miranda could feel herself fading . . . fading like the ghosts of the mother and her children . . . fading like all the spirits who had passed this way before her. And when she finally heard Etienne's familiar voice, it seemed like some distant memory that she couldn't quite recall. . . .

"Miranda."

That voice . . . I've heard that voice before . . . but where?

"Touch my hand, *cher*. Can you hear me? Go the mirror, and touch my hand."

Another shadow . . . passing by the mirror . . . pausing on the other side of the glass. Glass hazy again, dusty with time, washed with the tears of many grieving hearts . . .

"I know you're there—you've *got* to be there. Just take my hand . . . just reach for it . . ."

Sharp silhouette, fingers splayed, palm flat . . . those hands that I held, that held me, caressed me, protected me, wanted me . . . warmth, purpose, strength, life—

Weakly, she stretched her own hand to the mirror. Fingertips sliding uselessly away . . .

"Miranda," Gage said sharply, "look at the mirror. Take Etienne's hand. Do it now."

That hand . . . yes . . . that hand that I know . . . that I love . . .

With her last ounce of strength, she touched the shadow on the mirror. And instantly felt the connection—

Etienne.

"Come on, *cher*. Reach out to me, that's right, I can feel you—"

"Let your heart go, Miranda," Gage said softly. "Hold Etienne's hand . . . let your heart go . . . and follow it."

The world went upside down.

Every century, every day, every second of Belle Chandelle rushing past her, around her, each bright and bitter moment filling the mirror with images of long ago. In a dizzying blur, Miranda swept through the shadows and the sorrows and the spirits. . . .

And returned from the Other Side

She was still clutching Etienne's hand.

She was lying on the floor, with her friends around her, a blur of laughter and jokes and tears. Unspoken words in Etienne's eyes. Ashley, Parker, and Roo all talking at once. And Gage standing apart; hands clasped together behind his neck; a relieved and weary smile.

Miranda rose up on her elbows. She saw Roo walk over to Gage, the grateful hug she gave him, the modest hug he gave back.

But as Roo turned away, Gage's eyes met Miranda's.

Holding her in a gentle gaze . . .

As he touched one hand to his heart.

23

"Miss Nell wants us to come out there and eat," Roo explained. "Some new recipe she's trying. You know, for a crowd?"

Yawning, Miranda ran a hand through her tangled hair. Switched the phone to her other hand. Sat down on the porch swing and pulled her snuggly robe tight around her.

"Well, I definitely think the six of us qualify as a crowd," she agreed. "Is Miss Nell out at Belle Chandelle now? What time is it anyway?"

"A little after three. How's your coma?"

"No coma. Just mirror-itis. Luckily, Mom still thinks it's just a flu relapse. Although I *have* been getting a lot of I-told-you-so's."

"You should take advantage of your sick-leave. Stay home longer."

"No, thanks. One day is plenty. I'm sick-leaved out."

"Watch more comedy reruns. Enjoy more pampering. I mean . . . going back and forth through time takes a lot out of a person."

Miranda had to laugh. "Tell me about it."

"Anyway, Miss Nell said to come any time after five-thirty. You want Parker to give you a ride?"

"You know what?" Miranda said quickly. "I'm pretty sure I can borrow Mom's car. I'll just meet you out there."

"Okay."

The truth was, Miranda had her own agenda in mind. Something none of the others knew about, something she hadn't even been aware of herself till she'd slipped through that mirror for the final time, returning from the past to the present.

It had weighed on her mind ever since. With every memory of the attic and its occupants, a troubling insight had been forming in her mind, gathering substance and truth and reality. It had haunted her—not threatening this time, but with a strange sort of affection—murmuring into her dreams and then whispering her awake with gentle knowings.

She was right about it, she was certain.

The others weren't there yet when she got to Belle Chandelle; she'd purposely driven out early, after hanging up with Roo. Only Miss Nell's car was in the parking lot, and as Miranda walked toward the house, she could already smell the seafood boil—shrimp and crabs, potatoes and corn and onions, all boiled together with spices, outside in a giant cauldron. There was French bread baking too—butter being warmed, bread pudding in the oven, rum sauce gently simmering. When Miranda walked into the kitchen, Miss Nell was angled away from the door, leaning on the counter, poring eagerly over cookbooks. Miranda almost turned around and left. Maybe it was wrong to bring up this matter she wanted to discuss. Too intrusive. Too private . . . *too special*—

"Miranda! Come in! Has that flu finally run its course? I was so hoping you'd be here today."

Before Miranda could change her mind, Miss Nell had her wrapped in one of those perfect hugs. Maybe it was a sign, Miranda told herself—to go ahead with her mission.

"Are you here early for a sneak preview?" Miss Nell teased. "Did you notice the picnic tables? It's such perfect weather today, I thought we could eat outside. Plus, I think I'll be cooking for the work crews a few days a week from now on."

"That's great. No, I just decided to . . . see if I could help with anything."

"Honey, that's so sweet, but I think I have everything under control. Just some heavy stuff that can wait till the boys get here. Oh. And I brought something to show you." Clearing off a chair, she motioned Miranda to sit down. "Since you were telling me that day how much you like looking at old pictures . . ."

Miranda couldn't believe it. There couldn't have been a more perfect lead-in to what she had to say if she'd planned it herself. When Miss Nell placed the family album down on the table in front of her, Miranda immediately gave a squeal of delight.

"Gage? Oh my God, that *has* to be Gage—"

"It is," Miss Nell chuckled. "He looks like a little doll . . . those eyes and those dimples. See here, next to Etienne, he makes Etienne look like some criminal-in-training."

"He *is* a criminal-in-training," Miranda insisted. *He steals hearts, and batters down defenses, and sneaks in when and where you least expect him to.*

Miss Nell gave a knowing smile. As if all too aware of what Miranda was thinking.

Miranda was having so much fun. Family members and friends, summer vacations for Gage and his folks, pictures of Miss Nell's restaurant, historic images of St. Yvette and its charming transformation through the years. And on every page, snapshot after snapshot of Gage and Etienne.

The boys clowning around, competing, cutting up. School pictures and family holidays, the bayou in every season. And the rest of the group, of course—Ashley and Parker and Roo—keeping life interesting and entertaining through the years.

By the time Miss Nell closed the album, Miranda was sore from laughing. They'd gone through a whole pitcher of tea and finished off a bag of extra spicy pork rinds and talked till they were almost hoarse. But now, and unexpectedly, Miss Nell pulled a photograph from the album and passed it to her.

Miranda looked up in surprise. "What's this?"

"I was noticing how you looked at this one. As if you especially liked it."

Gage and Etienne side-by-side. Dark hair so much the same, but different; dark eyes so much the same, but different. The hard line of Etienne's jaw, the dimple in Gage's cheek. Miranda felt her throat tighten.

"Oh, Miss Nell . . . I mean—"

"It's my favorite too. I'd like you to have it."

"But—"

"Please. When they behave . . . irresponsibly—that picture will remind you of how good and wonderful they truly are."

Miranda ducked her head . . . felt a quick flush of embarrassment. Obviously, Miss Nell never missed much. And obviously, she knew her boys.

"I . . . need to ask you something, Miss Nell."

The woman's glance was totally open. "What is it, honey?"

Slowly, Miranda looked up. She gazed full into Miss Nell's black eyes, so very much like her son's.

"Gage and Etienne," Miranda murmured at last. "They're not . . . what I mean is . . ."

And she saw the expression on Miss Nell's face—a split second of acknowledgment, but no surprise . . . an instant of reflection, but no denial. Before Miranda could even say the words, Miss Nell's eyes told her everything that she needed to know. Immeasurable sadness . . . unbearable pain . . . and then finally . . . gently . . . surrender and relief.

"Gage and Etienne," Miranda could barely speak. "They're not cousins, are they?"

Straightening her shoulders, Miss Nell sat down again, directly across the table.

"No."

"They're both your sons. They're brothers."

Time crept by, and with it, a poignant silence. At last Miss Nell's mouth twisted into a brave, bitter smile. "Etienne's father didn't want another baby," she explained. "When I got pregnant with Gage, Lazare was drinking again, violent, the abuse worse than ever. I took Etienne and went to Jules and Frank's in

Mississippi around my due date. And I had my baby there. I told Lazare it was stillborn—which was believable, actually, considering the beatings."

Now Miss Nell's eyes were tearing up. She hesitated a moment, got her emotions under control. Cleared her throat and continued.

"He didn't care, of course, and he didn't question it. In fact, I'm sure he was relieved. Jules and Frank arranged Gage's adoption. I didn't want Gage to go through all the torture and humiliation that Etienne had. No child should ever have to endure that."

"And Gage doesn't know."

Miss Nell shook her head, absolute resolution. "And neither does Etienne. And neither one of them must *ever* know."

Reaching across the table, Miranda took the woman's hand. "Of course, I won't say anything if—"

"I'm dying, Miranda."

Time stopped. Pain stabbed from nowhere. As Miranda stared through a haze of shock, the whole world turned dark around her. Her sorrow was spilling over now; she could scarcely see Miss Nell for the tears.

"The cancer's back," Miss Nell said softly. "It's just a matter of time."

"Oh my God . . . Miss Nell . . ."

"Etienne doesn't know about that, either. And that's another thing you have to *promise* me—*swear* to me—you'll never tell him."

"But—but what if he figures it out? He—"

"Yes, he's always had a way of knowing things. But this one's different. He *doesn't want* to figure this out, Miranda. He *doesn't want* to know. He wants to believe I'm in remission, so that's exactly what I'm going to let him think. For as long as possible. For as long as I can hide it. And for as long as he wants to believe it."

"And how long . . . how long do you—"

"Well, it's a battle between my body and my will now, isn't it?" Despite the grim topic, a dimple flashed in Miss Nell's cheek. "And my will hasn't failed me yet. I just might outlive Belle Chandelle, who knows?"

She laughed. A courageous laugh. A determined laugh. A laugh that warmed Miranda's heart, despite the troubling shadows.

"Miss Nell." Her voice trembled. "I'm so sorry."

"Don't be sorry, honey. All of us are dying every day . . . just like all of us are living every day." Laughter faded now, Miss Nell's tone grew solemn once more. "The thing is . . . I always thought I'd be here a long time, to watch my boys grow up. Protect them. Keep them safe. But life didn't work out that way. And I don't want whatever time I have left with my boys to be bitter or sad or . . ."

Miss Nell pressed her hand over her eyes . . . shook her head. Miranda's face was wet with tears.

"But," Miranda had to say it, "don't you think Gage would *want* to know? About you being his mother? Especially if you're going to . . . not going to be here someday?"

"Gage has a mom and dad who adore him; a wonderful,

loving home; a great life." Her hand lowered back to the table, her voice grew urgent. "What more could a mother ask for her son? Why would I go and ruin that for him—because of things he didn't have any control over? Then there would be regrets, and guilt, and all those other things I don't ever want Gage to go through. I love him so much . . . *so much*. I don't want to put the burden on him of who I am."

"Miss Nell . . . you're incredible."

"Shh." With eyes gleaming tears, Miss Nell reached across the table. She took Miranda's hand tightly in her own. "I know that what I'm asking you to do is a huge thing . . . an enormous responsibility. To keep these secrets from Gage and Etienne. But I *need* you to do this for me, Miranda . . . *and* for them."

"I swear."

"Thank you, honey." Stretching from her chair, Miss Nell leaned over and kissed Miranda's forehead. Then she wiped the tears gently from Miranda's cheeks. "You remind me of somebody, Miranda. Somebody I used to know."

"Who's that?"

Sliding her fingers under Miranda's chin, Miss Nell gazed deep into her eyes. "Me. And you're a whole lot stronger than you think. Don't ever forget that."

There were sounds outside now, banter and fussing, laughter and commotion. Kicking into high gear, Miss Nell started toward the stove, stopped, and looked back at Miranda with a puzzled frown.

"Just out of curiosity . . . how did you figure out I was Gage's mother?"

"Would you believe the dimples?" Miranda teased.

"No, I wouldn't." Miss Nell laughed. "There are lots of people in our family with dimples. They're the bane of Gage's existence, poor thing."

An ache of tenderness went through Miranda's heart. "Watching you with them. Watching you love them."

And watching a dark-eyed mother with her two dark-haired sons. A mother whose love lasts forever . . .

The door burst open without warning. Etienne strolled in with Gage and Roo at his heels.

"Uh-oh—looks like we got ourselves some serious girl talk going on in here." Etienne elbowed Roo in the side. "Maybe you wanna be joining them, huh *cher*?"

Roo leveled him a look. "I don't do girl talk."

"Then maybe," Miss Nell said smoothly, "y'all wouldn't mind chopping some of this stuff for salad?"

As the prep crew got to work, Miranda slipped out of the kitchen. She could see Parker sitting on one of the picnic tables, Ashley drawn back between his knees, his kisses lazy on the top of her head. But Parker couldn't see Ashley's expression . . . the faraway dreams in her eyes. *And what secrets do* you *have, Ashley? That could change two lives in a minute?*

Lost in her thoughts, Miranda sneaked past them and headed away from the house.

The weather was beautiful. Cloudless sky, crisp breeze, and leaves swirling in every direction. A golden, glorious Southern day, and she was thankful to be alive.

She didn't hear the footsteps coming up behind her. Didn't

see Etienne till he caught her by the shoulders and swung her around to face him.

Swamp black eyes pinned her in a stare. And her heart was already racing.

"I thought you were mad at me," he mumbled.

For a minute Miranda stared back at him, trying to figure out what he was talking about.

"That's how come I didn't call you that night," he mumbled again. "After the boat, after I took you home. I thought maybe you were sorry about what happened. And so . . . I just wanted to tell you."

His voice was gruff, he was holding her so tight. She'd never heard him talk this fast before.

"Why would I be sorry?" was all she could think of to say.

"For how you got all embarrassed. And . . . well . . . for Gage."

A long silence passed between them. When Miranda finally shook her head, it was in mild disbelief.

"When you didn't call, I thought maybe *you* wished it never happened."

"Me? Now, why would I be wishing that?"

"I thought I was just one more of your . . . your . . ."

That hint of amusement, playing over his mouth. "One more *what, cher*?"

"One more . . . victory!" Miranda looked highly indignant. "Among hundreds, I'm sure."

"Hundreds?" As Etienne's eyes widened, he made a faint sound in his throat. "*Bon Dieu*, you're flattering me, girl. But I'm liking the compliment, just the same."

Turn the page for a peek at the novel that started Miranda's journey—

Walk of the Spirits

by

Richie Tankersley Cusick

He caught her face between his hands . . . covered her lips with a deep, slow kiss. When he spoke again, his expression was grave . . . and tender.

"I always thought I'd know what to do, how to keep you safe. But the other night, when I couldn't get you back . . ."

Shaking his head, Etienne looked away . . . fixed his gaze on the roof of Belle Chandelle.

"Gage . . . he saved your life, *cher*."

"You both did," Miranda whispered. "You both saved me." *And Parker saved me too, though I swore I wouldn't tell.*

"Yeah, well, don't be getting used to this teamwork stuff. I work alone."

"I'll remember that."

Stepping back, Etienne folded his arms, cocked his head, cleared his throat. "So I was thinking . . . maybe you might wanna do something this weekend."

"Etienne Boucher, are you asking me out on a date?"

"I'm asking what you wanna do, that's all. Like, if I can get me some time off, what would you like?"

"To see you smile again."

She hadn't planned on saying it—and from Etienne's reaction, it was the last thing he'd ever expected to hear.

"What the hell you talking about, Miranda?"

"Well, it's not as adorable as Gage's, but it's pretty darn cute. And I'd like to see it again. As much as possible."

He glanced away, vaguely embarrassed. Miranda tried not to laugh.

"Now . . . you were asking me about a date?" she prompted.

Sighing, he hooked one arm around her neck, steered her onto the path. "Well, yeah. If you're not gonna be too busy—"

"Hmmm . . . I *might* be busy. I guess it just depends on who I'd rather be busy *with*."

"Gage," Etienne groaned. "I'm right, yeah? Always gonna be Gage—"

"I'm not saying. It's a secret."

And as they strolled the tangled grounds of Belle Chandelle, Miranda couldn't help marveling at the irony of it all.

Grandpa made a pact with Etienne. A secret he never told.

And now I've *made a pact with Miss Nell. A secret* I *can never tell.*

"Secrets," Miranda said again, but more to herself than to him.

"What's that, *cher*?"

"Nothing." She smiled. "Not important."

Yes, Belle Chandelle was full of them. Just like St. Yvette and the world right here around her and that Other World beyond . . .

But some secrets were *meant* to be discovered. Shared and healed and put to rest . . .

And that's why I'm here.

And today's secrets are just the beginning.

1

She was tired today because of the screaming.

That horrible screaming that had woken her up last night, just like it had the night before. Screams out of the darkness that cut into her heart like razor blades; distant, muffled screams that trapped her and dangled her precariously between consciousness and full-blown nightmares.

"Miranda?"

At first she'd thought it was the hurricane all over again. Shrieking wind, screeches and groans of the roof and walls splitting and exploding around her. Or maybe her mother's cries of terror. Or her own hysterical weeping . . .

But then, of course, she'd realized where she was. In a different bed, in a different house—far from Florida, far from the home where she'd slept and felt safe. And those screams were so *real.* Much more real than *any* dream could ever be.

She hadn't had a decent night's sleep since they'd moved here to St. Yvette.

Naturally, Mom didn't believe her about the screams; Mom just kept telling her she was imagining it. And the harder Miranda tried to sleep, and the harder Mom tried to rationalize, the worse everything got. Miranda's energy was sapped. Her thoughts strayed down a hundred dark paths. It was impossible for her to concentrate on anything anymore.

"Miranda Barnes?"

"Huh?" Snapping back to attention, Miranda saw Miss Dupree paused beside the chalkboard, fixing her with a benevolent gaze. The whole class turned in Miranda's direction.

For a split second, Miranda wondered what they saw. A slight, not-very-tall girl with short brown hair pushed nervously behind her ears? A nice-enough girl with hazel eyes and a heart-shaped face and a light sprinkling of freckles across her nose?

Or the silent girl, the sullen girl, who, in her three days at St. Yvette High School, had yet to meet their eyes when they passed her in the hall? Who never spoke, never smiled, never bothered to be friendly?

They couldn't see the fear—that much she was sure of. The shock, the anguish, the grief, the emotions that choked her every time she let her guard down.

So she *wouldn't* let her guard down. Not with these kids, not in this school, not in this town. Not now. Not ever.

"Oh. Yes. I'm here," she mumbled. As her cheeks flushed, Miranda's hands clenched tightly in her lap.

"I know you're here, dear," Miss Dupree went on sweetly. "I was just explaining this little assignment we're all going to be working on."

"*Little* assignment?" a voice complained from the front row. "Come on, Miss Dupree, it counts for half our grade!"

"I'm well aware of that, Parker. And just think how much it would count for if it were a *big* assignment!"

The room erupted in laughter while the young man lounged back in his desk and grinned. *Parker Wilmington,* Miranda was already familiar with *that* name. She was sure she'd heard it uttered longingly from the lips of every girl in St. Yvette High, from giggly freshmen all the way up through her senior class. Tall and blond, sea-green eyes, those gorgeous, unruly strands of hair framing his handsome face, no matter how many times he shook them back. Star quarterback, not a single game lost last season. Self-confident swagger, cocky smile, and . . . taken. *Very and most definitely taken.* By the beautiful girl who was sitting next to Miranda at this very minute.

Miranda glanced quickly across the aisle. *Ashley.* Ashley . . . something, she couldn't remember. Ashley Something-or-Other with the long golden hair and the petite figure and the sexy little cheerleader uniform she was wearing today. One of those picture-perfect girls who would always be drooled over and sought after and passionately admired. *So of course she's with Parker Wilmington. Who else?*

Miranda didn't realize she was staring. Not until Ashley turned and beamed her a perfect white smile.

"Miss Dupree's broken us up into study groups," Ashley leaned toward her and whispered. "I asked her if you could be in ours."

It caught Miranda completely off guard. Study group? Oh, God, the *last* thing she wanted to do was be trapped in a group of strangers, especially curious ones. She'd felt the stares in the hallways, in the classrooms, across campus. She was all too aware of her novelty status here at St. Yvette High School as the Girl Who Lost Everything in the Hurricane. And soon, she knew, the questions would come—questions she couldn't handle, traumatic memories she didn't want to relive. So she'd tried her best to keep a low profile. Kept to herself and stayed invisible. Better that way, she'd decided, much better that way. She wasn't ready for socializing yet—not of any kind. She wanted to be alone—*needed* to be alone—to process all that had happened in the last few weeks, to sort everything out. What she didn't want or need right now were people feeling sorry for her or asking those painful questions or trying to butt into her life—

"I'm Ashley."

Again Miranda jolted back to the present. She was getting used to everyone's southern accents, but Ashley's still managed to fascinate her. Extra thick, extra rich, like warm, melted honey. She saw now that Ashley's hand was taking her own and giving it a firm, friendly shake. Conjuring a tight smile, Miranda kept the handshake brief.

"All right, class!" Miss Dupree motioned for silence. "You've had several weeks now to come up with your topics. Just a reminder: I want these projects to be socially oriented. Something that will get you involved in this town. Something to help you learn more about your community and the neighbors you share it with. I want to see some original ideas, people. Something creative and—"

"Gage wants to know more about *his* neighbor, Miss Dupree." On Miranda's left, a girl in black clothes and heavy black eye makeup stretched languidly in her seat. "The one who keeps getting undressed at night with the curtains open and the lights on."

In mock horror, Parker swung around in his chair. "Hey! *You and Ashley* are Gage's neighbors!"

"I *meant* the house behind him," the girl said calmly.

Clutching his chest, Parker gasped. "Gage! You pervert! That's Mrs. Falconi—she's ninety-six years old!"

This time the laughter reached hysteria. Miranda saw the girl give a slow, catlike smile, while a boy near the window—Gage, she supposed—blushed furiously and shook his head.

"Roo, stop it!" Ashley hissed, but she couldn't quite hold back a delighted grin. "Why do you always have to embarrass him?"

The other girl shrugged, obviously pleased with herself. "Because it's so easy. And he's so cute when he's embarrassed."

"All right, people, all right!" Clearing her throat, Miss Dupree struggled to keep her own amusement in check. "Thank you, Roo, for that fascinating bit of information. And should any of us notice a pervert lurking outside our windows tonight, we can all rest easily now, knowing it's only Gage."

The class went wild. Poor Gage went redder.

"Time to break into your study groups." Miss Dupree moved to her desk, then gestured toward the back of the room. "Oh . . . Miranda?"

"I told her she's with us, Miss Dupree!" Ashley spoke up quickly, while Roo regarded Miranda with undisguised boredom.

Miss Dupree smiled. "Then she's in good hands."

As the rest of the kids reassembled themselves, Parker sauntered back and eased himself down beside Ashley, giving her a quick kiss on the lips. Roo pulled her desk in closer. And Gage, flashing Roo an I-can't-believe-you-did-that look, made his way across the room and promptly smacked her on the head with his notebook.

Roo was right, Miranda decided: Gage *was* cute, embarrassed or not. The same height as Parker, but more slender, his shoulders not as broad. Soft brown hair, a little shaggy, big brown eyes, long dark lashes, and sensitive features, despite the huge frown he was currently leveling at Roo.

Gracing each of them with her smile, Ashley picked up a blue sequined pen. "Well, we're all here, I guess. Except for Etienne. Is he working today—do any of y'all know?"

"An alligator probably ate him." Roo yawned.

Trying not to be obvious, Miranda cast her a sideways glance. She could see now that Roo was short—not much over five feet—with a solid body, more curvy than plump. The girl seemed entirely unself-conscious in her long black Victorian dress and black combat boots. A silver crescent moon hung from a narrow black ribbon around her neck; silvery moons and stars dangled from her multipierced ears. Her bangs were long and thick and partially obscured her brows. And she had purple streaks—the same shade of purple as the heavy gloss on her lips—in several strands of her overdyed black hair.

As Roo's dark eyes shifted toward her, Miranda looked away. There'd been a few kids like Roo in her own high school at home, but she'd never gotten to know them. Never even spoken to them, really. In fact, she and her friends had jokingly called them the Zombie Rejects and avoided them at all costs.

"We definitely need his input." Once more, Ashley's voice drew Miranda back. "Etienne always has good ideas." She sat up straighter, pen poised over paper. "Oh, and Miss Dupree said Miranda can be in our group, okay?"

There were nods all around and mumbles of agreement. Parker winked. Gage shot Miranda a quick glance, while Roo still seemed bored. As Ashley made introductions, Miranda did her best to sound polite, but offered no more than that.

"So!" Ashley began cheerfully. "Out of all those ideas we had last time, which one are we going to do for the project?"

Parker shrugged. "They all sucked, and you know it."

"No, they didn't." Gage's voice was soft, gentle, like his eyes, just as Miranda had expected it to be. "I think the Symbolism of Cemetery Art is pretty good—"

"Good why? 'Cause you thought of it?" Roo asked.

"Good because it's . . . you know . . . interesting."

"Yeah, if you're a maggot."

"Well, it's better than Southern Belle Rock Bands."

Roo looked mildly annoyed. "The Development and Liberation of Women Musicians During the Antebellum Era, excuse me very much."

Ashley waved her paper at them. "Come on, we don't have much time. Maybe Miranda has some ideas."

"What?" Instantly Miranda felt four pairs of eyes on her. "Um, no. Sorry."

The truth was, she hadn't been paying much attention these last few seconds. It was something she was beginning to get used to—this zoning in and out of memories when she least expected it, when she was least prepared—but that didn't make it any easier. It still managed to catch her by surprise. *Sad surprise, lonely surprise.* Like just now, when Gage had mentioned something about art and cemeteries, a picture had snapped into Miranda's mind. She and Marge and Joanie in New Orleans over summer vacation, traveling there for a week with Joanie's parents. Shopping; flirting with those cute bellmen at the hotel; sightseeing around town—old buildings, museums, mansions, graveyards. *Was that only two months ago?* It seemed like years. The last really fun thing they'd done together before everything changed—

"What's this?" Leaning over Miranda's shoulder, Gage pointed to some scribbles on the front of her notebook. "Ghost Walk?"

Miranda looked down at the words. Yes, definitely her own handwriting, though she didn't remember putting them down just now.

"What the hell's a Ghost Walk?" Parker asked. His grin widened as he nudged Ashley in the ribs, and Miranda quickly turned her notebook over.

"It's . . . nothing."

"No, really," Ashley urged her. "Really—what is it?"

Don't make me talk about this—I had so much fun then—now it hurts too much to remember . . .

"Miranda?"

* * *